HAPPY ARE THE PEACEMAKERS

HAPPY ARE THE PEACEMAKERS

ANDREW M. GREELEY

PIATKUS

For Paddy Dowling, Parish Priest of the Church of the Three Patrons (Brigid, Patrick, and Columcille) in Rathgar, Dublin 2, where James Joyce, Stephen Dedalus, and Leopold Bloom were baptized.

4589940

Copyright © 1993 by Andrew M. Greeley

This edition first published in
Great Britain in 1994 by
Judy Piatkus (Publishers) Ltd of
5 Windmill Street, London W1

**The moral right of the author
has been asserted**

*A catalogue record for this book is available
from the British Library*

ISBN 0–7499–0257–4

Printed and bound in Great Britain by
Bookcraft (Bath) Ltd

The Beatitudes

THIS SERIES OF STORIES, FEATURING THE MOST REVEREND JOHN Blackwood Ryan, is orchestrated around the Beatitudes from Jesus' Sermon on the Mount. A variant form is found in Luke's so-called Sermon on the Plain, which is accompanied by parallel Woes. I choose Matthew's version, which is probably later and derivative, because it is so much better known.

The Sermon on the Mount is not, according to the scripture scholars, an actual sermon Jesus preached, but rather a compendium of His sayings and teaching, edited by the author of St. Matthew's Gospel, almost certainly from a preexisting source compendium.

The Beatitudes represent, if not in exact words, an important component of the teachings of Jesus, but they should not be interpreted as a new list of rules. Jesus taught that rules are of little use in our relationship with God. We do not constrain God's love by keeping rules, since that love is a freely given starting point in our relationship (a passionate love affair) with God. We keep rules because all communities need rules to stay together and because as ethical beings we should behave ethically, but that, according to Jesus, is a minor part of our relationship with God.

The Beatitudes are descriptive, not normative. They are a portrait of the Christian life as it becomes possible for those who believe in the Love of God as disclosed by Jesus. If we trust in God, we are then able to take the risks, the Beatitudes imply, never living them perfectly, of course, but growing and developing in their radiant goodness and experiencing the happiness of life that comes from such goodness, as do the various peace makers in this story.

To those who may object to the profanity of Dublin English as portrayed in this story, I reply that it is as much part of Dublin as St. Stephen's Green and the Liffey River, that in reality it is much less restrained than in this story, and that, as Bishop Ryan argues, God doesn't mind because She knows that the Dubliners don't mean anything by it!

From *Who's Who*

RYAN, JOHN BLACKWOOD. PRIEST, PHILOSOPHER; BORN Evergreen Park, IL, September 17, 1945; s.R.Ad. Edward Patrick Ryan, USNR (ret.) and Kate Collins; A.B., St. Mary of the Lake Seminary, 1966; S.T.L., St. Mary of the Lake Seminary, 1970; Ph.D., Seabury Western Theological Seminary, 1980. Ordained Priest, Roman Catholic Church, 1970; Asst. Pastor, St. Fintan's Church, Chicago, 1970–1978; Instructor, classics, Quigley Seminary, 1970–1978; Rector, Holy Name Cathedral, 1978– ; created Domestic Prelate (Monsignor), 1983; ordained Bishop, 1990; Author: *Salvation in Process: Catholicism and the Philosophy of Alfred North Whitehead*, 1980; *Truth in William James: An Irishman's Best Guess*, 1985; *Transcendental Empiricist: The Achievement of David Tracy*, 1989; *James Joyce, Catholic Theologian*, 1992. Mem. Am. Philos. Assoc., Soc. Sci. Stud. Rel., Chicago Yacht Club, Nat'l Conf. Cath. Bishops. Address: Holy Name Cathedral Rectory, 732 North Wabash, Chicago, IL 60611.

. . . She holds my mind
With her seedy elegance,
With the gentle veils of rain
And all her ghosts that walk
And all that hide behind
Her Georgian facades—
The catcalls and the pain,
The glamour of her squalor,
The bravado of her talk.

Fort of the Dane,
Garrison of the Saxon,
Augustan capital
Of a Gaelic nation,
Appropriating all
The alien brought,
You give me time for thought
And by a juggler's trick
You poise the toppling hour—
Of greyness run to flower,
Grey stone, grey water,
And brick about grey brick.

—Louis MacNeice, "Dublin"

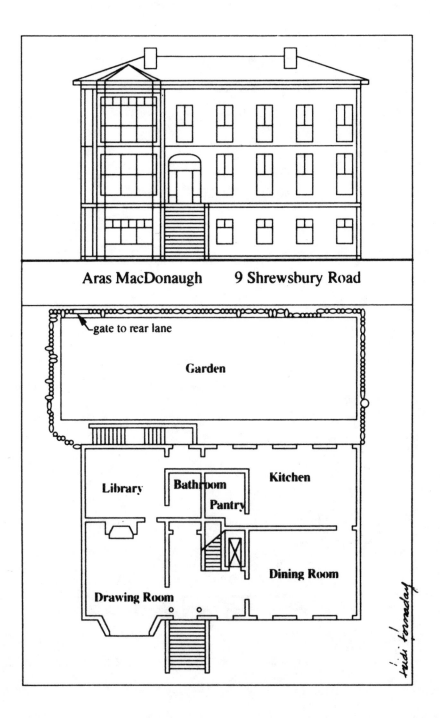

Aras MacDonaugh   9 Shrewsbury Road

gate to rear lane

Garden

Library   Bathroom   Kitchen
Pantry

Drawing Room   Dining Room

1

I MET THE WOMAN IN THE ELEVATOR OF THE SHELBOURNE HOTEL in Dublin a few moments before the Provos sprayed us with automatic weapons.

She was dressed in an off-the-shoulder white gown, gathered tightly at her waist, and a light black cape, a shapely silver-haired archduchess, radiant in jewelry, on her way to a ball at the czar's. Or, to get the country right, a reception for George I at the Vice-regal Lodge in Phoenix Park.

Okay, they didn't have archduchesses in Georgian Dublin, but this woman was too elegant and too lovely to be a plain old Anglo-Irish countess.

She dismissed me as I slipped through the door of the elevator with a quick flicker of her eyes. I no longer existed.

Eyes heavy with anguish.

She was tall, five feet nine or ten, and so slender as to seem almost thin. Her eyes were blue and her skin buttermilk white, as was required in this country. Her hair, piled in an aristocratic knot on the top of her head—no attempts to hide her height in this woman—suggested that she was either a young woman who was not daunted by premature gray or an older woman who had preserved her splendid figure by careful discipline and her face by skillful makeup.

In fact, I knew from my records that she was in her late thirties. But the records had not warned me that she was so beautiful as to make a lonely man's heart ache with desire. The last thing I was supposed to do was to fall in love with her.

Despite her cool pretense that I did not exist, she was aware, as women are, of my appraisal and my approval. She had been the target of lustful eyes before and knew how to ignore them; the lust in my eyes, I wanted to tell her, was respectful and protective. Well, mostly. But since, despite my dinner jacket and curly hair, I didn't exist in her world, I was not permitted to speak.

Just as well, I told myself. This archduchess is the prime suspect. You should not be enchanted by her.

But I was enchanted just the same. I wanted her for my own, to have and to hold, from this day . . .

Shut up, I told my respectful lust.

I suppose it says a lot about Tim MacCarthy, ex-cop and inveterate Irish-American bachelor, that at the present stage of his life desire propelled him toward the marriage vow and the marriage bed. It had not always been thus.

The sexual tension in the elevator increased; it did not bother her at all. It made my hands sweat.

Then the elevator cranked to a stop and the funny little priest joined us.

"It is necessary," he announced, "to realize that the noun 'guard' or 'garda' in Irish is both a singular and a collective noun. Thus it can mean a single cop on the corner or the entire national police force, as in 'The garda is expecting rain.' One must guess from the context whether this is the opinion of the cop on the corner or the whole police force. On the other hand, the plural, gardaí always means several guards, acting in unison or not. Thus we have 'The gardaí ran in opposite directions to avoid the rain.' "

An uninvited lecture like that certainly dispels sexual tension. That, for all I know, was the little priest's intention.

He was short, pudgy, and round-faced, with a high forehead and kinky brown hair speckled with gray, and his pale blue eyes blinked behind thick, rimless glasses. An inoffensive little man with an air of confusion about him, the kind of unimportant priest that you would hardly notice in this priest-ridden land unless he had launched into his odd talk.

I had never met him, but I knew him, of course; everyone in Chicago knew him.

My archduchess—she was already mine, you see—smiled and became even more lovely. She glanced quickly at me to see whether the funny little priest was somehow in charge. I lifted my shoulders, whose solidity I hoped she noticed, in denial.

"It is to be noted," he continued, "that this hotel was built in 1824 and occupies the site of Kerry House, constructed in the 1770s by one Thomas Fitzmaurice, the first Earl of Kerry."

I caught a quick glimpse of mischief in his pale blue eyes. That hint would stay with me through the next week; whatever else he might be and however odd he might seem at times, he was an imp, a benign if obscure leprechaun, or as we used to say in the Chicago Police Department, a real shit-kicker.

The pained eyes of the woman, the innocently playful eyes of the priest: I guess they're what my story is about.

The elevator opened and we entered the lobby of the Shelbourne. The little priest stared in one direction then the other, as if he were not certain which way to go.

"To the left, should you care to explore a few yards, you will find a plaque memorializing Oliver St. John Gogarty, who was forever pilloried in the opening words of a novel written by his sometime tenant as 'stately, plump Buck Mulligan.' "

At the hall porter's desk he ended his lecture. "If it were in the approximate location of Milwaukee, this city could become addictive."

The woman grinned broadly. The little priest had found her heart, which by rights was mine—even if his intentions were different from mine.

All right, I'd use him for my purposes.

"Ms. MacDonaugh," I said formally, "may I present His Gracious Lordship, the Most Reverend John Blackwood Ryan, Ph.D., D.D.—"

"*Honoris causa.*" The little priest beamed.

"—by the grace of God and the favor of the Apostolic See—"

"And its tolerant inattention."

"—titular Bishop of Ariopolis *in partibus infidelium* and auxiliary to the Archbishop of Chicago."

"One Cardinal Sean Cronin." The priest's blue eyes blinked.

"M'lord"—I strove to continue my formal introduction—"may I present Ms. Nora Marie MacDonaugh."

"Call me Blackie!"

Not exactly Ishmael, right?

The woman, a paragon of Irish respect for the clergy although she had lived in America for many years, bowed her head. "M'lord," she said respectfully, and reached for a ring to kiss.

The years in America had not erased the soft burr in her voice, a hint of bogs and mists and gentle rain.

"Uh, I seem to have mislaid that badge of office." The little priest fumbled in his pockets. "But I distinctly remember that somewhere I have the other badge . . . aha, yes, here in my inside pocket, oddly enough where I put it."

He pulled out a silver St. Brigid cross, probably the only such pectoral cross worn by a bishop in the whole world.

"Jesus, the light of the world," the woman said with reverential awe. "It's lovely."

" 'Tis." I sighed, faking the inimitable Irish sigh.

When this woman was mine, I would surely have to attend mass every Sunday. Fair enough trade with God.

"Well, Ms. MacDonaugh, Captain MacCarthy, I gather we are all intended for the function at the former lodge of the chief secretary in Phoenix Park." He led us by the concierge's desk and out into the street. "Might I suggest we share a cab . . . I note for the record that instead of St. Stephen's Green North, this street was once known by the more romantic name of Beaux Walk."

Nora MacDonaugh could buy all the taxis in Dublin if she wished, but she nodded in agreement, flattered at the possibility of conversation with a bishop, no doubt, even a funny little bishop named Blackie.

Why doesn't she have a limo? I wondered. And why is she staying in the Shelbourne instead of the Berkeley Court?

We walked out into the sunshine of the long midsummer Irish day. Across the street Stephen's Green glittered in a golden haze, a lush exuberant tropical garden it seemed on a humid evening. We stood under the marquee of the Shelbourne and the array of flags that welcomed everyone who came to it from "your focking Yanks to your focking Japs," as I heard a bellman say earlier in the day—in an unguarded moment using the favorite Irish word twice in one sentence, almost a grammatical requirement, it seemed.

A steady stream of early evening traffic, on foot and on the street, was moving rapidly by us. In Dublin you found little of the alleged Irish tendency to relax.

"Seamus." The bishop seemed to have taken charge. "We seem to need a cab for three."

"Right away, m'lord," said the massive bellman.

I saw the blue car slowing down as it neared us. But there was nothing suspicious about it. If I'd been expecting assassination, I might have reacted differently.

That's when I heard the firecrackerlike popping of automatic weapons and felt the faint swish of bullets over my head. Knight in armor that I was, I bore Nora MacDonaugh to the ground and covered her with my own body.

Real hero. Stupid hero. Lust-crazed hero.

Yet the result was not unpleasant. It had been a long time since I had a soft and trembling woman pinned beneath me. Moreover she didn't seem to mind the position at all.

Let us be like this in each other's arms across from Stephen's Green for all eternity, I asked the Deity. And to hell with Stephen Dedalus, too. And Leopold Bloom and James Joyce in the bargain. As the woman on the bus had said to me, James Joyce had a dirty mouth and a dirtier mind.

"Are you all right?" she asked.

"I think so . . . you?"

"Not even bruised, thanks be to God."

How could this supple and vulnerable woman have murdered two husbands?

We should get up, I told myself. This is, after all, a public place.

I helped her to her feet.

"The car, Officer," Blackie Ryan was telling a guard who

had raced across the street, "was a blue Renault with a Kerry license number, 90KY-295. As you doubtless perceived, it headed in that direction down Merrion Row into Baggot Street, formally Baggotrath Lane. Arguably they were using a Kalashnikov, a weapon from what used to be called the Soviet Union, I'm led to believe."

"Yes, Father," the guard said, and barked the information into his portable transceiver.

Not being a gallant knight, the bishop had not thrown himself or anyone else to the ground. Moreover, since he was the famous detective from Chicago's Holy Name Cathedral and, according to Commissioner Michael Casey, the only detective in the city more skillful than I, he doubtless knew the hunger that lurked beneath my phony gallantry.

" 'Twas the lads," the guard said nervously, "right here in Dublin and on the Green."

"Arguably," Bishop Blackie replied opaquely. "Arguably."

The pedestrians on both sides of the street, who had ducked for cover when the popping noise began, were emerging cautiously from the doorways and the stairwells into which they had scurried. Many of them gathered around us, but at a safe distance, lest the gunmen return.

"All right, now?" the guard ordered. "Isn't it all over? Move on, if you please." He turned to me. "Are you all right, sir?"

The term "lads" is normally affectionate among the Irish. But these days it had taken on a highly specific and very negative connotation; it meant the few hundred terrorists of the Provisional Irish Republican Army, the "Provos."

"We're fine, Officer."

"I'm all right," Nora MacDonaugh agreed, "thanks to Captain MacCarthy."

She smiled gratefully at me, a partial conquest.

Now I realized that I didn't want that conquest. My fantasies inside the Shelbourne were absurd. I had sworn off women; and this woman, for all her trembling softness, was, or at least might be, extremely dangerous.

"Am I a mess, m'lord?" she asked the bishop as she brushed dust off her cloak.

"Not noticeably," Blackie Ryan replied. "Herself will not see a speck of dirt on your dress. Nor, despite Captain MacCarthy's quick-thinking courage, any wrinkles on your gown."

Bishop, you're a fraud. You know my courage was unnecessary. But thank you anyway.

"Herself" was the *Uachtaran*, the President of Ireland, Mary Bourke Robinson, or simply "Mary" to most of the citizenry.

"Well, then," she said calmly, "shouldn't we take this taxi to Phoenix Park?"

Wasn't there still enough Irish in her that she spoke often in questions? And wasn't she self-possessed enough not to have to turn back into the hotel to rearrange her makeup?

As we wended our way along the south bank of the Liffey, the long June sunlight bathed the black river in gold, creating the momentary illusion that we were in a Disney World version of Venice, or maybe Amsterdam.

The bishop conducted a tour for us—"two cathedrals on the left, you will note, Christ Church and St. Patrick, both built in the Middle Ages. The opposition took them over at the Reformation and has neglected thus far even to give one back."

My own city is figuratively male—hog butcher to the world—or now, commodity broker to the world. Dublin, however, is womanly—a willful, contentious woman in the middle years of life who, depending on the volatility of her moods, could be either dazzlingly attractive or boringly dowdy, blossoming or gray as Louis MacNeice wrote, corseted and prim in her Georgian squares like Merrion and Fitzwilliam or unbelted and effervescent along the quays or in Wickow and Duke and Grafton streets, loving or angry, stubborn or fragile, inviting you into her arms or brusquely pushing you away, taking off her clothes to seduce you or bundling up in a tattered old robe to put you off, luring you into her bed or ordering you out of the room.

Then demanding that you come back into the room.

Was I confusing the city with Nora MacDonaugh? I stole a quick glance at her. It would be difficult, I decided, to think of her as dowdy. Besides, my erotic imagery for Dublin had taken shape before I met her. Dublin is a city that demands carnal womanly images, as James Joyce knew long before I did.

The bishop had maneuvered himself into the front seat of the cab, leaving Nora MacDonaugh and me in the back, intensely conscious of each other's presence and aware of the pleasant experience of body against body we had shared (and also of the danger we might have faced) but in conspiracy to pretend that the other was not present.

"Also the Liberties, neighborhoods so called because they were free from local taxes, weavers especially, both Dutch and Huguenot, and also distillers, hence St. James Gate Brewery, from which the magical Guinness comes forth. Note the large windmill base which towers over the region. Note, too, that Phoenix Park, which we now enter, was walled off by the Duke of Ormonde in 1761 and opened to the public seventy years later by Lord Chesterfield, thus giving back to the Irish people land that was always theirs."

"The park is seven miles in circumference," I added.

"Precisely," he continued, unabated. "When the Brits were finally expelled from the twenty-six counties of the Irish Republic, the Vice-regal Lodge in Phoenix Park, whence William Huble, Earl of Dudley, and Lady Dudley began their ride across Dublin on the afternoon of the first Bloomsday, became the *Aras an Uachtaran*, the House of the President. The home of his second-in-command was, appropriately enough, handed over to the ambassador of the United States of America. They also found a home for the papal nuncio here in the park, which might have been a serious mistake."

"See the light through the trees, m'lord," Nora interjected. "That's the light in the president's house, which we leave on at night to tell everyone that they are welcome in Ireland."

"Don't get too close to the house, however," I added. "They don't want any of the guests barging in."

My witticism was greeted with dead silence by my two companions.

"The name does not suggest a bird rising from its ashes, as in the Chicago seal." The bishop renewed his lecture. "Rather it comes from two Irish words which mean 'clear water.'"

"*Finn uisce,*" Nora murmured softly, and once more I heard the sound of the waves and of the wind over the bog. I imagined the smell of peat fire.

I was falling in love?

Yeah, and I knew it. Falling in love even with the sound of her voice.

At the gate of the vast area that was technically the United States of America, a handsome Marine noncom in full uniform checked our invitations against a list.

"MacCarthy, Timothy Patrick," I said.

"Very good, sir," said the gyrene.

"Ms. Nora MacDonaugh." I pointed at her.

"Yes, of course." He checked her off.

"And His Gracious Lordship John Blackwood Ryan, auxiliary Bishop of Chicago."

Blackie Ryan looked about as if to see whether there was someone else in the car with that name.

"Welcome, m'lord." The Marine grinned. "Your two relatives and their escorts are already here."

"Doubtless in anticipation of the early disappearance of food and drink."

"How did you get an invitation?" Nora demanded of me. "You're not a bishop."

"Clout," I replied.

"The house was built"—the bishop continued to talk—"in 1776, a year of another major event, you may remember. It became the house of the chief secretary in 1784, that worthy being the second-in-command of British imperialism on this island. After that form of oppression was finally ejected, the house of the viceroy became that of the governor general and now the president, and the house of the undersecretary, as I have remarked, became the papal nunciature. In 1927 the American ambassador moved in, thus showing what powers were important to the new government. Lamentably successive generations of nuncios permitted their house to degenerate and then moved out, leaving it to the Irish government. The government of the United States of America, on the other hand, has preserved and improved the property it rents."

"You've read a good guidebook, Bishop," I said.

"Shush!" Nora ordered me in tones that my mother would have used.

The funny little priest was enjoying greatly the sexual tension between the two of us. Arguably he was also preventing a fight between us.

"It is a large, rambling white stucco building, approached by a quarter-mile winding drive flanked by chestnut trees," he continued serenely. "You'll note the white fence on either side of the road which inhibits the cattle whose owners lease the land from said United States of America. You'll note when we go in the house that the coral room, the gold room, and the ballroom have been joined to accommodate this ritual in honor of Mr. Joyce and Mr. Bloom, an event which would doubtless have caused great puzzlement to the former and great laughter to the latter."

Nora and I broke up laughing, which is what the bishop wanted us to do.

We entered the splendid house, walked across the handmade Donegal rug, and glanced up a magnificent staircase. A string ensemble was playing chamber music somewhere. Mozart.

"Too elegant for South Side Irish," I whispered to the bishop.

"Arguably," he agreed.

Nora MacDonaugh was spirited away by the ambassador's wife. The bishop kind of dematerialized and I was left alone, a cop out of place.

You will not fall for her, Tim MacCarthy, and that's an order. There's every reason to think that despite her loveliness and her charm, she is a killer.

Maybe she realizes, too, that your show of gallantry was unnecessary.

2

"**I** SUPPOSE," I SAID TO THE *UACHTARAN* WITH MY MOST BOY-
ishly charming smile, "that you're weary of Americans
with a Mayo background claiming a common heritage with
you."

Herself laughed pleasantly. "Haven't I heard that often
enough? But wouldn't it be proof that I was not a Mayo
woman if it didn't delight me?"

Och, wasn't the woman a smooth one?

"Bishop Blackie," she greeted the little priest who was
trailing after me. "Isn't it wonderful to see you again? Your
nieces are beautiful young women. I hope the rest of your
family is in good form?"

More charm for the Roscommon man than for the Mayo
man.

I did not quote the proverb that in County Roscommon all
the Ryans are rogues but not all the rogues are Ryans.

Admittedly Blackie Ryan did not look like a rogue. But he
was, so to speak, a professional rival. Did he know why I was
in Dublin? Had he been sent in here for roughly the same
purpose, though by opposing forces? Nora MacDonaugh was
generous to the Church. They would not want a murder
charge against her.

Murder, murder, murder, I repeated over and over again.
That's why you're here. Not to bed a silver-haired Irish
beauty, even if it's a marriage bed you generally have in
mind.

My exorcism was only moderately successful. It collapsed
completely a half hour later when the dance music began and
I asked her if she would dance with me.

Mike Casey would have been profoundly shocked at my
behavior.

"Wouldn't I owe you at least one dance"—her smile was expansive—and dazzling—"and yourself saving my life?"

She fit nicely in my arms, a relaxed partner who put no barriers between herself and the man with whom she was dancing. She seemed to be saying that we both knew dancing was a mildly sexual exercise and there was no point in pretending that it wasn't. On the other hand, there was just enough reserve in her posture to let me know that I would be very unwise if I thought there was a possibility of anything further.

Her waist seemed so slim that one of my hands could encompass it. Her breasts, not large but delicately shaped and partially visible from my vantage point towering over her, were only an inch or two from my chest. People were watching us, an attractive couple, the rich and pretty widow and the curly haired blond ex–football player, aging but still in presentable condition.

"You're an excellent dancer, Captain," she murmured.

"Wasn't I about to say the same thing about yourself? In fact, the best I've ever danced with."

"You must have not only kissed but swallowed the stone, Captain." She flushed just a little.

"Well, 'tis at least nice to know that I'm not invisible like I was in the elevator."

Her eyes examined my face carefully, sizing me up, evaluating me, perhaps even making a decision.

"Women will always notice you, Tim Pat," she said. "They will pretend they don't until they make up their minds it is safe to admit that they've noticed you."

It was my turn to experience a warm sensation on my face.

"I'm now defined as safe, even perhaps harmless."

"Moderately safe." She laughed easily. "But not quite harmless."

There were lots of handsome women at the pre-Bloomsday reception arranged by the ambassador of the United States of America to Ireland—it was an opulent party with opulent music and opulent food and opulent drinks and perforce therefore opulent women. My partner was the most opulent of all.

"I didn't save your life."

"Oh?" She raised an eyebrow.

"If they wanted to kill you, or me, or the bishop, they would have done so. That's why the bishop didn't duck. He knew that once you hear the bullets, it's too late. Don't ask me how he knew it, but he knew it."

"But you did? And pulled me with you?"

"Knight-errant complex."

She laughed lightly again. "Sure, isn't it the intention that counts?"

"Mercy sisters?"

She nodded. "Who else?"

"It was a warning. Is there anyone who wants to warn you about anything?"

"Of course there are, Captain MacCarthy," she said promptly. "But I don't think the Provos have anything against me. Maybe they'll want money later on. Would you mind bringing me another glass of champagne?"

The dance music had ended and I was still staring into her tortured eyes with fascination.

"Immediately."

I returned with two glasses of the bubbly as quick as dignity and discretion would permit.

"Now you've gone and spilled some on your dinner jacket." She dabbed at the small spot of moisture on my jacket. "You should be more careful."

"You sound like my mother," I replied, my face feeling quite warm.

"Is that a compliment?"

"Highest I can pay."

"Then thank you."

We sipped our champagne silently until the music began again. She placed her empty glass and my half-empty one on a passing tray and offered her arms for another dance.

"Strauss, I believe."

"Richard," I replied.

"Rosenkavalier."

"It doesn't have to be the Provos," I said, returning to the subject of the automatic-weapons fire.

"I suppose not."

"At least," I said, my tongue getting out of hand, "it was worth the scare for the pleasant experience of holding you in my arms. Twice."

I counted it virtuous that I didn't say "being on top of you."

She flushed. "A terrible thing to say, isn't it, now, Captain MacCarthy, and yourself sent to prove that I killed my poor husband, God be good to him, and not to follow Leopold Bloom at all, at all."

Well, that was that. She knew and she was still smiling at me, mocking me just a bit.

"Is that what your sources told you?"

"Wasn't it something like that?"

"They didn't tell you that I absolutely refused to accept the job if that was the assignment?"

My face was burning again, now furiously.

"Sure, they might have, now." She was grinning at my embarrassment. "Haven't the exact words slipped me mind?"

The damn Irish are so clever with words that they have you coming and going, especially when they're tall and stately women. With irresistible breasts.

"I said that I would investigate the murder of James Larkin MacDonaugh and attempt to learn who might have set off the bomb in his room, but I would do so with no presuppositions as to who the killer might be."

"Did you, now?"

"Haven't I just said that I did?" Turning the Irish love of answering a question with another question back on her.

"And myself the prime suspect?"

She should have said "meself." Yank influence on her.

"Aren't you the one who most obviously benefits from Jim Lark MacDonaugh's death, Ms. MacDonaugh?"

"Since we're dancing together and yourself holding me so tenderlike, won't Nora do, Tim Pat?"

Her eyes twinkled mischievously. She had me on the run, knew it, and was enjoying it.

"Beyond that, there isn't any evidence against you."

"If I'm innocent, and let's say for the basis of this dance that I am, wouldn't I want the murder to be solved by a renowned detective, even if he is a Yank?"

"You might," I agreed.

"On the other hand"—she pretended to be weighing evidence about herself—"might I have not arranged the false assassination because I knew you'd play sir knight and meself trying to seduce you just like I did my husbands and then led them to their deaths?"

Even during the banter, the pain had not left her eyes. Now there was a hard edge of bitterness in her voice.

"You might."

She sighed, and hers, unlike mine, was thoroughly authentic. "Well, good luck to you, Timothy Patrick MacCarthy, as you try to figure that out."

"I've been very lucky on the board of trade," I said, referring to my amusements since I had retired the year before after twenty years on the police force.

"And very unlucky in love?"

Turned down twice at the last moment—once at the very altar—by women who liked me well enough but didn't want to be married to a cop who had been shot up a couple of times.

Not because of valor, I add quickly.

"Your researchers are pretty good," I admitted. "I'm not sure who is the detective just now."

"Oh, you are, Tim Pat, and yourself embarrassed to be mouse-trapped by a woman."

She even knew I had been a linebacker at the Golden Dome, a freshman on the famous team that had tied Michigan State in 1966, not good enough to make the pros, so it was the police force for me, just like my father, the week after I graduated. And night-school law. And now English literature in my spare time, of which I had a lot.

"Will you cooperate with my investigation?"

"I just might," she said thoughtfully. "I'll let you know before the evening is concluded . . . and now the music seems to be over."

"Does it, now?"

"Haven't I just said so?" She laughed again and eased herself out of my arms, which really didn't want to let her go.

"I have an open mind, Nora."

"Sure," she said, "wouldn't I have been thinking that it was filled with many things?"

Bitch.

She slipped away into the crowd and off the dance floor.

She didn't give me a chance to say, "Many conflicting things, Nora. And most of them respectful. Well, moderately respectful."

I'd say that later on.

I watched as she approached the table where the auxiliary Bishop of Chicago was sitting, in the company of two very attractive young women, one pale and the other dark, and two black-haired, handsome young men.

He was so inconspicuous, especially in the presence of his lovely companions, that you would almost think he wasn't there.

"That's part of his secret," Mike Casey had warned me. "You hardly notice that he's around and all the time he's absorbing every detail, including the ones that the rest of us never see."

Nora Finnegan Joyce MacDonaugh leaned over the bishop and whispered something in his ear. He peered around, as if trying to recognize where he was and what was happening. His eyes catching mine, he paused for a thoughtful second or two and then replied to her.

She was, I observed, watching me, too.

He seemed to nod. Or perhaps I was only imagining that I was a man approved.

How dare the woman ask a priest, even a bishop, she had just met, whether I was to be trusted?

And was I to be trusted?

The priest had probably said, "Arguably."

Was he right?

I wasn't sure myself anymore. The woman had bewitched me, deliberately.

"Breakfast at nine tomorrow in Bewley's on Grafton Street?" a voice whispered in my ear as I was talking to the cultural attaché from the embassy, a pretty enough if somewhat too enthusiastic young woman.

"Suits me."

Why a public tearoom, however famous, instead of the hotel? Don't ask.

"Mind, Grafton Street, not Westmoreland Road."

"Got it."

"Be careful," said the attaché.

"Why?"

"She's already killed two husbands."

"If I marry her, I'll wear my bulletproof vest to bed."

I excused myself from the cultural attaché and drifted toward the door. I was intercepted by the pale companion of the good bishop.

"Uncle Punk"—she smiled at the nickname—"I mean His Gracious Lordship Dr. Ryan, goes, 'Tell that nice blond ex-linebacker type from your alma mater that according to my best information'—and he always means that it is like totally certain when he says that—'the guards found the car and there was no one in it and nothing but spent Kalashnikov shells.' "

"I see."

She was a lovely young woman with pale alabaster shoulders and a gorgeous young body, the kind of young woman I had dated and kissed and occasionally fondled and sometimes even fallen in love with a score or more of times and almost married a couple of times.

No, that wasn't true; there was intelligence behind those blue eyes that rarely lurked in the eyes of my dates when I was at Notre Dame.

She did not seem flustered by my covert appraisal, which was not covert enough.

"He also goes, 'They think it's the same MO'—that means

modus operandi in Latin," she rushed on, "mode of operating—"

"I am not, young woman, totally unfamiliar with the Latin language."

She smiled, willing to share a great joke with me. "—of the Provos. But 'in all candor' he—that's Uncle Punk—'is not convinced.' Right?"

"Right," I agreed. "And you're . . . ?"

"Brigid." She smiled at me and turned back into the ballroom.

Brigid. Of course. Once priests wouldn't baptize children with that name. Now I had two nieces called Brigie. Brigie Jean and Brigie Maura.

I leaned against the wall, exhausted. If I had married someone like Brigid when I was that age, I now probably would have a daughter like her. If my wife had been as smart as Brigid seemed to be, I'd have a smart daughter. Who would naturally adore me.

Naturally.

But I had neither a wife nor a daughter and was, for all my nieces and nephews, alone in the world.

If you're Irish, there's nothing that's more fun than feeling sorry for yourself, especially when there are beautiful women in evening dress, dancing, expensive food and drink, and a good orchestra in the next room.

At first I had dated the intellectual ones, though I could not remember any glow of intelligence in their eyes like the light that shone from Brigid's. They didn't think I was intellectual enough. I didn't read the right kind of books and I wasn't socially concerned. Then I dated the less-than-intellectual ones. They thought I read too many books and was too worried about silly things like the Bomb.

"You can't do anything about it," one such had said. "So why ruin life fretting about it?"

In retrospect maybe she wasn't so dumb after all.

They tended to lose interest when they found out I was nothing but a rookie cop, a "pig in training," someone said one night at a bar.

Then there were the two I almost married, both of whom gave me a fair choice—either quit being a cop or forget about marriage.

Both choices were proposed after I had been shot up, the first time when I was in the hospital bed after I came out from surgery.

They had made fair offers. If a woman didn't want to be married to a man who gets in the way of bullets, one fired by a crazy and one by a drug lord, then she should decide that before marriage and not after.

Mature decision, right?

But if a man, who a lot of the time doesn't like being a cop all that much either, is given an ultimatum before he is married, what's he going to get after he's married?

Maybe if they had been willing to negotiate, it would have been another matter. But they weren't the kind of women who are inclined to negotiate.

My mother would have negotiated. She would have won, of course, but only after negotiation.

So I had settled into my bachelor existence again. After a while my hunger for women had subsided. Or maybe I had repressed it, as the psychologist said to me during the year I wasn't able to sleep much. Or maybe when you have seen often enough what drug gangs do to the bodies of women or what pimps do to the bodies of whores or what whores do to themselves, you lose your appetite for women.

It had seemed like that was what happened to me.

So I had been ready to stay on the force when I reached my twenty years. Why the hell not?

My parents had firmly vetoed that.

"Too long," my dad had said. "You're going native."

" 'Mista Kurtz, he dead,' " my mom had said, quoting Joseph Conrad in *Heart of Darkness*.

"You stayed thirty," I had protested.

"I was out on the street only half the time, the first half. You've been on it for most of your twenty years. You'll either get killed or kill yourself with hardness and cynicism."

"You're already halfway there," Mom added. "Maybe more than half."

They had been right; and they had given me the pretext I needed to get out.

I had resolved that life would not be empty. I had been playing around in the commodities markets and found I was pretty good at it. So I had continued to play and got better. I hadn't gone on the floor yet, but I figured that I might in another year. In the meantime, just so life wouldn't be boring, I had taken an occasional choice assignment as a private investigator, but only if the case was interesting and the fee was large.

A man had to save up for his old age, had he not? Especially when it is likely to be a lonely old age?

I had also enrolled in an evening program at Loyola with the thought that maybe I could get a degree in English and teach somewhere.

It took me six months to realize how hard and cynical I had become. As I wound down, women began to interest me again, but regret and, I admit it, fear inclined me to keep them at a safe distance.

So here I was after an encounter with one Brigid, shivering with self-pity and regret.

I left the reception, fleeing the music and the drink and the beautiful women and asked the Marine at the door if he could call for a cab. I wanted to return to my lonely room at the Shelbourne, where I could continue to feel sorry for myself.

She was not my date. Let someone else worry about how she got home.

Like her friend the bishop, with his two young women companions.

As I tried to sleep, conscious that she was on the same floor of the hotel as I was, I asked myself why I had ever taken the job.

The fee was nice, but I didn't really need the money.

It was the challenge of the puzzle. How had the bomb gone off in a locked room, ignited by a radio transmitter that was nowhere near the hand of the man the bomb had torn to tiny pieces, but was nonetheless in the locked room with him?

3

"TWENTY MILLION DOLLARS IN CASH," ARTHUR T. REGAN said to me in the offices of Jim Lark Enterprises in the Seagram Building in New York. "And control of a network of companies in Europe and America—food, transportation, liquor, real estate, a couple of hotels and resorts—wouldn't you kill for that?"

"No," I said. "I've killed men twice—once in self-defense, once to protect others. I wouldn't kill someone for all the money in the world."

"I was only speaking figuratively," Arthur T. Regan grumbled. "And Jim Lark leaves it all to her, not a cent to the children of his first marriage or to anyone else. And he changed his will just a week before she killed him."

Three and a half years ago James Larkin MacDonaugh had married a woman twenty-four years younger than he was. Two years later he had been blown up by a bomb in his Dublin home. His wife was the obvious suspect. But the Dublin police had reluctantly released her because of insufficient evidence.

"Before he died," I corrected him.

I did not particularly like Arthur T. Regan, as he always called himself. He looked like a handsome Tip O'Neill, tall, white-haired, and smooth. There was little trace of Ireland left in his voice and his eyes were small and hard—a tough businessman with powerful contacts all over the country and all over the world, a man who knew where every body was buried and every secret hidden.

I have never liked that kind of affluent mick. Despite their expensive clothes and costly sheen of good health, I always suspected them of being slightly bent, not much better than those who used to vote the dead and buried in the old days of Chicago politics—and maybe a lot worse.

"Whatever." He waved a jeweled hand and lighted a Havana cigar, without asking my permission.

"I wish you wouldn't smoke that," I said, "not when I'm in the office."

I'm a pretty mean bastard, too, you say?

I don't deny it. I'm a cop. Was a cop.

He frowned angrily and snubbed out his cigar.

"I worked with Jim Lark MacDonaugh for forty years," he said glumly. "We played hurling together for Tipperary; I was the captain of the team and he the star. I stood by him in good times and bad all the years together. I helped him build up his empire. He often said that without me holding down the fort, he could never have done it."

"Holding down the fort?"

"I'm the back-room man, I dot the *i*'s and cross the *t*'s in the contracts. I hire the lawyers and the accountants. I make sure there's enough money available from the banks for his deals. He's the great, charming adventurer. I mind the store . . . minded the store."

Arthur T. Regan sounded more bitter than sad.

"I see."

"Then, without a word to me—not a word, mind you—he marries this scheming bimbo and within two years changes his will to leave every penny to her, again without a word to me."

"I see."

I thought to myself, as I glanced at her picture in the news clips on his polished oak desk, that the bimbo might be interesting to meet, a statuesque, silver-haired bimbo with lovely breasts.

"Then she blows him into a million pieces."

"Surely he didn't leave you or his other colleagues or his family destitute."

"Huh?" Arthur T. Regan looked up, seemingly surprised. "Oh, no, everyone has trusts and stock and options and that sort of thing. No one is going to starve. But he left the money and the business to her. Without a single word to me. I was floored when the lawyers told me. Absolutely floored."

Long before probate, I bet.

"These other monies were available before his death?"

"Absolutely. We all own parts of some of the companies, but he kept the controlling interest in his hands and now it's in her hands."

"Even with inheritance taxes?"

"He told the lawyers he wanted her to be in control and they fixed it that way."

"I see. His children, as I understand it, are contesting the will."

"Sure they are. Nice kids, too. But they can't prove that Jim Lark was sick in mind or body when he gave the instructions to his lawyers. They'll be content with a modest cash settlement. Lord knows she has enough of that to give them."

"He was in good health, you say?"

"Absolutely. No one would have minded him marrying again. His kids were all married, little Agnes, the youngest—I was her godfather—just a couple of years ago. She was expecting her first child, his sixth grandchild, when he died, poor thing. Jim Lark had lived alone for five years, and living alone is no fun even if you're not much interested in sex anymore."

Tell me about it.

"Not interested in sex?"

"After a certain age"—Arthur T. Regan frowned more deeply—"it doesn't mean that much."

Not if I were to judge by the affection my mother and father showed for one another. But people are different, as every cop knows.

"Really?"

"A year or so after Dora died, I asked him about marrying again. He said he didn't see any point in it. It wasn't like he needed a woman all that much, to quote his very words."

"I see."

"Not that he was ever all that passionate, if you take my meaning. Dora and he had the three children and it kind of seemed that was that and they both decided there were other things in life besides fooling around in bed."

Fooling around—how often I had heard that.

"Anyhow, he hires this bimbo to run his Jim Lark Foundation. . . . I didn't like her from day one. She was one of these starry-eyed idealists from the late sixties. Loved to give money away."

In 1969, I calculated, Nora Joyce MacDonaugh would have been sixteen years old and only arrived in America for a job as a maid in the home of the man she would eventually marry. Hardly your typical baby-boom radical.

"Was there any sign of romance between them before the marriage?"

"Not in the least. Jim Lark, like I told you, had little time for women. It was adventure and power he wanted. He never even seemed to notice a good-looking dame when she came into the office."

"I imagine that you checked her performance as administrator of the MacDonaugh Foundation?"

"You bet I did," he snarled.

He had not offered me a cup of coffee, punishment no doubt for my refusal to permit him his Havana.

"And?"

"She gave a lot of it away to weird things—homeless people, AIDS victims, rape crisis centers, hospitals in Nicaragua, loony priests working with fucking tinkers in the rest of Ireland, that kind of shit."

"But no improprieties?"

"None that we were able to find. But she covers her tracks pretty well; we all know that."

"I see."

"Then one day he comes in and tells me that they were married the day before in the private chapel of the cardinal over on Madison Avenue." Arthur T. Regan slumped in his vast chair and fiddled with the extinguished cigar. "And herself twenty-five years younger than he was."

"She seems very attractive," I said, glancing at the picture, implying that if I were turning sixty, I might not mind a young woman like her in a flimsy nightgown next to me in my bed at night.

"I don't know whether they ever slept together." He sighed. "He was friendly to her, all right, but not the way a man is to a woman he's fucking regularly."

"Why then marry her?"

"So she could travel with him. He wanted her companionship and she insisted that he marry her. Look." He pulled out a stack of hotel bills. "Whenever they went anywhere, always a two-bedroom suite. Would you do that with a woman you're fucking two, three nights a week?"

I admitted that I probably would not, not unless I could afford it and I wanted to grant her all the privacy that she might need.

I wondered to myself what kind of a lifelong friend collects hotel bills to keep track of your sex life.

"And now she controls everything. She could fire me tomorrow. And the next day she could give it all to some fucking tinkers in the west of Ireland, saving a big hunk of it for her to enjoy the five homes."

"Five?"

"Five! The apartment here, the house out in Oyster Bay, the home on Shrewsbury Road in Dublin where she blew him up, the castle in South County Dublin, and the 'lodge' out in Baltimore."

"Baltimore?"

"In West Cork," he snapped, impatient with my stupidity in thinking he meant the city in Maryland.

"Is there any sign she intends to do this?"

"She is nice as pie at the board meetings, but her lawyers and accountants are sniffing around, and the rest of us don't like that," he growled. "She's up to something, that's for sure."

"Who's on the board?"

"This is the board of the whole shebang, the only one which matters." He ticked off the names on his fingers. "There's Micah Epstein, our outside counsel; Janet Armstrong, whose accounting firm reviews our inside audit; Paddy Quaid—he used to be lord mayor of Dublin, and he looks after the Irish holdings for us, particularly the dairy interests, which are very important to us over there; then there's Michael Davitt MacDonaugh, his brother who lives in London and is a banker; Charles Parnell MacDonaugh, who is a sheep farmer in West Australia; Liam Lynch MacDonaugh, an attorney in San Francisco; Julia Lynch, his only surviving sister, who raised him; his sons Dermot and Sean, both of whom live here in New York; and his daughter, Agnes, who lives in County Meath with her husband, Cormac Mac-Sweeney—his family has a big horse farm there. Then there's the woman herself, of course."

He snorted contemptuously.

"And the board, excepting the woman herself, unanimously agreed to this investigation."

"Precisely. We had an informal session here. Micah, Janet, Dermot, Sean, and myself are in New York. Liam flew in from California, we rang up Paddy and Michael and Agnes and Charlie."

"Not the elder sister."

"She's not really part of the board except in a technical sense. She's a bit of a recluse and never attends our meetings."

"I see."

"We're all very concerned about what this woman does with our companies. She has some grandiose notion that she can use all the money to bring peace to Ireland. Let me tell you, that would be pouring it down a sinkhole."

"Or into a bog," I said. "Tell me, why have you waited so long to call in a hired gun of your own?"

"We were hesitant about further scandal." He fidgeted. "Let-the-dead-bury-their-dead sort of thing. The children especially did not want their father's name dragged through the mud again."

"Now they do?"

"She's in Dublin now, poking around the books of the business. We ... they ... are concerned about what she's up to."

That seemed unlikely. More probable, I thought, was the explanation that Arthur T. had been pushing the family for further investigation for a long time and had finally carried the day, perhaps exploiting their dislike for the widow.

"She's staying at one of the homes?"

"Of course not. Part of her act is that she doesn't need or want all that money. She's at the Shelbourne."

"In a suite?"

"No. Single room. Part of the act."

"So you want me to reopen the investigation?"

"I want you to pin it on her. The Dublin *garda* tell me that they know she did it, but they can't prove it. We—all of the rest of us on the board—want you to get the proof and put her in jail for the rest of her life."

I went through my bit about not beginning with any assumptions about guilt. He accepted that condition with a wave of his hand. It didn't make any difference. She was the one who had done it. Just like she had rigged the apparent suicide of her first husband.

I had to admit that Nora Marie Finnegan Joyce MacDonaugh was the obvious suspect. But I didn't like Arthur T. Regan one bit. On the other hand he didn't try to impress me, which a man who was up to something himself might have done. His only charm was in the checkbook.

4

B ACK AT MY ROOM AT THE PENINSULA AFTER MY CONVERSAtion with Arthur T. Regan, I read through the clippings and the obituaries about the life of James Larkin MacDonaugh. He had been born in 1928 in Tipperary, seventh child and fourth son of a poor dirt farmer who had fought on the side of the "Irregulars" during the Irish Civil War. His mother had died at the age of thirty-two of tuberculosis shortly after his birth. He was raised by his oldest sister, Julia. He had gone to the national school in his hometown and then on to the Christian Brothers.

I paused in my reading. James Larkin was an Irish socialist labor leader in Dublin, who as head of the Irish Transport and General Workers Union had led the violent and disastrous Great Strike in 1913. So the family must have had some radical ties besides their affiliation with IRA radicals way out in the Tipperary farms? That didn't seem likely.

He grew up in the thirties and forties, a grim and impoverished time in Ireland. The civil war was over, Eamon De Valera was running the country and determined that even if the cost was acute poverty for the people of Ireland, he would maintain the nation's isolation from the rest of the world.

After he left the Christian Brothers, Jim Lark moved to Dublin and went to work for a chartered accountant. CPA.

I checked the list of relatives. Four of the siblings had survived, one in Australia, one in England, and one in San Francisco. Julia MacDonaugh, the eldest sister and apparently the only one unmarried, still lived in County Tipperary.

It would be worthwhile to find out how much money Jim Lark had left to his siblings and swarm of nieces and nephews. Had he set up trust funds for all of them? Did they resent his success? Did they wonder who he thought he was—standard Irish expression of resentment—as he became an international financial wizard? All details worth checking out.

He had played hurling—a game something like hockey except played on a field and dangerous as any game would be in which you equipped thirty Irishmen with clubs and urged them to have at each other—with the Christian Brothers and continued on the Tipperary team despite his move to Dublin. He had been the star of five championship teams and was captain of the All-Ireland team three times.

I glanced at his pictures from those years—a big, fierce-looking redhead, with a wild and slightly manic smile. I would not have wanted to tangle with him, not even with all my pads on.

At the same time he was thrilling the country with his athletic feats, he bought out the accounting firm for which he was working, probably with some help from those who admired his prowess on the hurling field.

Shortly after that, he married Dora Collins of South County Dublin, a young woman probably much higher on the social ladder than he was. That would have been in 1953, still hard times for most people in Ireland, but not for our young hurling star on the make. They had three children during the next ten years. By the time Agnes was born in 1964, he was already a millionaire, proof, it was said in an article in one of the Dublin papers, that Irishmen could be successful in European business so long as they worked hard.

But Jim Lark's success seemed less the result of hard work than of extraordinary quick wits and a corporate raider's instincts for when to buy and when to sell.

He would have made a superb trader, I thought, on the floor of the Chicago Board of Trade.

Dora died in 1984 after a long illness. Only fifty-two years old. Cancer presumably.

Pictures of her indicated that she was an attractive woman. Only three children? Did that mean they were practicing birth control? Or, perhaps more likely, maybe they weren't sleeping together, which was the Irish way of birth control in those days (in addition to late marriage). She died twenty years af-

ter Agnes's birth and would have been fertile for many of those years.

I felt guilty at such speculations about the intimate lives of two people who had gone on to whatever awaited them. It was none of my business what they did in bed and indeed whether they did anything at all.

Yet I was a cop, or at any rate doing a cop's job. And I would have had to wonder about Jim Lark's sex life, even if Arthur T. Regan had not tried to tell me about it.

Maybe Jim Lark had simply ruled sex out of his life with the iron resolution of which Irish males were once capable.

Still are, as far as that goes. As I myself proved.

Or seemed to prove.

Might a lovely woman, much younger than he was, and perhaps more sexually skilled from her first marriage than his poor wife ever was, awaken his sexual energies? They were married in 1989. He had two years of her. Maybe she brought him enough happiness for a lifetime. Certainly he looked happy in the pictures with her as they gave money to various worthy causes.

She looked pretty happy, too.

Three years before Dora's death, in 1982, Jim Lark was kidnapped by the IRA. Or so it was claimed. There was a certain skepticism about it in the Irish papers, but then the Irish papers, I had found, are skeptical about everything, especially about the doings of their rich and famous.

MACDONAUGH DISAPPEARS

the *Irish Independent* screamed.

Servants at Castle MacDonaugh in County Wicklow had reported to the guards that he had failed to appear for a supper with friends and business associates that night, although Mrs. MacDonaugh saw him leave Dublin with his driver.

Then the *Irish Times* proclaimed,

GUARDS FIND MACDONAUGH CAR AND DRIVER

The police had discovered the missing MacDonaugh Bentley on an abandoned farm near Mullingar, a long way from Castle MacDonaugh. The driver, who had been trussed up for forty hours, said that the car had been stopped by masked gunmen after dark in the Wicklow Hills. His only memory of the first day was that one of the gunmen had stuck a hypodermic needle in his arm.

Then the *Irish Press*:

IRA DEMANDS TEN MILLION FOR MACDONAUGH

The Provos had issued one of their usual pompous communiqués. An Irish revolutionary court had tried James Larkin MacDonaugh on charges of crimes against the honor and integrity of the people of Ireland. He had grown rich off the labor of Irish dairy farmers because the Free State government (as they called the duly elected Irish government with a reference to its former "dominion" status in the British empire) had joined the corrupt and imperialist Common Market. The jury had found him guilty and recommended the death sentence. However, for humanitarian reasons, the court had commuted that sentence to a fine of ten million Irish pounds, which must be paid within three days.

Then the papers were filled with accounts for several days of the pleas of his family and the stern warnings of the Irish government. Irish television must have had a grand time with the story.

I remembered vaguely seeing some of the drama on American TV.

I looked at the family pictures that the papers carried at the time of the crisis—two handsome sons, a pretty daughter, a faded wife, probably already fatally ill, assorted adorable grandchildren, three brothers, and a sister, looking like an Irish farm-family portrait of a generation ago—one Michael Davitt, a banker in London, another Liam Lynch, a lawyer in San Francisco, the third, Charles Parnell, a sheep farmer in Australia, all pretty clearly older than the kidnapped millionaire. Of the sister, an Irish country woman in a long black dress, it was said only that she "still lives on the family farm in County Tipperary."

The three men were all dressed in modern business suits, however. Why did they make me think of an impoverished farm family from the thirties or the forties? Was it that I knew that's what they in fact were? Or was I sensitive to their stern and somber faces, particularly Julia's?

Or was it because, not to put too fine an edge on it, they all looked like thugs, the sort of dark, frowning, grim men with narrow foreheads and thick hands you'd not want to encounter on a dark road at any time in Irish history?

The lawyer, the oldest in the family, about sixty-five perhaps, must have earned his degree in the United States, before Jim Lark made his money. But the other two could have been financially dependent on him, as could the lawyer by now.

Liam MacDonaugh's comment to the *Irish Independent* was scary: "We'll find out who did it, all right, and we'll settle up with them personally. Our family has always known how to take care of itself."

I looked at the man's picture again—Liam Lynch MacDonaugh.

The original Michael Davitt was the founder of the Irish Land League, James Larkin was a trade-union leader, Charles Parnell a political leader—all radicals. Who was Liam Lynch? I must remember to ask.

Then I studied Julia's picture closely. Was I imagining it or did steel sparks of hatred leap out of her eyes at the photographer?

Jim Lark MacDonaugh seemed in his pictures to be bright and cheerful, a pirate perhaps, but a genial and charming pirate, a man who would play reasonably fair in both hurling matches and life, not above an occasional trick perhaps, an elbow in the back maybe, and always ready for the main chance, but not mean or vicious or vindictive.

The rest of them looked like the dark side of the family. Did they represent the mother or the father? I wondered.

Knowing how Irish culture works, I would bet on the mother.

Then there were the headlines that announced that the Special Branch (their FBI and CIA combined) had freed MacDonaugh after assaulting a country house in County Meath. No shots had been fired and the three IRA terrorists had been captured alive.

Jim Lark, his arm around his wife and daughter in one of the pictures and grinning genially, thanked the government and the people of Ireland for their support.

In the back of one of the pictures, I saw Julia MacDonaugh, her eyes still sparking hatred.

Two months later all three prisoners escaped from the Portaloise, the prison in the center of the country where captured terrorists were confined.

The Irish papers, who seemed to think that the sun came up in the morning with a twisted and insidious plot on its mind, hinted darkly that all the recent events in the life of Jim Lark MacDonaugh were part of a sinister conspiracy in which the government and perhaps the CIA and the KGB were involved.

As best as I could figure out the hints, they were saying that the MacDonaugh family had paid off the IRA and the government and made a deal in which Jim Lark would be freed in return for the subsequent "escape" of those who had kidnapped him.

Given for the sake of the argument that there might be a plot, why would it have had to be so convoluted? Why was it necessary for the government to apprehend the kidnappers and then permit them to escape?

I thought of all the devious political plots in Chicago that my dad took great delight in recounting. Simple conspiracies would not do.

Three small clippings were attached to the last story about the escape of the kidnappers.

At different times and in different places in England and Ireland, police had found the bodies of all three escaped kidnappers, bullet wounds in the back of their heads. Brr!

Why would Arthur T. Regan have included that information in the thick dossier he had prepared for me?

Surely Nora Finnegan Joyce could not have been involved in the kidnapping. She was still working at her Irish bookstore and import shop on Fifty-seventh Street at that time and had yet to meet Jim Lark MacDonaugh.

As far as anyone knew.

I resolved to put some people working on all the living members of the MacDonaugh family and all the trustees of the Jim Lark Foundation.

At the bottom of the stack was a half-page picture from one of the English trash papers of Nora bare-breasted next to her husband on a yacht off the Riviera, taken by a snoop with a telephoto lens. YOUNG WIFE FROLICS WITH MACDONAUGH! said the headline.

I wouldn't call it a frolic, though he was certainly looking at her and obviously liked what he saw.

What man wouldn't, I reflected, and then quickly turned the clip over for the sake of virtue. The final Xeroxes were of arch comments from columnists in the Irish papers.

A particularly bitchy interviewer from the *Irish Times* made a big deal out of it:

> When asked how she felt about being the subject of a lewd picture in the British tabloid press, MacDonaugh replied with an indifferent shrug. "Wouldn't a woman who removes the top of her swimsuit in a private situation in that part of the world know she's running a risk that someone with a long-range camera will be watching, and not much care?"
>
> What did her husband think?
>
> "Of the picture or of me in half a swimsuit?"
>
> Both.
>
> "As to the picture, wasn't he furious until I laughed at it, then didn't he laugh, too? As to me, wouldn't you have to ask him, now?"
>
> Didn't she think that appearing that way in public merely encouraged men to objectify women?

"Ah, well, it wasn't public, now, was it? And, sure, wouldn't we all be in trouble if men were not enthralled by women's breasts?"

Tough, defiant lady. And with carefully prepared answers for bitchy interviewers.

I looked at the picture again, told myself that I was a voyeur, and placed it firmly back in the folder from which the clippings came.

I put the clippings aside and decided to watch the videotapes Arthur T. Regan had given me. Some of them were family videos, handsome kids and playful grandchildren. Jim Lark presided over the crowd like an ancient Irish king—indulgent, proud, and totally in charge, frantically so.

One of the tapes showed a family baptism party in Westchester County (I guessed) after Jim Lark had married Nora Joyce. He had grown a beard and seemed more content and at ease than in earlier tapes. His new wife was almost unbearably beautiful, not as thin as the woman in the clippings still on my table of the widow after Jim Lark's death.

The last tape was professional, an interview with Jim Lark by a very bright Irish television commentator about the state of the world economy and the prospects for Ireland which was made only two months before he died.

Much of the conversation was too allusive and cute for me to understand what was being said. However, Jim Lark seemed to be exactly the sort of man I had thought he would be—quick, witty, articulate, and very hard to back into a corner. He still had the body of an athlete and the twinkling eyes of a charming fellow from whom you would not want to buy a used car but from whom you would end up buying it anyway.

I gathered from the swift-paced dialogue that Jim Lark was bullish on Ireland, bullish on the world economy, and bullish on life.

He seemed to be a healthy and happy man.

I wished I had known him. I like that kind of man. Matching wits and heisting a few with him would have been great fun.

A very few for me.

Would he mind my claiming his wife after he was gone?

I imagined him saying that he would not mind at all, at all, not if I did it fair and square—then with a wink and a chuckle, well, more or less fair and square because in matters like that nothing is ever completely open and aboveboard.

I chastised myself severely for those thoughts. She was, after all, only an image on the tube.

Something had caught my attention in the previous video and I hadn't quite nailed it down.

I played it over again and saw what it was.

Julia MacDonaugh was hovering in the background, where she always was in any pictures in which the photographer was quick enough to catch her.

Despite the happy occasion of the baptism of a new baby, a cute little grandnephew, her eyes were cold with bitter fury.

I could not tell whether her anger was aimed at her brother or her new sister-in-law.

I turned off the video and picked up the final folder, materials on the death of Jim Lark MacDonaugh.

Whoever had done Arthur T. Regan's research for him was certainly thorough. And careful.

I presumed that Arthur T. was equally careful himself. He was the kind of man who would have gone over every single Xeroxed sheet to make sure that I had everything I could possibly want.

And would receive nothing that he did not want to give to me.

The next folder contained accounts in the Irish papers of MacDonaugh's death in January a year and a half ago; they were both shocking and obscure:

IRISH HERO BLOWN UP!

MACDONAUGH VICTIM OF IRA?

HUNT FOR MACDONAUGH KILLERS

NO NEW MACDONAUGH CLUES

Then later there was another headline:

MACDONAUGH WIDOW INHERITS ALL

Only in the last article, several months after Jim Lark's death, was there any mention that this was the second time that Nora MacDonaugh had inherited substantial wealth from the mysterious death of a husband. Chief Superintendent Clarke had commented about this coincidence and assured the Irish people that the Dublin police still considered the case to be open, deftly hinting that he thought it was more than a coincidence.

The facts of the case were straightforward: Mr. and Mrs. James Larkin MacDonaugh had arrived unannounced at Dublin airport at midday and, in the absence of a limousine, took a taxi to their in-town home on Shrewsbury Road. Since the servants had not been warned of this sudden trip to Ireland, no one was in the house. Ms. MacDonaugh had left the house in midafternoon to purchase scones and whipped cream for tea. She had heard a dull explosion and was frightened because of the possibility of terrorism, but she had no reason to think that her husband's life was in any danger. There had been, as far as she knew, no threats. Julia MacDonaugh, the deceased's sister, arrived at the house to meet her brother Michael Davitt MacDonaugh, whose wife and children were to visit with her at Castle MacDonaugh, the County Wicklow country house of Jim Larkin MacDonaugh.

Ms. MacDonaugh was knocked from her feet by the explosion just as she opened the door. They rushed into the house and found that the explosion had taken place in Mr. James Larkin MacDonaugh's study, the door to which was locked. Only when the guards from the station around the corner on Donnybrook Road, alerted by the sound of the bomb, arrived a few minutes later and battered their way through the door, was access obtained to the room. The remains of Mr. MacDonaugh were then discovered.

Where was Nora MacDonaugh? Did she have a key to the study? Did the guards arrive at the house on Shrewsbury Road before she came home?

The guard believed that the bomb had been electrically detonated by a radio transmitter. They were not ruling out the possibility of terrorist involvement.

There was nothing at all to suggest that the explosive device had been activated within the death room. No hint of a locked-room mystery. The walls and the door of the room must have been pretty solid if the bomb tore Jim Lark apart and yet did not open up the room.

The obvious conclusion was that Nora MacDonaugh had left the bomb in the room, gone to buy scones, and activated the device from somewhere outside her house.

They would need proof of that, of course. But such proof might be hard to come by if the transmitter was inside the room.

I looked at one of the pictures of husband and wife in a somewhat nasty feature article in an Irish paper published a couple of weeks before his death. It was a full-page shot with text in a single column on either side of the picture, Brit tabloid style.

His red hair had faded, but he was still a big man, not particularly fat, now with a full beard—which he had not worn before his marriage to Nora. He seemed to be smiling happily, though there was, I thought, a hint of unease around his eyes.

She was both beautiful and beatific, clinging to her solid husband as if her very life depended on him.

Prime suspect? Sure.

Killer? Probably. The guard thought so and they were professional cops.

Besides, what was he worrying about?

5

A FTER A RESTLESS NIGHT, I STRUGGLED OUT OF BED AT 7:30, soaked with sweat. I peered through the drapes. The sun was already high in the sky, and the Dublin Mountains, across the Green and looming in the distance, were shrouded in a yellow curtain of haze. Another day of heat and humidity. In Chicago during June, okay. But how come in Ireland?

There would be, if the previous day was any indication, two types of comments to be heard.

"Ah, sure, we're perishing with the heat!"

And "Ain't the day focking rapid and won't we be paying for it next week?"

In the mouths of many Dubliners these two assessments would be modified at least once in each sentence and possibly twice by a participle alluding to sexual intercourse.

"Rapid," as far as I could determine, was the superlative of the adjective "grand," the comparative case of which seemed to be "super."

The aforementioned participle could also modify these two adjectives.

Having thus reflected on the poetry of the Irish response to a hot day, I took a shower and went down to the coffee shop for a cup and a roll. I read the *Irish Times* and yesterday's copy of the Paris *Tribune*, which had unaccountably turned up at the gift shop this morning. The hotel was jammed with American tourists, doubtless come for the Bloomsday festivities.

At 8:30 I wandered out the door of the hotel and encountered Bishop Blackie and his two companions, both looking very young and very attractive in shorts and James Joyce T-shirts with cameras slung over their shoulders.

"Ah, Captain MacCarthy, I would like to introduce my niece Brigid Murphy." He seemed to hesitate as if trying to make sure he had the right young woman and then pointed at the blonde. "And my sister, Trish"—he gestured vaguely at the dark girl—"which, I believe, is short for Patricia. They are off for an expedition to the Boyne Valley, where, I believe, they intend to photograph any Druid that might survive in Newgrange."

"The family resemblance is obvious," I said.

Both young women laughed.

"You will doubtless be happy to learn that they are both graduates of the University of Notre Dame, an institution with which you might be familiar."

"I have heard of it," I admitted.

"You went there," Trish insisted.

"Played football," Brigid reminded me.

"In 1966," Trish added. "When Parsigian went for the tie against Michigan State and still won the national championship."

"I was a freshman." I tried to assure them that I was not four years older than I really was.

Brigid finished the litany. "Third-string All-American."

"On some teams." I laughed.

"Cop," they both said together.

"Who has fallen into the hands of not one but three private eyes . . . is the bishop in Ireland to chaperon you two Golden Domers?"

They looked at each other in surprise and then burst out laughing.

"Oh, no!" Brigid this time.

"Our mothers sent us along to keep an eye on him." From Trish.

"So he doesn't get lost . . ."

"Following after that poor dear Leopold Bloom."

The bishop beamed proudly. "Indeed."

I thought that it would be interesting to follow Bishop Blackie on the Bloomsday tour, but I had at the moment other fish to fry, other drums to march to.

I turned right from the hotel and walked along the south side of the Green, a street from which most of the Georgian homes had been cleared to make way for modern shops and banks. Hundreds of well-dressed men and women were rushing by in either direction. The street was filled with expensive cars. Only a tiny girl child from the "traveling people" (as the tinkers like to be called) who begged me for a pound reminded me of the poverty of Ireland and the twenty-percent unemployment rate.

I gave her a five-pound note, at which she squealed with eleven-year-old delight—and probably judged that I was a stupid Yank.

But as my father says, "Let it be on their conscience what they do with the money, don't let it be on our conscience that you didn't give it to them."

As I walked toward Grafton Street—one of Dublin's oldest streets and described in the late 1600s as so foul smelling that no one could walk down it—at the far end of the Green, I thought about the report that Arthur T. Regan's foot-slogging gumshoes had prepared on Nora Marie MacDonaugh, a report that was so totally professional and objective that I was surprised that Arthur T. had turned it over to me.

Maybe he was merely trying to establish how straight he was. Or maybe he found the report damning as written.

She had been born Nora Finnegan out on the end of Clew Bay in County Mayo, a place where they would say that the next parish was on Long Island.

She was an only child, born late in life to elderly parents, both of whom were now dead. She had attended the national school in the next village and then for five years went to the Sisters of Mercy school in Westport. She did well enough in her A-level exams to attend the University in Galway, but there was no money to pay for her expenses in that faraway place. At the age of sixteen she was invited by a visiting distant cousin from America and her husband to live with them and enjoy the benefits of American life. She accepted with grave reluctance because she was so close to her parents and she was all they had to live for.

Apparently the parents insisted. There was no opportunity for her in Ireland. She should take advantage of her cousin's generosity. There was also a hint that the cousin might have made a substantial financial gift to her parents.

Buy a teenager?

There was no clear explanation of how the cousin and her husband managed to get her through the American immigration system. In any case, she eventually became an American citizen, after her marriage to Ronan Joyce.

I couldn't quite get a fix on the motivation of her cousin, Ruth Joyce, Ronan's mother. She had always wanted a daughter and perhaps saw in the bright, pretty girl a surrogate daughter. In fact, Nora became something of a servant— perhaps what a daughter would have been in that odd house. The Joyces' only son was "delicate" and there was a lot of work to be done around the house.

How much work, I wondered, in a modern home in Riverdale with only three people in it? Why not hire a maid instead of importing a serf from Ireland? The serf was free, but the Joyces were not poor.

It sounded to me like they were a little crazy.

Nonetheless Nora did not complain. The neighbors who remember this strange ménage say that she was cheerful and helpful and transformed the atmosphere of this strangely morose family.

Young Ronan, who was said to be "too delicate" to attend college, underwent an astonishing change. Despite his parents' warning, he used some of the income from the trust fund his grandfather, a successful merchant, had set up for him, to buy a car and drive to Fordham every day for four years to obtain his college degree. He then enrolled in law school.

The elder Joyces gave full credit to Nora, who had somehow managed to pass a high-school equivalency test, for their son's revival. While they were apparently shocked at the announcement of an engagement between their son and his cousin, once they had been assured that the relationship was not an impediment to a Catholic marriage, they enthusiastically supported it.

The newly married couple moved into an expensive home

down the street from his parents. Ronan finished law school and joined a prominent Manhattan firm. While both couples lamented the fact that there were as yet no grandchildren, they seemed happy enough, the older and younger couple often going out to dinner and a film together. Nora enrolled in Marymount Manhattan, where she became an honor student.

I calculated how long ago that was. Nora and Ronan had married in 1973, when she was twenty and he twenty-four. Eighteen years ago. The investigators must have dug pretty deep to find out as much as they had. On the other hand, in a neighborhood like Riverdale, there would be many couples the age of Ronan and Nora Joyce who would remember that time and had not moved away.

Nora also became active in the local parish and helped out in the parish teen club. Other women her age remembered her as a person who was always cheerful and outgoing, "without a care or a worry in the world."

I thought about the pictures the investigators had gathered of that time, a more robust and always smiling Nora.

The woman with whom I had danced the night before seemed a completely different person. She showed no trace of either her Irish immigrant origins or of the happiness that marked her early years of marriage.

Some of the informants thought that they detected a problem in 1977. During that year Ronan, always inclined to be moody, seemed a little more serious than usual; Nora's cheerfulness and patience appeared on occasion to be wearing thin. The younger couple and the older couple were seen less frequently together.

The editor of the final draft of the investigators' report noted that these were retrospective opinions and hence one should exercise caution in accepting them at face value. Other neighbors reported that they had noticed no changes in the relationship, except that Nora seemed to be working very hard in her last year of school.

Then it happened. Two weeks before her graduation, on a pleasant spring day, Nora returned late from school. As she drove into the driveway she was surprised to see her husband's car already there. He had driven downtown that day, because he had a meeting with a client over in Paterson, New Jersey, and did not expect to be home until after the rush hour.

As she opened the garage door to her house, she heard a shot. She rushed to their bedroom and found Ronan stretched out on their bed, a gun in his hand and the back of his head blown off.

The *Daily News* and the *Post* made a big thing about the "suburban bedroom death." There were hints that Ronan Joyce had not committed suicide, but had been murdered. His wife said that Ronan had been depressed lately and that she had urged him to see a doctor. His heartsick parents denied that the dead man had displayed any signs of depression. They avoided Nora at the wake and funeral. The *Post* darkly hinted that the Joyces believed that their son had been murdered. "Sources" in the NYPD told the *Daily News* that traces of explosive had been found on Nora's hand and that the gun was not in her husband's hand but on the floor next to the bed.

At her own request Nora took a lie-detector test the day after the funeral. The results of the test were not released. The police reported that the paraffin-test results were not compatible with firing the gun, but rather with her shoving the gun away when she rushed into the room. The death was ruled suicide and there was no arrest.

However, Nora and her in-laws remained estranged.

Then, the day she graduated from Marymount, the *Post* reported that "sources" had informed them that Ronan had left the money from the half-million-dollar trust fund established by his grandfather to Nora. Originally the money, which had become his on his twenty-first birthday, had been bequested, in a will executed on that birthday, to his mother and father. Only six months before he died he changed the will and left it all to Nora. Though she would collect no money from insurance because of a death by suicide, she would still, once the house was sold and the joint savings accounts liquidated, have almost a million dollars after taxes, no small accomplishment for an immigrant who eight years before had been penniless.

In an editorial the *Post* had demanded that the police reopen the case of the "maid who married a millionaire and became a millionaire when her husband died of a bullet hole in his head."

Two days later a spokesman for the Manhattan county district attorney could find no grounds for reconsidering the original verdict.

I paused for a stoplight at the head of Grafton Street, the old Gaiety Theatre on one side of King Street and the glittering new multilevel St. Stephen's shopping mall on the other side.

There was certainly nothing unusual about a husband, a prudent and rising young lawyer, making a decision to leave his money to his wife. What was strange perhaps was that he would have waited so long to change his will.

I called back in my memory the wedding picture of Ronan and Nora. He was a handsome young man and seemed greatly pleased with his wife. Yet his family was surely strange. Who could tell what the conversations about money with his parents might have been like.

Arthur T's investigators had found some NYPD guys that remembered the case.

"It was touch and go," one of them was quoted as saying. "We kind of felt that she had done it. Why does a guy that young, with everything going for him, kill himself? But his prints were on the gun in exactly the spots they would be if he put the gun in his mouth and pulled the trigger. She would have had to somehow get the gun in his mouth, pull the trigger, and then wipe off her prints and put his on them in exactly the right place. It could have happened, all right, and she was a smart little number—she told us about the will when we were questioning her the day before we found out. Smart move.

"We questioned her pretty closely, let me tell you, because the first instinct in such cases is, hell, yes, the wife did it. She kept repeating her story, tears pouring down her face, and there was nothing we could do to shake it. Usually they don't have consistent stories and it's easy to break 'em down.

"Sure we read her Miranda rights, but she said she didn't need a lawyer and I guess she didn't at that.

"She was just a little too good to be true—young and a knockout and smart and a smooth talker. But, hell, you'd have a hard time persuading a jury that the kid was a killer just because she seemed to some cynical cops too good to be true.

"No, she claimed she didn't know anything about the weapon, claimed he must have bought it that day, which smelled a little fishy, if you ask me. But we gave her a paraffin test that day and only came up with traces. 'Course she could be wearing gloves, which is why his prints are the only ones on the gun. Not even a latent of anyone else.

"Well, one of the DA's men on the case wanted to go for an indictment and another said they'd get creamed in court.

"She turns around and comes in with a lawyer for a lie-detector test the day after the funeral. She sails through it. So the assistant district attorney in charge says, hell, we don't have a case anyway. Maybe she didn't do it.

"And some of us say, yeah, well maybe she did, but she won't be the first smart woman to walk after killing a rich husband. Maybe she'll try it again. Then I read in the paper a year ago that sure enough, another rich husband gets blown up and I start to wonder all over again.

"The thing that got us even then was that she could give no explanation of why her husband was depressed. Beats me. Either way. Maybe she's not smart enough to make up a reason. But you gotta figure she's smart enough to stage the whole thing, she's smart enough to cook up a reason. Or maybe she's telling the truth. Or maybe she's so smart she says she doesn't know the reason because that way we'll figure she's not so smart. Either way, know what I mean?"

I was ten minutes early for our breakfast at Bewley's, a tearoom founded in 1846 and what we Yanks would now call a cafeteria. I went into the tea shop, stood in line for a cup of coffee, a glass of orange juice, three scones, two rashers of bacon, and a handful of marmalade and jelly containers.

I'd had a couple of cases of clever wives who thought they could commit the perfect crime. I tripped up every one of them. What about this kid? If I were the cop in charge of the investigation, would I let her walk?

I didn't think I would. I'd leave it to a state's attorney or a jury to decide.

And a Cook County state's attorney would come to the same conclusion that a Manhattan county district attorney had come up with:

Who needs this case? She hires a smart lawyer, she walks for sure.

That didn't mean she didn't do it. Why would the poor guy shoot himself?

I found myself a small table in the corner of the crowded and historic old tearoom with the bright stained-glass windows, a historic work by Harry Clarke.

But two husbands dying and leaving fortunes to the same woman, that was too much to be a coincidence, wasn't it? She had to have been the killer.

I had taken a course once about probability. I take a lot of courses. It's better than sitting around a bar ogling women who are too young for you. Well, maybe not better, but more dignified anyway. Cops usually operate on the premise that there are no such things as coincidences. If a person is accused of the same crime twice, it's no accident.

The probability course shook me. Coincidences, even the most seemingly fantastic and improbable, do happen routinely. That someone will get hits in fifty-six straight games like DiMaggio did in 1941 is improbable, but not all that improbable. Quite the contrary; in a half century of baseball, it's likely to happen.

The guys I was working with then didn't believe me. Then we picked up a guy named Jimmie J. Smith for a shooting in a bar. He had the name that witnesses gave, he lived across the street from the bar, he didn't have an alibi for the time of the killing, the witnesses IDed him. What more did we need?

He claimed that it was someone else called Jimmie J. Smith.

Funny thing, but he was telling the truth. I picked up the other guy and he admitted the shooting. We would have looked pretty bad in court if we'd brought in the wrong Jimmie J. Smith. And we would have probably sent an innocent man to jail.

Cops don't generally think innocent. We only think enough proof for a jury or not enough. We assume that the people we pick up are guilty and that there are no coincidences. We're almost always right.

So sometimes, very rarely, we're wrong. And if we've cooked up some evidence, we're really up the well-known creek without visible means of transportation when the defense attorneys find out.

What about Nora Finnegan Joyce? Maybe there was a coincidence. Maybe cops in both Dublin and New York were wrong. Maybe it was all a coincidence. Maybe.

I found myself hoping so.

After she was cleared the second time of Ronan Joyce's murder, Nora Joyce sold her house and enlisted in a Peace Corps–type operation that the Marymount Sisters ran in Belize. She stayed there for three years and ended up running the operation. Then she came back to New York in 1980 because of some kind of tropical illness. Already, the pictures revealed, her hair had turned from black to silver. She bought a condo in Yorkville, the old German neighborhood in the eighties on the East Side, and opened an Irish gift-and-book store on East Fifty-seventh Street, strictly an upscale place. It was an instant success, in great part because of her charm and energy. She dated occasionally, but seemed to keep pretty much to herself. She was not active in any Irish organizations, especially not any of the IRA sympathy groups.

Jim Lark used to drop into the store occasionally to buy a book. The name James L. MacDonaugh didn't mean anything to her. While she went to Ireland often for purchases, she didn't read the Irish papers and paid little attention to Irish celebrities. One day she poured him a cup of coffee and they sat down to talk. This was probably in 1985, around a year after Dora died. She told him about her experiences in Belize and her idea about foundations. He told her that his foundation was languishing and he needed someone to take it over and run it right. He offered her the job and she turned the management of the store over to her assistant and took the new job.

The same day.

Two impulsive people. They saw what they wanted and went for it.

There was a formal picture of her from that time, taken for the announcement of her appointment as executive director of the Jim Lark Foundation (that's what he called it). She seemed every inch the successful and ambitious professional woman, prettier than most perhaps, but otherwise utterly composed and determined. And not quite so thin as she was last night.

No tormented eyes either.

Fifteen or sixteen years out of the bogs at the end of Clew Bay and she must have seemed an entirely different person to herself and to anyone who had known her as a frightened immigrant kid.

Frightened? That was my word. There was nothing in the report on her to suggest that she had ever been frightened.

Three years later she and Jim Lark were married. Two years after that a bomb blew him apart. She was no longer merely comfortable. She was fabulously wealthy.

One very successful woman.

"I suppose," she said, sitting down across from me, "you want to start with my intimate life with my late husband."

6

"**N**OT NECESSARILY." I JUMPED UP FROM THE TABLE, STAR-tled by her arrival and her opening line.

I was too late to help her with her chair. Still she nodded and smiled her gratitude. Routine response to courtesy.

"Come now, Tim Pat, you do, too," she said pleasantly enough.

She was wearing a light running suit, beige with red trim, a set of Walkman earphones around her neck, and a waist purse. Her striking silver hair was tied in a ponytail. She had been running, and her running suit, moist with sweat, clung attractively to her body. However, she radiated the scent of flowers instead of human perspiration—pretty strong perfume in that purse.

Everyone in the room was looking at her, the men doubt-less envying me.

"Kind of a hot day for running, isn't it?"

"And I'm sufficiently prudish when I'm in Ireland that I have to wear more than shorts and a running bra." She put a dab of marmalade on a piece of the scones she had brought.

"Not much breakfast."

"I'm usually not very hungry. Too thin perhaps." She looked away from me. "Five more pounds at least, maybe ten. Not like most women my age. I used to weigh more. But you know that; you've seen pictures of me at various stages of my life."

"Have I, now?"

"Haven't I just said that you have?" She displayed a trace of a mischievous grin for a brief moment. "And naturally you want to know about my intimate life with Jim Lark. Didn't your good friend Arthur T. Regan show you the hotel bills from our two years of marriage?"

"You have good sources."

"Don't I, now?" She sipped from her teacup. Black tea, in this respect American rather than Irish.

"What kind of a man is it who monitors the sex life of his boss and best friend?"

"A man like Arthur T. Regan." She folded her hands in front of her on the scarred and unstable little table. "When I was dressing this morning, I decided I would be utterly candid with you, more open about my relationship with Jim Lark than I have ever been to anyone, more open than I would be to anyone except maybe a priest or a doctor."

"Why?"

"To persuade you of my innocence, obviously."

She was looking at me, her eyes level with mine, a pose of total frankness and sincerity.

"Why do you want me to think you're innocent?"

She lifted one shoulder slightly. "I want you to find the real killers, I want justice for poor Jim Lark, I want the cloud out of my own life. Also, Bishop Blackie said you're a good man. I guess"—her eyes never wavered—"I want the good opinion of a good man."

"I see . . . and you believe Bishop Blackie?"

The little leprechaun glint appeared again, oh so briefly, and then quickly vanished.

"The kids who are keeping an eye on him go, 'Like Uncle Punk is *always* right. Totally.' Even the half sister calls him Uncle some of the time, for convenience, she says."

"And now you hesitate at the threshold of candor?"

"Indeed yes, Tim Pat." She refolded her hands. "Unveiling is mildly pleasant, even exciting, in the presence of a favorably disposed audience. It is also terrifying. I find myself reflecting that you would find my story interesting, no doubt, but there is no way I can persuade you that it's true. Hence it will not contribute in any way to my contention that I did not kill my husband."

"I'm not a jury, Nora."

"Yes, you are, Tim Pat."

There was no way on earth she could have learned that my

mother, and only in private, called me by that affectionate name.

"It's up to you, of course." I chose my words carefully. "My job is to piece together a story, kind of like a jigsaw puzzle, I suppose. The more parts of the story I have, the easier it is to make sense out of it."

She nodded. "I know that. I'm still scared."

"You also know that I'm not unfavorably disposed toward you."

She sighed. Her lovely breasts moved up and down beneath the thin fabric of jacket. "Half-prepared to believe me?"

"A fair description."

"I know that's all I can expect." She glanced down at the table and then looked up at me again. "All right. To begin with, I had a kind of teenage crush on Jim Lark before I knew he was anyone else but an occasional customer in my shop. So he was twenty years and more older than me; but he was a handsome, virile man who exuded charm and strength and wit. A woman couldn't help but find him attractive. When I went to work for him, I found that all the young women in the office had the same kind of crush, though a little more obvious than mine."

"You covered it up?"

"Certainly. I was not in the market for a husband, or so I told myself . . . there was never a hint from him that he might want me. He was always friendly, with that quick smile and ready laugh he had for everyone, but nothing more than that. We even traveled together to visit some of the grantees of the foundation. Once to Africa to a hospital some Irish nuns were running on a shoestring. There was never the slightest suggestion that we share the same room, much less same bed."

"Enormous restraint," I murmured.

She stared at me, wondering for a second or two whether my inappropriate words were snide. She decided that they weren't.

"Arguably, as the bishop would say. Then—oh, God, this is hard to say—then one day he asked me to marry him. Made a mess of it for a man so glib. Didn't talk about love, but about loneliness and companionship. I was enormously flattered that a man like him would want me. And at the same time I felt an incredibly powerful sting of desire. I fell in love with him on the spot. I was willing to give myself to him at that very moment in his office." She lowered her eyes. "You will think me a terrible woman."

"That's Clew Bay talking, Nora."

She smiled. "Isn't it, now. . . ."

"In truth, you are not really ashamed of your healthy and normal reaction."

She nodded. "Not at all, at all. Yet our courtship—it lasted only a couple of weeks—was incredibly restrained. I began to wonder whether he meant companionship literally. On our wedding night he was the one who was shy and scared—one of the most successful and hard-driving entrepreneurs in the world was frightened by a slip of a girl in a sheer robe. Can you believe that?"

"Yes."

"Jim Lark and Dora had been incredibly hung up on sex. They barely knew how to do it, much less enjoy it. It was not their fault. It was the way they were raised. You'll say the Irish are terrible prudes and I guess we are, but not all of us are that bad. Rony and I enjoyed one another enormously. We really did. From the beginning. I mean we weren't accomplished or anything like that. But we had fun. Jim Lark never had any real fun in bed before me."

I hoped that my silence would reassure her.

"So I became his teacher. Can you imagine that? A man of his position and importance and power and age giving himself to a woman so that she could teach him about sex? I don't claim to be any great expert on the subject, but I knew a lot more than he did. He had the strength of character to permit me to teach him. He was a very good pupil. He became in bed what he was in the rest of his life. Naturally I fell even more hopelessly in love with him."

Who wouldn't? I thought. You can teach me any day.

I contend that such a reaction is a normal and healthy male response to someone like Nora.

"Just a minute," I interrupted her so that she could put her emotions back together. Also I was hungry.

I brought back to the table two more rashers of bacon and another large scone for myself and the same for her.

"How did you know I was hungry?" She grinned up at me. "I guess talking about sex does make one hungry. Maybe if I talk about it more, I'll put on those ten pounds."

"The woman I danced with last night was fine the way she was."

Nora destroyed the bacon and the scone. Destroyed it altogether, as they say in Dublin's fair city.

"Anyway, to Arthur T. Regan's snooping on our hotel bills. If he had snooped back far enough, he would have found that Jim Lark also reserved two bedroom suites when he traveled with Dora. He was a man with delicate respect for women, a little too delicate maybe, but better that than the opposite. He said that the other room was in case I didn't want to sleep with him, 'on the odd night.'

"I told him that I would never not want to sleep with him and that I couldn't get enough of him. He couldn't get enough of me. We had two good years, Tim Pat."

Tears glistened in her eyes.

"More than a hell of a lot of people, Nora Marie."

"I know. . . . I swore to myself I wouldn't cry. I don't want to appeal to your sympathy, only to your concern for truth."

She dabbed at her eyes with a tissue.

I struggled for an appropriate response. "I think I can be objective and sympathetic at the same time."

They were the right words.

"Thanks." She put away the tissue and folded her hands again. "You're very sweet."

"For a cop."

"Retired cop . . . Anyway I've lost him. I will not ever marry again. . . . We made love just before I went out to buy the fixings for afternoon tea. We were both tired from the trip across the Atlantic and we wanted to nap. But we wanted each other more. It was spectacular love, Tim Pat. Later, when I pulled myself together, I thought that it might have been a wonderful hint of what he found in heaven. . . . Do you believe that's true?"

"Isn't your Man saying that it's the great sacrament?"

"St. Paul? Well, maybe it is. I hope so. But if we have to end our lives—and we all do, don't we?—maybe it was the happiest ending poor Jim Lark could have had."

She bit her lips, on the verge of tears again.

"So, you see, Tim Pat, I didn't kill him. I couldn't have killed him. I don't care what that terrible man Chief Superintendent Tom Clarke may tell you. I didn't do it."

I wanted to say that I knew she didn't do it. However, it would not have been professional to take sides that early in my investigation.

"What are you going to do with all the money, Nora?"

"Arthur T. Regan will have told you that I waste it on my crazy idea of bringing peace to Ireland." She polished off the remnants of her second scone, this time with a liberal scoop of strawberry jam. "I don't think you can buy peace. But I think you can support social and economic and educational projects which will help to shape the context for peace. I want to do all I can for my poor native land to find peace. I want to be one of the peace makers. Jim Lark said that he would spend the last years of his life doing that. I want to do the same thing for the rest of my life, however long or short it may be."

Her eyes shone now with enthusiasm and zeal.

"Happy are the peace makers, like your Man said."

She smiled. "He did have some pretty good insights, on the odd occasion. . . . Look, Tim Pat. I'm not a crazy. I'm not going to gut the companies and then sell them off. There's too many people depending for their livelihood on them. I'm just going to put all my share of the profits and the money he left me into a new Jim Lark Peace Foundation. I don't even want to run the companies, but you can be damn sure that I'll keep an eye on how they're run."

"Another couple of rashers?"

"No . . . all right, yes. And one more tiny scone, if you please."

When I returned, she greeted me with, "Haven't you spilled some of that orange juice on your nice sport jacket?"

Out came the tissue again to dab up what she could.

"You'll have to send it out when you return to the hotel, won't you?"

"Yes, Mother."

She bent over and laughed—good, honest Irish laughter.

"Sure, I'm the terrible one, giving orders all the time."

"From some people I don't mind . . . like my mother."

"She sounds like a grand woman."

"She's all of that."

Nora destroyed her second refill as competently and completely as she had finished off the first.

"So you think that someone is messing in the companies."

"I do. Jim Lark did, too. I haven't been able to find out who is doing it, but I know it's happening. You see, Jim Lark was kind of suspicious of organizational charts. He used them, but he combined the various interests so that only he knew the way around all of them. Arthur T. understood some of the back alleys and mountain trails, but not all of them."

"You think that Arthur T. is on the take?"

"I hope it's him, he's such a mean man. But there's no evidence that he is doing anything dishonest. Jim Lark thought he was as straight as the day is long. The man couldn't be cute even if he wanted to, he used to say."

"You're continuing the investigation?"

"Jim Lark would have wanted me to do that. I have a whole new set of audit reports with me."

"Anything in the reports?"

"Not that an auditor could see . . . Maybe a detective could find something if he wanted to look."

"If you want me to . . ."

"Isn't that why I told you about them?"

"Were Jim Lark's suspicions the reason for your sudden flight to Dublin?"

"I don't know. He had something on his mind that he

wouldn't talk about, but it didn't worry him very much. A bit of stuff to clear up, was all he said. But, as you know from the stories, his whole family was gathering."

"Did they like you?"

"Not all that much. Well, his kids did until they found out about the will. His sister and brothers barely spoke to me even then. They're strange, dark people, the very opposite of Jim Lark."

"You knew about the will, of course?"

"Certainly not." She waved her hand. "If I did, I would have insisted he change it back or at least modify it."

"Why?"

"So there wouldn't be ill feeling with his children, who are nice people. I miss the grandchildren terribly. They're such sweet kids. But I guess he wanted to make sure that the money went to peace making. Everyone has enough anyway."

"No one ever has enough money."

"I do. More than enough. Too much. Look, Tim Pat MacCarthy." She straightened up and jabbed a finger at me. "I live in my old condo in Yorkville. I take taxis not limousines, I stay in the Shelbourne, not the Berkeley Court, and in a single room, not a suite. My clothes are not super expensive, I buy inexpensive makeup and scent, the only jewelry I own Jim Lark bought for me. I fly business class, in New York I own a seven-year-old Chevy Celebrity. Julia lives in the house on Shrewsbury Road and Mick Dav in the castle. I sent word to the kids through my lawyer that the summer home was theirs this summer and every summer. What more can a woman do to prove that she's not money hungry?"

I would have to check all of this out. She knew that. So presumably she was speaking the truth.

"I don't know, Nora."

"I'm still the careful kid from Clew Bay who never had anything and was happy enough without it."

"Do you go out there anymore, Nora?"

"No." She shook her head sadly. "My parents are dead. There's nothing left for me out there. Maybe someday I'll run back and search for a few memories. . . . I do send something to the Mercy Sisters in Westport. I have since I returned from Belize."

"You say you were happy out there?"

"Wasn't I ever? I went to New York because I wanted to go to university. I thought I could earn money in America to help my parents in their old age. Doesn't every immigrant from this battered old island? Poor things, they were both dead by the time I would have been able to help."

"You wouldn't want to live that life again, however, would you?"

"Wasn't I spoiled the first two weeks in New York—inside toilets, showers, electricity, central heating, television. I almost thought I was in heaven."

There are a lot of details of the murder day that were in the reports of the Dublin police and about which I could ask Chief Superintendent Clarke when I saw him later this morning. I would not stir up painful memories for her.

"One final question, Nora. Why are you here in Dublin now?"

"Oh"—she smiled shyly—" 'tis a silly thing that I came to talk to Paddy Quaid about. Jim Lark had this wonderful idea—an Irish cream that's even better than Baileys. It really is, you'll have to do a blind test of it someday to see if I'm not right. It just needs a little fine-tuning, if you take my meaning. Jim Lark planned to produce it and market it all over the world. Jim Lark Cream, he wanted to call it, no shy man, my late husband." She smiled again briefly. "We put some money into development and marketing research, and of course into mixing just the right ingredients."

"Sounds like it will be tasty."

"Is it ever." She nodded enthusiastically. "Arthur T. Regan thinks it's a crazy scheme, and maybe it is. I want to be certain about it, but it's the kind of thing Jim Lark would want me to continue."

"I suppose Baileys don't half like the prospect?"

"I asked the man who came to me to talk about it, whether he believed in capitalism or not. He did." She grinned enthusiastically. "But he didn't think too much competition was a good thing."

"And you said?"

She wiped her lips with a napkin and stood up, sensing that our conversation was over.

"I said that they had beat the focking shit out of all the other creams, now 'twas time someone gave them a focking run for their focking money and the competition would be a good thing for focking Ireland."

"Four times in one sentence! Congratulations!"

She turned a deep shade of red. "I only talk that way when I'm dealing with your male-chauvinist Irish businessman."

"Not cops?"

"Not sweet cops anyway." She was easing us toward the side door of Bewley's.

"You wear your grief gracefully," I said, not wanting to respond to the sweet comment and thus by inattention saying something that would certainly rank as sweet.

"Sometimes." She sighed. "Then sometimes, Tim Pat, I think my heart will break and I'll die of sadness. Two men I loved . . . I'll not take the chance again."

I was not about to cope with that firm declaration.

Anyway, people can change their minds.

"Thank you for your cooperation," I said formally.

"Thank you for being such a gracious interrogator." She touched my hand. "I'd love to ask you whether you believe me or not, but that wouldn't be fair, would it, now? You haven't had a chance to put all the pieces together."

Just then she could have told me the moon was made of Irish cheese and I would have believed her.

"I'll stay in touch," I said lamely as we walked into the tiny walkway that linked Grafton Street to Clarendon Street and South William Street beyond, the narrow curving streets of Dublin in the early 1700s. The clear sky had been replaced by clouds moving in rapidly from the Irish Sea and the air seemed noticeably cooler, with a hint of rain.

In Ireland there is always a hint of rain.

"I'm going to drop in here." She gestured at the entrance

to the Clarendon Street Carmelite church, just across the lane from Bewley's.

"I'll join you."

St. Teresa of Avila's Church, as it is called properly, though everyone in Dublin calls it "Clarendon Street," may be the ugliest Catholic church in all the world, complete with blue lights and statues that would make one a follower of Leo the Isaurian (an Iconoclast Roman emperor). Nonetheless it was somehow a good place in which to pray.

What's she praying for? I asked the Deity. Is she giving thanks that she's taken me in completely? Or is she begging You to help me to believe her? Or is it all part of the focking act, You should excuse my language.

I'm not exactly a devout Catholic. I don't go to church every week, not since I became embarrassed at old St. Patrick's in Chicago because I was the oldest unmarried person in that congregation of attractive young singles of both genders.

I do believe in God, though I find it odd that He—or She, if you wish—would be interested in our prayers. Still, on the record, that seems to be the case.

So I said to Whoever was in charge, Okay, I hope You'll give me a hand in my investigation. And I'd be very happy if You work things out so she's telling me the truth and so I can clear her name. And I hope also that You'll forgive me if there's anything wrong with the terrible obscene images I have about her. If they're lustful, I hope You understand that they are respectfully lustful. Well, more or less respectful anyway.

I paused. That was going far enough, wasn't it?

And if you can without too much difficulty arrange it so that I can bed her, on a permanent basis, mind you, I wouldn't half mind.

It was a very Irish prayer.

Next to me Nora was praying with a slight frown on her face, as if she, too, were trying to figure something out.

I hope she's praying about me, I informed the Deity in my last petition.

Naturally there was no response.

Outside on Clarendon Street, she glanced at me. "Sometimes I wonder if there's anyone up there. Then I decide that if there's no one up there, then I'm not here. Right?"

"Sounds like good theology to me."

"Bye." She looked like she wanted to kiss me, but did not do so. "I'll see you."

If she had kissed me, she would have owned me completely. Probably she knew that.

The sky was even darker than it had been when we went into the church. I walked through the tangled streets of old Dublin, down Clarendon Street to where it ended and then over to Great George Street and finally Dame Street and around the corner to Dublin Castle.

I was early for the appointment, so I walked around the corner, by Christ Church Cathedral, a low-slung and quaint Romanesque church with Gothic flying buttresses, and down along the stores with cheap clothes on Thomas Street through the old section of Dublin called the Liberties. The early-eighteenth-century Guinness brewery, with many more recent additions, loomed like a fortress over the west end of the neighborhood. A city within a city and a subculture all its own, the Liberties were once the worst slums of Dublin and still seemed to my romantic imagination an unhappy and depressed neighborhood, as though tainted by ancient grief. Dean Swift bemoaned the poverty in the area when he wasn't worrying about his tragic love for Stella, and Reverend James Whitelaw, the vicar of St. Catherine's, surveyed the neighborhood house-to-house in 1798 and detailed the poverty.

You wouldn't want to walk down these by yourself at night, I had been warned. But in daylight the people who swarmed on the streets, young and old, quiet and noisy, attractive and plain—and more kids per cubic foot than any place I'd ever been—were as friendly as any other Irish. The outdoor markets on Thomas and Meath streets, a little like Chicago's Maxwell Street in days of yore, were lively and energetic. The neighborhood was a patchwork of ugly public housing, though not as ugly as that in Chicago and with much less graffiti, a few old five-story tenements, and the tiniest row houses I'd ever seen, some of which were already being gentrified.

Despite Ireland's economic problems, life in the Liberties was much better than it had been in O'Casey's time and infinitely better than de Tocqueville had described in the 1830s. If there were still a special culture in this old, old neighborhood, it was not likely to survive all that long. The Yuppies would take over with their expensive cars and their alarm systems on the front of the row houses. It would be the end of an historic sadness, exorcised by the ambitions of young professionals.

Life out on Clew Bay, I reflected, turning to my current favorite subject, was better not so long ago than life in the Liberties.

I thought about Nora again, more objectively, I told myself, in the context of the Liberties. She was a very clever woman, no doubt about that. She knew how to use her seeming fragility and her erotic appeal most effectively on a man.

Could I seriously believe that she never turned her allurements on Jim Lark? He was, by her own admission, an attractive man despite the age difference and an attractive man with a lot of money. Did she want me to believe that she sent out no subtle sexual signals to him and that she was totally surprised when he suggested marriage?

Unlikely, very unlikely.

She was very clever, she had to have been to move from Clew Bay to Shrewsbury Road in two decades. Was it not reasonable to assume that she had deliberately charmed her distant American relatives to bring her back to the United States with them?

In fact, was it not unreasonable to assume anything besides that? She had seduced her way from poverty to enormous wealth—how could I think otherwise? Maybe the seduction was not fully self-conscious, but it was deliberate just the same? Nora Finnegan knew what she was doing. I was just the most recent target.

Yet if it was all an act, if the tenderness of the love she described between herself and her late husband was an act, too, then she was the most clever woman criminal I had ever met.

I walked over to the Liffey and strolled along Ushers Quay, Merchants Quay, and Wood Quay, where the Vikings first settled. Across the river, and outlined against the dark sky, the Four Courts loomed. An elegant Georgian structure designed by the great architect Gandon, it had been rebuilt after its destruction (and much of the documentation of Irish history with it) in the Irish Civil War in the twenties. Underneath ESE Quay the Poodle River, once the source of Dublin's water and the pool from which came the name Dub Lin (black pool), flowed through a grate into the Liffey. Life in Viking Dublin had been, as they say, nasty, brutish, and short—not that it had been much better in either the Liberties or County Mayo in the middle of the last century.

There was a lot of history concentrated in those few blocks around Dublin Castle, most of it tragic.

How did Nora MacDonaugh fit into that history?

She had learned how to survive, as many other Irishwomen had since the Vikings came up the Liffey a thousand years and more ago. She had also learned how to survive and prosper, which was more than many others had been able to do.

Don't trust her, I warned myself sternly. And don't let her act fool you.

Right?

Right.

It was raining when I entered the castle to interview Chief Superintendent Tomás Clarke.

7

"**O**F COURSE, SHE KILLED HIM," CHIEF SUPERINTENDENT Tom Clarke insisted, "the woman's a bleeding tosser. She plays with his goiter for a while, lets him knob her, goes out of the house to buy the odd scone for tea, and then focking blows him apart."

I had only met Tom Clarke a few moments before in his smoke-filled, airless office. Yet I knew him well and didn't like him. He was the cop I might have become in a few more years if I hadn't retired when I did.

"I see."

He was about my age and, indeed, was built like I am, but he was overweight and out of condition. His tie, spotted with breakfast food, was open at the neck and his shirt already wrinkled. His once handsome face was turning to seed like the rest of him, and his razor must need a new blade. His salt-and-pepper hair hadn't seen a barber's scissors in a couple of months.

"I don't mind you poking around, so long as you don't bollix things up on me," he continued, lighting a cigarette. "Your good friend Mike Casey says you're all right, not a right focking yobo at all, at all. And them that gives the orders"—he jerked a thumb toward the higher floors of the building—"says I should go along with you. But I don't think you'll find a focking thing that we didn't focking find."

He had not opened the office window when I entered and began to cough. "That window," he had said, "hasn't been opened since the day Mick Collins took this place over from the bleeding Brits."

Dublin Castle isn't really a castle at all, but a group of buildings of varying ages and tastelessness gathered around what was probably once a medieval courtyard and is now, naturally, a parking lot. The Irish have restored one building that looks like a medieval keep. But they are in no hurry to make the site of a millennium or so of English oppression a picturesque tourist attraction.

He knew I was a fellow cop, so he was somewhat more gracious than he would have been if I were a layman.

"I don't imagine I will," I agreed. "But I have to go through the motions."

"Yeah, I know what it's like. But it's all the same MO, if you take my meaning. Miss Yo-Yo Knickers lets a guy pork her for a while. Then when he has had enough good rides, he makes out a will in which she gets everything, and then *bang*, he's dead."

I marveled at the Irish fluency in obscenity. We were no match for them.

"It sure looks like it," I agreed.

"Focking coincidences don't focking happen."

No point in telling him about focking probability theory.

"Not usually."

"Mind you, the focking gobshite is smart, one of the smartest I've ever met. She's got away with murder not once but twice. Not many pull that off. Someone will get her eventually."

"I sure hope so."

"Not that she's not a focking looker; it would be focking deadly to get into her box and ride her a couple of times, but a man would have to be pissed out of his focking mind to risk it."

"It certainly sounds that way."

"The focking thing is that we focking know she did it, but we haven't any focking proof."

Only three times in each of his last two statements. Nora can do it four times and it's not habitual with her.

"Tell me about how it happened."

"Well, she and poor old Jim Lark decide, suddenlike, to fly into Dublin. Some kind of gathering of the clan or something like that. No one seems to know why. She doesn't call the servants to fix the place up, allegedly because it's too late when they leave Kennedy. But that makes the house empty, which is what she wants. She shags him—"

"How do you know that?"

"Wasn't he focking naked except for a robe when we found the pieces. No trace of any other clothes at all, at all. . . . Then she gets out of the house just before the bomb goes off to buy scones and cream for tea, if you're willing to believe that!"

"Where?"

"A bakery right at Ballsbridge at the top of Merrion Street."

"Why go to a bakery? Couldn't a woman of her importance call for scones?"

He winked at me. "Isn't that a good question, now? Sure, she pretends to live like everyone else, but why would anyone want to do that unless they had something to hide, if you take me meaning?"

"The bomb?"

"There wasn't much left of it when we got there, as you might imagine. The bomb boys say it was the kind the Provos are using these days. You get an ordinary business envelope, you put a few ounces—five or six maybe—of sheet explosive inside it and a couple of wires and a little thing that can be activated by remote control, like the things you change TV stations with or like garage-door openers that the plushies out in South County use, thinking they're focking Yanks."

"I know the kind."

"Yeah, so long as you can get the demo, the rest is easy. You can pick up the transmitter in any electronics shop in the world."

"Who makes it?"

"She buys it from the Provos." He shrugged. "Or from one of the focking yobos who make it for the Provos."

"How does it get into the house?"

"Someone puts it under the door. Or maybe she puts it under the door when she leaves to buy the scones . . . can you picture that? Going out to buy scones after a geezer has porked you? It focking stinks."

"It sounds that way."

"But it's just about a perfect alibi. The people in the bakery all know her. Hell, everyone in focking Ireland knows her with her bare tits hanging out of the English papers. She's right outside the door of the bakery when they hear the focking explosion."

"It is indeed a great alibi."

"Just like a couple of old folks in New York see her going into the house just as the gun goes off. Too focking good, if you ask me."

"Does she bring the bomb into the country?"

"Maybe someone slips it into her hands at the airport or in the ladies'. She puts it in the attaché case she carries and the transmitter into her purse. A lot better than risking a customs search, though the bleeding tossers out at the airport don't search much, especially the luggage of the wife of focking Jim focking Lark."

"I don't suppose they would. . . . So all you'd need would be the gizmo that transmits the signals with her fingerprints on it and you've got her."

"Then it's the rest of her natural life in Limerick Prison."

"But you couldn't find it?"

He shifted uneasily in his chair. "No trouble finding it."

"Oh?"

"It's in the room where the explosion was."

"With her prints?"

"Nah, only with his, just like the gun in New York."

"Wait a minute, let me get this straight. The gizmo is in the room where he died?"

I knew it was, but I wanted to hear him say so.

"Yeah."

"And with his prints on it?"

"Yeah."

"So he blew himself up?"

"Right," Tom Clarke said sardonically, and lit another cigarette. "He presses the button that focking blows himself up and then, having been blown up, walks across the room and deposits his odd bits and pieces around the desk where the bomb was."

"Could there have been a delay mechanism?"

"Bomb says there wasn't. It was instantaneous detonation."

"Wow!"

"A focking pisser!"

"Could it have been another radio device?"

"Nope. The people that make it tell us that this one was altered a little so that it was keyed to this bomb. The Provos do that. We tried it on a couple of dozen other remote-control devices and it didn't send out the radio signal for any of them."

"Might the force of the explosion have thrown the gizmo off his desk and across the room?"

"That explosion would have torn your gizmo apart just like it tore apart old Jim Lark."

"Yeah . . . so someone uses it from outside and then throws it into the room afterward?"

"That's what we figure."

"There's the problem of how they get Jim Lark's prints."

"A thousand ways"—he shrugged his shoulders—"they could do that."

"The wife, I suppose I should say the widow, could have done it."

"That's what we think. But, see, she walks right home after she leaves the shop. It takes ten minutes. By the time she's at the house, the guards and her sister-in-law Julia are already there."

"She could have someone drive her, couldn't she?"

"That's what we figure, but we can't find any driver. Anyway, it would be cutting it awful close. She must figure the bomb will bring all kinds of people into Shrewsbury Road and the local guards would be there in a couple of minutes. You gotta time it perfectly. A car comes by just as you press the button, picks you up, drives you over to Shrewsbury Road, dumps you in front of your house, and you dash in and throw the transmitter into the room you've blown up."

"And what if someone sees you dashing into the house?"

"Yeah, that's what her focking lawyer said."

"Of course, she could have had someone else detonate the bomb."

"Sure, that O'Neill guy who's riding her these days might be the one. He's at the back of the house. He opens the back-door as soon as he hears the explosion, runs into the house, opens the door to the study where the brains and guts of Jim Lark are scattered about—nothing bigger than six inches square—throws in the transmitter, locks the door, and disappears out the back. It's risky, but she's got him wrapped around her little finger."

"O'Neill?"

"Marty O'Neill, a guy about thirty, real good-looking. Kind of ran errands for Jim Lark. Gofer, as you Yanks call him. Slippery."

"He's intimate with the widow?"

"If it walks like a focking duck and talks like a focking duck, it sure as hell is a focking duck, right?"

Three times in one sentence, but all modifying the same word. Nora was ahead.

"I guess."

"If you tell me a guy travels with her most of the time and is always with her at business meetings and that she seems to depend on him, then I say he's focking shagging her, right?"

"I suppose so. . . . Is he here in Dublin now?"

"You bet your focking life he is! Staying over at the focking Berkeley Court, mind you, so it won't look bad. But you follow him around, you'll find he's porking her some-where every night."

"You have him under surveillance?"

"Nah! What good would it do to trail that gobshite? What does it prove now? Maybe in Chicago you got enough cops to go around, but we don't."

"No police force in the world has enough."

"Trouble is that he has a good alibi. A dozen people will swear he was in London all that day. Flew over on the last plane when he heard about the explosion. Can't shake it."

"Someone else, then?"

"That seems to be the best bet. We worked her over pretty good during the next two days when she was 'helping us with our inquiries,' harder than you Yanks would, harder than we ought to, especially with a woman. No physical stuff, mind you. We don't have to do that anymore. The psychological stuff is just as good. Some of our women constables are pretty good at it with other women. Get their confidence, you know. Didn't budge her a focking inch, focking little Miss Yo-Yo Pants."

Regardless of Marty O'Neill, I wanted to smash his ugly face. Instead I said, "Didn't trip once, huh?"

"Not once. The coolest killer I've ever known. Hell, after what she went through, a lot of birds would have admitted they killed their own mother."

"Professional hit man, then?"

"That's what we figure. From out of the country."

"It would have had to be a pretty quick spur-of-the-moment contract, wouldn't it?"

"That sort of thing can be done," he said indifferently, lighting yet another cigarette.

The trouble with a cop that gets mired in his own cynicism is that he never can admit that there's something he doesn't know. The outside hit man who punched the radio transmitter from the back garden of the house on Shrewsbury Road was a deus ex machina, a fiction to explain a crime that he could not solve. It was only a remote possibility that an outside professional could have been called in at the last minute and pull off such an intricate crime—even if he had been prepared for it before.

A smart pro wouldn't touch it.

And what was the rush anyway? Why would Nora be in such a hurry to dispose of her husband? Tom Clarke had not offered an explanation for that; so he didn't have one.

"So the guards and Julia MacDonaugh arrived at the same time," I continued. "And her brother-in-law Michael Davitt MacDonaugh right after her. She let them into the house and they charged into the library where the explosion occurred?"

He shifted uneasily again. "Not quite. You see, the door to

the library was locked. Julia MacDonaugh didn't have the key. When Miss Yo-Yo Pants showed up, she said that she didn't have one either. So we had to break the door down."

"Who had a key?"

"Supposedly there was only one key, and Jim Lark had it. The grieving widow"—he sneered—"said he never locked the door and she had no idea where the key was."

"So you broke the door down and found the radio transmitter *inside*?"

"Yeah. The key and the transmitter on the shelf with the rare books right inside the door . . . and Jim Lark spread out all over the room."

"Literally?"

"Focking literally. He must have been leaning over the envelope when it blew. Biggest thing we found was a hunk of thigh. It was quite a blast, blew out all the windows in the house. They were all covered with bars except the one in the WC." He pulled out a diagram. "And no one but a focking midget could get in or out of that."

I pored over the diagram.

"Not the door, however?"

"Massive oak. It was a little loose on the hinges, that's all. All the doors in the house built that way."

"Bathrooms were not in the original house, I suppose?"

"Nah, they put them in later. When the house was built, there were three staircases, one in the back for the servants"—he pointed at the diagram—"one in the front for the family, and another one in between for himself when he wanted to sneak out without being noticed"—he leered—"for whatever purpose. So when he was fixing this house at the time he married Dora Collins back in fifty-three, he tore out the staircase and put in two bathrooms, one up here next to the husband's dressing room—from which the old fella used to sneak out back in the last century—and one below it next to the library. The hot-tub thing upstairs was Miss Yo-Yo Pants's idea. That way he could knob her underwater."

He laughed obscenely.

"All solid construction, laddie," he continued. "No way

anyone could get out of those bathrooms, especially because the guards were there in a couple of minutes, as anyone would know they would be. Julia, too, though that was an accident."

I would have to check all that out in the afternoon when I visited Julia.

"What was their reaction when you finally opened the door?"

"The widow screamed and then vomited. Like I say there were bits and pieces scattered all about. Not much left of him."

"How did you ID him?"

"Who the hell else would it be? There were no clothes, like I said, because she had just shagged him. But we found pieces of the robe she said he was wearing."

"And the sister?"

He shifted uneasily again. "She's a hard one. The guards that were there say she merely stared at the rubble and said something like, 'Well, you finally got what you were asking for all your life.' "

"Brr!"

"Yeah, but there's no way she could have done it. Same for the brothers. They're thugs, all right, but they all had alibis."

I almost said that they could have hired the postulated hit man, too. They knew that Jim Lark was coming to Dublin for some kind of meeting. If one of them had something to worry about, now was the time to strike. Being in the country made it easier for them to organize the plan.

I didn't necessarily believe that had happened, but I didn't exclude it and I wondered why Tom Clarke did.

Probably because he was so convinced that Nora was the killer. That happens to cops. You're so sure that you've got the right suspect that you don't look beyond your nose for another one.

Sure, each of the brothers had plenty of money, as Nora had said earlier that morning. But no one ever has enough money, as I had told her. I didn't clarify what I meant because she went on to her spirited defense of herself. Had the banker in London made some bad investment or perhaps embezzled a few pounds? Was the sheep farmer up against a big mortgage? Or Jim Lark's own kids, were any of them up against a wall?

Maybe not, but a smart cop would find out. Tom Clarke was not only a brute, he was a careless brute. Whatever he might have been ten, fifteen years ago, he wouldn't work for me very long today.

"So that's where it all stands?" I said.

"Yeah. I don't like it, but what can I do? The people upstairs"—he jerked his thumb upward again—"they say you haven't got a case, so go on to something else."

"And the Provos?" I said softly.

"Who do you mean?" he grumbled.

"Our mutual friends from up north." I nodded my head toward Ulster the way in Chicago I would nod my head toward the West Side when I was talking about the Outfit.

"Bollix!" he exploded. "If them focking tossers had blown off Jim Lark's gooter, they'd be claiming credit the next day. This time they denied it completely. They don't deny something unless they haven't done it."

"They kidnapped him once."

"Did they, now?"

"That's what the papers say."

"Well, do you believe everything they say in the papers in America?"

"And the three terrorists who kidnapped him and then later escaped are all dead."

That caught him by surprise. "Are they, now?" he said, trying to cover up, but not quickly enough to fool me.

"I'm wondering if there's some connection between the two incidents, especially since our mutual friends make the same kind of bomb."

It was a question that any halfway intelligent and relatively honest cop would have asked.

"Yeah," he said, staring at his desk glumly.

I waited.

"Look, a lot of people think there was something funny

about that so-called kidnapping. I wouldn't be at all surprised if the MacDonaughs and the government and the Provos made some kind of deal. But let me tell you one thing. If they did, neither you nor I nor anyone else is ever gonna find out about it. It's buried deep in ten layers of shit. Know what I mean?"

I knew, all right. "Too bad you weren't able to clear it up right away."

"Yeah. The big fellas wanted me to, but they didn't want to go into a courtroom with a weak case against a grieving widow."

"Especially one you couldn't break."

"That's focking true."

Whatever might lie beneath all those layers of shit, the ones who had piled it up had ample reason for not wanting anyone to start poking around in it. Better that Nora Finnegan Joyce MacDonaugh walk, especially if you really couldn't prove anything against her, than stir up that shit.

I understood, all right. Moreover Tom Clarke wanted me to understand.

"One more thing." I stood up to leave. "Who's Liam Lynch?"

"It's a common enough name." He was puzzled by my question. "I suppose the best-known man by that name was the fella that was the chief of staff of the Irregulars, the Republicans that is, during the Civil War. They said he was responsible for the death of Mick Collins. Died of a bullet in the belly at the end of the war. He was twenty-six or something like that."

"Thank you much, Chief Superintendent. May I take along this diagram of the house?"

"Wasn't that why I had the focking thing made?"

I shook hands with him and left the office. He'd given me a lot to think about and I'd given him some things to think about, too.

But not for long. He was a busy cop with lots of stuff on his platter. The murder of Jim Lark MacDonaugh was not on the platter and there were shadowy forces that didn't want it there.

And after my talk with Tom Clarke and despite Martin O'Neill, Nora MacDonaugh looked a little better than she had while I was walking through the Liberties.

Anyone that Tom Clarke didn't like couldn't be all bad.

8

I'M PRETTY GOOD AT SHORT-RUN TOTAL RECALL. AS I WALKED back along Dame Street toward the Green, I dictated the results of my morning interviews almost verbatim into my pocket recorder, leaving out some of Clarke's obscenity and my own personal response to Nora.

The rain was over, the clouds were clearing off, the sun was turning the steam rising off the streets into a fine silver mist.

And I felt like a teenage boy who had discovered his girlfriend had another boyfriend. I'd have to learn more about Marty O'Neill. And why hadn't she told me about him?

In the Green, sitting near the pond and talking to three very tiny tots and their beaming mother, was His Gracious Lordship John Blackwood Ryan. He was wearing a green windbreaker over his clerical shirt, from which his Roman collar had vanished, but the St. Brigid pectoral cross was plainly in view.

As I came close to him I noted that the writing on the windbreaker said "South Side Irish."

The kids scurried away with their mother.

"Not the South Side of Dublin, I would wager," I said, sitting down next to him.

He blinked at me through his Coke-bottle glasses, which were smeared by raindrops.

"Ah, the ingenious Captain MacCarthy. I trust you had a pleasant breakfast."

"Depends . . . What brings you to Dublin, Bishop?"

"Your man over there in the black marble"—he nodded toward the Henry Moder bust of James Joyce—"who is forever 'crossing Stephen's, that is my Green.' "

"For the fun of doing Bloomsday?"

"Arguably. Also because I am writing a book on James Joyce, Catholic theologian."

"That will stir up a lot of trouble."

His sigh sounded authentic. "It is much to be feared that it will not. It is most difficult to cause controversial scandal in the Catholic Church today. But patently your man was a profound Catholic theologian. Only one such can utter the blasphemies he uses."

"I see. But he claimed not to believe."

"On the level of intellect"—the bishop sighed again—"the poor dear man thought he did not, though he went to Holy Week services and said that without the intercession of St. Patrick, he would have never finished *Finnegans Wake*. On the level of metaphor, however, he was irredeemably Catholic; and religion is metaphor before it is anything else."

"Indeed," I said, using one of his favorite words.

"He was one of the greatest Catholic theologians of all times, as I presume is patent to you. And the story has a happy ending, as all good Catholic stories must."

"He and Molly make it up the next morning?"

"I think you can take that as given."

"But she was having her period."

"I am led to believe from well-informed authorities that there are various methods for dealing with that obstacle."

I let that comment pass in silence.

"Consider, for example, Molly's argument for the existence of God at the end," the bishop went on, "surely one of the most effective forms of that argument ever stated."

He then quoted the passage.

" 'God of heaven theres nothing like nature the wild mountains then the sea and the waves rushing then in the beautiful country with fields of oats and wheat and all kinds of things and all the fine cattle going about that would do your heart good to see rivers and lakes and flowers all sorts of shapes and smells and colours springing up even out of the ditches primroses and violets nature it is as for them saying theres no God I wouldnt give a snap of my two fingers for all their learning why dont they go and create something I often asked him atheists or whatever they call themselves go and wash the cobbles off themselves first then they go howling for the priest and they dying and why why because theyre afraid of hell on account of their bad conscience ah yes I know them well who was the first person in the universe before there was anybody that made it all who ah that they dont know neither do I so there you are and they might as well try to stop the sun from rising tomorrow.' "

"Indeed," I said again.

"As the worthy Anthony Burgess puts it, her God is the God of the creator; the God of Stephen's mother is the destroyer. Her vision is not mean and nagging and tearful and self-pitying, but humorous, drenched in light, born of the sun."

"A god who blesses sexual love? Not the God about whom the Jesuits taught your man?"

"No indeed. But that he half believed in that God is established, I think beyond any doubt, by the fact that Molly, poor dear, immediately moves to a recollection of her first encounter with Leopold on Howth Head."

"It was probably Nora Barnacle's argument. The critics say Joyce found his ideas for Molly's reverie from listening to his wife Nora."

"Note that Molly Bloom, surrounded by mystical roses at the end of the story, was born on September eighth, the birthday of the mother of Jesus. In truth, just as he had to leave Ireland to be Irish, so perhaps he had to leave the Church to be Catholic. He understood, you see, that if the Word was made flesh, then the erotic is sacramental. The rest of us didn't perceive that at the time, so in effect he excommunicated us and became, in his judgment, the only Catholic in the world."

"What I felt for Nora MacDonaugh last night is a sacrament?"

"Only if it were sufficiently passionate."

That was an interesting way of looking at it. As Bishop Blackie talked a decision was shaping up in my head.

"I see," I replied.

"One must keep in mind," he continued, "that, as your man perceived, the emptying of self in erotic love is a revelation, a hint, a metaphor for the self-emptying of God in the Incarnation of Jesus."

"Arguably," I said.

"No." The bishop waved his pudgy little hand. "Definitively."

"*Ulysses* is a good book," I agreed, in what was one of the great understatements of all my life.

"I often think"—he waved at another tot, who waved back like she and the bishop were lifelong friends—"that with a good editor, the book would make a superb popular novel. Sure to rise to the top of the best-seller list. The same with the book about Mr. and Mrs. Porter."

"You mean Anna Livia Plurabelle and her husband?"

"Yes, by whatever name H.C.E. might be called . . . Speaking of everyone coming here, I invite you to share"—he picked up a briefcase and removed from it as though it were buried treasure a flat package wrapped in white paper—"a bite of Chicago pizza, bought at the Chicago pizza place on the side of this very Green, within hailing distance of your man. You will find, I think, that it is reasonably authentic."

He broke off a very large piece and gave it to me. We munched silently for a few moments and dreamed of our beloved city by the lake.

"I want your help," I said impulsively.

"Indeed." He did not seem surprised.

"On some other case, it's all right for us to be rivals. Not this one."

"Rivals?" He produced two small cans of diet Pepsi from the pockets of his windbreaker.

"Mike Casey says that you're the only detective in Chicago that's better than I am."

"Mike Casey . . ." He seemed to be trying to place the name.

"The former commissioner."

"Ah, Mike the Cop. Indeed. His good wife would insist that he was better than either of us, but we'll let that pass."

"I'm personally involved in this one," I said. "I don't want to goof up."

"The inestimable Nora." He nodded.

"Indeed . . . may I tell you what I learned this morning?"

"Fascinating," he replied.

So I told him in summary, as objectively as I could, the results of my two interviews.

"Fascinating," he said somberly when I was finished.

"I need a reality check. I'd like you to be it."

"I take it as intolerable to even suggest that the numinous Nora might be responsible for the deaths of either of her husbands. We must rule out that possibility as unthinkable."

"Why? Because she is pretty and respectful to priests and gives money to the Church and worked in a third-world country for a couple of years?"

I sounded angry.

"All proof of excellent virtue . . . but hardly proof of innocence."

"Then why do you say she is innocent?"

"Because as one who is not enamored of her as you are, I can see that her guilt is unimaginable and not worry about self-deception. You can take it that her innocence is established beyond all doubt."

"I want to believe that."

"Most assuredly you do. However, for your own investigation, you need to maintain a certain skepticism. Nonetheless in the back of your head you may be unshakably convinced of her innocence."

"Why? Because Blackie Ryan says so?"

"There are worse reasons." He sighed.

"So it's all right to fall in love with her?"

"Ah, as to that, I cannot say. Moreover such a question presumes that the matter has not already been decided."

"I'm captured?"

"Not inextricably."

I opened my recorder and gave him the tape of my morning dictation. "You'll have to excuse the chief superintendent's language, Bishop. I cut most of it, but I had to keep some."

"I doubt that I'll hear anything original."

"And here's the diagram of the house on Shrewsbury Road."

"Fascinating!"

I explained it to him much as Clarke had explained it to me.

"Remarkable!"

"What we have is a locked-room mystery . . . a man blown up by someone who was locked inside a room with him or perhaps by himself."

"Arguably." He turned somber again.

"Clarke thinks it may be an outside hit man, a professional called in to push the button."

"Most improbable."

"Do you have any ideas?"

"I would not, if I were in your position, worry too much about the locked room."

"Oh?"

"That is not the problem." He sighed loudly. "Not at all."

"But how could it have been done?"

"I can think of three self-evident explanations, one of which I will not share with you because I think it is the most probable of the three and I do not wish to prejudice your further research."

"Three explanations?"

He ticked them off on his finger. "The first one we will defer for the present. Consider, however, the second. For whatever reason, perhaps because he has discovered that he has incurable cancer, James Larkin MacDonaugh decides to do away with himself. He does not want his wife to be sad over a second suicidal husband, so he devises an elaborate plot, not anticipating how the police will react to it. He locks himself in his room as she goes off to buy scones. Puts a radio mechanism along with the key on a shelf inside the door where they will be instantly recognized when the police rush in. And then calmly goes to his desk and pushes the button on a second radio control mechanism. The latter is placed directly on top of the bomb so that it is destroyed at the same time he is."

"That could have happened, all right," I agreed dubiously.

"I don't say that it did happen." He appeared to be searching for his watch and then discovered it on his wrist. "As I thought, my young guardians will be returning from the Boyne Valley, eager for some other strenuous amusement. . . . As I say, I don't think it could happen, but it might have."

"The sending device the guards found . . ."

"No one can say whether it was tuned to the receiving device because the receiving device was destroyed by the bomb."

"True enough."

My head was beginning to whirl. I needed a drink.

"A third possibility"—he rose from the bench—"farfetched but not to be ignored, is that for his own reasons, James Larkin MacDonaugh wanted to disappear for a time and perhaps dispose of someone else in the process. He persuades the someone else to don his robe, goes to a safe corner of the room, and presses the button. Then he locks the door from the inside, leaves the key and the sending device on the shelf, and departs from the house by a means of which he perhaps alone is aware."

I stood up with him. "I thought that Clarke had accepted the obvious ID too quickly."

"As you say"—we started to walk across the Green toward the Shelbourne—"the good chief superintendent is a tired, harried, and cynical man. He merely accepts the obvious a little too easily."

"So who did it?"

"We don't know yet, but I'll wager we'll find out by the time the sun sets on Bloomsday. . . . You did say you prayed with the numinous Nora?"

"Yes?"

"Sulivan says that to pray is to admit that one is empty and hungry."

"Fascinating," I replied, not wanting to admit that I didn't know who Sulivan was and also not wanting to admit that I was empty and hungry.

"You should investigate Newman House on the other side of the Green, along what was once called Leeson Walk. One Buck Whaley, who lived there before the Church acquired it for the Catholic University, now called University College, is reputed to have jumped from the second story into a carriage with a woman with whom he was enamored. More spectacularly he journeyed to Jerusalem to play handball against the walls of Old City on a fifteen-thousand-pound bet."

"Those were the good old days."

"Arguably. Not only Newman and your man are to be associated with the house, but also Gerard Manley Hopkins, who spent his last years an exile living on the top floor in a servant's room and teaching Greek—before they buried him in Glasnevin Cemetery, where later Paddy Dingham would be interred."

"Poor man."

"Indeed, Timothy. The Jesuits treat their heroes well only after they're dead."

"A lot of history in this city, Bishop Blackie."

"Arguably too much ... I fear that if I am not there promptly, the young persons will grow impatient."

I walked to the south side of the Green with him and then turned toward Ballsbridge and Shrewsbury Road. As I walked away I saw the two young women bound off a minibus and hug him enthusiastically.

I held back only one important point—and he'd learn that from listening to the tape: Perhaps the numinous Nora was having a love affair with her late husband's young and good-looking administrative assistant.

Arguably.

9

"**A**YE," SAID THE FORMIDABLE OLD WOMAN, "I'VE BEEN EX-
pecting you. I won't say you're welcome because
you're not, but come in and I'll make you a cup of tea and
show you the house. You may come in, Philomena."

Philomena was an aging wolfhound who greeted me with
a mildly interested sniff on the single step at the door of her
house. Apparently I passed muster.

Shrewsbury Road is on the boundary between Ballsbridge
and Donnybrook, two nineteenth-century suburbs of Dublin
Town, the latter a site for fairs and drinking and carousing
and "donnybrooks." It's just off Dublin's embassy row and
behind the offices of the embassy of the United States of
America, a hideous circular building in imitation of Edward
Durrell Stone at his worst (Phoenix Park being the ambassador's home). The neighborhood is surrounded by parks, athletic fields, a golf course, the grounds of the RDS, the Royal
Dublin Society's agricultural and horse-show premises, where
the annual spring show must be held even if there is revolu-
tion or civil war. Though thus sheltered from the rest of the
city, it is an easy walk from Sandymount Strand and the
Sandymount and Sydney parade stations of the DART—
Dublin Area Raid Transit.

I could have taken a taxi from the Green or maybe walked
over to the DART station behind Trinity College (Pearse station, after one of the leaders of the Easter Rising) and ridden
south for a couple of stops.

Instead, since I needed the exercise and since now the day
was quite lovely, and since, finally, I wanted to think, I decided to walk, a forty-five-minute stroll at the most.

I walked along Baggot Street up to the Grand Canal, where
boats were already queueing up for the coming weekend, and
crossed the canal at Wilton Terrace. Then I strolled along the

rows of Georgian buildings into Pembroke Road and Merrion Road. I walked over the bridge that gave Ballsbridge its name and the Dodder River (and thus traversed two of the seven rivers of Hades that Leopold Bloom, traveling in the opposite direction, had crossed on his way to Glasnevin Cemetery for the burial of Paddy Dingham) and passed the RDS and the American and British embassies. Finally I turned right at Shrewsbury and entered a radically different world. I was in the midst of the dwellings of the super rich of Victorian Dublin. Their urban dwellings anyway, since they probably had homes on their estates out in the country—the "big houses" of story.

Shrewsbury Road was Chicago's Astor Street with older trees, greener lawns, larger homes, and stone or brick walls—a short, quiet and elegant thoroughfare, under a cathedral of greenery, which would have done Paris credit. Behind the walls and the shrubs and the fences, gravel and an occasional paved driveway led to the front door, usually just a step off the ground and often decorated by a Philomena-like creature.

The typical driveway seemed to require both a BMW and a Mercedes.

Number nine was the biggest house on the street, just across the way from the entrance to the Chester Beatty Museum, where Egyptian relics were stored. Jim Lark must have loved living there, an impoverished kid from a rocky farm who had won, while still in his twenties, a beautiful and cultivated young bride and one of the finest homes in the city—while all the time the family out in County Tip was paying ground rent to the bloody English lords who technically still own it—even to this day.

The names of the fence posts of the homes—Pitchrain, Runnymeade, Glenlissa—revealed their origins and perhaps even their present owners. Not what you would call Celtic names, not by a long shot.

I studied the house for a few minutes from the street. He must have made an awful lot of money at an early age to be able to buy this red-brick Victorian mansion with its towers and turrets and bay windows and multiple chimneys and, from what Tomás Clarke had said, to reconstruct it for his new wife.

Even if the house had been run-down and was picked up cheap, reconstruction even a third of a century ago must have cost a lot of money.

I would have to inquire of Paddy Quaid, with whom I was supposed to meet in Davy Byrne's Pub on Duke Street just around the corner from Grafton Street, later in the day, about the reconstruction.

Like virtually every other house on the street, "Glendora" bore on its front wall a large alarm box with the name of the security firm that protected the premises, in this case the thoroughly American ADT. Crime was a problem for the affluent in Dublin, too.

So, remembering with a shiver the hate-filled eyes of Julia MacDonaugh, I pulled the cord at the front door of the house.

No butler answering the door of this mansion. Herself, tall and lean and grim in black, opened the door and bid me enter with the blunt statement that I was not welcome.

There were no spikes of hate shooting from her eyes, as I had feared. If anything, she seemed sad and weary. At seventy-four maybe she had reason to feel that way.

Much of the time it was hard to understand her. Her west-of-Ireland brogue was thick, her speech allusive and filled with strange metaphors, and her train of thought either confused or perhaps deliberately confusing.

Yet she served the tea—including sandwiches, biscuits (cookies to us Yanks), scones and cream, fresh raspberry jam, and a "drop of sherry." By the latter she meant a large "jar" for me and one for herself, too.

I might not be welcome at all, at all, but the Irish are genetically programmed to be hospitable.

"Och," the old woman said, pouring my tea in an almost unbearably elegant drawing room, "hadn't I told him all along that it was too much?"

She had issued a strict prohibition to Philomena. "Stop bothering the Yank, you worthless hound."

The pooch had ignored her and shared my scones with me until I told her "no more." At which point she curled up at my feet and went to sleep. Some watchdog.

"This house?" I asked.

"Isn't it a terrible big place? It's like living in a mausoleum. Don't I keep hearing footsteps behind me? And wasn't the woman, too, with all her airs and manners?"

"Nora Joyce?"

"And herself almost young enough to be a daughter with indecent clothes and her bold ways. And the other one, looking on me as though I were dirt every time I came to town to call like a decent woman should, wasn't she the terrible snob?"

I gathered she meant Dora Collins. I looked at the painting of Dora on the wall, an apparently sweet young woman in an off-the-shoulder dress with a deep neckline—the romanticized portrait deemed appropriate for rich young women in the British Isles for a couple of centuries, the kind of portrait that would make a young woman look beautiful if the observer didn't pay too close attention to the face.

Dora's face was pretty enough, not striking, but surely pretty.

On the other side of the drawing room—in which one could have entertained several hundred people with plenty of space to spare, was a realistic portrait of Nora in a white blouse and a brown skirt. Nora could afford to be realistic.

"Aye," said my hostess, noticing the direction of my eyes, "aren't they a pair, now? What business did Jim Lark have marrying either one of them, and themselves so far above his station?"

"Nora is a country woman from West Mayo, isn't she?"

"She should have stayed where she belonged, shouldn't she, now?"

I didn't know quite what to make of that bit of seeming Irish bull, so I let it pass.

"Ah, and would you look at him over there, all dressed up like he were some kind of ghost?"

On a third wall, over a huge fireplace, was a dramatic portrait of Jim Lark himself, looking like Silken Thomas or Red Hugh O'Neill or Brian Boru about to go into battle. He was wearing the white robe and red cross of a knight commander of Knights of Malta. His face was split in a manic smile, a warrior who would love every minute of the battle.

"Fascinating," I said, taking a leaf from my new ally's book.

"Wasn't I saying to him often enough who do you think you are, living in fancy homes and wearing fancy clothes and marrying fancy women? Won't it catch up with you soon enough? And it did, now, didn't it? Will you have another small drop?"

"No thanks, Ms. MacDonaugh. I wonder what your hospitality would be like if I were welcome."

She snorted.

"Didn't I raise him myself from the first minute after Ma died and Da brought him out of the room and put him in my arms and he mine to raise? Wasn't he the only son I ever had and himself a darlin' little redhead?"

Tears glistened in her dim old eyes.

"I bet he was."

"And now dead and gone before his own time and it's all his fault, isn't it, now?"

It may have been the sherry, which was excellent, by the way (bought by someone with good taste), but I was having a hard time following her conversation.

"Who killed him, Ms. MacDonaugh?"

"Ay," she said bitterly, her eyes finally flashing rage, "weren't there lots who had reason to do it, and not all them would have called themselves enemies either, would they?"

"Family and friends?"

"Ah, now, haven't worse things happened?"

"Like his wife?"

"I haven't said that, have I, now? Ah, there were things going on that you wouldn't believe."

"Like?"

"Betrayal." She spat out the world like a bullet. "And himself knowing about it and not doing anything about it. Should I not blame him more than anyone else?"

"Martin O'Neill?"

"Ah, that shite-faced little gombeen man, I never did trust him at all, at all."

She was a hater, all right, but it didn't seem that she hated her youngest brother, except perhaps for permitting himself to be killed.

"You'll have another small jar?"

It was good sherry, so I agreed, though I knew it would make me light-headed—cop or not, I am not what you call a long hitter.

"What did he do wrong, Ms. MacDonaugh?"

"He didn't listen to me." She got up and began to remove the china.

I stood up to help her. She didn't protest my feminist gesture. She probably expected it.

"About what?"

"About staying in his right station and not pretending to be someone who he was not. Isn't that what killed him, now?"

"That and his wife?"

"Ah, isn't she the cute one, now? Sure, she's not telling all she knows, is she, now?"

I began to suspect that I'd get nothing at all from this strange, bitter old woman.

"Jim Lark has always been good to his family, hasn't he?"

"Too good by half, if you ask me."

"Not to you?"

"I never wanted a thing, I'm living here only because the woman insists that I stay here where I'm safe."

"Nora?"

"Haven't I just said that?"

Dear God, give me patience.

We brought the china to an enormous kitchen. No peat fire here.

"You'd want to be seeing the room, I suppose?"

"Yes, ma'am."

We took the "lift" to the second floor—elevator to speak

American English—which Jim Lark had also added to the house. We turned to the right, Philomena following us with a sleepy yawn, and walked down a sumptuous corridor and stopped before a massive oak door. Herself threw it open.

The two of us entered the death room. The wolfhound, however, stubbornly refused to accompany us. Rather she sat at the door and watched us carefully until we were ready to leave.

"The library" was smaller than the Harold Washington Jr. Memorial Library Center in Chicago, but it was a real library and not merely a tiny study. Three of the walls of the huge room were actually lined with books, the fourth overlooked a garden one could observe through high Georgian windows. The furnishings were in oak and black leather and the carpet a dark maroon. Thick beams outlined a high ceiling decorated with gold leaf. Next to the windows was a large, highly polished and empty oak desk. Except for the bright lights that Julia MacDonaugh flicked on, it might be unchanged since the time when Victoria was a young woman.

No, there was one other modern blemish, a large console TV behind the desk.

"Restored after the blast?"

"Ay. Every last bit of it. Even the books that were damaged. The woman."

She said the last word with what I thought was a sneer.

"She won't live here?"

"Isn't she afraid of all the ghosts?"

"Does she say so?"

"Doesn't she know they're here?"

I paced off the dimensions of the room, looking for secret passages or priest holes or something of the sort. Obviously the place was not old enough for a priest hole. Had Tom Clarke considered the secret-passage theory? Most likely he had; it was an obvious if unlikely possibility.

Julia MacDonaugh watched my efforts impassively as if she'd seen it all before.

"Was Jim Lark like his brothers?" I asked as I noted dimensions in my book.

"Aren't they unfit to carry his shoes for him?" she said bitterly. "Wasn't I saying that he was a fool to trust them?"

"A touch of gombeen?" I observed, meaning sharp and slippery.

"Aren't they worse than that?"

Not a woman of nuanced opinions, Julia MacDonaugh.

I went into the bathroom. It had not been damaged by the blast, so no restoration was necessary. By the standards of Ireland thirty-five years ago, it was probably luxurious. By the standards of contemporary American hedonism, it was spare—a combination shower and tub (on legs) with a thick royal-blue shower curtain, a tile floor that must be cold on your typical Irish morning, an old-fashioned radiator (also on legs) that probably didn't give enough heat, a small unglazed window through which perhaps a child could slip out, low ceiling without an exhaust fan, dim mirror over the washbasin, painted heating and water pipes that almost certainly gurgled. Good enough for a second-class hotel maybe.

I pushed aside the shower curtain. An old-style shower head, controlled by a single handle, hung in the top of the wall at the head of the tub. Push it all the way to the right for hot, move it back to left for cold; and be prepared for scorching or freezing if you guess wrong.

A new and more modern head, removable to spray the various crucial parts of your anatomy, had been implanted lower in the wall—with two pipes going to the ceiling. On either side of it were faucets, one marked red and the other marked blue, a recent innovation.

Why not redo the whole thing?

Probably because it didn't seem necessary. All a man needed, Jim Lark might have said, is one of them new shower heads for the odd time that he might want to take a shower in here.

Fair enough.

I tried to open the window, but it wouldn't yield to my repeated shoves. While I was shoving I glanced down at the garden below. It was ablaze with flowers, yellow, red, deep blue, dainty pink.

"Your man works hard on the garden, doesn't he, now?"

"The gardener?"

"Didn't I say so?"

I flushed the toilet bowl to make sure about the gurgling pipes. They sounded like a noisy waterfall.

Then I stood on it and poked at the plaster ceiling. It was as solid as Tom Clarke had said it was. No escape here.

"May I see the master bedroom?" I asked.

" 'Twas said you could see everything in the house, wasn't it?"

"Was it, now?"

By whom? Arthur T. Regan, I suppose.

Philomena tagged along at my side, not so much to keep an eye on me, it seemed, as to play the role of my assistant. Anything I inspected carefully, she sniffed. If I didn't pat her head at that point, she shoved it under my hand.

The bedroom was almost as big as the library. The Victorians of Shrewsbury Road did not share the passion for small rooms that was typical of their era.

One would exhaust oneself chasing a prudish wife around such a room.

It was decorated in the froufrou and lace of the era, doubtless an accurate restoration—though the electric blankets, revealed by telltale cords and dials, were a modern addition. As was the massive big-screen TV—fifty-five inches at least—opposite the bed.

Even the bed itself was a standard double bed, not the queen or king size that American couples prefer today.

No trouble finding your wife in such a bed.

There were two bathrooms, one for the woman of the house on the far side of the master bedroom, furnished in the style a Victorian bathroom might be furnished if it had all the modern American conveniences, including a king-size bath and a separate shower stall.

The one off the man's dressing room, on the other hand, was utterly and completely modern California—two sunken tubs, one for bath and one for hot tub and a shower with multiple nozzles and clear glass through which one could admire a person of the opposite gender while that person was showering. The floor was covered with blue carpet, sufficiently thick that one might pin the aforementioned person of the opposite gender on it in the midst of certain amusements.

The toilet did not gurgle.

"The woman," Julia MacDonaugh said again.

"Aye," I agreed.

"Terrible, sinful thing." She inclined her head toward the spa.

"Aye."

"And herself from a cottage in the west of Ireland," she continued bitterly, "where all the water came from an outside pump."

"Aye."

So she hated Nora. And her own brothers. And Jim Lark for dying. And probably everyone else in the world.

"She would have worn him out anyway, wouldn't she?"

"Aye."

"And himself old enough to be her father?"

"Wasn't he, now?"

"They both were old enough to know better."

"Isn't that the truth?"

We then entered the husband's dressing room, a small and very masculine place, oak and black leather like the library. On the wall hung a framed enlargement of the British tabloid picture of the topless Nora.

I think I gulped. I'm sure I did.

"The most heinous thing in the whole world." Julia sighed. " 'Tis sinful even for a woman to look at it."

"Nice composition," I replied, wondering what kind of man would dare to buy a picture like that of his wife.

I left the dressing room hurriedly before my guilty imagination began to run riot.

We completed the tour of the home. Like the master bedroom the rest was an accurate Victorian restoration with modern electricity and plumbing and deftly installed central heating.

Too big and too much like a museum for comfortable living? And too cold and drafty despite the central heating, which would never warm those vast high spaces?

Probably. But I wouldn't mind trying it for a while. I might even get used to it. It would depend on the wife whom I might chase around the master bedroom or ogle through the clear glass of the shower.

There may have been some dust in the house, but I didn't see a speck anywhere. Did the old woman do it herself? Or did servants come in by the day—there being no sign of life in the five servant rooms at the back end of the third floor.

I looked down the servant stairway.

"Goes down to your kitchen?"

"Ay, and then back into the garden."

We walked down those narrow and squeaky stairs into her kitchen. I snatched a final biscuit from the tray.

"Them's the steps to the garden." She pointed at a small doorway. "In them days there wasn't much time for the servants to go into the garden, poor dear things."

I opened the door and walked down a tight single flight of stairs. The door was locked.

"Here's the key." She jabbed it in my back.

I opened the door and peered into the glorious garden, resplendent in the afternoon sunlight.

"Ay, the man does a good job indeed."

"And no one to admire his work but an old woman."

"There's nothing wrong with an old woman having a garden of her own to admire, is there, now?"

She snorted again.

I walked around the garden, overwhelmed by its loveliness and the powerful scent of the flowers. It was surrounded by an old stone fence, at least ten feet high, hidden almost completely by ivy.

A high gate, tipped with barbed wire, protected the driveway between the end of the fence and the house.

"That gate is always locked, is it?"

"No point in asking criminals from the North Side to come in and steal something, is there, now?" She was trailing after me.

The North Side of Dublin—north of the Liffey River—is where poverty and unemployment and crime abound. Thus Dublin violates Stephen Potter's dictum that problems are always in the south.

"That gate at the side of the house is the only one?"

"Isn't it always locked?"

"Who would be having the key?"

She shrugged her frail shoulders. "Your man, who else would be needing it?"

Probably there were a master set of keys somewhere in the house with the garden key on it. And a key to the library?

But what difference would it make if there were a library key there now?

Nora had testified that Jim Lark had never locked the door to the library and that she had never seen the library key.

She might have meant that she had never seen a key which she knew to be a library key.

"Is there a key ring with all the keys in the house?"

"Isn't it in the closet inside the front door? Would you want to be seeing it?"

Why not?

Each ring carried a neatly labeled tag. One read "library," another "garden gate."

If Jim Lark had wanted to lock the door to his library, he would walk down the stairs from the second floor—which the Irish, like the English, would call the first floor—or possibly from the third floor if he had started from the master bedroom. He would have had to come down the broad stairs that rose at the opposite side of the house from the front door, turn at the stained-glass window on the first landing, and take the key off the ring. Still apparently clad in the robe from their lovemaking, he would, I imagined, have done this after Nora had departed to purchase the "fixings" for afternoon tea.

No reason not to do that. There were no servants in the house to watch the master wandering about in dishabille.

Still it was curious. Why lock the library? From Nora? From Julia? From Mick Dav?

Did Jim Lark trust Nora? Could he have ridden her—Tom

Clarke's vocabulary was affecting me—although he distrusted her?

It didn't seem to fit the character of either. But I didn't really know Jim Lark MacDonaugh, did I?

And I had only Nora's candid testimony that they had made love just before his death.

"Thank you for the tour."

"Wasn't it me obligation to do what I was told? And would you like another sip of sherry against the cold?"

"Ah, you'll be the death of me, woman."

Philomena accompanied me out of the house and down the driveway to the gate. Then she returned to her post on the step. Had she been in charge of the door on the day of the crime? If she were, she would have hardly been an obstacle to a stranger.

Outside on the road, I turned to survey the house again. It was sheltered by large trees and a hedge as well as a shoulder-high stone fence. Yet the lawn in front was open enough, so that a passerby looking in the gate could see someone walking up to the door—if there were a passerby.

I knew that I should take a taxi back to the Shelbourne and sleep off the effects of the sherries. Instead I decided I would walk at least part of the way and dictate a detailed description of the house and its current mistress for the good Bishop Blackie.

I might as well do it while, like Stephen Dedalus and presumably James Joyce, walking into eternity along Sandymount Strand.

10

"**I**F YOU DON'T MIND," I SAID TO THE DEITY, WITH WHOM I had become quite familiar in the course of the day, what with the blue lights of Clarendon Street and Bishop Blackie's lecture, "I'd just as soon walk into eternity from somewhere else."

The clouds had returned from the Irish Sea and with them fog and a touch of mist and a smell of dead fish. Sandymount Strand was nothing more than a vast and dirty segment of tidal beach, not able to hold a candle, for example, to Grand Beach in the state of Michigan in the United States of America. Moreover the segment of the strand on which Bold Jimmy Joyce (as they often call him in Dublin, comparing him in mockery to Bold Robert Emmett of song and story) and Dedalus had walked had been built over by a school and a road.

"When my time comes to walk into eternity," I added to the Deity, who ought not to have been concerned about such matters, but who, according to reports claiming to have an accurate reading of Her interests, seemed to care about me, "if it's a beach, Grand Beach will do nicely."

But I was not either James Joyce, Stephen Dedalus, or Leopold Bloom. Nor was Nora Finnegan Joyce MacDonaugh Molly Bloom, not by a country mile. Nor Gertie MacDowell nor Anna Livia Plurabelle for that matter.

I had walked down Sandymount Road and through the picturesque little triangle called Sandymount Green to reach the strand. Dublin's Yuppies had obviously expropriated the road. Its quaint mix of row houses, semidetached villas, cottages, and bungalows—with an occasional gray stucco manor house—glittered with fresh paint. The driveways were different, however. They contained either a Mercedes or a BMW but not both. The street swarmed with young mothers and their children, sometimes two or even three in strollers. Irish kids seemed both well behaved and well loved. Their parents seemed to enjoy them, indeed to have fun with them. The kids did not hesitate to smile and wave at the tall Yank when he smiled and waved at them. And their mothers—all, it seemed that day, young and attractive—blushed happily when the Yank complimented them on their children.

Maybe they even flirted a little with the big Yank, though that was most likely in his imagination as he fantasized about what it would be like to have a sexy young wife and three gorgeous children.

I had too much of the sherry taken altogether, you say?

Had I ever. But not so much that I wasn't proud of myself because I had not showed off for the bishop.

I didn't say to him when we were discussing Bold Jimmy Joyce in the Green that I knew what your man meant when he pictured Stephen reflecting on Sandymount Strand, "God becomes man becomes fish becomes barnacle goose becomes featherbed mountain."

The barnacle goose, a seabird, was his Nora, Nora Barnacle, the woman who kept him alive with her love and who was the model for all the women in his stories. Bold Jimmy meant that just as God became man through the Incarnation and Christ became a fish (in the symbol of the early Church), he himself became man in the hands of a woman who anchored him in the feather bed of married love and taught him the vision that the most important thing in life is love, the opposite of "force, hatred, history, all that."

I'd read a couple of books on the way over, too, Bishop Blackie. I think he's a Catholic theologian, too.

And I'm in love with my own Nora.

So I finished recording my report for the good bishop, having apologized for any hint of tipsiness in my voice with the explanation that I was by no means a long hitter. I did not add that I was terribly distracted in my recording by pleasantly, even virtuously, obscene images of my Nora.

Suppose, I reflected as I looked for a three-masted ship that would represent, according to some scholars anyway, the three crosses on Calvary, that a person or person unknown had access to the house on Shrewsbury Road. Suppose that person knew—or had been told—where the key ring was. Suppose that person took both the garden ring and the library ring. Suppose that person went to the library floor (their first, our second). Suppose that person had somehow or the other detonated the explosion that killed Jim Lark MacDonaugh without destroying himself in the process. Suppose that somehow this person then locks the door, places the key and radio sender on the library shelf right next to the door, and leaves by a way that he himself knows about or has been told about. Suppose he sneaks down the servant stairs and out into the garden and hides among the flowers and the trees and the bushes. He waits till it's dark and takes a chance on opening the garden gate and slipping out into the night, risking that the guards around the house don't see him.

It was not, I knew, a scenario that a professional killer would buy. A terrorist might. Or someone desperate to protect himself. Or herself.

Nora? Or someone who was working for her?

Not very likely. Why take that kind of a chance when there were so many easier ways to dispose of an aging husband?

Why leave the key and the transmitter?

To create a mystery that would becloud the issues?

A smart and creative trick.

All right, Nora was smart and creative.

The scenario was perfect as it stood, except there was no explanation of how the killer could get out of the library. It fell apart at that critical point.

Who would know about the keys? Almost any one of a hundred people?

So my scenario was fundamentally flawed, and even if it wasn't, it did not narrow the list of suspects.

It certainly did not, however, point at Nora.

Or did it? Could I think rationally about the woman?

Anyway, the good bishop had pronounced as intolerable the thought that she was the killer.

Who was I to argue with a good bishop?

Nonetheless, as he implied, it was my professional obligation to consider her a suspect until I had evidence that she was innocent.

That she was innocent would remain in background mode, as the computer experts would say—in virtual memory. Fair enough. Could I love her in virtual memory?

The good bishop had said that was up to me.

But did it make any sense to love her even in virtual memory until I could close the case—or the good bishop and I could close it?

Moreover how can you love a woman whom you've known, I glanced at my watch, for less than twenty-four hours?

I had shared an elevator with her (and the good bishop), held her in my arms briefly while bullets spattered over our heads, danced with her in the lodge of the chief secretary turned ambassador of the United States of America, listened to her self-revelation in Bewley's, and prayed with her in the blue-lighted Carmelite church in Clarendon Street.

One can desire a woman with much less contact. But love her? Consider a life together with her?

Nonsense.

I ought to have ended my reflections there and retreated from any further confrontations with eternity on Sandymount Strand.

This was, however, the same strand on which later in the day, Mr. Leopold Bloom achieved an orgasm from looking up, from a substantial distance, the underwear of the lame Nausicaa, Gertie MacDowell, while the benediction of the Blessed Sacrament was taking place in the Star of the Sea Church behind him as the congregation sang the *tantum ergo* and skyrockets were exploding in the sky—nice mix of symbols!

And said Gertie MacDowell, not after all the pious Irish virgin that in fantasy she thought herself, also achieved orgasm in response to Mr. Bloom's distant fascination.

I looked around for the church and then remembered that the park at the head of the beach was landfill over the beach where Gertie and Mr. Bloom staged their brief encounter. I'd have to find it on the way back.

Gertie, a romantic and pious young woman, trained by the good sisters, knew what she was doing to the hapless and eager Mr. Bloom and reveled in it.

An interesting view, I thought, of the complexities of a young woman, both virgin and seducer. Like Madonna. Are they really that way? Who knows? What man knows what's going on in their imaginations?

Was it possible for two people to achieve sexual satisfaction *in distans* that easily?

It was perhaps one way to do it.

Mr. Leopold Bloom must have been in a bad way if the cotton undies and stockings of Gertie MacDowell could turn him on. Joyce had a thing about young women on beaches, like the girl at Clontarf (whom Dedalus had imagined as a "seabird" in a coded reference to Nora Barnacle)—another bold young thing. There were other young women during his exile, according to the recent revised biography. Well, we all have our turn-ons.

How would Mr. Bloom have reacted to contemporary women's underwear, more daring than any of the prostitutes in "Nighttown" would have dreamed of wearing—and available for all to see in store windows and on the first floor of the new St. Stephen's Green's shopping mall? Or, perhaps even more scandalously, in the windows of Brown Thomas on Grafton Street?

What would an American woman like my Nora—well Irish American—in form-fitting shorts and a running bra have done to him?

Yet we hardly notice such phenomena, save for transient admiration. Times change.

And men remain the same, Tim Pat. Men lust after women and women play their own intricate games, like Gertie MacDowell and Molly Bloom.

I was certainly discreetly ogling the good bishop's young relatives last night, though they're hardly the kind you'll find in cotton bloomers on Sandymount Strand, are they?

Long ago girls like them might give me dirty thoughts, but it's other sorts of women who bother me today.

Like?

Like herself, naturally.

Who's herself?

Nora, who else?

In her lingerie?

Yeah, but you're not likely to encounter that on Sandymount Strand either.

That's not the point.

Well, smart-ass, what is the point?

The point is, eejit, that she is afraid of you but also likes you.

Yeah?

That's not a bad position to have a woman in, like poor Gertie, defenseless here on the strand.

Yeah?

Yeah.

You mean that her candid talk with me was a come-on?

Are you kidding?

She was trying to prove her love for her husband.

I won't deny that. Can't a woman have two agendas at the same time?

So she is interested in me?

I ask you again: Are you kidding?

Is she beginning to lift her skirt for me like poor Gertie did for Leopold here, first steps of seduction?

What do you think?

At least I haven't done the male equivalent.

Oh, fock off, you bleeding tosser! Who you focking trying to kid!

I've only known her for twenty-one hours.

My dialogue partner declined to continue the conversation. He had left me not only dizzy from the drink taken, but also with a mean headache.

With the headache came a recollection of Martin O'Neill, the handsome gombeen man who was Nora MacDonaugh's as-yet-unmentioned administrative assistant.

Well, fock him, too, my dazed brain said pugnaciously.

Farther down the beach a group of kids, wearing wet-suit jackets, were receiving instructions in windsurfing. Since I indulge in that amusement, I wandered down to watch them. I'd need more than just a wet jacket to venture into the Irish Sea.

When I drew near them, I discovered that they were girl kids, fourteen, fifteen, and sixteen years old, and that their instructor was a woman person who was no older than the good bishop's relatives. Girl kids windsurfing in the Irish Sea! Some of them revealing bikinis—and delectable young breasts—beneath their open wet-suit jackets!

What was happening to Ireland!

The species had come a long way since Gertie MacDowell in her cotton drawers under her long skirt; most of the change was an improvement, I decided.

And men still admired the breasts and desired the bodies of young women.

Well, you wouldn't want that to change, would you?

As I walked back to Strand Road from the wet beach—and as the mist turned to rain again—I attempted, foolishly, to picture what life with Nora might be like, with and without lingerie. Could she be the girl of my dreams for whom I had waited, one way or another, for a couple of decades?

Probably not.

But possibly yes.

Go for it, I told myself with an inebriate's self-confidence.

Or arguably, as the good bishop would have said, the confidence of a retired blitzing linebacker.

I walked back on the beach road to the Star of the Sea Church, just to make sure it was still there, and prayed inside it for all young women who seek happiness in human love, particularly the kids learning to windsurf on Sandymount Strand.

"Take care of them," I pleaded with Herself. "And take care of my Nora for me, too."

The Deity raised no objection to my use of the personal pronoun before Nora.

On that happy thought I ambled away from the beach on Newbridge Road and passed number nine, where Paddy Dingham's funeral cortege began. Death and sex—the two obsessions of Mr. Bloom, the Jew on a Greek quest in a Catholic city. Was sex a hedge against death, perhaps a hint that there was something stronger than death?

Arguably.

I boarded the DART at Lansdowne Road, in the shadow of the great football stadium, and rode to Pearse Street, a short trip. Then I walked through Trinity College, pretending not to notice the young women in T-shirts and shorts plastered against their bodies by the rain, to my meeting with Councillor Paddy Quaid in Davy Byrne's Pub on Duke Street.

Quaid was reputed to be one of the most adroit politicians in Ireland. Unfortunately he had entered the fray only in his forties and hence didn't fit in with the factions that dominated Irish politics. He had been elected often to the Dublin Corporation and had served as lord mayor twice, but had never been elected to the Dail, the Irish Parliament. Now he was reported to be thinking about standing for the European Community Parliament as a successful businessman who could plead Ireland's case more effectively in that body than any mere politician.

I was looking forward to meeting a certified Irish pol. How, I wondered, would he stack up to an Irish-American pol, of whom we have had one or two in Chicago?

11

I ARRIVED AT THE PUB WET AND CHILLED. THE "SOFT" MIST HAD turned into a hard rain when I had left the DART at Pearse Street. I was reluctant to hail a taxi for the short ride to Grafton Street, especially since that once smelly thoroughfare was now a pedestrian mall—always crowded with people, unlike State Street in Chicago—no longer that great street at all, at all.

The Boer War memorial arch at the top of the street was known to Dubliners as "Traitors' Arch," hardly a charitable recollection of the Irish soldiers who died in that war.

So I had rushed across the quadrangles of "Trinners," by the marvelously sculpted statue of Sweet Molly Malone at the top of Grafton Street—the "Tart with the Cart," the Dubliners called her—and down to Davy Byrne's.

Molly Malone was a gift to the city on its thousandth anniversary, as was the naked Anna Livia in a fountain on O'Connell Street (the floozy in the Jacuzzi) and the two elderly women on a bench in front of the woolen mills across the river on the ha'penny pedestrian bridge (the hags with the bags). Given the statues' nicknames, it was certain that no one ever promised the gift givers a respectful response to their generosity.

I was a few minutes early, so I grabbed a pint (of Guinness, what else?) and found myself a table in the back corner of the public bar.

Behind me there was a cartoonlike portrait of the Bold Jimmy Joyce. It was unlikely that the owner and his staff or most of the "regulars" had ever read the book, but they knew that he was an important man and, more to the point, that a lot of Yank tourists came there to have a pint of the best in a tavern that Leopold Bloom had visited on June 16, 1904.

Did I, in my rain-soaked tweed sport coat, look like a Yank? Probably. There was no way you could hide it.

As I waited for Paddy Quaid I thought about Mr. Leopold Bloom, who would have been four years younger than me when he ate a lunch of cheese sandwich and burgundy in this place.

What kind of a cop knows about *Ulysses*?

One that realizes he ought to quit after twenty years, especially when his mother and father tell him he should.

Noisey Flynn had asked about Molly's health. Bloom hadn't the slightest notion how to cope with his woman. What man does know how to cope with his woman? Bloom could only fret about Blazes Boylan.

Martin O'Neill.

Cut that out. You've known her for less than a day.

Molly was born on September 8, the Feast of the Nativity of Mary the Mother of Jesus. The good bishop would make much out of that symbol—woman as goddess, woman as mother. As he ate lunch Bloom remembered the love between him and Molly on Howth Hill, the big headland at the top of Dublin Bay. Molly remembers the encounter at the end of the story when she decides, somewhat ambiguously, to give herself again to her husband.

So Bloom won in the end, or so it seemed. Molly standing naked at the side of his bed. A nice guy who didn't finish last.

In this pub Bloom had also fantasized about Molly's underwear. He would buy her a new petticoat. Petticoats of that kind were out of fashion these days. But obsession with women's undergarments was not. Nothing necessarily wrong with that.

Then, though I'd known her only for a day, I permitted myself some fantasies about Nora MacDonaugh in various stages of dress and undress. For the rest of my life.

They were pleasant and reassuring fantasies for a horny old bachelor.

Paddy Quaid, sometime lord mayor of Dublin, was late. So

I drained my pint, felt a little warmer and drier, and, with total lack of prudence, collected another pint.

Besides the other Yanks, whom I had no trouble picking out, the rest of the clientele looked prosperous—businessmen, shop managers, senior clerks and professionals gulping a "quick one" (or two or three) before returning home to familial bliss.

Better a quick couple than two martinis.

When I had disposed of most of my second pint, I then realized that all I had eaten since breakfast was a piece of Bishop Blackie's Chicago-style pizza and the small sandwiches, scones, and cookies at the house on Shrewsbury Road. I figured I ought not to drink any more Guinness without something in my stomach. Perhaps I should imitate Mr. Bloom and sample one of the pub's cheese sandwiches.

Then Paddy Quaid appeared and I forgot that I was hungry.

There was no doubt that it was the councillor when he finally strode into the pub.

" 'Tis himself!"

"Ah, good day to you, Councillor!"

"How ya doing, Paddy!"

"Grand to see you, Paddy!"

"Give it to them, Paddy!"

It was unclear what "it" was or who "they" were and it didn't much matter.

"A word with you, Councillor, before you leave?"

Jim Lark's other mate from the Tipperary champions of long ago was as genial as Arthur T. Regan was grim. A big man—I'd probably give away a couple of inches and thirty pounds to him—with a solid, bulky body and hair that was still mostly brown, he worked the crowd with a professional pol's skill. There was a genial smile, a clap on the back, a good word for each of them, even an inside joke for some of them.

He would do well in Bridgeport, our royal borough in Chicago.

An expertly tailored dark gray suit encased his huge frame. A careful razor cut had arranged his thick, wavy hair. His conservative blue-and-red silk tie must have cost at least thirty pounds. The tan on his square, distinguished face had been applied by an expert. Paddy Quaid, looking maybe ten years younger than his middle sixties, was money and power. Every one of us in the room knew that from the moment he entered.

Patrick Michael Quaid had come a long way from his origins as the son of a small creamery manager in the County Tip. But then most of the people in my story had come a long way, all riding on the coattails of Jim Lark MacDonaugh.

I stood up to walk toward him. He was at my side before I could take a step.

"Glory be to God," he exclaimed, pumping my hand. "Art said a big blond football player, he didn't say how big! Sit down! Sit down! I'll get us a couple of more pints. Yours looks like it's dying a happy death."

"I should—"

"Not a word, not a word." He shoved me into my chair. "You're my guest as long as you're in my pub."

I wondered how many pubs in Dublin he called his pub. Probably a lot. Not that there was any sign that he could not absorb the "creature" unharmed. A smart politician ought to have a lot of pubs he could call his own.

I don't trust pols generally (I make an exception of our currently reigning mayor in Chicago) and I wasn't sure I would want to trust Paddy Quaid, but I'd let him do his act for me.

"Well, now, here we are!" He plunked the two pints of the dark liquid on our table. "It's Tim, isn't it?"

"My ma called me Tim Pat. I go by that name here."

That was a nasty beginning, designed to slow him down.

"Tim Pat it is." He sat down heavily on the chair across from me. "Is your ma Dublin born?"

"County Cook," I said, still fencing. "Her mother was from Mayo and her father from Kerry."

"Ah, a grand mixture that is, grand altogether. And your da?"

"Clare all the way, his parents that is."

"So you're a real man of the west, are you, now? And your da was a cop before you? A captain just like yourself?"

So he knew all about me?

"He was that."

"Well, 'tis grand to have you here in Dublin, grand altogether. Was it Notre Dame you played on? And yourself a linebacker at that? And an All-American, too?"

"Third string."

"We see a lot of American football here, on the telly, I mean. Your Chicago Bears are my favorite. The Holy Saints preserve us, did I like your man Jim McMahon!"

"Fragile," I murmured.

"Aren't we trying every year to have Notre Dame play here in Lansdowne Road—you know where that is, sure I thought you would—but we haven't been able to work it out yet."

"They'd want a lot of money up front."

"Too true, but Jesus, Mary, and Joseph, says I, who is to blame them, isn't that right."

" 'Tis."

The small talk was essential as a lead-up to the reason for our conversation. Dealing with the Irish in any country, there was no other way.

Not at all, at all.

I had worked my way through my fourth pint before we could become serious.

"I appreciate your finding time to talk to me, Mr. Quaid."

"Paddy! Nothing else but Paddy!"

"And yourself lord mayor of this fair city."

"Past lord mayor." He put a strong and solid hand on my shoulder. " 'Tis only an honorary thing here. We take turns and are glad to be rid of it when it's over. Nothing like your man in Chicago. By the way, I've been meaning to ask you, is he as good as his father was?"

I gave my standard one-word answer when asked that question.

"Better."

"Glad to hear it, glad to hear it."

"Now, about Jim Lark MacDonaugh?"

His facial expression changed instantly from geniality to grief, even to my cynical eyes a sincere change.

"Sure, don't I know that and meself reluctant to admit that he's gone."

"You know why I'm here, I take it?"

"Hasn't Art been on the phone to me every day about it? He's convinced that the lass herself did it."

"So he told me."

"Do you believe it, Tim Pat?" His face tightened into a frown.

"Usually in a murder case one looks for the person who is most likely to benefit from it, especially if it is a spouse." I spoke with caution, not sure that my response would not be phoned back to Arthur T. as soon as we left the pub.

"But the Dublin police have found no proof that she did it at all, at all, have they, now?"

"Nonetheless they're convinced that she's the criminal."

"Without proof that isn't worth shite, Tim Pat."

"And they've stopped looking for evidence."

"Have you found any yourself?" he asked eagerly, almost too eagerly.

"Not yet."

"Do you think you will?" he persisted.

"I have come to try to solve a crime, Councillor, not to pin a murder rap on anyone. I'm keeping an open mind on Ms. MacDonaugh and everyone else. What do you think?"

"I can't imagine the lass killing him. As far as I can see, they really loved one another, the first real love in poor Jim Lark's life."

"I see."

"After a certain age, as you know, Tim Pat, it stops being important to most of us. But then a man like Jim Lark, rich, wealthy, good-looking, well, he gets another chance. I think he was very lucky, not that his life wasn't a long run of good luck."

"Until the end."

"Right you are," he said glumly. "But, don't you see, I

hardly knew the woman until they married. Just an attractive and efficient woman I'd see around the New York office. Arthur T. said she was a bimbo and I figured that likely enough she was and that was a shame for poor Jim Lark."

"You changed your mind."

"Not at first, mind you, I was always the suspicious one on the team, the one looking for tricks. Jim took the risks, Art counted the numbers, and I was suspicious of the other side. It worked well enough, God knows."

"But then?"

"Well, like I said to Art, if the woman is a bimbo, she's a smart and generous and loving bimbo, so what the hell difference does it make? You've met her, have you, now?"

"Yes."

"Don't you agree?"

"It's my job to keep an open mind."

" 'Tis that, 'tis all of that." He rubbed his hands fervently. "Another pint?"

"Just one more."

That would make five, plus the two jars of sherry; way, way over my own legal limit.

"Now where were we?"

"Talking about Jim Lark MacDonaugh."

"So we were and you weren't telling me who you thought the killer was."

"I have no idea," I said candidly, "or perhaps I should say I have lots of ideas, but not much support for any of them."

"Do you think we'll ever know?" He sighed. "In this world, I mean?"

"Maybe."

"Well, I'm sure it's not the lass. She's a fine woman, much more of a woman than the first one."

"Oh?"

"Mind you, there was nothing wrong with Dora, though she a bit too much prissy South County Dublin upper middle class for my taste. Not the kind of woman you could have a good roll in the hay with on the odd Saturday evening or Sunday morning before mass, not at all, at all."

"I've heard hints of that."

"She thought she was marrying down, but it was alright because she could tame this new-rich dirt farmer from the west into the same kind of life she knew growing up a surgeon's daughter in a big bungalow in Dalkey. Teach him good manners and proper diction, if you know what I mean."

"I think I do."

Davy Byrne's was filling up with smoke—or so it seemed in my condition.

I was not so "pissed out of my mind" as to be unable to perform my professional task, not quite.

"She never did realize that he streaked through that world like a jetliner. She deplored his County Tip brashness, but she had no idea of how to cope with the world of international finance. Tell the truth, I think she never knew it existed, couldn't imagine anything better than a Dalkey villa."

"I know that kind of person."

"The lass started at the bottom just like we did, so she sailed right through that pissant South County snobbery."

"It would appear so."

Paddy Quaid was too "cute" a politician and businessman not to have made up his mind exactly what he was going to tell me and how he would tell it. So I let him proceed at his own pace.

"Did Jim Lark approve of your political interests?"

"Approve?" He laughed. "Didn't he know that I'd always been interested? And wasn't he the one who pushed me for years into running for the corporation? Go for it, Paddy, he says, you'll be *taoiseach* someday—that's our prime minister, you understand?"

"Your man seems to have a stranglehold on it?"

"Charley Haughey, is it? Well, he's the smartest politician in Ireland, maybe in the world. I came along at just the wrong time, looks like."

"There's always the EC, isn't there?"

"Ay, but I'm a bit long in the tooth for it now."

He sighed and we were silent for a few moments.

"Mind you, I was the closest person in all the world to

himself and he never said a word against Dora. Never spoke much about women at all, if you really want to know. Not a word like 'that's a nice little ass over there, isn't it?' Or 'how would you like to get your gooter in that one's box?' Sort of thing men say all the time and don't mean any harm by it, you know what I mean."

I nodded. "Box" didn't exactly strike me as a particularly apt descriptive word, but I was not about to stop his flow of words with a pugnacious drunken comment.

"Take that house below on Shrewsbury Road. He bought it and had it rebuilt, from top to bottom, and I mean from top to bottom, to surprise her with when they came home from their honeymoon at Lloret de Mer—Costa Brava, you know, used to be a great place before the tourists moved in on it—and didn't she turn up her nose at it. Thought it was too grand altogether."

"She told him that?"

"Not in so many words. She was a grand one for hints and suchlike. But he knew. Never said much about it. And they continued to live there just the same."

"Sounds like a bitch to me."

That was the Guinness talking.

"Well, you might use that term." He nodded wisely. "Though not in his presence, God knows. She was sweet enough most of the time and a grand mother for the kids. The real problem with her was that she never had any fun, didn't think it was quite proper, you know what I mean? Not just riding fun, but any kind of fun. Himself was the sort of man who loved fun, laughing and clowning from the first day I met him."

"Tell me more about him."

"He was everything, Tim Pat. He was the show, the game, the life for all of us that knew him. I'll never forget the day he came to me—we were both working at the chartered-accountants office above Townsend Street, a tiny hole in the wall, but he'd bought it with money he'd borrowed from the hurling team's fans. I wasn't an accountant at all, but Art was. He brought us both into the office, meself as a kind of manager, without much to manage, tell you the truth, and Art doing the work on the books. We were both there not because we knew anything about accounting in Dublin but because we were his mates. Always because we were mates."

"A loyal man."

"The best ... It was already 'Jim Lark MacDonaugh, Chartered Accountant' on the window and in the best gold leaf, too."

"What happened that day?"

"Ah, where was I? Oh, yes, he comes in and tosses some papers on my desk and says, 'Paddy, we've just bought a creamery above in Drogheda. Go on up there and take care of it.'

"Well, it was no small company either, let me tell you. And the three of us lads in our twenties."

" 'Where did the money come from?' Arthur says.

" 'Go along with you.' Jim Lark laughs. 'I'll worry about where the money comes from.'

"That's the way it always was. He'd make the deals. I'd take over the management. Art would worry about the money and us nothing more than kids from Tipperary."

"You seem to have done all right."

"Not too bad, all things considered." He waved a modest hand. "Do you mind if I smoke?"

This time I didn't admit that I did. So he lit up a Havana.

"But if it wasn't for him caring for his mates, I'd be managing a small creamery out in the west and Art would be repairing motorcars in a nearby town, getting on in years by now and never enough money."

"As it is ..."

"As it is, he has his fancy places in America and I head the largest creamery group in the British Isles and watch all Jim Lark's other interests here, and let me tell you there are a lot of them—hotels, golf courses, housing schemes, property."

"It started with the creamery, did it?"

"Jim Lark kept telling us that the Common Market, which most sensible Irish businessmen feared and opposed, would be a godsend for Irish dairy farmers. Art told him he was dead wrong. I thought he was wrong, too, though I never argued with him on those subjects anymore. Now, he'd have me check out companies before he bought them, find out what kind of gombeen men we were dealing with. I was pretty good at that."

"He did a lot of buying?"

"Get loans on what we had and buy something else, even if we hadn't paid off the first loan. Irish banks wouldn't touch him, so he turned to the bleeding Yanks—'cuse me, Tim Pat. You know what I mean."

"Sure." Bleeding Yank, focking Yank, what difference did it make?

"Well, there were some banks out on Long Island that didn't mind taking a flier. That's when he began to establish a base in America. Dora never liked that either. She only went over a couple of times with the kids."

"But they're more American than Irish, aren't they?"

"True enough. He sent them to schools in America."

"Wasn't that strange?"

"I says to him, people will think you're high-hatting your native country. And he says back, 'Fock 'em all, Paddy'—he didn't use that kind of language as much as the rest of us—'I love Ireland but I love my kids more. They'll get the best and America is the best. They'll say I'm high-hatting no matter what I do.' "

"So he moved back and forth to America a lot?"

"He crossed the Atlantic as easy as I cross the Liffey. ' 'Tis closer by far than a walk out to Mullingar,' he'd say. I told him he was keeping Aer Lingus in business. He tried to buy them once, but the government wouldn't let him."

"So that's the way it went, huh?"

"I'm getting ahead of my story. With the money from the Yanks we bought up the creameries, and then, after Ireland joined the Common Market, we piled up the money like I never dreamed we would. Suddenly all of us were rich."

"Quick rise to success?"

"Indeed that . . . and let me tell you, I would do it all over again. I don't have any regrets about making a lot of cold, hard stuff, not at all, at all . . . and despite what Their Reverences say at mass on Sunday. They take it easy enough when we give it to them. . . . One more?"

"I haven't finished this one." I held my hand over my glass.

"Well," he said when he came back, showing no signs of the drink having had any impact on him, "I was telling you what it was like. He'd always send me out to do the deals and tie up the loose ends, whether it was a hotel in Galway or a new creamery or a new house to build somewhere or other. He had no interest in details or administration, tell the truth; mind you, he could do administration or details if he had to, but it bored him. He'd say, 'You're the politician, Paddy, you see to it.' Or 'you're the numbers man, Artie, you take care of it.' "

"And it all worked, that's for sure."

"And it was always fun, too. I mean we had some close shaves and we lost a few, some that we should have lost and some that we shouldn't have lost. But it was never dull."

"I can imagine." I sipped a tiny amount of my Guinness.

He was quiet for a few long moments; then, staring into the dark liquid in his glass, he said thoughtfully, "Have I made him sound reckless, Tim Pat?"

"Kind of a buccaneer, big chances and usually big winnings."

He nodded. "I thought I might have given the wrong impression. He wasn't that way at all. He never took unnecessary risks, not even at the beginning. He just calculated the odds very shrewdly. He was the quickest man at the odds I've ever seen. Hardly ever lost a poker game back in the days when we had time to play. Whether it was buying that house on Shrewsbury Road for almost nothing and fixing it up for not much more—sure, wouldn't it be worth two million pounds today?—or launching this Irish-cream scheme to go head to head with Baileys, or marrying a wife—he always reckoned the odds and bet with them. Not the way you and me would, maybe, but quicker and smarter."

"Even on Nora?"

"He says to me, 'Well, now, Paddy, what do you think of me new wife?' And I'm astonished that he'd ask me a question like that. So I says to him, I says, 'She's a fine-looking woman, Jim Lark.' And he says, 'You think I've been a bit reckless and impulsive, don't you?' And I says, 'I've never known you to be either.' And he says, 'Well, I wasn't reckless with her either. I figured it was time I have me a woman like her and I sized her up a long time to make sure she was the right one. And she was.' And I says, 'Did she know you were sizing her up?' And he laughs that big, loud, happy laugh and says, 'Ah, Paddy me boy, you can't let them know that, can you, now?' "

"You think it was another good risk?"

"I'd never seen him happier than he was with her."

"And herself?"

"My own wife asks me that. And I says I watch her real close like when he comes in the room and I think she melts every time she sees him and wants him to knob her on the spot, you take my meaning? Even if she's twenty-five years younger than him, she adores him."

"A different story than the one I hear from Mr. Regan."

"That dried-up old bastard, pardon my expression, doesn't have the faintest idea what it's like to pork a woman or be porked by a man, not a clue."

Apparently Paddy Quaid thought he did. I wasn't so sure that he did comprehend what it was like from the woman's perspective. I wasn't sure I did either.

"So she didn't kill him?"

"I can't see it—hiya, Mick, how you doing? See you in a few minutes. . . . Nah, Tim Pat me lad, I can't see it."

"You think she's going to take away the companies from the rest of you?"

"Why the hell should she do that? She's got enough to do with her peace foundation, which is a damn good idea, if you ask me, despite what they say in the papers. Poor old Artie is getting weak in the head, if you ask me. Crazy old widower. She's not given the slightest sign of it."

"He says she's got people going over the books?"

"Wouldn't you if you were in her position?" He pounded the table. "Jim Lark, for reasons of his own, left the whole shooting works to her. She's got to keep an eye on it."

"Do you think Mr. Regan is hiding something?"

"You know . . ." He eased a large gulp of Guinness into his mouth. "You know, I've thought that myself. It wouldn't be like Artie, but you never can tell about people, can you? The woman's been an obsession with him from the beginning. I told him once that I thought he had the hots for her and he was furious at me, which doesn't prove I'm wrong, does it, now?"

"She's certainly a very attractive woman. . . . Who killed him, Paddy?"

"Ah." He sighed. "That's the big question, isn't it? If you ask me, it had something to do with his changing the will. That would figure, wouldn't it?"

"Then it should have been done before he changed the will, shouldn't it?"

"Not necessarily, Tim Pat, not necessarily. Maybe he changed it because of something he found out. Someone cheating in the family maybe. Or maybe the killer thought the police would pin it on her. After all, he might have thought she was in the house, and himself not knowing that she'd slipped out for a few moments to a shop on Merrion Road. It could have happened that way? Couldn't it, now?"

"She could have detonated the bomb from the bedroom, then run downstairs, locked the door from the inside, put the key on the detonator inside, and slammed the door shut."

"If she had been in the house when the guards came and herself screaming at the door, they would have suspected her on the spot. As it was, I gather they were pretty rough on her at first until someone went around to the bakery shop on Merrion Road by the bridge and inquired. They said she was right out in front of the store when the bomb went off. But my point is, whoever set the thing off might have thought all the time she was upstairs unless himself told him."

"Did you try to tell this to Chief Superintendent Clarke?"

"That asshole is a typical cop, not interested in anything

but his own ideas." He threw back his head and roared with laughter. "Begging your pardon, Tim Pat."

I laughed with him. His was an easy laugh to join.

"I'm not your typical cop. I got out."

"Tommy should have, too . . . but do you take me point? If Nora hadn't been at the bakery, they probably would have accused her. I'm not sure about a conviction, but if someone wanted to reverse the will badly enough, they might have taken that chance."

A long shot perhaps, but a mind twisted with hate might have devised such a plan.

"What was the meeting about for which the family was gathering?"

"Blamed if I know. It must have been family, not business. The two overlapped, you see, because Jim Lark was always good to his family, brought them in on the board and everything. We didn't pay any attention to them, but they were always there. When it was business, those of us who weren't family would always be at the meeting. When it was family, we didn't come."

"You didn't know he was even in Ireland, if I remember correctly?"

"Not a bit of it. I was working late over at the new financial services center on the Liffey—we'd only moved in about six months before from our place in Liberty Hall, you know the place—"

"Oh, yes."

Liberty Hall was a "glass skyscraper," minute by Chicago standards, on the Liffey, a monstrosity built on the site of the old trade-union building.

"With my assistant, Clare McNulty—she's really a kind of vice-president of our Irish operations, very bright woman—and the first thing we know, someone comes rushing into our offices to tell us the radio was saying that Jim Lark has been blown up. I don't believe it. I take a taxi down below to Shrewsbury Road. It's dark when I get there—mind you, it's January—but there's crowds all over the place. The guards have already taken the poor woman away to the station, the press is everywhere, and at first the guards won't let me in. Finally I tell them who I am and they let me go up the stairs ... and ..." His eyes began to water. "And I see the little that's left of him. . . . Excuse me, Tim Pat."

I sat silently while he pulled himself together.

"He was my life, you see. I wouldn't say it to many people, but in a way more than my wife and kids. The work goes on, sure enough, but there's no joy in it anymore, don't you see?"

"I think so."

"Take this crazy business with Jim Lark's Irish cream. He wants to take on Baileys, teach the rest of Ireland a lesson about capitalistic competition. Now, mind you, it's not a bad idea. Baileys Irish Cream is the top liqueur in the world, number one in the States, Britain, France, Germany, and Italy, as well as Ireland. They do a tremendous business in Japan, can you imagine that? They got some twenty competitors or rivals, but they're not up to Baileys. And the formula is a deep, dark secret, to make things mysterious for you while you're drinking it."

" 'Tis the quality of the cream, I believe."

"Oh, 'tis all of that, but everyone knows the farms where the cream comes from, so that's no great secret. Our game isn't to make something as good as Baileys—what's the point in that, now?—but something better! Jim Lark says to me, 'Paddy we have a lot of focking cream on this island, let's make up a new Irish cream and give the Baileys people a run for their money. Sure there's enough cream around and enough drinkers out there, too.' "

"One of his more reckless schemes, I'd say."

"Oh, all of that, but do you see, we put some money, not much, into research and development, a little bit of marketing experimentation before we put up our own distillery, or more likely, buy one. Maybe development so far costs half, three quarters of a million pounds." His soft brown eyes glowed with excitement. "A million and a half before we go into the market, if we do. For R and D that's nothing, don't you see, nothing at all, since it's our American company that's funding it, so we have a tax write-off. If it doesn't work, we don't lose anything that matters; and if it does, we pull off another big one."

"So you're going ahead with it?"

"Yeah," he said, his shoulders drooping a little, "the lass wants to. But like I say, the fun's all gone out of it."

"I'll have to sample it sometime, when it's ready."

"We're not finished with development now, but you're welcome to have a taste."

I tried to remember what other questions I had. Did he know that I'd too much of the drink taken? Probably not. I'm a pretty good faker.

"His family . . ."

"Bad business, Tim Pat, bad business altogether. Stupid, if you ask me. Behind the door when God passed out brains. Sure Liam's a lawyer and Dav is a banker and they've done well enough, but too cute by half. Fool themselves coming and going."

"You guys didn't pay much attention to them?"

"We listened politely. Then we'd ignore them and go ahead. They'd sit there and glower."

"They seem the glowering kind."

"A century or two ago, they would have been Whiteboys or Ribbonmen, what you'd call terrorists today. Or members of the mobs that used to come to the patterns—patron-saint festivals—and attack each other with clubs. I wouldn't want to cross them in their professions. Neither would anyone else, unless I miss my guess. Too cute by half and too brutal, too."

"Are they mixed up with our friends in the north?" I nodded in the direction of the six counties.

"I'd think they'd play their own terror game rather than someone else's."

"Interesting . . . Did they kill the three men who kidnapped Jim Lark?"

Paddy Quaid stared at me, stopped cold by the question.

"You know that, do you, now?"

"I do."

"I don't know, Tim Pat, and I don't want to know," he said

grimly. "And I wouldn't ask the brothers if I were you. It might not be healthy."

"I'll note your warning."

"Those were terrible days. I wanted to negotiate with the lads; so did Dora, and the poor woman already dying. The government wanted to resist. Hell, it wasn't any of their lives. I did my best to get through with some of the contacts I have ... every politician and major businessman in the country has his contacts, and don't let anyone tell you differently. But the focking Special Branch was all over the focking place and you couldn't tell whether you were coming or going, do you see? The brothers just stood around and murmured about settling it themselves. And that wicked old woman did nothing but mutter curses in Irish. She's a deep one. She'd put poison in your tea as quick as she'd look at you. They were no help at all."

"Could they have paid the money?"

"Where would they get it? And you can take it from me, our organization didn't pay them a cent. Funny, because we would have if we could have. Some think the government itself paid because Jim Lark was a 'national resource.' They might just have done that, some of them are cute enough to play it that way."

"Do you think that happened?"

"If you want to know what I think, Tim Pat MacCarthy, I think the official story is the truth. The government doesn't mind telling us the truth about the lads when it suits its purpose. The Special Branch really did have a tip, they really did storm the country house and free Jim Lark. The three prisoners really did escape from Portaloise, even if they were the first and the last to do it. I'll tell you one thing: Jim Lark always believed the story, and he ought to have known, wouldn't you think?"

"Did he know about the later deaths of the kidnappers?"

"Not from me. Nor did he ever mention it to me. It didn't make the papers here."

Interesting. Why not? Well, leave that for the moment.

"One more question, Paddy?"

"Sure you don't want another pint of the best?"

"I'd be really fluttered then."

"Not a big, strong man like you ... Well, if you don't mind, I'll have a small one myself."

Small was a euphemism. There are no small pints.

I watched him work his way over to the bar, slapping backs, shaking hands, shouting at those whose hands he couldn't reach. Like any really good pol he fed on such activity. Well, more power to him, in both senses of the phrase. Did he really miss Jim Lark as much as he said he did?

"Well, now," he began when he'd struggled back, and plunked another "jar" on the table in front of him, "what is your last question?"

"His family was Republican, I gather?"

"For whatever that word means these days, they were."

"His brother is named after the chief of staff of the IRA during the troubles."

"He was indeed."

"I understand that some of his uncles were killed at the time."

"Ay, 'tis true. One of them was with Liam Lynch when he got it in the gut. Was killed the next day by the Free State troops. I think he lost uncles on both sides."

"Yet he certainly seemed unsympathetic to the current nationalists in the north."

"Well, 'tis a complicated matter, Tim Pat MacCarthy. I can't expect a Yank, even a bright Yank like yourself, to understand it, because we don't half understand it ourselves. There's a lot of folk from solid Republican families who want no part of what's going on above in the six counties. Mind you, they'd stand for a free and United Ireland, the republic one and indivisible and that sort of shite, but they don't want to spend any money, much less any blood on the cause, don't you see?"

"Yet Jim Lark went further than that, didn't he? As I remember, he supported the Anglo-Irish agreement in which the Dublin government renounced any claim to the six counties unless a majority of the people up there voted for union."

"He did indeed ... and to be candid about it, I disagreed with him there, though it was only a matter of emphasis. I say to him, I say, 'Jim Lark, it's one island after all, and they're colonists even if they've been up there for four centuries. By rights we ought to throw them out.' And he'd laugh and say, 'Hog shite, Paddy, just plain hog shite. Who's the "we" that's going to do the throwing? You? Me? My kids? It won't work. The secret is to build prosperity and to make money here and leave the rest to the future.' He took a lot of heat for that attitude, but he just laughed and said when Charley—he meant Charley Haughey, who is the *taoiseach* today and opposition leader then—was willing to march up the Bann toward Belfast, he'd be right behind him. It shut them all up. If there's one thing I know as a man who has to stand for reelection, it's that if I explicitly supported the IRA, I'd be turned out of office the first time my constituents got a chance to vote against me."

"Our friends in the six counties kidnapped him once, might they have killed him this time?"

"Sure." He shrugged skeptically. "They might have. The lads might do anything. They might kill all the wealthy men in Ireland. Tony O'Reilly, for example, who has more money than even Jim Lark did. But why? They're not crazy. Or maybe they are crazy, but they don't do things that are, from their point of view, without rhyme or reason. And when they do something, damn well better believe they claim credit for it. This time they deny responsibility, and vehemently enough so you know they mean it."

"I see."

"If you have any more questions, don't hesitate to call." He stood up. "And Clare has an appointment with you in the lounge at the Shelbourne tomorrow at half five?"

"She does."

"Good! Good!" He rubbed his hands again. "Anything we can do to help." He paused. "Speaking about the Shelbourne, one more story about Jim Lark. 'The Shelbourne,' he says to me, 'is a right focking hole. No matter how often they try to renovate the old girl, she still ends up looking like a whore.

Why don't you hop over to London and see if Tony Forte will sell it to us. We'll gut the place and redo it, make it the best hotel in Ireland, the place where all the beautiful people have to stay, instead of the Berkeley Court. Call it the Jim Lark Shelbourne, or maybe the Jim Lark.' I says to him, 'The old whore is profitable now, why put a lot of money into it?' And he says for the hell of it and because we'll charge higher rates since we're the best and pay it off in five years."

"Obviously you didn't do it."

"Tony Forte wouldn't sell it for love nor money." He slapped me on the back. "Good luck in your hunt."

He turned to work the room again and I edged my way out into the rain and the mists. It didn't seem cold anymore. Maybe that was because of the warmth inside me.

I struggled up the Green toward the hotel, only a couple of blocks away, and murmured whatever I could of my recall into the recorder for the good bishop.

I'd talked to three suspects so far—counting Arthur T. Regan. They all seemed to have flawless alibis—Regan was in New York; Quaid was in his office with a witness; Nora was in front of the bakery at Ballsbridge. Regan was convinced that Nora did it. Quaid was just as convinced that she did not. His portrait of the marriage was virtually the same as Nora's.

Could he and Nora be in collusion? They obviously liked one another. But why should they collude?

He had made an extremely important point that I had missed: perhaps the killer thought that Nora was in the house, in which case suspicions against her would have been much stronger. She would indeed probably have been put on trial— and if the jury was permitted to hear about Ronan Joyce, she might have been in deep trouble. Her alibi was completely fortuitous.

I had acquired a lot of information about Jim Lark MacDonaugh, indeed more than I really wanted. He had cold-bloodedly stalked a second wife more to his taste than his first wife. He had played poker on an international scale for the pure hell of it. Some of his ideas, if not crackpot since they turned out to be profitable, were designed to call attention to himself. The Jim Lark Shelbourne indeed. Neither his wife nor his best friend seemed to mind or even notice.

James Larkin MacDonaugh was growing more obscure in my imagination, like a picture fading out as a camera loses focus. He didn't quite seem to fit together.

Yet people loved him, even that poor old woman out on Shrewsbury Road. Come to think of it, she had an alibi, too. Wasn't she walking up the path to the house when the bomb went off? Didn't her brother Michael arrive at the same time?

A radio transmitter might have been in her purse or his pocket.

How then would it have gotten to the library shelf?

"There's probably something I'm overlooking in all this, Bishop Blackie, but in my present state I've missed it completely. I'll never be an alcoholic, that's for sure. There's a couple of more things I should check on, a call to a demolition expert at the Chicago PD and to a doctor in New York, but I'm afraid that'll have to wait till tomorrow afternoon after I return from Castle MacDonaugh."

Before I went to my room, I did remember to do two things. I sent a fax to America asking for information on the other members of the MacDonaugh family. Undoubtedly the always careful Arthur T. had checked them out. Since he had reasons for everything he did, there must be a good reason why he didn't give his data to me. Come to think of it, I reflected as I carefully wrote out the message to my colleagues in Chicago who were specialists in the financial world, Arthur T. seemed to have a strong need to believe in Nora's guilt.

Was he attracted to her, too, as Paddy Quaid had suggested?

A man would have to be devoid of hormones to work in the same offices with the woman and not fantasize about her.

Fascinating, I told myself as I tried to weave a straight line toward the elevator, though I'm not exactly sure at the moment why.

I had used one of Bishop Blackie's favorite words. What was I supposed to remember about him?

Oh, yes. I wove back to the desk, asked for an envelope as soberly as I could, thought about leaving the tape with the hall porter, and decided against it.

Once I reached the elevator, I carefully removed the tape from my recorder, put it in the envelope, scrawled the good bishop's name on it, and waited till the elevator halted at my floor.

Then some good angel reminded me that the bishop was on the third floor and I was on the fourth. I walked carefully down the steps, made sure I had the right room, and slid the envelope under the door.

Then I climbed even more carefully up the steps and stumbled toward my own room.

I noted in passing that Nora's door, only two doors from mine, was firmly closed, as it should be.

Then I entered my own room, threw everything but my shorts on the floor, and collapsed into a sleep that I knew would end with a hangover.

12

I WOKE WITH A START—THE ALCOHOL EFFECT GONE AND MY hangover beginning. I lay in a pool of sweat. Why? The windows were open, weren't they? It was a warm night by Irish standards, despite the rain, and the humidity was thick.

What time was it, then?

Then I heard the noise again, the noise that had awakened me, a very faint, muffled scream.

Nora!

Not even thinking of a robe, I charged out of my room and down the dimly lit corridor. The door to her room was ajar. I pushed it open and roared in. In the faint illumination of the streetlights on the Green through the drapes, I saw two men, in the required black sweaters, pants, and ski masks, on top of her. One was holding her motionless, the other was pushing a pillow down on her face. She was struggling feebly, as if her breath was fading.

Without pausing for a strategy, I blind-sided them like I would hit a quarterback from Southern California.

They weren't ready for me. They rolled off her and fell on the floor. I heard her gasp weakly.

It's not enough, if you're a cop in a tight spot, to have a linebacker's bulk and strength when you're up against pros. You have to know more tricks than they do or they'll kill you.

I knew a lot of tricks from the martial-arts mat, but I hadn't used them in a long time. These two were probably younger and in better condition. I'd have to get them before they had time for an instinctive reaction to explode in their brains.

As they struggled off the floor in confusion, looking for the location in the semidarkness of the battering ram that hit them, I dove on one guy, grabbed his wrist, and broke his arm. He was a sufficient pro to muffle his scream. I jumped up and dug my knee into his groin to give him something to think about.

"Kill the focker," he groaned through gritted teeth.

I saw a flash of blade in the faint light and ducked. The man plunged past me toward Nora. I threw my arm around his throat and yanked him back, almost strangling him on the spot. While he struggled for breath I twisted one of his arms behind his back and broke it.

He muffled his scream, too.

They were both little guys, I noted. So I threw this one who was sobbing with pain out the doorway into the corridor. He landed with a thud.

Nora was still gasping behind me, struggling with desperate effort for breath. At least she was still alive.

The other one was coming at me again. I didn't see a knife, but I suspected brass knuckles on his fist. He was coming pretty slowly.

So I hit him in the general area I thought his jaw might be. He rocked back toward the doorway. I picked him up and heaved him out on top of his inert companion.

"Let's get the fock out of here!" one of them groaned.

They hobbled down the corridor and around the corner, presumably toward the staircase at the back end of the center wing of the building. I thought about following them, even if, as I was suddenly aware, I was wearing only my shorts.

I would take care of them later. I flicked on the light, shut the bolt on the door, which I noted had been jimmied open, and turned toward Nora.

"Tim Pat?" she choked.

"Lancelot du Lac."

She tried to laugh and gasped deeply again.

She was wearing a thin, almost transparent, lemon-colored sleep shirt—the perfect woman in distress for M. du Lac. I turned off the ceiling light, turned on the small lamp at the bedside, and took her into my arms.

"It's all right, it's all right," I repeated as I held her and soothed her. She gasped and sobbed and struggled for breath and shivered in my arms.

I was aware for the first time that I was breathing heavily, the retired alley-fighter cop turned Lancelot was not in quite the excellent physical condition he thought he was.

His instincts were still good.

Toward the fair lady I had saved and whom I held protectively in my arms I felt great tenderness. Not the tenderness that comes before lovemaking, however. Not yet.

Slowly she relaxed. Her breathing became more easy and regular. Her sobbing stopped. She cuddled closer to me.

We remained that way for what seemed like a long time, eternity on Stephen's Green, not Sandymount Strand.

"My lungs hurt." She tried to speak.

"They will for a while," I said. "No permanent damage."

"My throat is sore."

"Advil for a day or two."

"They were trying to kill me."

"They were indeed."

"One of them wanted to rape me first. He said it was a shame to waste the opportunity. The other said there wasn't enough time. They were both young, Tim Pat." She stiffened in my arms. "They'll be back."

"No way."

"You saved me life. Thank you."

"Thank God, Nora," I said. "*He* woke me up."

"She." She tried to laugh again and ended up gasping.

"Easy, easy, just relax."

So she just relaxed.

Then she stiffened again. "Get out of my room, please, Captain MacCarthy," she said in a hoarse but firm voice.

"I thought I was Tim Pat."

"Not in my bedroom." She pushed me away. "At night and myself naked."

"You're not naked," I argued.

"Yes, I am, for all practical purposes."

"I guess you're right."

"Give me my robe . . . over there on the chair, eejit."

The robe in matching lemon but much more substantial

was neatly folded on a chair where it could be picked up and thrown on instantly in the morning.

"Give it to me and turn your back. No, go into the bathroom and put on one of those terry robes."

"Yes, ma'am," I said docilely.

"Not designed for a linebacker," I apologized as I came back from the bathroom. "My shoulders are too big."

"I'm sorry I called you an eejit." She was curled up in a knot at the head of the bed. "I'm upset."

"You have every reason to be," I said grimly, just beginning to feel inordinately proud of M. du Lac.

"You saved my life, for whatever it is worth. I'll be eternally grateful to you. But please leave me alone."

"No."

"Why not?" She seemed surprised.

"You might go into shock. You're in no shape to be left alone."

"I'm fine."

"No, you're not."

"Is my nose broken?"

"I don't think so." I touched it lightly.

She didn't scream.

"Nope."

"*Please* go," she begged me.

"Only when the police come."

"No *police*. I hate the Dublin police. They'll accuse me of something awful again."

"I'm here as a witness that two masked attackers tried to kill you."

"They'll say I seduced you like I seduced both my husbands."

"Did you?"

"The first one sure, but we loved each other. Not the second, at least I didn't realize I was doing it if I did."

I reached for the phone.

"No!" She pushed my hand away.

"You need protection."

"I can take care of that in the morning. I'm quite capable of hiring a private security service for myself."

"Between now and then." Both our hands gripped the phone, not exactly struggling for it, but contending anyway.

"I don't care whether they kill me or not," she said, struggling with cough spasms.

"Do you mean that?"

"I thought I was going to die. Then I wanted to die. I had nothing to live for. Then there was this terrible hope. As if someone was telling me I couldn't die because there was a lot left for me to do."

Classic near-death experience, though she hadn't stopped breathing.

"Then this enormous linebacker person saved my life." She was about to cry. "He's a nice man. . . ."

"A good man."

"Right. A good man, but I wish he'd leave my bedroom."

I took the phone away.

"No, *please!*"

"Not the cops, just inside the hotel." I gave a room number.

"Cathedral, Father Ryan." As though he were always awake, anticipating a hospital call.

"Tim MacCarthy here. I'm in Nora MacDonaugh's room."

"Ah."

"Not so exciting as it sounds. Two goons tried to smother her. She's all right now. But she doesn't want to call the guard because of the bad experiences she's had with them. Can't say I blame her. The guy on her case is a real asshole. Tried to mess up her head."

"Put her on." Not a request, but an order.

I handed Nora the phone.

"Yes, Bishop."

She spoke as if she were a grammar-school child who had been called on the carpet by a crotchety old monsignor.

"Yes, Bishop.

"Yes, Bishop.

"Yes, Bishop, it was Tim. Who else?

"Oh, no, Bishop, I'm not afraid of him." She looked at me shyly. "I'm afraid of me.

"Yes, Bishop.

"How did you know that?" She laughed hoarsely.

"Yes, Bishop. Thank you, Bishop."

She replaced the phone and then sat up straight in bed.

"His Lordship said you should stay here and have a friendly conversation with me until he calls and says he's made appropriate arrangements. I am supposed to pour you a drop of Bushmills." She stood up, rather unsteadily, and moved carefully toward the wardrobe. "And have a friendly conversation with you."

"Did he, now?"

"Didn't I say that?" She gasped in spasms but removed a bottle with a green label from the wardrobe. "Would you mind bringing two tumblers from the bathroom? Please."

" 'Tis yourself that has the heavy hand," I said as she filled both glasses.

"No need to pour a second time. I have a jar each night before bed. It beats tranquilizers."

I forbore saying that sex might be more fun than Bushmills. Even green-label Bush.

"I don't know how the bishop knows that I have the bottle here. He didn't say that I had green label, so I guess there's something he doesn't know. . . . Your health." She leaned against the wardrobe. "And my deepest gratitude, Monsieur du Lac."

I toasted her in return and sipped from the tumbler. It was powerful stuff.

"Gorgeous." She sighed, still leaning against the wardrobe.

"It clears the sinuses," I said, struggling to regain my voice.

"And doctors say it's good for the heart. Jim Lark"—her face clouded and then cleared quickly—"taught me how nice it was at the very end of the day—just one jar, mind you. Ordinarily."

"Very good." I touched a drop of the single malt with my tongue. "Very good indeed."

As a prelude to sex? I'd fall asleep first.

"Now, shall we sit down and have a friendly conversation?"

"Yes, ma'am."

"I apologize again for my rudeness."

I almost said I love you, but this was a friendly conversation.

"No problem ... You recover your poise very quickly."

She waved her glass to dismiss my compliment. I noted that she sipped from it very cautiously.

She looked terrible. She also looked devastatingly beautiful.

She tucked her legs under herself on the chair, primly soothed her robe, an archduchess receiving one of her inferior servants for his early-morning instructions.

"Why did they want to kill me? Yesterday you said it was a warning, didn't you?"

"What have you done since last night?"

"Talked to you in the morning, studied these audit reports, which you must take, by the way, when Bishop Blackie and I release you from captivity."

Was that her fantasy? That she had me all tied up in knots? Well, maybe she did.

"Either one of those might have done it. Someone is afraid of you, of what you might find."

"The one who killed Jim Lark?"

"Maybe."

"Do you still think I might have killed him?"

"No ... Well, personally I know you didn't. Professionally I have to keep an open mind."

"Of course ... When did you make up your mind about me?"

"Last night." I hadn't realized that myself. "After I left the reception."

"Leaving me to fend for myself."

"You weren't my date."

"Too true." She looked down at her glass. "What makes you think I'm innocent? I have a bad history, don't I?"

"I don't think, Nora Finnegan Joyce MacDonaugh, that you'd be a good enough faker to carry it all off. I don't think you're much of a faker at all, less than most of us maybe. That's cop gut instinct, but mine is not wrong much."

"Not even about women?"

I laughed and tried a larger sip of the whiskey. It certainly did clear the sinuses. "I haven't usually followed the instinct when it warned me about women, worse luck for me."

"I suppose you want to know more about me and Ronan." She lowered her eyes and swished her drink around in the glass. "And myself admitting that I had seduced him."

"And adding that you loved him."

"You already know more about me than anyone else living or dead, you may as well know the rest, for your professional opinion, so to speak."

"If you want to."

"Not much sense in hiding now, is there? He was a lovely boy, you see. There was nothing wrong with his health at all, at all. His parents couldn't help themselves, poor dears. They had to dote on his health because they were old and he was all they had. They didn't want him to slip away from them, the father even more than the mother."

"I know the kind."

"Not this extreme. Rony and I were shy with each other at the beginning, but I think we liked each other at first sight. I talked him into Fordham. All he was wanting was a little shove."

"The parents resisted?"

"No. They worried and the game was that he didn't want to worry them. But he didn't want to lose my respect either. Even for someone who had been dominated by possessive parents all his life, the young girl is more important than the parents."

"A fight all the way . . ."

"Ah, but a subtle one." She continued to dispose of her whiskey at a more rapid clip than I. "You'd hardly have noticed. Well, as you might imagine, Rony and I fell crazy in love with one another. He was such a nice boy, so kind and patient and witty, too, poor dear man."

She stopped for a minute, alone with her memories.

"I made him laugh; he was a pretty serious and gloomy kid, but there was a lot of laughter inside him. In those days I'd laugh and sing a lot when I was working around the house. Soon he was singing with me; that's when I knew he was starting to love me. I was so happy that someone finally loved me that I loved him right back. Everyone said, even after we were married, that I could make the gloomiest person in the world laugh. . . ."

Her voice trailed off.

"That was so long ago and I was such a young fool."

I remained silent, letting her find her own way through her memories.

"The laughter's all gone, Tim Pat. Now they want to kill me in my sleep."

I hadn't seen her laugh much, that was true, but still there was an occasional leprechaun glint in her eye.

"The laughter can come back, Nora. There's always a hint of it in your eyes and on your lips."

"It did for a while, Tim Pat." She sighed. "It's gone for good now."

"I don't believe it."

"Believe it," she said. "Where was I? Oh, yes . . . poor dear Rony and me . . . They didn't want him to finish college. I mean they did and they didn't, if you take me meaning. I told myself that he needed some extra gumption to push through that last year. So"—she lifted her shoulders—"I gave it to him."

"I see."

"I mean, I was deadly curious and so was he and we loved one another. So I went to his room one night when the old folks were asleep, after thinking about it for a long time, and I undressed while he watched me, and his eyes leaping out of his head, and we both lost our virginity and had a grand time."

"Good for you."

"Ah, wasn't it ever. We were young and silly and we had a super time fooling his parents. After he graduated and told them he was going to law school and we were going to be married, they were very angry at first and then overnight changed their minds.

"They figured they wouldn't have to fight me for him like they might have to fight some other girl. And they didn't. Rony was all mine anyway and I never did dislike the parents. Sometimes I thought that his ma, deep down, had brought me across the Atlantic for him. Wouldn't that have been something?"

"She was very wise if she did."

"So I made it my business to keep them happy, which was easy enough, poor dears, and to keep Ronan happy, too . . . and yourself saying I'm not a faker."

"I didn't say you weren't shrewd."

"I'm not being shrewd with you now, Tim Pat MacCarthy."

"No more than usual."

She laughed. " 'Tis true, but I'm trying to be as naked about myself as I was over there on that bed."

"With only a little bit of cover that, like you said, doesn't make any difference."

"All right." She blushed. "And meself near choking to death."

"You were very beautiful, Nora. Even more beautiful than I thought you would be. You'll be beautiful all your life."

"Don't say things like that to me," she begged. "I can't bear to hear them."

"I'll say what I want."

"It wasn't as if you hadn't seen that picture of me in the *Illustrated London News*. I'm sure your man put it in the file."

"I barely glanced at it."

She laughed skeptically. "And yourself staring at me bare boobs in the picture at the house on Shrewsbury Road, too."

"Did Jim Lark buy that from the photographer?"

"He did *not*." She was outraged. "Wouldn't I have been furious if he dared to do such a thing? Wasn't I buying it myself and giving it to him for a Christmas present! And wasn't he howling with laughter when he saw it on the wall!"

"Nice touch," I murmured.

"Just a few weeks before he died." She sighed, her humor quickly gone.

"I'm so sorry, Nora Marie," I said. And I really was.

"Well, what's done is done." She bit her lip for a moment and then, grief banished, continued. "At first I felt embarrassed and violated. Then I realized that laughter was the way to fight back, so I made it a focking joke."

"And dealt nicely with that gobshite from the *Irish Times*. Now go on with your story."

"Rony and I were terrible happy. You'd be thinking that I was one of your dominating Irish wives, but I wasn't at all, at all. Rony had a lot of backbone in him, he really did, and I didn't mind that either. He was on his way to being a strong man."

Two tears rolled down her cheeks.

"What happened?"

"No children. Weren't all of us wanting to have some brats, the parents especially? And it wasn't that we weren't together often enough, God knows. Some false alarms, but no morning sickness for me."

"You went to a doctor?"

"After a couple of years. We tried everything, some of the stuff pretty indecent, if you ask me. Nothing worked. I could have lived with it, you see. But the doctor said himself was the one who was sterile and it was a terrible blow to his pride. Silly, if you take me meaning, but, alas, 'tis the way you men are. He was a grand lover, but he was not a man unless he could father a child."

"The parents?"

"We didn't tell them anything about it, but they guessed, of course, and they blamed me. Their little comments, if you know what I mean, became more pointed."

"You could have adopted?"

"Sure we could. But poor dear Rony had not grown up in a normal family. He had to have a child that was his own.

Mind you, he was already a big success at law, making scads of money, but he wanted a brat of his own. Then he became depressed and morose—not sullen, mind you, he couldn't be that way. And not much interested in lovemaking either. He was already sterile and he thought he was turning impotent. The doctor warned me that he was worried about him. I was terrible worried about him myself. I wanted him to see a psychiatrist. He said what good would that do. Afterward I thought that if I hadn't been so concerned about college graduation ... but what could I have done?"

"You didn't tell this to the police?"

"I didn't want to seem to be disgracing his memory. I was a silly little kid. If it had come to it, I would have asked the doctor to testify, but it wasn't necessary."

"Is the doctor still alive?"

"He is. He's still me doctor."

"May I get a statement from him?"

"Why?"

"To put in the file of this case. It will help to clear your name. Permanently."

She stared at me, silent.

"Ah, sure, Tim Pat, why not? It's all water under the bridge anyway, isn't it?"

"It is, but you're not."

"All right." She scribbled a name and phone number on a note sheet and gave it to me. "Put it in your file. . . . Wasn't I hoping that Jim Lark and I would have a brat, but it didn't work out that way."

I took the sheet from her and put it in the pocket of the terrycloth robe that I'd have to wear back to my room.

"You're still young enough to have a couple of them."

"I'll never marry again," she said firmly. "Never again. I won't destroy another man. It was my body that killed them both. If they hadn't wanted me, they'd both still be alive today."

"Nora Marie, that's the most damn fool Irish superstitious thing I've ever heard in all my life and I forbid you to say it, even think it in my presence, ever again. Do you understand me?"

She was startled by my vehemence. "Yes, Captain MacCarthy," she said meekly.

"You do understand?" I poked a finger at her, a captain giving orders to a rookie patrol officer.

"Yes, sir." She grinned tentatively.

"You admit that it's superstitious nonsense."

"I don't—"

"You gave those two lucky men more happy years than most of us get in all our lives, and I'll tolerate no other response from yourself, is that clear?"

She stiffened as if she were prepared to fight me. Then she sank back in the chair and closed her eyes.

"Are you sure of that, Tim Pat?"

"I am, woman."

I expected an argument. I had intervened intolerably in her most personal thoughts and feelings. Instead she sighed and said, "Sure, doesn't part of me know you're right? Ah, but isn't it good to hear you say it?"

"Now tell me about Marty O'Neill!"

She sat up again. "What's wrong with Marty O'Neill? He was Jim Lark's administrative assistant and now he's mine. No one suspects him, do they? He was off in New York."

"I'm told you travel with him."

"Well, I do sometimes." She seemed confused. "He's very helpful and it's easier and safer to have a man around, but—"

"Is that all he is?"

"Ah, I bet that terrible Tom Clarke is planting ideas in your head, Tim Pat. Is he watching us?"

"Not closely. I suppose he checks occasionally. He doesn't have the time or the manpower to do anything else. Clearly they weren't watching you tonight."

"And it's made you jealous, has it, now, Tim Pat?" She was smiling at me affectionately, as a mother does at a dear but difficult little boy. As my mother smiles at me most of the time.

"It has raised some questions I need answered for my investigation. You didn't tell me about him."

"There isn't much to tell. He's efficient. He's reliable, and, Tim Pat, he's gay."

"Gay?"

"Isn't he over at the Berkeley Court with one of his lovers?"

Oh.

I'd have to check that out, but there was no reason to doubt her word. Did asshole Clarke know he was gay?

"Did Jim Lark know?" I tried to cover my embarrassment.

"Not at first. When he found out, he wanted to fire him. I gave him a stern lecture and he changed his mind."

Another flash of insight into that relationship. Jim Lark MacDonaugh wasn't the only tough partner. Not at all, at all.

"You can check up on him."

"I will, but I believe you."

"Maybe you should interview him, too. He says that Jim Lark had a lot of things on his mind when we made that rush to Kennedy. He isn't quite sure what they were."

"All right, I will. . . . Random question, did he know about the will?"

"I don't think so. It was a secret to everyone but Jim Lark's personal lawyer in New York, and only two weeks before he died. I wonder if he had some kind of hunch. . . ."

There were a number of other things I'd have to check when I escaped from my pleasant prison. I'd have to jot them down because in my present hung-over condition I might forget.

Thought about the hangover made me realize that I was risking an even worse one by drinking the whiskey. To my astonishment both our glasses were empty.

"Let me fill your glass." She picked up the bottle.

"No thanks."

"Are you a short hitter, Tim Pat?" Again she wrapped me in her affectionate maternal smile. I don't need a mother, woman. I've already got one who does very nicely. She's a lot like you, come to think of it.

"In a manner of speaking. I had two sherries and five pints of Guinness yesterday and I'm a wreck."

She shrugged and filled her own glass halfway up again. " 'Tis a pity." She sighed. "A terrible pity, but you shouldn't mix your drinks. I bet you had the sherry with Julia. Did you like it?"

"It was very good sherry." I sighed in my turn. "Too good."

She giggled. "A terrible pity altogether . . . and isn't it one of my few extravagances? I mean I always buy the best liquor. Jim Lark said that it was not the thing to economize on. . . . How do you like Julia, by the way?"

"An angry bitter old woman."

"Julie!" She laughed. "And am I not uncertain about your instincts now? Julie's a pussycat, a pushover, isn't she, now? I bet she told you that the whirlpool next to the master bedroom is a sinful, indecent thing, didn't she?"

"She did."

"Ah, what a terrible woman she is! I bet she didn't tell you that she uses it every day for her poor old bones, as she calls them. And she and some of her friends sneak in and play poker and sip at my sherry every day, too, and all of them cheating, too. I bet she didn't tell you that, now, did she?"

"She did not."

"And she gave you that line that she wouldn't tell you that you were welcome, but she'd still make tea for you."

"She did."

"She's my source, Tim Pat."

"What!"

"Aggie—that's the youngest of my stepchildren, if you can call them that, the cute little redhead—tells Julie what happens at the board meetings and the wicked old woman passes it on to me. Aggie probably knows that. She feels she has to hate me because of the will, but she finds it pretty hard."

"That's a different version of Julia MacDonaugh."

"You're not very good on judging Irishwomen, are you, Tim Pat?" She grinned slyly. "And yourself with such a high opinion of your own instinct?"

The phone saved me from further embarrassment.

Nora answered the phone. "Yes, Bishop. Yes, he's still here. A nice talk, Bishop. He had only one drink, but he's still a good man."

She handed me the phone.

"This whole business is deplorable, Timothy," Bishop Blackie began.

"It sure is."

"Totally unacceptable."

"I agree."

"It must be brought to a conclusion shortly."

"Indeed."

"Your investigation proceeds successfully, it would seem?"

"If you say so."

"You may leave the exemplary Nora's room now, if you so desire. She is adequately protected, though I doubt that her new and more or less invisible protectors can do so much damage in as short time as you did."

"They've been picked up?"

"They have . . . ah, I made certain representations . . . they are wanted for various reasons."

"She'll be happy to hear that."

Nora nodded in happy agreement.

"Very good, Timothy, I'm sure I'll hear from you."

"I'm going back to my room to sleep for a couple of hours."

"Virtuous."

He hung up.

No, good bishop, just hung over.

"He says I can go home now."

Nora nodded. "Thanks for the visit—and the conversation."

She walked me to the door. Outside, the sun was already coming up, an early sunrise in this high latitude.

"And thanks for saving my life." She unlocked the door. "Many, many thanks."

"You are very graceful, Nora, and very beautiful."

"In my sleep shirt?" She giggled.

"No, in your robe. You handle terror, suffering, and tragedy with incredible grace."

She looked like she was about to kiss me. Then we both thought better of it.

"Good night, Nora Marie."

"Good night, Tim Pat. Or good morning or whatever."

"Whatever."

"Tim Pat," she called after me.

"Yes?" I turned around.

"You forgot the audits!"

I went back to her door. A demure smile on her face, she piled them into my arms.

"Something to keep your mind occupied."

" 'Tis not the mind I'm worried about, 'tis the imagination."

"Go 'long with you." She closed the door firmly.

No one was in the corridor, so I hurried to my room in my mixed ensemble of shorts and a robe not designed for a linebacker's shoulders.

In my room I scribbled some more reminders on the back of Nora's notepaper and, remembering to put the Do Not Disturb sign on the door, fell into bed.

My dreams were incredibly pleasant.

13

"**P**OOR NORA HAS A TERRIBLE COLD," TRISH RYAN INformed me. "Listen to how hoarse she is."

"Irish weather," I explained.

I had met Nora again at noon on the gun platform of the Martello Tower at Sandycove, five miles down the beach from Sandymount, where Joyce lived with Oliver St. John Gogarty—Buck Mulligan—for a couple of weeks and where the first scene in *Ulysses* is set. I had stopped there as part of my random exploration of the Bloomsday track while driving to the Wicklow Hills and Castle MacDonaugh. She was in the company of the good bishop and his vivacious companions. It was Saturday morning and my schedule called for a conversation with Michael Dav and Liam MacDonaugh at the castle and then a late-afternoon interview with Clare McNulty in the lounge of the Shelbourne.

All three women were affecting slacks, blouses, and sweaters in the now bright and crisp weather. At the foot of the tower, the waters of Dublin Bay, snot-green, scrotum-tightening waters according to Joyce, were pounding against the rocks. The furious bay didn't look much like a mother, as your man said it did.

Despite her ordeal of the previous night, Nora seemed as young and vibrant as the two others.

" 'Plump, stately Buck Mulligan,' " Brigie Murphy observed. "What a put-down for a man he didn't like. An eternal put-down. More people will know that about Gogarty as long as there is an English language than will ever read a word he's written."

"The chapter is a parody of the mass," Nora added to the babble of Joycean show-offs. "Isn't that terrible!"

"It shows he knew what the mass was." The Bishop sighed. "And that he even had a theology of the mass. The book may be said from one point of view to be a tract on the Most Holy Trinity."

"Bloom represents the Father," Brigie informed me as though she was reciting from lecture notes, "and Stephen the son, and Molly, naturally, the Holy Spirit, Who we all know is womanly anyway."

"And thus," Trish added solemnly, "Joyce breaks down the old dichotomy between virgin and prostitute, between pure woman and erotic woman, which is like totally neat, right?"

I claimed I couldn't agree more, but I didn't think such agreement won me any points.

I wasn't sure how this foursome had been assembled. It looked like Blackie had simply appropriated Nora. Nor were any protectors visible from the top of the tower. I was pretty sure they were around somewhere.

I was constrained to join them for lunch at the old shrine of Glendalough in the Wicklow Hills before going on to Castle MacDonaugh. I had time, so I decided why not. I wanted to be with Nora every minute I could.

Nora, her face flushed and her laughter rich and easy, seemed much younger than her thirty-eight years, a silver-haired adolescent only a few years older than Brigid and Trish. The vivacity of the bishop's supervisors had captured her. She had been their age once, but never with the freedom and great expectations for the future that they enjoyed.

Over tea and sandwiches in the hotel next to the shrine, a mysterious and haunting place whose archaic loveliness spooked me, the two of us rarely spoke to one another. Rather we talked to the enthusiastic young women and the bishop.

But our eyes crossed often as those of lovers or about-to-be lovers often do. In her eyes I saw gratitude and admiration and perhaps a beginning of something else, something that she wanted to hide still, but not entirely.

I don't know what she saw in my eyes—perhaps the memories of mostly naked women cuddled in my arms—but if she recognized my desire, it didn't seem to offend her.

If I didn't end my investigation quickly, we both might be

in trouble that neither of us wanted—well, about which both of us were highly ambivalent.

"Thank you again," she whispered, and touched my hand as our party left the hotel. "I like having a retired linebacker around when someone is trying to kill me."

"Anytime."

We said no more because the odd trinity caught up with us.

"Captain MacCarthy, Uncle Punk," Trish informed us, "goes that you two ought to take tomorrow off and go to the beach if the weather is nice."

"Sandymount?"

"Barf city," Brigie replied, "a gobshite place."

Nice mix of two slang traditions.

"Bull Island is supposed to be like totally rapid," Trish reassured us. "Isn't it, Nora?"

" 'Tis grand altogether."

"Will you two come with us?"

"Well . . . like we'll be there to keep an eye on you, but . . ."

"Like by ourselves in another car . . ."

"In case there are any neat boys in Dublin, which I doubt."

"They all migrated," I said. "Well, I tell you what." I turned on my Golden Dome charm. "I'll ask herself if she'll drive up with me in my rented Renault, but you two will have to promise—"

"What!" they demanded imperiously, wary of my conditions.

"Is it not patent"—the bishop's eyes blinked rapidly—"that the good captain feels like an old man when you call Nora by her Christian name and him by his formal title?"

"But he's not old," Trish exclaimed.

"Not *really* old," her niece agreed, and then shyly: "We can call you Tim or maybe even Timmy like my bro?"

"Better Tim Pat!" Nora informed them.

"Grand!" they exclaimed together.

"And," Nora continued with a playful smile, "I'll be happy to keep an eye on him so he doesn't try to act like some neat boy."

"Excellent!"

"After mass at Clarendon Street; the bishop will say it, of course."

"If they permit me."

It was true enough that the two young women were in charge of Bishop Blackie. They took turns driving the rented red Mercedes, they directed him in and out of the hotel, they ordered his food and drink for him, including a pint of the "wine of the countryside," by which was meant Guinness, naturally.

Yet I was perfectly prepared to believe that John Blackwood Ryan, Ph.D., D.D. (*honoris causa*), etc., etc., while he enjoyed the attention and the care, was more than capable of taking care of himself. He lurked behind the persona of inefficiency because it suited him to do so and because it made people less nervous about his wisdom.

Let other people worry about the details while he pondered the important things.

"Your man," he remarked as we were splitting up, "as is obvious at the ending of the book, suspected that the body of the beloved is a powerful hint of the nature of whatever energy is responsible for our world. In this he was, of course, profoundly Catholic. Thus reverent desire for the aforementioned body may be taken as desire for God."

"Does reverence depress the desire?"

"Arguably not. It is said by those with more experience in such matters than I that it enhances the joy."

Nora and I had not fooled the bishop for one moment. Probably not the sharp-eyed aides-de-camp either. I had tried to fool them. I wasn't sure that she had bothered.

As I picked my way back into the hills, searching for Castle MacDonaugh with a road map in my hand, I realized that I was being gently eased by the bishop and his crew—no, not so gently—toward Nora. What was a dream, a fantasy, a remote imagination the night before last could become a reality. Neither of us had made up our mind definitively, but we saw the possibility and were not rejecting it out of hand.

We were both of us also terrified by it, attracted to each other and repelled at the same time.

What was my present position on that subject—besides desire, reverent or mostly so, for her lovely body, one which I had told her the night before in all honesty would always be lovely?

The truthful answer to my question of whether this was the woman for whom I had been waiting for twenty years, more or less, was at a minimum that she was the best prospect to come down the pike in a long time.

Could I tell that in two days?

Not with complete confidence, but . . .

Hell, it had been a very crowded two days, hadn't it, now?

Yeah, but you can never know what a woman will really be like.

That's true, God knows.

And you're a bachelor, set in your ways, and an odd one at that, a cop and a literate cop that might be too clever by half, aren't you, now? You'd be good at shagging her, but there's life together and doesn't she have a mind of her own?

I like that.

All the time?

She's more like me ma than any woman I've ever known.

That seemed to be a pretty good argument.

I wasn't sure that I'd take the risk. In fact, I still doubted that I would.

Passion, however, can blot out good intentions.

I was half hoping, as they say in Ireland, that it might.

I was so preoccupied with Nora that I passed the sign on the road that said CASTLE MACDONAUGH and did not consciously notice it when I passed it.

A quarter mile down the road I said to myself, "That sign did say Castle MacDonaugh, didn't it?"

I backed up and turned around, no easy task on the narrow and hilly road, and returned to where I thought I had seen the sign.

Sure enough, there it was, a huge sign, just so you

wouldn't have any doubt. CASTLE MACDONAUGH—HOME OF JIM LARK MACDONAUGH.

Not a suggestion that he wasn't alive and well ... which in one of the good bishop's scenarios he might very well be.

A smartly uniformed guard—looking like an aide to a president or a queen—blocked my way.

"No tours till Monday, sir."

"Captain MacCarthy to see the brothers," I said.

In Ireland, as in that other island across the Irish Sea whose name escapes me at the minute, titles and ranks are very important.

"Yes, sir, Captain." He saluted me sharply. "Drive on directly, the big house is a half mile down the road, through the roads and into the park."

Jim Lark ran tours, did he? He certainly didn't need the money. But the tours would enhance the image in which he seemed to delight.

Would he show off his woman the same way he showed off his house?

Sure he would. As far as that went, who wouldn't?

He'd do it more carefully, however, than put a sign out on the highway.

I drove cautiously up the curving road and entered the "park," a vast lawn, on which roamed a couple of well-fed deer. At the back of the park, or perhaps in the center of it, was the castle.

It wasn't a castle in the sense of being a medieval keep. Rather it was an enormous nineteenth-century country house in which must have lived some very important Anglo-Irish lord.

I stopped the car to look at its smooth gray facade, glowing softly in the early-afternoon sunlight. Probably the house was in much better condition than it had been when the lord lived there—better plumbing and electricity and central heating for sure, and almost certainly a swimming pool somewhere. One could put up with the satellite disk above the gables as a trade for such conveniences.

The woman whom I thought I might marry owned all of this.

Her wealth hadn't bothered me before. Now I was not so sure. I could become the kept male in her entourage, a useless but amusing appendage to her life, a gooter in her box on the odd occasion.

You're being an eejit altogether, Tim Pat MacCarthy. The woman isn't interested in all the money. She leads a decent, quiet life. She might argue with you, and God knows she has a mind of her own. But she'd never overwhelm you with her money. She'd not spend much time in this place at all, at all.

Fair enough.

So long as she'd spend some time here.

Not bad, though, for a man and a woman both of whom had grown up in two-room stucco cottages in the west of Ireland, not bad.

Conspicuous consumption, all right, but Jim Lark would say it was proof of what an Irishman could do with a little hard work and ambition. He could even own an English mansion, a lot bigger than Parnell's home at Avondale and almost as large as the granddaddy of all country houses—Powerscourt.

And you could bet your life that Jim Lark had a supply of water around and the means to pump it so this place would not burn down the way Powerscourt had.

I pulled up to the front door on a graveled drive that looked like it was manicured every morning. My Renault was out of place next to the Bentley and Mercedes parked ahead of me on the drive.

"Captain Timothy MacCarthy to see the brothers," I said to the butler who answered the door.

"You're expected, Captain."

The brothers were waiting in a drawing room that seemed big enough for a dozen squash courts. They were both slumped in easy chairs near the window, with glasses in their hands. There was an empty chair in which, I gathered, I was supposed to sit.

"Captain MacCarthy, gentlemen," the butler announced.

Neither stood up to greet me.

"Drink?" one—Liam, I suspected—asked me.

"No, thank you."

"Sit down," said the other.

I sat.

"How soon you gonna bring down the whore for us?" the first demanded.

"Put her in Limerick Prison for the rest of her life for the butches to play with," said the other, laughing hoarsely. "They'd have a lot of fun with her."

They were both older than Jim Lark, in their late sixties, with black hair turning gray and lines softening their hard faces; but they both seemed healthy and alert, despite the gin they were drinking—slick and well-preserved thugs, with hard eyes and dangerously low brows.

Not men to be fooled with.

"My assignment is to try to solve the mystery of your brother's death," I said meekly.

A good cop knows when to seem meek.

"You doing it?" demanded Mick Dav. "You're over here wasting our money, are you?"

"I'm progressing reasonably well, sir."

"Then you'll pin it on the whore. She killed him, no one else had any reason to."

"Jim Lark was so hot in the pants for her that he gave her all our money. We want it back."

Hard, dangerous men. Whiteboys and Ribbonmen, as Paddy Quaid had said.

"As I understand it," I began, looking at the one I thought was Mick Dav, "you came up to the house just after your sister Julia, just after the bomb exploded?"

There was a touch of Irish brogue in them both, but their accents were more English and American than Irish.

"Just after the guards," he muttered. "Jim Lark brought it on himself, living in that fancy house with that whore."

"And you, sir." I turned to Liam, the lawyer who lived in San Francisco.

"What the fuck does that have to do with getting the whore?"

I closed my notebook and stood up.

"Gentlemen," I said briskly. "You are perfectly free not to cooperate in my investigation. You have no obligation at all to give civil answers to my questions. As I told Mr. Regan, I have to investigate all elements of the case. If I am to find something that the Irish police have missed, I must be given a free hand. Should I limit myself to one suspect, my investigation will have no credibility. Additionally it would be a violation of my own professional integrity."

"Bollix integrity," Liam snarled.

"Fine." I turned to leave. "I'll inform Mr. Regan that you will not cooperate."

"Sit down," Mick Dav grunted.

"Don't order me around, Mr. MacDonaugh," I shot back at him. "Unless you tell me you will cooperate and cooperate civilly, I'm leaving."

"We'll cooperate," he said glumly.

"And civil answers to civil questions? Counsellor"—I turned to Liam—"I presume you know what that means?"

"All right. Ask your questions."

I sat down.

Bastards.

They were the kind of men who might well have sent two thugs into Nora's hotel room to smother her. If they were responsible, they knew I was tougher than they were.

I'd break their arms, too. Real tough guy, this literate cop.

"Well," Liam Lynch, the American lawyer, said in a tone of voice that for him might pass as civil, "since you asked, I was coming in from the airport. Jim Lark called a family meeting, so I flew over from San Francisco to London. Heathrow was closed for a couple of hours, so I realized I might be late for the meeting. Sometimes, Mick here and I try to coordinate coming over, but in that madhouse at Heathrow it usually doesn't work. When I drove up in the limo that Jim Lark had sent for me, I told the driver to take me to Shrewsbury Road instead of out here. By the time I got there, the police were all around." He shrugged. "There wasn't going to be a meeting, was there, now?"

"What time was the meeting to be?"

"Dinner, half seven."

"You and Julia came in early?" I turned to Mick.

"The three of us, and Charlie Parn when he'd come up from Perth, would stay out here—the bitch doesn't like the place—and drive in for his meetings. This time Julia wanted to get in before dinner and visit some of her friends. Himself never minded if we came early, only if he came late."

"I see. . . . Were these meetings called often?"

"Too damn often, if you ask me," Liam snorted. "It's a long flight to be taking from San Francisco just because Jim Lark is in the mood."

"Your brother Charles Parnell MacDonaugh was not invited?'

"He was dispensed from some of them." Mick sneered. "Especially if they were sudden like this one. It's a long, long way from west Australia, no matter you come east or west."

They were genuine nasty men, each with a chip on his shoulder and a grudge against the world. Why did Jim Lark put up with them?

They were family, were they not?

"His children?"

"Spoiled brats, if you ask me," Liam grumbled. "When he wanted them at one of his family meetings, he had the meetings in New York, though with his favorite having a kid inside her, maybe he would have made the others come over here. Turns out that he didn't invite any of them."

"There were meetings like this just of the siblings?"

"Jim Lark figured he could have any kind of meeting he wanted anywhere he wanted." Mick, the nastier of the two, spat out the words. "He paid the bills, so that was that. Usually they were a waste of time because he never paid any attention to us anyway."

"Some of the meetings included others who weren't family?"

"If they were official board meetings." Liam sighed patiently. "In Dublin he'd invite Paddy Quaid and maybe that fat McNulty whore. Paddy is a director, too. But they weren't invited this time. So it was just a family meeting."

"About what?"

"I don't know where this is getting us," Liam complained. "But we didn't have the foggiest. I talked to himself"—he nodded at Mick—"before I flew over, and he said he didn't have a clue either."

"Sometimes he'd tell us and sometimes not. This time he didn't. . . . Sure you don't want a drink?"

"I don't drink when I work," I lied. The truth was I wanted to be stone sober when I drove back through the Wicklow Hills to Dublin.

He replenished both their drinks, full Waterford whiskey tumblers, without a drop of water or a hint of ice.

"Like I say," he continued when he had returned to his chair, "we didn't have a clue, but it was obvious enough after she blew him up."

"Ah?"

"It figures"—the American spread out his hands—"that he was going to tell us about the new will and she was afraid we'd talk him out of it, so she killed him first."

The will was only a couple of weeks old at the most and apparently only the lawyer knew about it—not even Nora, if she were to be believed (and whatever my imagination was dreaming, professionally I still had to be skeptical). Would Jim Lark assemble the family to tell them that they had been disinherited?

Maybe. He was a man who liked a big show.

"She talked him out of our money." The Brit's eyes narrowed into a single beam of fury. "And then killed him."

"No one had any idea that the will would be changed?"

There was an uneasy silence while they debated whether to tell the truth.

"You have to wonder." Liam, the smoother of the two, spread his hands again. "Don't you? A man in his sixties marries a good-looking hooker twenty-five years younger without telling anyone in the family before—not that he ever gave a fock about what we thought. So we wondered, sure. Hell, we wondered a lot. It was our money, wasn't it?"

"You thought it might be coming?"

"You'd never know with Jim Lark. If he marries a bimbo with good tits, you think it might come all right, but you don't want to believe he'd do it to his own flesh and blood."

"It was our money," Mick agreed. "We really didn't think when push came to shove he'd take it away from us. We were wrong."

They were giving themselves a perfect motive for murder—kill their brother before Nora could persuade him to change his will. Were they being too clever by half? Were they so confident of their alibis, which, after all, were pretty good, that they could afford to take the risk I might become more suspicious of them.

"Did she seem hostile to you?"

"Nah." The American lawyer drained half his glass of gin. "All sweet and friendly. Won over Jim Lark's dumb kids real quick. Their own kids called her 'Nana Nora'—can you imagine that shite?"

"We warned them that she wasn't up to any good, but like Jim Lark, they thought they were too smart to listen to us. She's so nice and Daddy's so happy, Aggie says to me—well, now they know better."

"Gobshite," his brother agreed.

"Jim Lark didn't heed your advice?"

They both laughed meanly.

"Usually didn't ask for it . . ."

"And didn't listen to us when he did ask for it."

"Jim Lark"—Liam frowned moodily into his glass— "forgot who he was and where he came from and who helped him to get there."

"I see."

"Who do you think paid for his schooling with the Christian Brothers? Who worked hard every day in the fields so Julia's little sweetheart could get dressed up in fancy clothes and go off and learn his numbers?"

"Who bought him his first soccer ball?"

"Who cheered for him at every game he ever played?"

"Who lent him the money for the trip to Dublin so he could take that focking chartered-accountant's focking job?"

"Who paid for his new suit that day?"

"He owed everything to us. And he gave it all away to that cunt."

"I'd like to shove a hot iron pipe up her box."

"He wasn't generous to you?"

"Yeah, sure, he gave us trust funds and that sort of thing." Liam sneered. "Got us clients, paid for kids' education, but we were never part of it like we deserved to be, not like those gobshites Paddy Quaid and Artie Regan."

"Paddy focking Quaid and Artie focking Regan."

"We should be where they are by rights."

"Aren't we family? Isn't that better than hurling mates?"

"What was so good about them?"

"Two gobshites! Focking gobshites!"

"He'd listen carefully to them and not pay any attention to us!"

"When we disagreed with them, they won, every focking time!"

So that was the source of their anger and frustration. They were left out. I wondered why. Perhaps Jim Lark did not trust their judgment, and with good reason.

Mick filled up both their drinks, this time without asking me. Did they drink this way every day, all day?

"Do you think they are in league with the widow?"

"Artie isn't, that's certain." Liam nodded his head for emphasis. "He's afraid she'll take his job away from him."

"But I wouldn't be surprised by anything Paddy does. He's too cute a politician for me to ever trust. I told Jim Lark, but he just laughed at me."

"I wouldn't be surprised if he ends up in Artie's place."

"Take this cow-piss Irish cream of theirs. It's the worst asshole idea I've ever heard and she's letting him put money into it."

"Didn't Jim Lark start it?"

"He wanted to see his name on a bottle."

"He wanted to see his name on every focking thing in the focking world."

The gin was taking its toll. The heads of both men were lolling on their chests. The conversation would be called on account of darkness—the darkness in their heads.

"Would he lend you money for business ventures?"

"Sure," said Liam, his voice already a little slurred, "and with all kinds of advice about how he had made his money, focking asshole."

"Be careful like I was. Choose your colleagues carefully. Gobshites."

So he had bailed them out of trouble.

"Mrs. MacDonaugh hasn't taken away anything yet, has she?"

"Says she's going to put our money into that focking foundation for peace in Ireland."

"Focking peace in focking Ireland."

"She lets you use the houses here, doesn't she?"

"For the moment."

"Least she can do after she's stolen everything from us."

"Thank you very much, gentlemen." I snapped the notebook shut and stood up. "I appreciate your cooperation."

Their replies were guttural murmurs. When they faded, they faded quickly.

I got out of the drawing room as fast as I could. The butler was ready at the door.

"Good afternoon, Captain MacCarthy. Nice to have you visit us."

"Thank you ... Is that the scene every day?"

"The brothers do like their little drop, sir."

I'd met some real winners in my career as a cop, but these guys were at the top of the list.

Would they kill their own brother if they needed the money? They just might, they just might. Their resentment against him was so white-hot, they might do just about anything, especially if they suspected he was about to disinherit them.

But because they were furious at him, it didn't follow that

they actually had killed him, not without evidence of how they had done it.

Moreover, if the legend was to be believed, they had disposed of the IRA men who had kidnapped him. Perhaps blood ties were even stronger than money.

I had been advised—by Nora—to take the old Military Road (built in 1798) into Dublin because it was easier to reach from Castle MacDonaugh and the scenery was lovelier.

She had no way of knowing that there would be a roadblock on the way into Dublin—two unarmed guards, a squad of soldiers with guns at the ready, and some pleasant-looking folks in a car in civilian clothes who were surely Special Branch—a unit that these days specialized in being smooth and polite. After a twenty-minute wait, I pulled up to a young and pretty *ban garda*, brown hair tucked neatly under cap— with what looked like a cast-iron jaw.

"Could I have your name, sir?"

"Timothy Patrick MacCarthy."

"Your destination?"

"Dublin."

"And where are you coming from?"

"The MacDonaugh house."

"I see." She considered me carefully. I was obviously a Yank and maybe just a little too glib.

"Identification, sir?" she said politely but coldly. "And registration, please?"

I gave her my American driver's license and the rental-car agreement.

"Yank, are you?"

"Yes, ma'am." With women patrol officers—or police constables—the rule is that the more polite you are, the better off you will be. If they're young and pretty, you better be extra polite because they're especially likely to think you're engaging in sexual harassment.

"What are you doing in Ireland, sir?"

"Some looking around."

She was considering my license like it was an indictment for murder one.

"You have your American passport, sir?"

"In my room at the Shelbourne."

"Shelbourne, is it, sir?" Almost an accusation, a bleeding Yank tourist.

"Yes, ma'am."

"It's not the law, but it's better if you carry it with you, especially out in the country."

"It'll try to remember, ma'am."

She seemed reluctant to give my license back to me.

"It says here that you're a captain. What kind of captain?"

It says "captain" on my license so all traffic cops will eventually ask the same question, though if they're Chicagoans, God help me, they've heard of Timothy Patrick Mac-Carthy. Maybe once too often.

"Cop," I said.

She looked up from the license. "Yeah, you got a cop's eyes."

"You don't," I said. "And that's a compliment."

"Focking Yank cop." She blushed and gave me the license back. "Know just when to butter up a woman *ban garda*."

"Not too early and not too late . . . and you guys are just plain *gardaí* now. The *ban* has been dropped, just like in America, everyone is a patrol officer."

"Aren't you the clever one! Timothy Patrick MacCarthy, is it, Captain?"

"Jewish," I said.

"I can see that. . . . What kind of work?"

"Homicide." Which was my last assignment.

"Ugh." She shook her head.

She was very pretty indeed when her iron jaw relaxed, and she had a fine young woman's body—trim and with all the proper curves.

"You get used to it. . . . You want to look in the boot to keep the inspector happy?"

"Not a bad idea, Captain." She winked at me.

I flipped the lid of the trunk. She glanced at it and nodded.

"All right, Captain, you can go ahead. Sorry for the delay."

"I understand, ma'am. People from the north?"

"Gobshites . . . one of the worst. Tosser calls himself Brendan . . . hey, Seamus, let this fella through, he's a Yank police captain."

"If you say so, Nessa," the army officer shouted back with a broad grin. He liked Nessa, too.

"I do. Good-bye, Captain, I hope you enjoy your trip to Ireland. Come back again sometime."

"I will, ma'am."

"Jesus and Mary go with you," she said in Irish.

"Jesus and Mary and Patrick be with you, Nessa," I replied in Irish, exhausting my vocabulary. "Now and for the rest of your life," I added in English.

She blessed me with a wondrous smile and waved as I pulled away. Her colleagues grinned and waved me to the head of the line and saluted as they let me through the barrier.

I could have proposed a drink at the Shelbourne when she was off duty and she would have accepted, virtuously telling herself it was a chance to learn more about police work in America and on her guard for my making a pass at her, which I wouldn't do.

Lucky for her and worse luck for me I hadn't asked.

If Jim Lark could claim a woman twenty-four years younger, why I couldn't I consider one twenty-two or so years younger? A conversation over a drink would quickly reveal whether, after shying away from a generation or two of young and pretty American cops, there might be reason to consider settling down with an Irish one.

Nessa was her name. It wouldn't be hard to find her if I tried.

I knew I wouldn't try.

14

Dᴇꜱᴘɪᴛᴇ ᴛʜᴇ ᴅᴇʟᴀʏ ᴏɴ ᴛʜᴇ Mɪʟɪᴛᴀʀʏ Rᴏᴀᴅ, I ᴡᴀꜱ ʙᴀᴄᴋ ɪɴ my room at the Shelbourne by 4:30. I dictated my "report" for the good bishop, as I now defined my notes. There were no answers to my requests for information, but it was Saturday. I put in two calls to doctors' offices in New York. On Saturday neither was in, as I had suspected they wouldn't be. I left messages on their answering machines.

"My name is Timothy Patrick MacCarthy. I am a retired police captain from the Chicago Police Department. I am investigating a case in Dublin, Ireland. I need to ask you some questions about . . ." I then told them what I wanted and gave them references to check about my credentials. "I will guarantee that I will hold whatever you tell me in the strictest confidence. I'll call you again Monday morning, American time."

You think I should have waited and caught them off guard. No way with a reputable doctor. You give him time to think about it and to check you out, then you ask him the question.

On a hunch, I tried a police number in Chicago.

"Riordan."

"MacCarthy."

We exchanged the usual profane insults through which cops express affection for one another.

"What are you doing messing with bombs?" he protested at the end of our ritual. "Why don't you leave that shit to someone who knows something about it!"

"I wasn't anywhere near a bomb." I laughed. "You know me, one of those things shows up and I'm Lake County."

"Yeah, well, for that thing you sent me the specs on, Lake County wouldn't be far enough. You say the guy was bent over it when it went down?"

"Yeah."

"Much left of him?"

"Very little."

"Didn't figure to be. It would have blown the walls out of the place."

"Solid oak doors and thick walls . . . old-time construction?"

"You'd have to know the vectors of the blast. Maybe not. Make the damage in the room all that worse. You can't be precise about these things, but it would have been a hell of a big blast."

"Anyone else in the room?"

"If he wasn't bent over it? They're history. Archive 'em."

"That's what I was wondering about."

"You don't want to get near one of those things. Sure, they key 'em to a specific radio frequency, but a car telephone signal could set it off. Then you'd be in the history books, too."

"How far away can you be to transmit a signal to the explosive device?"

"Quarter mile, maybe even half mile. You don't have to be all that close. And stay away from those things, they're dangerous."

"I'll remember that." I shivered. "Thanks loads for the information."

Car signal . . . the thing could have gone off anytime. Maybe it was too early or too late.

And it would have wiped out anyone and everyone in the room.

Then I sent a fax to a contact I had in Sidney, Australia, in which I asked him to do some digging for me on the subject of one Charles Parnell MacDonaugh, a subject that fascinated me.

If it were such an important meeting, why hadn't he been compelled to come to Dublin? Had the Dublin police checked out his alibi with any vigor? He seemed to be an unidentified wild card in the case.

I went down to the lounge for my appointment with Clare McNulty. She was already waiting for me, a Guinness in front of her. It was not hard to pick her out—a dark-haired, plump, but hardly fat woman in her middle forties, smartly dressed in a brown suit and with just the right amount of makeup and jewelry for a very successful businesswoman.

"Ms. McNulty?" I asked formally.

"Captain MacCarthy?" She shook hands firmly, but not quite like a man would.

That was the theme of our talk—a formal conversation with a competent business administrator who a man would be expected to treat as an equal without her having to act like a man.

As she shook hands it occurred to me that if one liked a woman of Junoesque proportions, one could do much worse than this one.

Then I reprimanded myself for being obsessed with women's bodies.

"I'm very glad you could find time to talk to me on Saturday, Ms. McNulty."

"Isn't it the least I can do if it helps to solve this terrible crime?"

A waiter came by and I ordered a Diet Coke with a twist. Clare McNulty's eyes widened.

"I have only a few questions. I am inclined to think that the crime might be connected with the sudden visit of Mr. and Mrs. MacDonaugh to Dublin for what was presumably a family meeting. Am I correct that you spoke with him often on the phone?"

"Oh, yes, sir," she said primly. "He was not one to watch too closely any of the ongoing ventures here for which we are responsible. He trusted us completely. But he would call with the odd question. If Councillor Quaid was absent at a meeting, he would speak to me. I was usually able to help him."

Modest and self-effacing, but she made the point. She was running the show.

"Was there any hint in your last conversation with him that he was concerned about anything?"

"No, sir, there wasn't." She lifted her Guinness and then put it down, deciding not to drink till my blasphemous Diet

Coke with a twist arrived. "He was always a cheerful and pleasant man on the phone. I'm not sure that he'd ever show that he was worried even if he were."

"Any special interest about which he might want to call a meeting of the family?"

"I've thought of that many times, sir." My drink safely delivered, she raised her pint and savored a healthy taste. "And again today before I came up here to talk to you. We didn't even know he was in the country until we heard about his death."

"Was it unusual for him to come in without giving you advance warning?"

"Very unusual, very unusual indeed. He'd call ahead out of courtesy and because he'd want servants and supplies at the house in Shrewsbury Road. There are always people out at the castle. . . . You've seen the castle, sir? Then you know it's open for tours. Actually it pays for itself from the tour income. A very clever man, Mr. MacDonaugh, God be good to him."

She sniffled, but restrained her emotions.

"Yes, indeed . . . you and Mr. Quaid were working together at your offices at the time of the blast."

"Not actually in the same office, Captain MacCarthy. He had the corner office, overlooking the Liffey. His secretary was in the next office, and I next to her. We have a fairly large staff here in Dublin, as you might imagine."

What was the woman worrying about? Maybe nothing more than being questioned once again by a cop.

"And were both there when you learned of the death of Mr. MacDonaugh?"

"Yes, sir. Working day was over and everyone else had gone home. The Councillor had a meeting of the Corporation to attend, or rather it was a reception at Mansion House, and I was reviewing one of the audits that we routinely do. A young woman from the company which has offices on the floor below came running up to say that she'd just heard on the radio that Mr. MacDonaugh had been hurt in a terrible explosion below on Shrewsbury Road. He isn't even in the country, I said to her. She says that they said on the radio that it was the IRA.

"I hurried into the Councillor's office and told him. We could neither of us believe it and we turned on the telly in his office, but the news was over. He called the Dublin Corporation and then the castle, but no one knew anything. So he decided that he'd better go out there. I waited a couple of hours and then he called and told me the terrible truth. We both wept on the phone, if I may say so, sir."

"Perfectly understandable."

"Thank you, sir."

"Did he say what the guard thought had happened?"

She hesitated. "Well, he said that at first it looked like the lads, but now they suspected his wife."

"Did he agree with them?"

"I think he did. Later he changed his mind."

"And you?"

She put down her pint. "I told the Councillor that I disagreed with him, and that if you asked me about it, I'd have to tell you the truth. I think she did it and that she's got away with it."

"You have any reason for this conviction, Ms. McNulty?"

"I never liked or trusted her." Her controlled demeanor began to fade. "She was much too young for him. She pretended to be someone important and she was nothing but trash from out at the end of Clew Bay, little better than a tinker."

"I see. . . . You think her motives were the inheritance?"

"What else could they be?" Her hands were trembling. The woman was furious and did not want to reveal it to me.

"Has she been a problem for you here in Dublin since she gained control of the company?"

"We had no choice but to accept her. Mr. MacDonaugh had designated her as trustee to administer the estate until his will was probated. She has complete control. We must do what she says."

"Has she been demanding?"

"She's always very polite, but her auditors from New York are asking questions all the time."

"It doesn't seem to bother Mr. Quaid."

"He's innocent when it comes to women. He says that we have nothing to worry about. I tell him that she's looking for an excuse to sell everything so that when the will is probated, she can put it all into her foundation."

"An interesting possibility."

"I'm absolutely convinced." Her lips were trembling. "You just have to look at her to know that she's a cheap little thing."

"You disapprove of the foundation?"

"It's a disgraceful way to pour down the drain the money that Mr. MacDonaugh worked so hard to obtain."

"Peace in Ireland?"

"Money can't buy that, as any fool knows."

"To whom ought he to have left control?"

"To his children, of course. Who else had the right to it?"

"That seems a reasonable position . . . not to his brothers?"

She turned up her nose. "Disgraceful people."

"How might she have committed the crime?"

"I'm not a detective, sir. She's clever and sneaky." Her face twisted with pure hatred. "No mistake about that. How else would she get him to change his will?"

"I understand."

She hadn't meant to reveal her anger. But she thought that she should run the Irish branch of Jim Lark's empire without any interference. Hadn't she run it that way for years?

"I'm sorry, Captain MacCarthy, for losing my temper. I feel very strongly about this matter . . . we all loved him so much."

Her tears began to flow. Had she been in love with Jim Lark? Had his lighthearted charm won her heart? Did she overinterpret what he meant? Did she think she might eventually become mistress of Castle MacDonaugh? Was she outraged at the woman who had taken her place?

And the biggest question of all: Might she want to dispose of the hated replacement? Efficient and competent woman that she was, she would have found a way to do it. With the children in control, she might have even more power, certainly not less.

I hadn't considered her a suspect before. I merely wanted to check on Paddy Quaid's alibi and learn if she had any hints about the purpose of the sudden meeting.

Now I had a suspect. Was she afraid that she might become one? Probably not; fear would have choked off her rage.

"I never had the privilege of meeting him, Ms. McNulty," I said soothingly. "But from everything I have heard he was one of the most remarkable men of our time. I can understand the grief of those who knew him and worked with him intimately for many years."

"Since I left school"—she gained control of her tears—"I've worked for them. It's been my life."

"I'm sure your life will continue and prosper, once the grief is healed."

I shook hands with her, escorted her to the street, offered to get a cab for her. However, her own car was parked on the other side of the Green. We shook hands again.

I watched her disappear in the trees across the street after she had passed the abstract monument to Wolfe Tone, which the Dubliners have characteristically called the "Wolfehenge."

There were as many twists in her character as in the monument.

I had reassured her that I suspected nothing. And I had no real reason to suspect anything—save the possibility of the fury of a woman scorned. Without more evidence than I had or was likely to get, that possibility was worthless.

I walked over to the Green and glanced at the flowers radiant in the afternoon sunlight, almost a tropical garden—focking rapid. I needed exercise to work off the remnants of my hangover, then a good supper and an early night in bed to prepare for the ardors of the beach on—what was it?—Bull Island.

While I was changing into my running clothes, the phone

rang. I grabbed for it. Maybe it was more information from America.

"MacCarthy?"

"Tim Pat?" A gentle and melodic voice.

"You got it."

"My name is Brendan."

The same name as the terrorist Nessa and her crowd were hunting down.

Keep your cool, MacCarthy.

"Hello, Brendan."

"I want to tell you two things to begin with, Tim Pat."

"All right."

"The first is that I'm calling from a public phone, so you can't trace me."

"No way I could do that anyhow."

"And the second is that we mean no harm to you and yours."

"I see."

"I mean that sincerely, Tim Pat," he pleaded. "I really do. We're on the same side, in a manner of speaking."

He chuckled lightly.

"My friends and I had nothing to do with what happened there last night. Nothing at all, at all."

"I'm glad to hear that."

"We mean no harm to the lass. We disagree with her, but we think she has some good ideas, if you take my meaning."

"I think I understand."

"Good." He chuckled again. "And 'tis a good thing we don't want to hurt her—good for us, that is, after what you did to them fockers last night."

"I played football, Brendan. American football."

"For Notre Dame, wasn't it?"

The man was a charmer, all right. I was beginning to like him, although now I was certain that he was IRA and probably the one that Nessa and her colleagues were hunting.

"It was indeed."

"Just let me finish this second thing I want to say, Tim Pat. If we wanted to dispose of you, we could gun you down in the street without any trouble or put a bomb in your nice Renault."

"I don't doubt that."

"We are not going to do that . . . and we had no part of that focking drive-by the other night either."

"If you did, I'd be dead."

"Too true. So now you know you can trust me."

It was my turn to laugh. "Up to a point, Brendan, up to a point."

He joined the laughter with me. "No more than that, no more than that at all, at all."

"So that's settled."

I would wait for him to tell me why he was calling.

"I'd like to have lunch with you. On me."

An invitation to lunch with the oldest terrorist group in the world. On them.

"Lunch, is it, Brendan?"

" 'Tis . . . in public, where everyone can see, so you'll be in no danger. We wouldn't have to do this to kidnap you, if you take me meaning."

" 'Tis true."

I'd let him tell me the reason for the lunch.

"You're wondering why we want to treat you to lunch?"

"Am I not waiting for you to tell me?"

"It won't be a grand meal, mind you, just ordinary food."

"I'm not a man with grand tastes, Brendan."

"Didn't we see you in Bewley's the other morning with the lass?"

"You don't miss much."

"Ah, we try, Tim Pat, we try. . . . Well, the point is we're not involved in this matter you're investigating. We want no part of it. There's some as trying to involve us against our will and we'll have no part of it, if you take me meaning."

"Not exactly."

"Isn't that why I'm wanting to talk to you?"

"Indeed?"

"The thing is we think if anyone is going to find out who killed your man, it will be you. Fine with us. But they might try to say that the killer is one of us. I want to convince you that's not true beforehand."

"I see."

"No, you don't, Tim Pat, not at all, at all, and after I explain it to you, you still might not. But I want a chance to explain it to you, do you see?"

"I do."

"So I'm inviting you to lunch. Do you know the DART?"

"I do."

"And the town of Bray at the end of the line?"

"I've heard about it."

"Well, you take the DART below to Bray and you walk up into the town to the main street where the Catholic church is and then you turn left. Halfway down the street on your right, there is Ray Carroll's Pub. It's just an ordinary pub, not one of ours."

"Sounds easy."

"Monday at half twelve?"

"I'll be there."

"If you can't, I'll understand. But it's to your interest to hear what I have to say."

"I'll be there."

"Without a gun?"

"I never carry one."

"It wouldn't be a good idea to carry one this time, Tim Pat."

"I don't like guns, Brendan. You can hurt yourself with them."

He sighed loudly. "Wouldn't I be knowing that. . . . So you promise you won't be carrying?"

"I do . . . for whatever my promise is worth."

"Ah, you're an honorable man, Tim Pat, we know that."

"And you?"

"When it's for the good of Ireland, sure I'm honorable."

And if not . . . ?

Better that I didn't ask.

"Do you know who the killer is, Brendan?"

"Monday at half twelve, it is, Tim Pat."

The line clicked.

My hands were sweating ... as if I had talked to Michael Collins himself on the phone.

I would have more to think about on my run along the banks of the Liffey than Nora.

15

"**I** CANNOT GUARANTEE YOUR SAFETY." BLACKIE FROWNED. "Not on a venture like this."

"I understand."

We were returning from seven o'clock mass at Clarendon Street and breakfast at Bewley's. The good bishop had somehow persuaded the Carmelite fathers to let him say the seven o'clock—or, as "the girls" insisted, to "preside over the Eucharistic liturgy." He had preached on "Happy are the peace makers" and warned that their happiness did not dispense them from the same diligence and prudence as the warmakers.

The congregation had nodded in silent agreement.

"The little Yank is a good preacher," a woman coming out ahead of us said to her husband, "isn't he, now?"

"Ay."

"Where would he be from, I wonder?"

" 'Tis a good question."

"And who is he?"

"He's Bishop Ryan from Chicago," the good bishop's half sister had piped up. "He's my brother."

"Roscommon man, is it?"

Knowing the bias against Ryans from Roscommon, Trish replied saucily, "County Cook."

The three "girls" had dressed to the nines—pastel spring dresses and the highest of heels. It was Sunday in Ireland and you dressed for it even if you're going to duck into Bewley's after the Eucharist because everyone in there would be wearing their Sunday best, too.

The bishop, despite the horrified remonstrances of his young relatives, had marked Sunday by donning a Chicago Bears windbreaker. He was able, however, to find his Roman collar.

As for myself, I had been roundly condemned by "the girls" (as the three referred to themselves) for not wearing a tie.

I was "terrible," I had been told, though all six blue eyes twinkled at the accusation.

In Bewley's we had "destroyed the place altogether" with the vast breakfasts we had eaten, Nora in particular, who, by my count, had demolished six rashers of bacon.

My hungry eyes had watched her every move.

"Aren't you're eating me up with them terrible silver eyes of yours, Tim Pat MacCarthy," she had murmured across the table when the other three went to collect seconds on our various comestibles.

"Woman, I'm not," I lied.

"A decent woman would be half-scared to spend a day at the strand with you, wouldn't she?"

"Only half-scared?"

"Go 'long with you!" She had slapped my hand, very gently, in reproof.

I figured it was all right to continue to eat her up with my eyes.

We were drifting toward love, in many different senses of that word; we half knew it, as the Irish would have said, and we were half-scared of where we might drift; but intrigued by what was happening, we lacked the will to end the drift.

Each of us knew, I suspected, that we might be hurt. We half didn't want to take the risk.

Only half.

Walking back to the hotel on the south side of the Green, the sun already blazing brightly in what promised to be another hot and humid day, I had told the good bishop about my phone conversation with the man who called himself Brendan. And he had warned that it might be risky.

"You assume that he's the Brendan your *garda* constable was seeking?"

"Seems reasonable."

"I have no contacts with whom to make representations in those quarters."

"I had not thought that you did."

"It's not like the Outfit in Chicago, where everyone has contacts, should they be needed."

"Dubliners have the same kind of contacts with the lads."

"We are not Dubliners.... I don't like it, Timothy. We may be able to have some sort of general safety net, but nothing more."

"We're no more interested in bringing in Brendan than he seems to mean us harm."

"Regardless ... I suppose it is a calculated risk. Perhaps the dangers may be minimized."

"I'm an experienced cop, Bishop."

"I understand.... You told me that you had retired from the CPD because you'd been shot twice and you felt that, among other things, you did not want your luck to run out."

"I was also afraid of turning into a bitter and dangerous cynic like your man over at the castle."

"Indeed. But consider these facts: In the last several days you've been shot at, fought with two murderous thugs, and conversed with a dangerous terrorist with whom you propose to meet."

" 'Tis true ... my instincts, which are still pretty good, say it is all right to meet him."

"Arguably. I impress on you, nonetheless, the need for caution."

"That's part of my instinct."

"If the man is who he claims to be, he may be one of the most dangerous men in the world."

"No more dangerous than a cornered drug dealer in a Chicago slum."

"Arguably. Fortunately his aim was inaccurate."

"I ducked. I'm not sure of the lads' involvement in this, but I think they may have an important clue. Hell, why do they need us, unless they think we can do them a favor?"

"Arguably."

That seemed to settle it. He didn't tell me not to rendezvous with Brendan.

"You didn't mention the other thing that has happened to me during the last couple of days."

"Ah?"

"I'm falling in love."

"Patently."

"Like a teenager with a crush."

"Clearly."

"You're not warning me off of the relationship?"

The good bishop chuckled and looked up at me with blinking eyes. "Would it do any good, Timothy Patrick MacCarthy?"

"None whatever, I suppose. But I would still like to know whether you disapprove."

His eyes continued to blink. "Of the enjoyable Nora? Hardly."

"For me ... and vice versa?"

"I would not"—he grinned—"inveigh against such a relationship from the altar of Holy Name Cathedral."

"You expect me to bring her home to Chicago?"

"Naturally."

That was that ... a nice clear challenge, which I kind of liked.

"However, in both matters we have discussed, I urge you to be cautious and prudent."

"Good cops always are."

At the Shelbourne Brigie polished her uncle's glasses with the comment that he simply couldn't do it for himself and he departed for further "inquiries" about "your man across the Green," nodding in the general direction of the Henry Moder bust of Bold Jimmy Joyce.

Brigie and Trish went to their rooms and promised to look us up on the beach, especially if there were no interesting boys available.

"Well, woman," I said to Nora. "Are you too afraid of me to keep our date on the strand?"

"It's not a date, and yes, I am afraid of those terrible blue eyes of yours, and yes, I'll be ready in a jiff to ride up there with you . . . and would you ever wait till I ring you up because I'll need help carrying everything."

She turned and ran into the hotel ahead of me, a shy and skittish colt.

Prudent and cautious, the bishop had said. Naturally.

I was involved in a difficult investigation; why was I also involved with a woman?

It was a day off, wasn't it?

I dressed in a swimsuit and my spare running suit and gym shoes and threw some things into a blue-and-white shoulder bag that said "Chicago Police Department." So, as a matter of fact, did the cap I was wearing. The phone rang.

"Would you ever give me a hand?"

"Woman, haven't I told you that I would?"

I knocked on the door of her room. She opened it cautiously.

" 'Tis yourself?"

" 'Tis."

"Would you ever carry this basket for me? It has a bite of lunch."

"From the heft of it, woman, it's a meal for twenty."

"I'll carry the beach umbrella."

She was wearing a floral-print dress, a cover-up over her swimsuit, I presumed, and beach clogs. Her silver hair was tied in a severe ponytail, so that the delicate lines of her facial bones were emphasized. She had discarded her Sunday jewelry and scrubbed her Sunday makeup off her face.

What would Nora Finnegan Joyce MacDonaugh look like in a swimsuit? I wondered.

I could hardly wait to find out.

She carried a bag on either shoulder and a collapsible beach umbrella in her arms. This was a serious expedition to the beach. Strand.

"Have a nice day at the strand." The doorman smiled when he brought my car.

We piled our stuff into the boot.

"I'll drive," she informed me.

"Will you, now?"

"I will."

"And why?" I gave her the key.

"Because"—she entered the car on the driver's side—"I know the way to Bull Island. . . ."

I closed the door and went around to the other side.

"And you're a Yank who doesn't drive on the proper side of the road and you're a short-hitting Yank who may some of the drink take on the strand."

"But I've none of it taken yet."

"We'll establish the precedent, if you take my meaning."

I did.

She drove us skillfully through the heavy traffic of Baggot Street.

"Have you been to Irishtown?"

"I have not."

"Then we'll go through there and Ringsend, as your man did on his way to the funeral."

"Mr. Bloom?"

"Who else would I be meaning?" she said, impatient with my slowness.

"But we'll not continue his route," she continued. "We'll go over to Liffey on the toll bridge and along the strand of Clontarf, though you won't be able to see much of it unless we stop."

"Where your man had dirty thoughts about the girl in her knickers?"

"They weren't dirty," she insisted. "Stephen had a religious experience watching her."

"A religious experience admiring a woman's thighs?"

"What's wrong with that?"

"I want to establish that it's all right for me to admire a certain woman's thighs."

She thought that was pretty funny. "And yourself having a religious experience, is it, now?"

"Who can tell?" I sighed contentedly.

"Besides, haven't you already seen the woman's thighs?"

"In the dark, where I couldn't properly enjoy them. But I'll tell you one thing. Even in the dark they looked promising."

"You're a desperate man."

The word did not indicate a reproof.

The two of us enjoyed the sparring. If I won her, there'd be a lifetime of it.

"And you didn't like the big house?" she charged, changing the subject.

"A focking monstrosity, as the woman guard called it."

"A woman guard, is it? What was her name?"

"Nessa."

"Nessa, is it? And where did you meet her?"

"At a roadblock on the Military Road. They were searching for one of the lads."

"Were they? And was she pretty?"

"Gorgeous."

"Nice boobs?"

"Tell the truth, I didn't notice."

"Liar. Men always notice. They can't help themselves, poor dears."

"Well, now that you mention it, they were impressive, but not as impressive as some others I've seen lately."

"I'll not have you talking that way."

"I'm just stating facts."

"Boobs and thighs and arses, men can't think of anything else about a woman."

"Yes, they can," I argued in defense of male humankind, "but we'd all be in trouble if they didn't notice those, too, as you yourself said to that bitch from the *Irish Times*."

She laughed. "Would we ever!"

The argument was thereby proclaimed a draw.

She lectured me about Irishtown, a swamp on the edge of the city to which all the Irish were banished by the English occupiers in the fourteenth century. In a generation the English occupiers had become at least as Irish themselves.

"The culture has a way of absorbing people," I observed.

"Does it ever!"

"And what are you, Nora Marie, Yank or mick, Dublin or west?"

"Ah, isn't that an interesting question?" She sighed loudly.

"Well, I suppose you'd have to say that I'm all of them and none of them, if you take me meaning."

"I do."

"Now, these darling little houses along the Dodder." She pointed out the window. "That's where a lot of your Yuppies live, they've gentrified the old workers' homes."

"Cute," I said, "in the American sense of the word, painted window frames and doors."

"You wouldn't want to raise a couple of brats in them, would you?"

"I would not."

"Imagine what it was like living in them with seven or eight brats." We had left the gentrified section of Irishtown and come into what was still the poor section along Brigid Street. The homes were no longer cute, but poor and dreadfully small.

"Probably better than a cottage in the west."

She nodded. "A lot better. They don't have as many brats in them now. Only two or maybe three."

She drove slowly because little "brats" of both genders were swarming in the street in their Sunday-morning finery.

"Aren't they adorable? And even if their da is on the dole, their ma dresses them up for Sunday morning."

Silently I wished I had a few brats of my own, neat, quiet, and orderly brats, unlike my nieces and nephews.

She was thinking the same thing surely.

We turned into Irishtown Road and then crossed the Liffey on the new toll bridge. Herself paid the toll. Naturally. Then we turned onto Clontarf Road.

"Do you want to see the strand? It's a bit of a mess these days."

"It's where your man beat the Danes, isn't it?"

"There were more Irish troops on the other side than on his. He's no more an Irish hero than the fockers in the north."

"Okay. Let's take a look anyway."

It was, as she said, not much of a beach, especially at low tide, just dirty sand and puddles of dark water—not a hint of the great battle or of Stephen Dedalus's young woman with her skirt pulled up and tucked into her drawers.

"I think the Board Failte ought to spruce up this place and have young women wandering along it just like the lass in the story."

"You would think that," she replied.

We returned to our car.

Bull Island, she explained to me, was formed against the northern wall of the Liffey estuary. The various walls had, through the years, created the island from drifting sand. It contained two golf courses, the Royal Dublin and St. Anne's, and an internationally famous bird sanctuary. The "bathing place" had been formed in recent years as more sand had piled up against the wall.

"Are you playing golf, Tim Pat MacCarthy?"

"I've been known to."

"What's your handicap?"

"Six."

"Hmm." She was impressed.

"And yours?

"The same."

"I'm impressed."

"Shouldn't you be. . . . Would you want to play today?"

"I didn't bring my clubs."

"We could rent some."

"I'd rather lie on the beach and ogle young women."

"I should have expected that."

We parked the car and struggled with our equipment through the dune and to the beach itself.

It was magnificent—a wide spread of soft clean sand against a backbone of grass-covered dune. The bay, calm and peaceful under a serene blue sky, invited the unwary into its waters. Although it was still early on Sunday morning—and many Dubliners had yet to awake for mass—there were already a lot of people on the strand.

Malibu. Only maybe better.

"Isn't it better than your Grand Beach now?"

"In some respects."

Having chosen a spot at the corner of dune, she busied herself setting up the umbrella and arranging our "rugs," as she called the large beach towels.

"I like Chicago," she said. " 'Tis a lovely city."

" 'Tis."

"I've thought of living there."

Brigid, Patrick, and Columcille!

"The city would be honored!"

"No, eejit, put the basket in the shade. You don't want our lunch to melt, do you, now?"

"Sorry, ma'am." I complied with her instructions.

"I'm sorry I called you an eejit, Tim Pat."

"It's an affectionate term, usually."

"I shouldn't have used it."

"Forget it. . . . Why would you move to Chicago?"

"I'm enough of a Yank that I want to live in America most of the time. The foundation has a small staff, so it would be easy to move. That way Sean wouldn't have me looking over his shoulder all the time."

We sat on our beach towels under the shade of the umbrella. It was already getting hot. I took off the jacket of my running suit. She untied her ponytail, and her long silver hair tumbled to her print dress.

"Sean?" I glanced around in search of the protectors Bishop Blackie had assembled for us. They must be very good indeed because I saw no trace of them.

"My stepson. He has an M.B.A. from Columbia and works for a big company in New York and makes tons of money. Jim Lark was fixing, as he put it, to make him CEO of Jim Lark Enterprises. I want to do the same thing, but he is so angry at me because of the will that he won't even discuss it."

"Nice boy?"

"Nice man, very nice. He's only a year younger than I am. I reckon that if I'm in Chicago with the foundation, he won't be afraid of me looking over his shoulder all the time. We got along very well until Jim Lark died and the will came out."

"The children liked you?"

"At first they were suspicious, as they had every right to

be. Then they became very friendly. Especially Aggie—she's the youngest and the only daughter. Dermot is a psychiatrist."

"Glory be to God!"

"And he's good at it, too. I used to tell him I didn't want him trying to figure me out, and he'd laugh and say that would be too much even for a Jewish training analyst. . . . Their brats called me Nana Nora. Aggie cried when she told me that none of them had ever seen her father so happy."

"You miss them?"

"And their brats . . . I'm hot." She stood up, unbuttoned the front of her dress, and pulled it over her head.

She was wearing a white bikini, classic style, not one of your more daring newer types, and she was astonishing lovely, beyond my expectations. She was a tall woman, taller than I had realized, and her slim waist made her seem even taller and more stately, with silver hair falling on white shoulders. Moreover, despite her seeming fragility, her muscles were solid, robust arms and robust legs, the latter also long and neatly curved. No wonder her handicap was the same as mine.

"Well," she said impatiently as I gazed at her silently, "why don't you say something?"

"I'm searching for the right metaphor, Nora Marie. Maybe for a start I could say an Irish Diana."

She grinned. "Not bad for a start; but I'm too thin."

"No you're not and I'll not tolerate that nonsense. A few more pounds wouldn't do any harm, but you blind a man's eyes the way you are."

Embarrassed finally, she sat down next to me and began to smear herself with number forty-five suntan lotion. "No skin cancer for me," she insisted.

I continued to watch her, reveling in every delightful move. "Why do you think Jim Lark changed his will?"

"I don't know." She anointed her legs. "My guess is that he would have named Sean CEO at some point in the near future, probably when he was forty. Then Jim Lark could search for other worlds to conquer. With Sean running the company and me holding the purse strings and expanding the foundation, he probably figured that when he died, everything would be in good order."

"Makes sense."

"If he had told me, I would have warned him that he couldn't do that to his family and colleagues." She rubbed the oil on her milk-white belly. "But he didn't ask. I suppose he wanted to keep the brothers completely out of it. And this was the way to do it."

"So maybe he was going to announce the new arrangement at the meeting."

"Here, put some of this on my back. Please." She gave me the lotion container. "In retrospect I think that might have been his idea. But I don't know what the rush was."

I unfastened the top of her swimsuit. She deftly caught the front so that it wouldn't fall off.

"What about Arthur T. and Paddy Quaid?"

"Jim Lark told me once—when he talked about how Sean would be the perfect manager for Jim Lark Enterprises—that Paddy was too busy with politics and too dependent on that terrible McNulty person and that Artie was too rigid for the job. He also didn't like Artie's attitude toward me."

"Oh?"

The secret of the art of spreading suntan lotion on a woman's back is to be gentle enough to suggest a caress and efficient enough so that she doesn't think you are trying to seduce her—which, of course, may well be what you're up to. You also come within a hairbreadth of her breasts without actually touching them. Through years of practice I have become pretty good at it.

"You're pretty good at that," she said, soothed by my attention. "From the first day after we were married, Arthur didn't bother to hide his contempt for me. He was crude and clumsy. Jim Lark wanted to fire him. I talked him out of it."

This would all be grist for Bishop Blackie's mill. Mine, too, if I ever had a rational thought for the rest of my life.

I fastened her top. "Straps?"

"Leave them until I want to swim."

"In that water?"

"Sure, isn't it refreshing?" She took the lotion out of my hand. "Thank you. Now I'll do your back. I'll not be responsible for your skin cancer."

"Fair enough . . . It would have been hard on Arthur T. and Paddy after all the years going back to County Tip."

"Not on Paddy. He didn't want complete control and he likes Sean. That woman would be furious. You know, sometimes I think she believes that I took Jim Lark away from her. Isn't that terrible altogether?"

" 'Tis," I said.

She was doing a much better job on me than I on her. But women have an advantage in the suntan-lotion game. Since culture expects them to be more gentle, they can caress you and not be accused of attempting seduction.

"As good as my mother would do." I sighed contentedly.

"Your *mother*?" She peered over my shoulder to look at my face and see if I was joking.

She discovered I wasn't.

"Yep. A grand woman."

"Dominating Irish-mother type, keeping her son home?" she asked suspiciously as she carefully covered my back again, just so she didn't miss any part of me.

"Threw me out of the house when I graduated from the Golden Dome. Said she didn't want me under her feet and interfering with my father and her."

"Interfering with what?"

"What do you think?"

"All done . . ." She abandoned my back. *"Really?"*

"Absolutely."

She inspected my face again to make sure I wasn't joking.

"It doesn't ever have to end, does it, Tim Pat?"

"I don't know about that. I just know that for some people it doesn't end."

She nodded thoughtfully. "I suppose not. I'd like to meet your mother someday."

"No way."

"Oh?" She was about to lose her temper.

"The two of you would make common cause against me and I'd be in great trouble."

"Silly." She pounded my arm.

"So if the killing came from within the company, you think it would be either Arthur T. or Clare McNulty."

"I'm not accusing anyone. Arthur was in New York and that woman was in the office with Paddy. How could they have done it?"

"I'm talking about motivation."

"For all his faults, Arthur T. is loyal. I'm not a good one to judge what Clare McNulty might do. She's good at her work, but I think she's just a little crazy. . . . Would you want to sleep with her?" She turned to look at me.

"She's not unattractive in an outsize sort of way." I spoke very carefully indeed. "So there might be a certain appeal to her. But after a few minutes of conversation, it would all slip away."

"Seductive till she opens her mouth?"

"Very mildly so till she opens her mouth."

"I thought so. I'm going to lie in the sun and collect some warmth against the return of real Irish weather."

"May I join you?"

"If you keep your distance."

"Was I thinking of anything else?"

"Yes, you were."

We lay next to each other in the sun, eyes closed, drinking up the warmth. A super day on the strand, grand, rapid.

"Did anyone know about the change in the will?"

"Only Micah Epstein, Jim Lark's lawyer. He is as tight-lipped as the Sphinx."

"His office staff?"

"Maybe. But would someone have a typist on retainer just in case a will came in?"

"If they suspected a new wife might persuade a change."

"I didn't do that."

"Some of them might have thought you would try."

"Maybe." She sighed, tired of the talk about the crime.

I thought about it myself, despite the attractions of the

beach. If we postulated a spy in the lawyer's office, then we opened up the possibility that anyone might know of the will. Or might know that it had been drafted.

To hell with it for the moment.

What about Nora?

What about her?

You're enchanted.

That's an understatement. She seems to like me, too.

She's trying to seduce you, just like she did her first two husbands.

Nothing wrong with that.

You don't have to get defensive.

Well, let her try.

She'll have you wrapped around her little finger in another day or two.

Nothing wrong with that either. But she has her doubts, too.

That's true. Strong doubts. She might turn and run almost anytime.

Yeah.

Would you run after her?

Don't know.

The subject of my inner dialogue spoke. "I'm going to read."

"Fine, I guess I will, too. More suntan lotion?"

"After we swim."

She put on huge sunglasses with white rims and settled down to Maeve Binchy's new novel.

I opened a commentary on *Ulysses*, but devoted most of my attention to Nora.

She glanced up a couple of times and then returned to her book.

Finally she closed the book and took off the shades.

"The way you're staring at me, Tim Pat," she protested, "you make me feel naked."

"I'm sorry," I mumbled. "I didn't meant to be rude. I'll stop."

"Do you think you can?"

"I doubt it."

"Then don't bother trying, so long as you know you are embarrassing me."

She put her shades back on and opened the book.

"A lot?"

"A lot."

"Offensively so?"

"No," she answered promptly, and then added, "not completely."

It was, I thought, a clear signal that I could continue to admire her, always reverently, as the bishop had said.

Well, more or less reverently.

"When I'm finished with this chapter," she murmured, "we'll go swimming."

"Do I have to?"

"Yes."

So she finished the chapter and we went swimming, first putting our car key and all other valuables in my CPD bag and, towels over our shoulders, brought it to the edge of the slowly rising tide. She gathered her hair back into a ponytail, but wore no bathing cap.

"I'll fasten your straps," I announced, removing her towel from her shoulders.

"I'll do it."

"No need."

So I did it. Sure, woman, I'll fasten straps for you for the rest of your life.

"The only way to do it," she informed me, "is to run into the water until it's up to your belly and then dive in."

"I'll take your word for it."

She followed her own prescription and swam a strong crawl out into the Irish Sea and then back to where she could stand. I, on the other hand, touched the historic waters with a tentative toe and wondered if hell could hurt any more.

"Come on, coward."

"I don't deny it."

But a man will do almost anything for love. So I dashed

into the water and, as ordered, dove when it was up to my stomach.

I thought I would die of an instant heart attack.

"Yow!" I screamed.

"Isn't it grand!"

"Focking awful."

She tugged her swimsuit into place and swam out toward Wales again. Reluctantly I followed.

The water didn't get any better. But I'd be damned if I would let her stay in it any longer than I did.

Eventually, breathless, laughing, and somehow hand in hand, we struggled ashore, picked up my CPD bag, threw towels around our shoulders, and hurried back to our place on the sand.

"Terrible refreshing, isn't it?"

"A cure for concupiscence."

"I doubt it." She turned toward me. "Not for long, anyway. But long enough for us to begin lunch."

"Suntan oil first?"

"I suppose so."

We went through our act again. The "scrotum-tightening" Irish Sea, as Jimmy Joyce called it, did not make the ritual any less appealing.

Nora then opened the heavy basket she had been carrying. First, out came a bottle of Bushmills green label and two Irish crystal tumblers, wrapped carefully in napkins.

"To warm you up after your dip in the sea."

"One glass, only."

"I'm driving."

"You too."

"Don't worry about that." She poured a modest amount into the tumbler for me.

We toasted one another, and sure enough, I did feel warm again.

Then came the white tablecloth and the rest of the meal— ham-and-cheese, egg-salad, roast-beef, and tuna-salad sandwiches, buttered scones with the jelly already spread, a bottle of very expensive burgundy, and truffles and cream puffs with whipped cream.

Goblets for the wine, of course.

We both ate like it was going out of fashion. When I reached for my third sandwich, she turned away shyly.

"Still staring, are you, Tim Pat, still drinking me with them terrible silver-blue eyes of yours, like you're drinking that burgundy."

"Richer woman than burgundy, but I'll stop."

"Ah, don't do that." She sighed. "Sure am I not half enjoying it anyway. Have another sandwich. Tuna salad."

Grand.

"Don't fill your glass to the top," she warned. "Won't you be spilling wine on the tablecloth?"

"Yes, ma'am."

"Sorry for being bossy," she said contritely. "Aren't I the awful nag?"

"Nope. I probably would have spilled the wine. If I resent the orders, I'll tell you. Don't worry about it then."

She touched my cheek and sighed. "Ah, you're the sweet one, Tim Pat."

"Yes, ma'am," I agreed.

We ate on, she as much as I. Her appetite had returned.

"Your figure is indestructible," I protested, sinking my teeth into another ham and cheese. "But this feast will destroy mine altogether."

"I bet. . . ." Wineglass in hand, she placed a finger gently on one of the scars across my chest. "Someone shot you?"

"They did."

"Does it hurt?"

"Not anymore."

Her hand rested on my chest and her fingers explored its musculature carefully, curiously. "Did you think you were going to die?"

"Yes."

"You won't take chances like that ever again?"

"Never," I lied, thinking of my trip to Bray for lunch on the IRA tomorrow at half twelve.

Her fingers continued their delicate exploration. If she didn't stop, I'd need another, and longer, dip in the Irish Sea.

"Nothing wrong with your figure at all, at all, Tim Pat." She smiled up at me.

"Turnabout is fair play, huh?"

"Only women stare much more discreetly." She moved her fingers away.

"May I breathe now?"

"Go 'long with you! And isn't it the young ones."

Brigid and Trish, in bikinis that were at the most symbolic, swarmed up to us with breathless stories about the various "truly gross" Irish boys they had met and about some "excellent" ones with whom they were about to establish contact.

They also finished off our sandwiches and helped demolish our desserts. We did not, however, offer them any of our precious burgundy.

"Swim it off in the sea," Trish asserted.

"Lent begins when we go home," Brigie agreed.

"Gorgeous young bodies," Nora said to me as they ran off. "And don't pretend you didn't notice."

"They're kids, Nora. You're a woman."

She pondered that. "I was never a kid, Tim Pat. I had a husband by the time I was their age."

"Those were different times."

"Not so different. Midseventies. I'm not complaining. It would have been nice to be a kid."

So we drank some more burgundy and then lay down in the sun again.

Somehow or the other, one of my hands, operating on its own, found its way to her belly, on which my fingers drew aimless designs. The rate of her breathing increased and she closed her eyes and bit her lip as my unruly hand continued its explorations. Despite explicit instructions from me, it found its way to a breast. It crept insidiously under her swimsuit in search of a nipple.

She didn't resist or forbid me.

It was a moist and full breast with a hard nipple.

"Please don't, Tim Pat." She sighed. "It's very nice and I'm not angry at you at all, at all. But please."

I waited a few more seconds and then obeyed her.

"Sorry," I said.

"Don't be sorry." She sighed again. "I didn't say I didn't like it. I only asked you please not to."

"I understand."

What else did you expect, you eejit, and on a public beach, too.

I didn't intend to do it.

Focking bullshit.

"Oh," she said a few minutes later, "I forgot when the kids were here. We must have the taste test."

"Taste test?"

"Right." She removed two pint-size plastic bottles of beige-colored liquid. "One's Jim Lark Cream and the other is Baileys. Taste each of them."

She produced, also carefully wrapped in napkins, two Waterford cordial glasses and filled each of them. Finally she offered me several crackers to clean my palate after each taste.

I went through the motions of the experiment. One glass clearly contained the mother of all Irish-cream liqueurs. The other tasted terrible, the sort of taste that leads you to suspect that the veterinarian will call you and tell you that your horse has a kidney infection.

She was watching me anxiously. I'd better come up with an appropriate answer.

"Well," I said, "this one is Baileys."

"That's right."

"No doubt about it . . . and this one is very different, a kind of surprise taste. It'll take some getting used to, but then I think I'd like it a lot."

Lie!

"That's what we've been thinking. It's distinctive and better, but it has to be obviously better the first time. We'll keep working on it."

Love for her late husband had affected the taste buds of even this intelligent woman.

If I had spoken the blunt truth, I would have said that the Jim Lark Cream had tasted like liquid shit compared with Baileys.

So we finished off the wine and swam again and argued. The arguments were revealing. Nora Marie Finnegan Joyce MacDonaugh was a woman of wide knowledge and opinions, always strong, on many different subjects—art, music, literature, politics, economics, love, religion. On most issues she was to the left of me. On love—discussed clinically and objectively—we were both romantics. And on religion she was a traditional Catholic with a deep distrust of church leaders (save for "that adorable little man," meaning, of course, the good Bishop Ryan) and liberal ideas about what the traditions meant. She also insisted that "they don't have a clue about what focking means to married people or how it draws a man and a woman together despite their fears."

That line made me gulp. But she didn't seem to be applying it to us.

It was then that I became fully conscious of what had been happening for most of the day. Nora Finnegan Joyce MacDonaugh was watching me closely. All the time. She was measuring my every expression, noting my every word, not critically or suspiciously, but with fascinated interest, a combination of affection and amusement, the way Irishwomen watched their men (and their boy children) in a place like Bewley's.

It was much more an invasion of my privacy than my fantasizing about her naked body was an invasion of hers. I was embarrassed but pleasantly so.

We had a fierce argument about American aid to what used to be the Soviet Union. She thought we had been too stingy altogether. I contended that we ought not to pour money into a sinkhole of impossible distribution systems.

It was fun arguing with her because she argued pretty much like my mother, fiercely and with wild exaggerations, but fairly and without animosity. She'd admit it if she'd made a mistake and refine or even change her mind if you were persuasive enough—but you had to be pretty damn persuasive.

"You're fun to argue with, aren't you, now, Tim Pat?"

"Wasn't I about to say the same to you, Nora Marie?"

" 'Tis the Irish Sea again for the both of us."

"If you say so."

"Haven't I just said so?"

So we swam and collapsed again on our towels and I fell asleep. I must have been out for an hour or more.

She shook me gently. "Wake up, sleepyhead, 'tis time for us to have a bite of tea and go back to the Shelbourne."

"Sorry I dozed off."

"Didn't you sleep just like an innocent baby?" She was wearing her cover-up and her hair was back in its ponytail.

"I'm not an innocent babe, Nora Marie."

"I'm not so sure about that."

We gathered our belongings, found our car, stopped for a tea and a scone (hard) at a roadside stand, and drove back to Dublin—herself at the wheel, of course, because I fell asleep again.

Great, ardent lover, this Timothy Patrick MacCarthy.

She accepted my invitation for a quick bite of supper in the hotel coffee shop after we had showered—in our respective rooms, need I say—and dressed in casual clothes.

She continued to examine my every move, thinking that I didn't notice because she had forgotten that cops are trained to notice everything. In her ongoing contemplation of the delightful puzzle of Tim Pat MacCarthy there was a touch of vulnerability that would break a man's heat if he noticed, and of course he wasn't supposed to notice.

"I think I may kiss you after supper," I told her.

"You'll do no such thing," she informed me pertly.

"Why not?"

"You had lots of chances before and now it's too late." She smiled impishly at me.

"When?"

"At the embassy party."

"I left early."

"You shouldn't have left without me."

"I wasn't your date."

"You could have become my date and I'd have had to kiss you good night."

"You're teasing me."

"I am *not*."

"When did I get another chance?"

"When we were swimming today."

"I was freezing to death!"

"Coward! And myself in that indecent swimsuit all day long!"

"Well, I don't care what you say, I'm still going to kiss you after supper. I'm an ex-linebacker, and when I want a kiss, I get one."

"You will *not*!"

"I will *too*!"

"I'll run away."

"I'll catch up with you!"

"We'll see!"

After we had polished off our sherry trifle with heavy cream, we rode up the elevator, the two of us giggling.

"No," she said.

"Yes," I said.

"No." She tried to run as soon as we left the elevator.

I grabbed her, almost tackled her.

Thank heaven there was no one in the corridor. The two of us were giggling like a pair of teens.

She squirmed and twisted and dug her elbows into my gut.

I picked her up and carried her to the door of her room. She laughed hysterically all the way.

"Brute," she sniggered as she pounded my chest, "beast, chauvinist."

She was, I realized, pathetically light.

"No," she said when I had set her back on her feet and pinned her against the door of her room.

"Yes," I insisted, tracing the outline of her face with the fingers of one hand while I pushed her shoulder firmly with the other.

"Oh, all right, get it over with!"

She was ready for me. Her lips met mine halfway. The kiss was very gentle and affectionate, a preliminary reconnaissance to see what the other was like.

"Not bad." She sighed. "Not good but not bad."

"Never had to fight for a kiss so much in all my life."

"Oh, Tim Pat . . ." Her body slumped against mine in surrender.

I had planned a second kiss, as I'm sure she did. Neither of us expected the intense contact that actually occurred.

We separated after what seemed like a light-year or two of passion.

"And the bishop said you were a good man!" She sighed. "A lot he knew."

"That was very nice, Nora Marie."

"It was that, Tim Pat. Thank you."

"Thank you."

"Good night." She sighed. "And I really mean good night."

She really did; so I said good night, too.

Then we both entered our rooms, I to the audit reports and she, I suspected, to her memories.

More terrible than I could ever imagine.

The audit figures blurred before my eyes. I wanted to think about Nora's figure. Maybe I would be welcome in her room. No way. Not tonight.

What if I don't come back tomorrow. She shouldn't lose a third lover.

Maybe I should take a long run.

You're too sleepy to do that.

You'd better do it anyway. Clear your head and get a good night's sleep before you face the IRA tomorrow.

"All right." I sighed, struggled out of my chair, and prepared for a run.

The phone rang.

"MacCarthy."

"Tim Pat?"

My heart did several excited flip-flops.

"Nora?"

"I need a date for a dinner party tomorrow night. They just called me. Would find a dinner companion for me. They're usually terrible. Since you've already kissed me against my will, I suppose I have to ask you. Black tie."

"I don't have one."

"Bollix!"

"I'd be delighted, Nora Marie. What time?"

"Half seven?"

"Super!"

"Grand!"

"Rapid!" we exclaimed together.

As I ran I prayed to the Deity that this would be not the last time in this life I heard her voice.

16

"**Y**OU HAVE EXAMINED THESE AUDITS IN SOME DETAIL?" THE good bishop was poring over reports about the financial condition of Jim Lark Enterprises, both in Ireland and around the world.

"I've gone over them a couple of times," I said. "The only thing I see is that it is a very healthy empire in most respects, a few troubled hotels and resorts still recovering from the depression, and some developments about which it is too early to tell, but otherwise fine."

"Indeed."

"I did have a couple of courses in accounting, you know."

"Doubtless. Yet there may be patterns."

"Be my guest. Do you have a theory?"

"Certain patterns emerge."

"You know who did it?"

"Oh, yes. Proof, however, is another matter."

He *knew*. I didn't believe it.

Nor had he asked a single question about our day in the strand.

Probably thought he didn't need to.

Probably was right.

"We had a rapid day at Bull Island yesterday."

"Indeed."

"Nora seems reasonably happy."

"The woman collects strays." He did not look up.

"Strays?"

"A young man weakened by emotional stress and an older man with little sexual satisfaction in his past. Certainly; strays."

"And a bachelor cop, too, huh?" I said with a touch of asperity. "I guess that puts me in my place."

He looked up at me as if he were surprised at my reaction, which I was sure he was not.

"It would depend on where you wanted your place to be, would it not?"

"I'm not sure yet."

"Ah."

Was I really a stray, a cause for a woman who looked for odd men to dedicate her life to? A holy Roman martyr looking for a cause for which to offer herself?

Wasn't our kissing encounter last night proof that I had something more to offer?

I decided to change the subject.

"I'm going down to Bray in a few minutes, walk around a little."

"I urge caution."

"Then I'm going to talk to Martin O'Neill at the Berkeley Court."

"Capital." He was not paying much attention to me.

"I expect by the time I return, some of my information from America will be here."

"Capital."

"Then I have a date with Nora tonight."

"Ah?" I had not surprised him or stirred his interest.

"Black tie. Some political and journalistic thing over in Merrion Square."

"Capital."

"Then tomorrow I'm going out to Meath to see the MacDonaugh children. The Americans are over here with their kids on holiday—uh, vacation."

That made him look up from the pages of figures.

"Your report from yesterday states that it was the late Mr. MacDonaugh's intent to make, ah, Sean MacDonaugh the president of the empire and that the elegant Nora wishes to do the same thing, but the children are too angry at her to co-operate?"

"That's right."

"Most unfortunate." He sighed. "Most unfortunate. The

spreading waves of evil continue to exert their insidious influence. We must contain them."

"Indeed."

"The makers of peace must reassert themselves."

"I'll buy that."

"At some point the children—ah, Sean, Dermot, and Agnes—must be pressed to reconsider their position vis-à-vis the exemplary Nora. No useful purpose will be served in prolonged estrangement."

"By me?"

He shrugged. "Arguably."

"If you say so."

"Who else is able to effect a reconciliation?"

He returned to the audits and I drifted toward the door.

"God go with you, Tim Patrick MacCarthy, and the Mother of Jesus keep you from all harm, and the three patrons, Brigid, Patrick, and Columcille, protect you on your way."

"Uh . . . thanks."

It was a pretty heavy and solemn blessing. Yet he didn't seem all that worried about me.

Maybe he figured that I was good at calculating the odds. After all, I was a successful commodity trader, was I not?

But why was I the one to effect a reconciliation between a woman I'd known for only a couple of days and three hurt and angry young people I had never met?

You're the miracle worker, Bishop Blackie, not me.

On the way out I checked my box. There was a fax message from Australia.

The police in Perth do not think much of your friend Charles Stewart Parnell MacDonaugh. He has killed two men in barroom fights, both times, according to witnesses, in self-defense. They had him up for trial on one of the offenses, but the jury didn't think they had enough evidence. Moreover, one of his bitter enemies out on the range died in a car explosion several years ago, a man who was about to buy the mortgage on MacDonaugh's land. He is also supposed to have good contacts with the local Mafia in Melbourne.

He is deeper in trouble now than he has ever been in his long and nefarious career. I gather that he owes the Mafia and they are pressing him.

As you suspected, a man named Charles Stewart flew from Perth to Singapore on Qantas on January 12 and thence to London on Singapore Airlines. He returned to Perth on January 17, meaning he probably left London on the sixteenth.

Parny MacDonaugh has good alibis for those days, but he always has good alibis. Our inquiries at Perth suggest that Charles Stewart looks very much like Parny. Good hunting.

I put the fax in an envelope and asked the hall porter to see that it was delivered to Bishop Ryan's room.

I was very proud of myself. My secret hunch had paid off. Charles Parnell MacDonaugh had been in Dublin at the time of his brother's death. He had arrived under an assumed name and had departed mysteriously the day after someone had murdered Jim Lark. Now we had to find evidence that he was in Dublin. He had the opportunity and he had the motive. It would be hard to go beyond such circumstances and prove that he had committed the crime, but his history of car bombing made it seem a pretty good case—enough to force the Dublin Guard to reopen the case.

And to lift the suspicion from Nora. Not a bad service just before I went off to meet the IRA.

Dublin had cooled off again, the sky gray and dull, a fresh breeze off the Irish Sea.

I walked down Kildare Street past the national museum and library, the latter a place where Stephen had dazzled his friends with a lecture on *Hamlet*—an effort on Joyce's part to express his anguish about fathers and sons, and his frustrations with his own father. On the right-hand side of the street with only a guard in front of it, stood Leinster House, a monumental eighteenth-century home built by the Duke of Lein-

202 / Andrew M. Greeley

ster. When he left behind his previous home on Henrietta Street, he moved the center of fashionable Dublin from Mountjoy Square north of the River Liffey to Merrion Square south of it, thus creating the social-class difference between the north side (which is one of the themes of the film *The Commitments*) and the south side of the city—and making Mr. Bloom's address at 7 Eccles Street, near Mountjoy Square, distinctly unfashionable.

Maybe tomorrow or the next day I would wander by the empty lot on which that world-famous house once stood.

I cut around behind Trinity College and into Westland Row. Under the dark and somber arch of the railroad bridge—now replaced by the DART trestle—Mr. Bloom had paused to read the silly letter from his woman pen pal. There was no note for me at all at all this dull morning.

Had she forgotten about me already?

Well, at least we had a date tonight, a real date. Our first. And doubtless our last.

Out of loyalty to Mr. Bloom I ducked into the sternly classical St Andrew's Church (which Joyce called All Hallows).

You know what I want, I told Whoever might be listening. It's all Your fault that I can't do without her. What? Oh, sure, I *can* survive without her, but the point is I don't want to. Is it wrong for me to want her as much as I do? If it is, that's Your fault, too, for creating us male and female.

There was no discernible reply to that complaint.

As I rode up the escalator of the Pearse station, I felt very sorry for myself, an exercise in which we Irish Americans yield nothing to the mere Irish—or the real Irish if you please.

There was a DART train waiting for me. I was on the edge of rushing in when I realized that the Irish drive their trains like their cars on the wrong side of the tracks (as we would see it) and that therefore the train I was about to board would take me to Howth at the other end of Dublin Bray, where I wanted to go.

I walked down to the ground level and over to the other side and just missed a train going in my direction.

Well, I was in no hurry. Time to go through my list of available suspects. I pulled out my notebook and scribbled down a list.

Nora MacDonaugh—wife of the victim. She had the best motive of anyone, but she may not have known of the motive. Her first husband had died under mysterious circumstances. She also had perhaps the best opportunity, if one could figure out how she had activated the bomb. According to my friend Riordan, you might be able to set the bomb off from as much as half a mile away. The Klyemore bakery was less than that. No one had seen her push a button, but she could have done that in her purse and then discarded the transmitter in any dustbin (trash can to us) on Merrion Road. The transmitter inside might have been another left there as a blind. Pretty good suspect if you could prove any of your suppositions. Professionally she still looked like a good bet, but how would I know? I was in love with her.

The good bishop had cleared her, but he wasn't infallible, was he?

I didn't like that line of reasoning.

For the moment I would assign general infallibility to himself.

Arthur T. Regan.

Current second-in-command of Jim Lark Enterprises. My employer, but that didn't mean a thing. Killers have hired detectives before to pin the murder on someone else. He hated Jim Lark's new wife so deeply and so patently that Jim Lark himself was offended. Maybe he also lusted after her. Arthur T. indeed owed his job to Nora's defense of him. He didn't know that probably, and if he did, he no doubt hated her even more. If the will were to be changed—and he was the one most likely to have a spy in Micah Epstein's office—he would have been at her mercy. If he knew the will had been changed, giving control to the woman he hated, he might have murdered Jim Lark in an outburst of anger and with the intent that Nora would be blamed. Or, perhaps more likely, if he anticipated his bewitched friend from hurling days would change the will, he might kill to prevent such a change. How about opportunity? He couldn't activate the bomb from New York, but he could have hired someone to do so. How would I ever prove that?

Paddy Quaid.

Sometime lord mayor of Dublin, member of the City Corporation, head of Irish operations, also a boyhood friend of Jim Lark. Much closer to the scene, but with a tight alibi. Moreover, motivation was less clear. His job was not likely to be in jeopardy no matter what happened. He got along well with both the MacDonaugh children and the widow, whom he seemed to like and support. Besides, his interests were political rather than economic. The only likely replacement for him was Clare McNulty, and he surely knew her weaknesses and understood she was no threat.

Clare McNulty.

Again close to the scene and with the motivation of deep hatred for both Nora and Jim Lark MacDonaugh. Hell hath no fury. Also the opportunity because she was in Dublin. She and Paddy had alibis that canceled each other out and they were unlikely to be in collusion.

The sister.

Julia was a woman filled with hatred. She had been in the vicinity at the time of the explosion and might have detonated a bomb. But why would she kill the boy she had raised and still worshiped? Because he pretended to be bigger than he really was? Not very likely.

The brothers.

The kind of reckless, angry, ruthless men who would try anything. Hated Jim Lark because he paid little attention to them and showed no gratitude for their contribution to his success. Stood to lose vast sums of money if the will was changed. Might have acted to prevent the change and thus did themselves in. Too clever by half. Mick Dav was close enough to the crime to have done it, although Julia was something of an alibi for him. Information from my sources would reveal if any of them were in deep financial trouble out of which they could climb on expectations of inheritance after the will was probated.

The children.

I hadn't met them yet. By all accounts nice young people. Furious now at Nora, but once fond of her.

Martin O'Neill.

I hadn't seen him either. Administrative assistant to Jim Lark and now to his widow. Motive and opportunity unknown. Alleged by the guard, or at least by Chief Superintendent Tom Clarke, to be the widow's lover. Alleged by the widow to be gay.

The Irish Republican Army, a.k.a. the lads.

They had kidnapped Jim Lark once (maybe) and might well have killed him. But what would have been their motives? They were terrorists, all right, but not irrational in the context of their convictions and goals. They killed only for a purpose that would serve their cause. How was their cause served by Jim Lark MacDonaugh's death—any more than by the death of any other wealthy Irishman? Moreover, far from claiming credit for executing an enemy of the Irish people, they vigorously denied responsibility. Brendan had pleaded innocent in his conversation last night.

Whoever was embezzling money from somewhere in the Jim Lark empire.

It could have been almost any of the above. Or anyone else, person or persons unknown. Was there really theft? Jim Lark had thought so. Nora did, too, but then she thought the Jim Lark Irish Cream he was planning to market was better than Baileys. She loved him so much and missed him so desperately that she'd do anything she thought he would want her to do. Yet she had found nothing in more than a year and a half of searching. Trying to find a flaw in vast reams of computer output when all you have is a hunch is like looking for the proverbial needle in the haystack. Bishop Blackie had hinted he knew what to look for, but what did that mean?

Maybe the good bishop was just a bit of a fake. Certainly he was a superb showman.

James Larkin MacDonaugh himself.

He might have chosen the explosion as a spectacular method for suicide—especially given his love of self-display.

He would go down in history as the victim of terrorists, a way out that he might like. Moreover, he was a shrewd and ruthless man beneath the veneer of devil-may-care charm. After the death of his first wife, he wanted another woman who would open up to him the mysteries and wonders and pleasures of sex. He had clinically evaluated Nora for a number of years before going after her, a version of the story that made a lot more sense than Nora's romantic account. He might have just as shrewdly plotted his own end.

Or someone else might have died in his place. Who? Person or persons unknown. Why? Anybody's guess.

He was an unlikely suspect but not one to rule out completely.

Two critical unanswered questions: Why did he change his will and why did he call the meeting?

Nora had a tentative answer to both. He wanted to appoint his son Sean CEO or at least COO of the empire. Nora and Sean, a generation younger, were cordial to one another and would provide a nice balance for the future. He was not planning to die, but he wanted them both to know that he had prepared for such an event. Perhaps the purpose of the meeting was to announce to members of the family this change. Or perhaps only the appointment of Sean.

Plausible enough, but we'd need testimony from a dead man to confirm it.

I pulled the list of suspects out of my notebook, tore the page into tiny pieces, and scattered them in front of the approaching DART train.

I had nothing, not a thing. Maybe the information I was expecting from America this afternoon would provide a clue.

If not, what should I do? Call Arthur T. Regan and report failure. Then devote my time fully to my still uncertain pursuit of the woman who was on the top of the list of suspects? Tail between my legs, go home to the United States of America a failure? Consult with the good bishop, who claimed to know—or at least to recognize a pattern?

Ergo, meathead, as we used to say when I was in the seminary.

Yeah, I studied for the priesthood. Not for long, but for a few years. And after the time when every intelligent kid on the South Side of Chicago went off to Quigley.

Given the wife and children I had acquired, I might just as well have stayed there.

The DART (and the article is used in Dublin, if not in San Francisco) is a modern, high-speed transit system (the cars are green, naturally) built in part on the roadbed on which once ran the world's second oldest railroad line—from Dublin to Kingstown, before and after known by its proper Irish name of Dun Leary. (The first was from Liverpool to Birmingham.)

Since the Irish economy could not support car ads in every space, there were poems, jokes, and bits of information posted in the empty spots. Only in Ireland would you find a sonnet in a car ad.

One of the bits of information informed riders that the old steam train back in the 1830s needed nineteen minutes to make the run from Dublin to Kingstown (which was the ferry head for the ships that came from Hollyhead in Wales). Now, with the most modern rail beds and high-speed trains, the run took sixteen minutes.

Only in Ireland that sort of irony.

The line cut through Irishtown and Sandymount and then rushed to the edge of the bay. The clouds had cleared off and the view of the bay as the train sped south was spectacular. Not the Seven Mile Drive or the Corniche or the Costa Brava or the Amalfi Drive or, to my prejudiced eyes, Duneland Drive on the south end of Lake Michigan, but still lovely, a soft and serene meeting of land and water, the blue of the bay on one side, as we sped into South County Dublin, and the greenery of parks and golf courses on the other—a very Irish blend of land and sea.

Bray was the southern end of the line. Above the town was the solid rock of Bray Head, the southern end of Dublin Bay, just as Howth Head (beloved by Mr. and Mrs. Bloom and perhaps the image that rekindled their love affair) clearly etched in the distance against the now suddenly pure sky, marked the north end of the bay and the north head of the DART.

In the old railroad station I bought two candy bars to hold me till half twelve and began my exploration of Bray— always know the lay of the land, a good cop says.

It had been a resort town in the Edwardian era, whose beachside hotels attracted the elite of Dublin and many of the famous writers in the British Isles. As I walked along the strand I marveled at how different expectations were in those days. Most American tourists, even those who were not all that affluent, would not be satisfied with such small buildings and the tiny rooms inside—with only one "bathroom" to a corridor or two at the most. Give them a motel or perhaps a Hilton.

Yet to the Edwardian ladies, their bodies pinched by terrible corsets, and gentlemen, in their hats and frock coats and vests, Bray must have seemed like the height of seaside luxury. The strand was still there and a boardwalk on which vendors had set up their carts. But why come to such a dirty strand when the clean soft sands of Bull Island beckoned only a brief ride away on the DART?

I crossed through an underpass and entered the main part of town. My first stop was Martello Tower Place. The towers had been built by the Brits as a ring around Ireland to defend the island from a feared invasion by Bonaparte. A fire built on the gun platform was supposed to be visible on the next tower in either direction. If the Frenchies landed near you, you started a fire and thus sent word to headquarters in Dublin or wherever. The tower on the land side of the Bray railroad station had, like some others (including *the* tower in Sandycove), been converted into a home, this time with a large glass enclosure over the top.

Your man had lived in one of the homes in the shadow of the tower—I wasn't sure which one—as a boy. Indeed the famous Christmas scene, both funny and tragic, in *Portrait of the Artist*, had occurred there.

Poor Jimmy Joyce. Poor everyone who had to work out a

relationship with a father. Especially a strong father. Who was already a legend in the CPD when you signed up.

Well, we did all right, I guess. Through no fault of mine.

I strolled into the town, still forty-five minutes before my lunch with the Provos. Or the IRA. Some of the old resort villas along the street had been converted into Yuppie town houses. Others were being converted. New town-house developments were growing up. Once a resort town and commercial center, Bray was fast being transformed, courtesy of the DART, into a flourishing commuter center for professional men and women.

Its main street, over which loomed an enormous Catholic church, bustled with pre-lunch-hour pedestrians and cars. A prosperous little town, this Bray. And just busy enough so that it would be hard to pick out any IRA operatives that might be on the street.

Were they watching me?

Were Bishop Blackie's friends, whoever they might be, also watching?

I wasn't able to pick out either group, and I'm pretty good at picking up trails. Or I used to be.

Sure enough, halfway down the street was Ray Carroll's Pub, a snug little place for ordinary folk, not for your gentry. I did not cross the street to look at it.

No point in doing that anyway. And I don't want to give anyone the impression that I'm scared.

I wasn't particularly scared anyway. It was a lovely day in Ireland and I was half in love. My adrenaline would start to flow about 12:25, and that would be enough to give me just the right edge.

I could be as good a fraud as any sweet-talking terrorist.

I strolled back down the main street to the church and drifted inside to have a brief talk with Whoever is in Charge.

If it's all the same to You, I'd just as soon come out of this conversation alive and well as not. And I'd also like to have the woman as a wife, if you wouldn't mind. Forgive me for saying so, but I think I'd be a better husband to her than her two previous men. The only bad rap on me is that I'm an aging Irish bachelor and I think I could overcome that. She may not love me yet. But I think she genuinely likes me, if You don't mind my saying so, and that's not a bad basis for spending the next thirty- or forty-odd years together.

If it's what You want, get me out of this town and give me the courage to go for her like I used to go for the quarterbacks when they threatened the team named after Your mother.

And not to give up if she tries to scramble.

I walked into Ray Carroll's at precisely half twelve.

A slender, handsome blond fellow, in his middle twenties perhaps, wearing slacks and a sweater just as I was, and with a broad smile, stood up as I entered and strode over to shake hands.

"Sure, Tim Pat, wasn't I saying that your man would walk in just at half twelve?"

I returned his smile and cordiality in kind. "What else would it be now, Brendan?"

He led me to a quiet table in the corner on which there were already two pints and an array of sandwiches for our lunch.

"Sit with your back to the wall, if you wish."

If I were reckless, I'd decline, and he'd know I was reckless.

"Thank you," I said, and sat with my back to the wall.

" 'Tis good to meet you, Tim Pat," he said enthusiastically. "I'm a great Notre Dame fan, as you must know."

"I met some friends of yours out on the Military Road yesterday, Brendan."

"Did you, now?" He raised an eyebrow.

"At a roadblock."

"Ah, *those* friends, is it? Well, they're fine lads and lassies and I would have liked to have stopped and passed the time of day with them, but I had other things to do, if you take me meaning."

"I think I understand."

"Now let's talk about football."

So we talked about the differences among American, Canadian, Irish, and Australian football and rugby and soccer. Brendan was an expert on the origins of and relationships among these games and admitted that while he had national- istic reasons for liking Gaelic football, he still would rather watch American football on the telly.

"Sure there should be one of them teams right here in Ire- land."

"You'd fill Lansdowne Road every week if there were."

I'd met sociopaths in my life, but there was no hint of that in his lively brown eyes. Brendan's interest in football was authentic enough. He was a bright and appealing young man who, for reasons of nurture or nature or racial memory, had joined the world's oldest terrorist organization. He knew how to use his charm to disarm, but that didn't mean he was a to- tal fake.

He was also very dangerous. I was sitting with an end-of- the-century version of Michael Collins. He would kill me as quick as look at me if he thought it would serve the purposes of the "organization."

"Well," he said, "I suppose you wish this crazy Irishman would stop babbling away and get down to business."

"I'm Irish, too, Brendan." I sipped a bit of malt, not much in case it was doped. "And I know the way the game is played. I have all day."

"Ah, aren't you really Irish now? Let me, if you don't mind, take a sip of your pint, just so you'll know there's nothing in either of them."

"Be my guest."

"All right, now let's get to the point. We don't like this MacDonaugh business at all. He was no hero to us, but we didn't kill him. We didn't even kidnap him. Someone else did that and tried to blame us. The men they arrested weren't ours."

"All dead, aren't they, now?"

"Sure you're a smart cop, Tim Pat." He slapped my shoul- der. "Nothing wrong with that at all, at all. Unlike some of my friends I don't expect every Yank to be on my side, but I do expect you to know where I'm coming from."

"I think I understand that, Brendan."

"Difference over means, not ends, if you take my meaning."

"Something like that."

"Well, about them fellas that pretended to be us when they lifted your man, let's just say they're dead and not worry about who killed them."

"If it doesn't have any impact on the death of Jim Lark, I don't give a fock who did it, Brendan."

"All right," he said, rubbing his hands just like Paddy Quaid had done. "All right, that's out of the way."

"Fine with me."

I now half believed that Brendan was on the level, that he had no hidden agenda, and that he wanted to tell me something important, but, *modo hibernico*, that would be filled with allusions and indirections that a poor Yank would have a hard time figuring out.

"You saw the headlines in the papers the day your man was killed."

"Copies of them."

"Instantly they blamed it on us."

"And you denied it promptly."

"We did that . . . and a lot of good it did us. Well, them that was responsible are still trying that. Like shooting at you and trying to smother that poor lass. Tell me, Tim Pat, man to man, is she good in bed?"

"I have no firsthand knowledge, but I assume she might be."

"Grand, grand." He rubbed his hands together again. "We didn't do them things. We had no reason to do them, if you take me meaning. Yet they're using some of our contacts and our equipment—it was our kind of bomb that sent Jim Lark to his Maker, as you well know."

"Who is doing that?"

He waved the question away. "That's neither here nor there at the moment. My point is that they're doing it and they're going to keep on doing it. Everyone jumps to the conclusion that it's us."

"I see."

"Mind you, they're them as might have been on our side at one time, kind of on the fringes like, if you take me meaning. But they're not on our side anymore."

"Can't you take them out yourselves?"

"We could, Tim Pat, you're absolutely right we could. And don't think we haven't discussed that. But my friends and I decided that there'd be a lot of dust up if we did and that it was much better for us if this bright cop from America takes them out instead."

"You want me to do your work for you?"

He beamed happily. "I knew you'd see it, Tim Pat. I says he'll catch on right away. I'm not saying you should liquidate them. I'm just saying that you should catch them."

"That's what I'm trying to do."

"We know that and we're sure you will, you and that cute little bishop fella. Ah, how I wish that one was on our side. Well, that's neither here nor there."

"So?"

"So when you do nail the fockers, there may be some signs that they're with us. They're not, you can count on that. They're with themselves and always have been."

"You want me to resist a snap judgment that the organization is behind it all?"

"Got it," Brendan said simply.

"I see . . . but Brendan, why do you care?"

"Public image, Tim Pat, I'm sure you know about that, sound bites and that sort of thing."

"The organization is worried about its public image?"

"Times are changing, times are changing. We don't mind being called killers—fock, man, we're soldiers that have been fighting a war since before either of us were born. But when they call us senseless killers, it makes us look like a lot of lunatics. All right, maybe some of us are. But we have a cause, too, and we want those who don't agree with us to understand it and not write us off like a lot of crazies with guns and bombs, if you take me meaning."

"I think I do."

However, for all his charm and intelligence, Brendan was as crazy as the rest of them. He had the idea that the organization's cause, properly understood, would not seem like terrorism. But the Irish in the twenty-six counties of the south of Ireland understood the cause and yet ninety-nine out of a hundred voted against Brendan's party in free and open elections. They understood the cause, all right, and maybe half approved of it. They wanted no part of the violence.

So Brendan, a sensitive and intelligent young man, had deluded himself into thinking that if he could spruce up the image of the organization—the "new" IRA like the "new" Nixon or the "new" Bush—he might win some more support in Ireland and the rest of the world.

Revolutionaries constantly delude themselves.

In this case it was all right with me if they did.

"You took the risk of coming down here and evading your friends out on the Military Road to ask me not to blame you when I solve the crime?"

"Tell you."

"Same thing."

It wasn't at all, at all. The warning was clear, blame them and I'd go on the execution list. All right, I had no reason to blame them.

He nodded. "I wouldn't have done it, Tim Pat, if we didn't think it is important."

"All right, Brendan, I'll make you a promise. When we solve this crime, the least I will say is that some people have tried to blame the organization, but that I believe the attempt to be a clumsy fraud and that in my judgment the organization is not involved in the slightest. Fair enough?"

His soft brown eyes considered me thoughtfully. "Couldn't ask for more, Tim Pat, couldn't ask for more." He shook hands with me. "It's a deal and thank you. Now I should be moving along. Someone like me shouldn't linger too long in one place." He winked. "If you take me meaning."

"One more thing, Brendan," I said as we walked rapidly to the door. "You know as well as I do that I was going to ask you for a hint."

"Too true." He laughed. "Too true." He glanced quickly in either direction. "You'd do me a great favor if you walked back toward the church where you were praying—I hope that God would help you have a ride on the lass—and I'll be going to the left."

"The hint, Brendan?"

"Blazes Boylan."

"Who?"

"The lad who was screwing your man's wife."

So terrorists as well as cops read Joyce.

"I don't . . ."

"It's not quite the same, Tim Pat, but it's sort of in the same direction, don't you know. . . . Good-bye, Tim Pat. Luck with the lass."

He disappeared into the crowd.

What the hell!

My head whirling, I walked back to the church and passed it by. Then I went back and thanked Himself.

I want more than a ride, I assured Him. Her. Whatever.

Then I turned toward the DART station, found a public phone kiosk outside the door, called the Shelbourne, and asked for the good bishop's room.

"Father Ryan."

"MacCarthy, from the DART station. Still alive."

"Patently and excellent."

"I'll report back after I have talked to Martin O'Neill."

"Capital."

"They gave me a hint."

"Did they, now?"

"Blazes Boylan."

"Fascinating."

"You know what it means?"

"Oh, yes, a very interesting metaphor."

"It fits your pattern."

"Naturally."

"Delighted to hear it. Have you seen Ms. MacDonaugh?"

"I believe that she and my niece and sister, having returned from a morning expedition to Glasnevin Cemetery, are now engaged in an activity which the women of our species subsume under the rubric of shopping."

"She can afford it."

"Patently."

I hung up, bought two more candy bars and an ice-cream cone, and waited for the next train to pull in.

Nothing made any sense at all anymore.

17

MARTIN O'NEILL DIDN'T LOOK GAY.
I know enough about such matters to know that gay is a sexual orientation and is not necessarily related to appearance or mannerisms. A man can be broad-shouldered, masculine looking, whatever that means, and still be gay.

And I didn't care much what his sexual orientation was, save that if he were gay, one more accusation against Nora would fall, together with one that I expected would be destroyed by a message waiting for me back at the hotel.

If I were a woman, I would have found this polite and soft-spoken young man with the cleanly cut face and thick blond hair to be very attractive. But women can usually tell, much more easily than we do.

"I have two puzzles which are driving me up the wall, Martin," I said as we sat in the Dubliners pub in Jury's Hotel where he had suggested we meet. "Did anyone know of the change in will and the reason for the change, and what was the reason for the meeting?"

"And I suppose whether there was a connection between." He sipped his pint.

I had taken the DART to the Lansdowne Road station, an interesting little rococo station built in the last century so there would be a stop available for the Royal Dublin Society horse show, a crucial event in a land addicted to the breeding, raising, and, above all, the racing of horses.

The DART runs under the grandstand of the stadium, an idea not yet tried in the U.S.

Then I walked west a couple of blocks to the Berkeley Court, where Martin met me and suggested the Dubliners, something that ought not to be missed on a Dublin trip.

Fair enough.

"Indeed." I agreed with his assessment of the issue.

"I may be of some help to you, sir," he said politely, "but I'm not sure how much."

"I see."

"I knew that there was a new will. Mr. MacDonaugh had given it to me to put in his safe. Naturally I did not read it or tell anyone about it. It was hard not to guess what the general shape of the changes might be, though I was surprised later to learn how radical it was. Then, looking back on how he always behaved, I think I understood it a little better."

"You sound like you approve of the changes."

"It was not for me to approve or disapprove, but if you mean did I think that the change would be healthy for Jim Lark Enterprises, the answer would obviously have to be yes."

"Ah?"

"No one was nearly so well qualified as Ms. MacDonaugh to oversee what Mr. MacDonaugh had built. She has the intelligence and the vision to adjust his work for the next generation."

"Together with Sean MacDonaugh?"

"As CEO of the enterprises. Mr. James Larkin Mac-Donaugh often remarked that the combination would be an excellent one. She would administer the foundation and he the company, though she would have total ownership."

"He remarked this to you?"

"Yes, sir."

"And to anyone else?"

"Not that I'm aware."

"You told anyone?"

"Of course not, sir."

A truly confidential secretary.

"It sounds like a recipe for conflict, if you ask me."

"Not given Ms. MacDonaugh's personality. 'She'll only intervene to stir up a little imagination,' he'd say."

"Would Sean MacDonaugh approve of this arrangement?"

"He refused several times to take on the responsibility as president of Jim Lark Enterprises unless his father removed himself by giving him a ten-year contract as CEO. He loved his father, but he had more sense than to try to work under him."

"Did you ever hear him explicitly discuss his relationship with Ms. MacDonaugh?"

"No, sir, but he seemed cordial with her."

"You judged that they would have worked well together?"

"They would have respected one another's responsibilities. I know of no reason for conflict between them. She had particularly cordial relations with Sean MacDonaugh's wife, Eileen."

"Besides the will, were there any indications that Jim Lark MacDonaugh was thinking of stepping down and turning over the administration of his affairs to the next generation, so to speak?"

O'Neill hesitated.

"The fact that the will had been changed made me sensitive to the issue, sir. Beyond that, it would be hard to say. . . . Mr. MacDonaugh was a very private man. For all his wit and charm, he was very hard to read. I believe that I was the only person whom he told that he was about to marry. He asked me what I thought of the idea. He didn't know I was gay then, but I suspect that it would not have mattered. I said that I thought he showed excellent judgment. Why he would ask me and no one else escaped me completely, and still does."

"What happened when he found out you were gay?"

"He fired me. Ms. MacDonaugh made him apologize and rehire me," he replied dispassionately. "Nothing changed in our relationship after that."

"Made him apologize?"

"She's a very strong-willed woman, sir. Much stronger than the late Mr. MacDonaugh. But his apology was genuine enough."

"Strong-willed yet fragile?"

"Oh, indeed, yes. Her experiences in life would have made her that. I had the impression that Mr. MacDonaugh found the combination appealing."

"You did, too?"

"Naturally."

"Did Mr. MacDonaugh and his son Sean argue?"

"Their relationship was friendly, sir. They disagreed on occasion, but then would laugh it off over a drink. It was hard to argue with Mr. MacDonaugh."

"How so?"

"He was elusive, Captain MacCarthy. Before you argue with a man, you have to be able to pin him down. Mr. MacDonaugh was impossible to pin down. I had the impression that he had no taste for direct personal conflict."

"What would Mr. Regan have thought of the new arrangement?"

"He would not have liked it, sir. He had known Sean MacDonaugh as a babe in arms and would have found it very hard to report to him. And he disliked Nora MacDonaugh."

"What would he have done?"

"He would probably have retired."

"That would have affected the company?"

"Not in the least. He was an anachronism and he was the only one who didn't understand that. Now he has more power than he ever did, because Ms. MacDonaugh has been reluctant to assert her authority as executor over him so long as she is under a cloud."

I paused. This intelligent young man seemed open and honest, though he was certainly loyal to Nora. He had every reason to be.

"Another pint?"

"Thank you, Captain MacCarthy. This is not an easy matter to discuss, as you might well imagine."

I collected the pint for him and a second Diet Pepsi for myself.

"Why the sudden family meeting?"

"I have no idea, sir. Mr. MacDonaugh merely came into my office and said that he and the wife would be flying over to Dublin that night and would stay at the house on Shrewsbury Road and that they'd be back in a couple of days and that he wanted to meet with his brothers and sister the next afternoon—that usually did not include his brother Charles because of the distance from Australia. I asked him if I should inform Charles, too, and he said that it was not necessary."

"Did you think then that he might be preparing to hand the reins of Jim Lark Enterprises to his son?"

He hesitated. "It's hard to sort out what I thought then and what I thought immediately after the . . . the event. As best as I can remember I made no particular estimate beforehand as to the reason of the meeting. Mr. MacDonaugh would cross the Atlantic as casually as we would cross the East River. Dublin and New York to him were as close as Dublin and Galway."

"There were never any ripples in his relationship with Ms. MacDonaugh?"

He permitted himself a smile. "If there were, Captain MacCarthy, they were quickly smoothed over. He adored her, he loved her, and he did what she told him to do."

Keep that in mind if you should think of marrying her, Timothy Patrick MacCarthy.

"Because he feared her?"

"Hardly. Because he knew she was almost always right."

"No decline in his affection and respect?"

"If anything, there was more of both the last time I saw him alive."

"Who do you think might have killed him?"

"I don't know that—"

"Come on, Martin. You must have an opinion. Everyone else does."

"I must admit," he began cautiously. "Well, sir, his brothers were a constant source of financial drain. Not large sums of money surely in relationship to his overall wealth, but nonetheless substantial amounts of money. They did not request help, they demanded it. And they never expressed gratitude for it. They acted as if he had caused whatever problem they had encountered and that he was therefore responsible for extracting them from the problem."

"They would not have fared well in the new order of things?"

"No, they would not. They still make demands on Ms.

MacDonaugh, as executor of his estate, though they are contesting the will. Under advice of counsel, she declines to respond."

"I should hope so. They would have the motivation to try to prevent a change of will?"

"I wouldn't attribute to them anything quite so rational, Captain MacCarthy. There is no telling what they might do if they were sufficiently angry. But this, I hardly need say, does not constitute proof."

I had about exhausted my questions. If this man were part of a murder plot, it would be very difficult to break through his smooth exterior of discretion and self-possession. Who would he plot with anyway? Nora? In theory perhaps, but hardly in practice.

"Ms. MacDonaugh did not know about the change in the will?"

He permitted himself a smile. "I rather think not. She would have vociferously disapproved."

"You admire her greatly, don't you, Martin?"

His smile widened. "I don't find her sexually attractive, Captain, except in the aesthetic sense. If I were straight, I'm sure I would. As it is, you can quote me as saying that regardless of sexual preference, I adore her."

"Like her husband you would not dream of disagreeing with her?"

"That's not true, sir," he said mildly. "You can win an argument with her, but you had better have good reasons and present them forcefully."

I wouldn't mind doing that, at all, at all.

I thanked him. We left the hotel together, he to return to the Berkeley Court next door and I to walk down Pembroke and Baggot streets back toward the Green. Big white clouds were rushing across the sky at a high altitude, and dirty gray ones, their unruly children, were scurrying beneath them. In America such a combination would mean rain. In Ireland, it might and then again it might not.

I walked back to Jury's on a hunch and turned my charm on a woman assistant manager, a petite and neatly shaped woman a few years younger than I was. She responded by turning her charm on me. She had more of it than I did.

Nonetheless she did lead me to her office behind the registration desk and offered me a cup of tea and some biscuits.

Naturally I accepted.

"Middle of January, is it, Captain MacCarthy?" She filled my teacup.

" 'Tis." I picked up a "biscuit" and began to nibble on it.

"You're working with the *garda*, are you?"

"In a manner of speaking."

"You won't get me in trouble for breaking the law?" Her impish blue eyes glittered.

"Would I be doing that, now?"

She wasn't wearing a wedding ring and she knew how to flirt. I told myself sternly that I was not interested.

"You just might. . . . Wait here a moment."

I decided that I was interested. I would have hardly noticed her appeal—or Nessa's out on the Military Road—if Nora had not sensitized me to womanly attractions again. Or so I explained my resurgent lust.

"Here's our ledger for those days." She returned, a prim frown on her face and laid it in front of me on her. "I don't want to be here when you examine it."

"Yes, ma'am."

When she had left the office and closed the door, I opened the ledger. Sure enough, a certain Charles Stewart from Melbourne, Australia, had registered on the fourteenth of January and departed on the sixteenth.

I closed the ledger. Why use such an obvious name? Or if you were just coming to a family meeting, why use any other name than your own?

The brothers were supposed to be too clever by half. Was this one more example of that trait?

I closed the ledger and opened the door of the office.

"Thank you very much," I said to the assistant manager.

"You found what you were looking for?" she asked anxiously.

"I did."

224 / Andrew M. Greeley

"You'll not tell."

"Not if you don't tell the guard that I was here first."

"Not a word." She winked. "Not a word."

"Would you be remembering a Mr. Charles Stewart who was registered here at that time?"

"Would I ever? And wasn't I wondering if he was the one you were looking for?"

"You can remember him after a year and a half?"

"Wasn't the kind of man you'd forget." She shivered. "A white-haired giant with a dangerous look about him. He frightened the poor housekeeping girls on the floor something awful. We all were very happy to see him leave."

"I can imagine."

"Where are you staying, Captain MacCarthy?"

"At the Shelbourne, God forgive me."

"We're much nicer."

"I won't dispute that."

"You'll stay with us next time, then?"

"You can count on it."

Trying not to think about Nora—and the magic that exploded when our lips touched—I dictated my report of the conversation with Martin O'Neill and my discovery at Jury's.

"I have the impression," I said as I crossed the Grand Canal, "that pieces are falling into place. Jim Lark was preparing for a changing of the guard, perhaps so that he could devote more time to his adored wife. Perhaps, too, he wanted to spend the rest of his life as a statesman working for peace in Ireland. Perhaps he was tired of the constant risk taking. Surely he must have been weary of his brothers and Arthur Regan. Here in Ireland, he was advising Paddy Quaid to have a run for the European Parliament, which meant being even less involved in the Irish interests of his empire. If I have any reading of the man, Clare McNulty must have set his teeth on edge. Get rid of the lot of them and let Sean deal with them. He'll be stricter than I am and good enough for them.

"As I say, that seems to be what was going on in his mind and the reason he called the meeting. Why so sudden? He was an impulsive man, at least in some respects. When he had finally made up his mind, he acted.

"But does this scenario offer us any explanation for his murder?

"I can't see that it does.

"I now suspect that Parny MacDonaugh is deeply involved. We won't be able to prove anything, but if I turn over my information from Australia to the *garda* or to Arthur T. Regan, who will pass it on to them, they'll have to reopen the case. I hesitate to do that because they'll probably want to go after Nora again. However, short of involving them and the Australian police I don't see how we can collect more evidence.

"Just the same, there are a lot of pointed questions someone must ask Parny."

18

"**T**IM MacCARTHY," I SAID AS I KNOCKED AT THE DOOR.
"Come in," said a woman's voice.

I entered the bishop's room. His nieces, in shorts and T-shirts proclaiming Bloomsday (with pictures of Leopold on the front and Molly on the back) were curled up, legs beneath them, on couch and on chair, poring over audits. Trish was wearing outsize granny glasses.

"We're reading audits for Uncle Punk," Brigid said, barely wasting a quick glance on me.

"You can wait for him to come back," Trish agreed. "If you have nothing else to do."

"I can't imagine waiting in more charming company." I took the remaining chair.

My compliment elicited a bare movement of two sets of young lips.

They were no longer two coordinated voices in a chorus. I now was able to distinguish between them. Trish, the half sister, was the dark one, a trifle less lush than her niece, and quieter and more thoughtful. Brigid, or Biddy, as Trish called her, the pale one, seemed devoid of inhibitions, possessed an outrageous sense of humor, and took the lead in conversations. However, she frequently turned to Trish for confirmation of her opinions, suggesting that she deferred to her aunt's superior wisdom or intelligence.

They had undoubtedly grown up together, knew each other's moves perfectly, and were well aware that they were a devastating combination.

It was pleasant enough to chat with these attractive young beauties, so long as you were on your toes for dialogue with them.

Biddy: Uncle Punk has this, like, group of friends who help him. He calls them the North Wabash Avenue Irregulars.

Trish: Like the Baker Street Irregulars, you know.

Me: I've read Sherlock Holmes.

Biddy: (laughing) So he goes, like, we're candidate members, which is neat because we're both accounting majors, so he's, like, would you find the holes in these audits?

Me: Accounting?

Trish: We're both going into the M.B.A. program at the University of Chicago in September. We want to be businesspersons.

Biddy: Who wants to be a lawyer, barf city. There are too many lawyers anyway.

Trish: Are you a lawyer, Tim Pat?

Me: Yes, went to night school.

Biddy: Did you pass the bar?

Me: Sure did.

Trish: Have you studied *everything* in night school?

Me: Just about. It's better than hanging around the singles bars.

Trish: Fersure.

Biddy: You have a date with Nora tonight?

Me: Can't keep a secret around this place, can you?

Biddy: Are you *dating* her, Tim Pat?

Me: One date does not dating make.

Trish: Would you like to be dating her?

Me: (guardedly) I might.

Biddy: Do you love her?

Me: As they say around here, it's early times.

They both seemed to accept that evasion.

Biddy: We think she likes you a real lot.

Me: I thought she had better taste.

Trish: You made the sadness go out of her eyes and put laughter there.

Me: Grave responsibility.

Biddy: We hope you'll be good to her.

Me: I'll try.

Trish: My brother says that you can tell whether you love someone as well as being in love, if your concern is more about the other than it is about yourself.

Me: A wise man, the good bishop.

Biddy: IF you, like, love her and IF you marry her and IF she comes to live in Chicago like she goes she might, would you buy a house in Grand Beach?

Me: A lot of hypothetical conditions in there, Biddy.

Trish: But . . .

Me: (sensing there is no escape) It would be an attractive possibility.

Biddy: Are you a typical Irish bachelor?

Me: That depends. I was almost married twice and they both called it off. So I don't know.

Trish: What happened?

Me: The last time I had the misfortune to be shot two days before the wedding.

Trish: Gross!

Me: Yeah, it was pretty tacky.

Biddy: And she wouldn't marry you?

Me: Would you marry a man who was so careless as to be shot in a convenience store two days before his marriage?

Biddy: If I loved him enough.

Me: Maybe she didn't love me enough.

Trish: Were you, like, a hero or something?

Me: An unmarried and hospitalized hero, if I really were one. You could make a case that I was showboating.

Biddy: You gotta tell us, you know, what happened!

Me: (with, I trust, becoming modesty) The alleged perpetrator, a white male about nineteen, entered a suburban convenience store and pulled a gun on the elderly man, Mr. Alonso DeCenzo, who owns the store. He demanded all the money in the till, a little less than twenty dollars, it later turned out. The subject then remarked that he was going to waste him. Captain MacCarthy, who was off duty and had previously entered the store to purchase a box of tea bags, then intervened and identified himself as a police officer and requested that the subject put down his gun. Captain MacCarthy then attempted to disarm the subject. In the ensuing struggle, Captain MacCarthy was critically wounded. However, he did succeed in disarming and apprehending the subject. Mr. DeCenzo summoned police officers from that jurisdiction.

Biddy: You sound just like the cops who say those things on television.

Me: Brigid, I *am* one of the cops who say those things on television. Or at least I used to be.

Trish: Drug addict?

Me: Yep, put on probation by the judge on the condition he seek treatment. He killed another convenience-store owner the following year.

Biddy: And she wouldn't marry you!

Me: Nope.

Trish: But he would have killed you, too.

Me: Undoubtedly. She said I should have drawn my own gun and killed him. Maybe she was right. She's a lawyer, by the way.

Biddy: (firmly) Nora would never do a thing like that!

Me: Arguably.

I was saved from further cross-examination by the arrival of the good bishop himself—in his Chicago Bulls windbreaker over a collarless clerical shirt—who, as he looked around his room, had the expression of someone who was sure he was in the wrong place.

"I'm being cross-examined about my intentions with regard to Ms. MacDonaugh," I informed him.

"The lamentable but incorrigible propensity of the gender to play matchmaker, especially prevalent in our ethnic group."

"Here's the tapes." I unwound my legs and rose from the chair. I felt my bones were creaking, either because I hadn't done my running or because his young relatives had made me feel so old.

"Ah."

"You'll find the one on Brendan very interesting. I'm going to check my room for faxes from America."

Biddy: Was he like totally cute, Tim Pat?

Me: Totally, Biddy. And dangerous as they come.

Trish: Like, you know, crazy?

Me: No, as sane as you and I. Maybe not as sane as your brother here. But caught up in a rigid view of the world that makes actions we'd think irrational seem the most sensible thing to do.

Trish: Will he ever get better?

Me: If he lives long enough, maybe.

Biddy: How long?

Me: Till he's thirty maybe.

Biddy: Will he?

Bishop Blackie: They rarely do.

Feeling chilled by that judgment, I slipped out of the counting room and went up to the next floor. I paused briefly at Nora's door, shrugged, and then went on to my own. The faxes I was expecting were there. Most interesting.

I called a doctor's office in New York. He was not in. Could I call back in an hour?

I called a second one. He was waiting for me.

"Oh, yes, Captain MacCarthy. Nora told me you'd be calling."

"I understand that you were prepared to testify back in the seventies about her first husband's mental condition."

"Indeed I was. As a matter of fact, I wrote out a statement at that time and had it notarized in case she ever needed it. I don't think she kept her copy, but I still have the original. I'd be happy to fax it to you."

"That would be a big help. Can you tell me roughly its contents?"

"Certainly. If I may say so, I'm surprised that law enforcement agencies have not asked me for it before."

"So am I."

"Briefly that I had been treating them for infertility problems, that her husband was virtually sterile because of low sperm count, that our attempts to facilitate conception had been unsuccessful, and that her husband, discouraged by our failures, had become temporarily impotent and terribly depressed. I add that, despite his success at the law and the happiness of his marriage, his self-esteem was not very robust and that his depression seemed to be approaching the pathological. Both Nora and I urged him to seek psychiatric help, but he resisted for fear of how his parents might react. Finally I note that on the last day of his life I felt that he had become suicidal. I called Nora repeatedly to share this fear with her, but she was in her car, coming home from school. By the time she answered the phone, he was already dead."

"Did you share this information with the police?"

"I was perfectly prepared to do so, but after she passed the lie-detector test, she said that my testimony was unnecessary. If the case had gone to trial, it would have been another matter, of course. But as it was, she wanted to protect her husband's reputation and his parents' peace of mind as best she could. When the matter was finally settled, I insisted on recording my testimony in writing in case the issue should ever arise again."

"Admirably succinct, Doctor."

"Thank you, Captain MacCarthy . . . I always thought that she deserved better in life. . . . Then she seemed so content with her second husband. It was a terrible tragedy to have lost him. She's a resilient person, God knows, but there is an upper limit to what resiliency can accomplish."

"I understand. If it's not out of line, she has always been capable of childbearing?"

"She told me to answer whatever questions you might ask. In response, yes, indeed, she is quite capable of bearing children. I'm not sure, however, that she would be willing to undertake a third marriage, but that is merely speculation."

"I see."

I thanked the doctor, sat on the edge of my bed, and pondered his responses. Nora had not killed her first husband. The doctor's testimony would have diminished speculations that she might have killed her second husband. It would not only impress a jury, it would persuade them that she was a gallant woman.

One who would play her high cards only when she had to.

It impressed me.

It was now my professional as well as personal opinion that she was innocent.

232 / Andrew M. Greeley

Good. I could enjoy our date tonight with a clear conscience.

Well, more or less clear.

I considered calling the other doctor, but reasoned that he
was probably not in his office yet.

I gathered together my faxes and left my room. Then, at
the head of the stairs, I remembered something and went back
to the room.

I heard my voice at the door to the good bishop's room. I
knocked.

No answer.

I knocked again louder. "Tim out here."

I thought I heard someone say, "Come in."

So I did.

The bishop turned off my description of my interview with
Brendan.

Biddy: *Cree-py!*

Trish: Poor dear man!

Bishop: Remarkable.

Me: Is he telling the truth?

Bishop: Arguably.

Biddy: Everyone has to be concerned about their image
these days, don't they, Trish?

Trish: Totally.

Me: (sitting on the edge of the bed, the only available
space) My sources from New York provide interesting information. First, Martin O'Neill is certainly gay. Second, Nora's
doctor wrote out an affidavit at the time of her first husband's
death which certainly confirms the suicide verdict. Thirdly,
Arthur T. Regan, for all his righteousness, has engaged in
heavy speculation in the stock market and has not done all
that well. He is not, however, in deep financial trouble and
his stock in Jim Lark Enterprises would keep him in the style
to which he has been accustomed for the rest of his life, but
without any margins around which to play.

Bishop: Not a successful speculator like yourself.

Biddy: Are you a trader, too? Is there anything you're not,
Tim Pat?

Me: Married ... The brothers are another matter. They have been in trouble as far back as records go. Jim Lark consistently bailed them out of their messes, but they are incorrigible. Currently Charles Parnell MacDonaugh is about to lose his sheep farm in West Australia, Liam Lynch MacDonaugh is faced with a severe judgment from an American tax court, and Michael Davitt MacDonaugh faces indictment in Britain for embezzlement. These are all troubles that have arisen since Jim Lark's death. He had picked up the pieces for them just before he died.

Bishop: Fascinating.

Me: They're trying to obtain loans on expectations of changing the will, without too much success so far. They want to settle now, take the money and run. The children want the will completely overturned and are prepared to fight.

Biddy: (as if she were already more than just a candidate for membership in the North Wabash Avenue Irregulars) Do any of them have financial troubles?

Me: It seems not. They all lead comfortable lives, well within their incomes.

Bishop: Fascinating.

Me: What did you think of my discoveries about Parny MacDonaugh?

Bishop: Admirable.

Me: Did he do it?

Bishop: He was up to no good when he was in Dublin, that much is certain.

Trish: He might have come to Dublin for the family meeting under an assumed name because he was afraid of his enemies in Australia and then left in a hurry because of his record as a bomber.

Me: (mildly upset that she had thought of that possibility when I had not) Arguably.

Bishop: We must investigate the matter further. He does make an attractive suspect, particularly if, ah, our information is leaked to the papers.

Me: I can take care of that.

Biddy: What do you have in those bottles?

Me: The materials for an Irish-cream taste test that herself asked me to administer. We need six glasses.

Trish provided them. I filled three with Baileys and three with Jim Lark Cream.

Solemnly my three colleagues sipped from them.

Biddy: That one's Baileys, isn't it, Trish?

Trish: Totally.

Bishop: Unarguably.

Me: And the other?

Biddy: Barf city!

Trish: Yuc-ky!

Bishop: Fascinating!

Me: Nora is so much in love with her husband's memory that she can't perceive that, not that it matters very much.

Bishop: (considering his glass) Fascinating!

Me: It's a phrase that they would use locally, so I'll use it: This stuff tastes like liquid shite!

(Young people giggle.)

Bishop: (continuing to stare at the glass) It must be acknowledged candidly that the Irish seem to have the dirtiest mouths in the world. On the other hand, it must be vigorously argued in their defense that their poetic use of scatology, obscenity, and blasphemy must not be held against them, because they don't mean anything by it.

Biddy: If you're going to do your running and get ready for your date with Nora, you'd better start now.

Me: Yes, ma'am. What kind of cologne should I wear?

Biddy: (feigning outrage) Really!

Bishop: (still examining his glass of Jim Lark Cream) Fascinating.

Exit me.

I did manage to run for a half hour and adequately shower before struggling into my black-tie regalia.

However, when I got out of the shower, I called the doctor in New York. He was in the office and would be happy to talk to me.

"I'm surprised no one asked me before," he said. "Jim Lark MacDonaugh had only about a year to live."

"What!"

"He was suffering from a rare form of untreatable carcinoma. I estimated eleven months of normal life and then a final month of rapid weakening, followed by a relatively painless death."

"I see. . . ." I shivered under my terrycloth robe. "How did he react?"

"The way one would expect from Jim Lark MacDonaugh. His jaw tightened for a moment and then he laughed and said something like, 'Well, I had a good run for it. I suppose I should tidy up the loose ends while there's still time.' "

"That's all."

"That's all. I presume that the malignancy would have appeared in the autopsy."

"There was not enough of him left for an autopsy."

"Oh."

"Could I trouble you to fax over a brief note repeating this."

"Not at all . . . I would have told the widow—wonderful woman, by the way, made an enormous difference in his life—but I presumed she knew."

I thanked him and buzzed the good bishop's room.

"I thought as much." He sighed.

"I'll have to tell Nora," I said, "but not right away."

"Capital," he agreed. "I will, ah, withhold the information from my romantic young assistants."

I continued to shiver.

19

"**I**'M READY IF YOU ARE." NORA KNOCKED LIGHTLY ON MY door.

"Tying me tie." I opened the door.

"My, you keep a neat room for a man. Here, let me do it for you."

She laid aside the trench coat she was carrying and put the finishing touches on my tie.

"There." She patted it in place.

"You look lovely." I kissed her forehead chastely. "Beautiful date."

"Thank you."

"Did you have that champagne sponged off your dinner jacket?"

"Yes, ma'am!"

I knew that I could not tell her about Jim Lark tonight. Perhaps not ever. Maybe I'd depute that task to the good bishop.

She was dressed in a black minidress, the sort you might wear to a cocktail party, with a thin strap around her neck, practically no back, and a neckline that plunged not quite as far as it might have—a concession to modesty, no doubt. Above her breasts rested a pendant with a single topaz. Her hair, restrained by a black band, fell down her naked back— silver on alabaster.

"Your hair is lovely," I said, knowing that such a compliment pleased a woman perhaps more than any other.

"Oh, thank you, Tim Pat." She blushed a little. "It's authentic, you know, touched up a little myself, but still essentially what it pretends to be. It'll turn white in four or five years."

"And you'll touch that up more than a little?"

"Certainly not!"

"Not a lot of fabric was wasted on that gown," I observed, holding her coat for her and kissing the back of her neck.

"Black tie means an excuse for women to look sexy," she said primly, as if she were perfectly within her rights to dress any way she wanted. "Wait till you see the other women."

"I can hardly wait."

"Don't stare at them. Let's walk over to Merrion Square. It's not raining yet and the house is just around the corner."

The other women at the dinner party were also lovely and well preserved and sexy. They were dressed much like my date. I felt that I was drifting into a harem, located, of all places, inside an elegantly restored Georgian house just down the street from where the Duke of Wellington was born. And a stone's throw away from the homes of Daniel O'Connell, William Butler Yeats, George Russell, and Sheridan Le Fanu.

That crowd covered just about everything Irish.

I reflected that even ladies of the evening in Dublin during the various times of those worthies probably wore a good deal more than these brilliant business and professional women.

So much the better for their dates and their spouses.

My Nora was the most glorious of them all.

And the brightest and the most witty during the sparkling conversation that began over cocktails, lasted through dinner, and then went on with scarcely diminished vigor through the rest of the evening.

I couldn't follow most of it because the talk was poetic and allusive, conveying much of what was being said with a wink, a shrug, an unfinished sentenced, a roll of the eyes. My date's Irish brogue became thicker as the evening wore on and I often understood only vaguely what she had said.

Nora continued to watch me closely, critical, amused, vulnerable, perhaps, heaven save me, adoring.

"Why don't you ask Captain MacCarthy about that?" she said at one point. "He's a retired police officer."

"Ah," said one of the men, a journalist, I think, "isn't that interesting, now?"

"Full colonel." Nora beamed proudly.

"I wore the eagle only once in my life," I said, waving a hand. But then, perhaps a bit too much of the drink taken and too much of the women admired, I launched into a discourse on my theories about the decriminalization of victimless crimes, theories that would have shocked my sometime colleagues on the CPD. For a few moments I was the center of attention, perhaps my allotted ration for the evening, carefully calculated in advance.

"Very interesting, Captain," said the journalist. "Very interesting indeed; you sound like you're an attorney, too."

"And a commodities trader," Nora added, her face flushed with approval.

So we talked about commodities and Ireland's great hope for its new financial services center on the north bank of the Liffey.

"So far," one of the women said, "all that has happened is that some of our businesspeople have lost their money."

There was general laughter around the table.

The conversation passed on to other subjects, and I wisely avoided bringing up either law enforcement or trading again. I also kept my mouth shut when they turned to Bloomsday and poked clever fun at the things the Yanks did on that day.

So I was very proud of myself when we left, after midnight, to walk back to the hotel. I was deflated immediately.

"You were terrible," she snapped at me. "I was ashamed of you."

"Really?" I gulped, feeling the same unease then as I did when I had offended my mother. "What did I do wrong?"

"You stared at me all evening long. You made me feel like I didn't have any clothes on at all."

"Well, you weren't wearing all that much. . . ."

"I don't consider this a matter for laughter."

Big chill.

"You said that I couldn't help myself."

"That was on the beach, not at a dinner party."

"You didn't seem angry at me during the dinner party."

"That was then. This is now."

"There was so much lovely womanhood. . . ."

"That's the whole point, you were supposed to stare, circumspectly of course, at all of us and not just at me."

"I should have shared the wealth."

"It is NOT funny."

"I can see that. . . . Anyway, you've been watching me for the last couple of days."

"I have NOT."

"Yes, you have. You forget I'm a cop and I notice small things in a woman. You were checking me out every minute."

"I was NOT checking you out."

"You admit you were staring at me, too."

"That was different."

"You were wondering what I'd be like in bed."

"I was NOT."

I know when there's no point in arguing with a woman. We walked back to the hotel in silence.

At the door to her room, I said, "Good night, Nora."

I did not try to kiss her good night.

"Good night, Tim Pat."

In my own room, I undressed and donned the wrinkle-free lounging robe I carry on airplane trips.

What the hell was wrong? It wasn't me, I was sure of that. Something was eating her; she was pushing me away because she didn't want my help.

I thought about it for a while and figured that it was none of my business. Time to go to bed. Right?

Instead I opened the door and peered down the darkened and silent corridor. The Bloomsday enthusiasts were either asleep or still out drinking. I tightened the belt on my robe.

Why the hell not?

I knocked lightly on the door.

"Yes."

"Tim."

The door opened instantly. "Thank God you came." She released the front of her satin robe, which she was holding together. "In another minute I would have come to you."

Under the robe she was wearing the assortment of lingerie

that enables a woman to appear in a frock like hers—a festival of delight for male fantasy.

All right, Leopold Bloom, we are the same gender.

"I'm so lonely, Tim Pat." She threw her arms around me. "So terrible lonely. And so sorry for being a bitch."

"I'm terrible lonely, too, Nora Marie."

"Isn't it awful to come into a hotel room and know that you're the only one that's going to be in it?"

"Hotel rooms are the loneliest places in the world."

We clung to one another like the two pilgrims we were, lost in the darkness and passing each other in the storm.

Finally, aware that we were both on fire with need, I pushed the robe off her shoulders and undressed her, my fingers anxious and clumsy.

We both giggled.

"Ah, you haven't struggled with this lot for a while," she murmured.

" 'Tis the woman that makes me anxious, not the hooks."

"You'll get no help from me."

"I want none."

We continued to giggle, exorcising our fear by choked laughter.

She was passive while I worked slowly and gently at my delicious work, her head bowed shyly and turned to one side, her face pink, her body submissive.

"You enjoy my undressing you," I argued.

"Do I ever!"

"I'll do it permanently on a contract basis."

"Oh, Tim Pat." She sighed as I finished. "You're driving me out of my mind."

"That's the general idea."

"You're so different from the others," she moaned. "I knew you would be."

Those words, as I removed my own clothes, changed it all.

The other men in her life, I realized dimly, had used her, not indeed contemptuously, but needing her to struggle out of their own problems. Now she should encounter a man whose concern was her and not himself.

My desire was furious. I had been celibate for too long, longer than she surely. But I focused my hunger into the service of my love for her. I must do everything for her comfort, her reassurance, her joy. I was destined to heal her loneliness, if only for a few transient moments.

Afterward, in reflection, I understood that is what I was about. Then it was pure instinct.

At first her eyes showed surprise and then fear. Then everything else inside her dissolved into joy and her eyes widened in pleasure.

I don't flatter myself that I am a particularly sensational lover. But for Nora that night I was more than just competent.

She was my concern, my only concern, my total concern. Then, recalling Trish's quote of the good bishop, I realized that I loved Nora and told her so, repeatedly as I led her, hand in hand, up the mountain of pleasure.

When finally we were finished and she lay against me, her head on my chest, her breasts on my belly, she said, "Don't you take everything that a woman has away from her and then give it back again all shining in exuberant glory like a great garden after a rainstorm?"

"Do I?"

" 'Tis a metaphor, eejit, but it's how you make me feel."

"For the record, my love, at my age in life I'm not into one-night stands or mistresses."

"Um." She sighed and cuddled closer.

"When this case is resolved, I have every intention of dragging you toward a marriage bed."

"No," she muttered sleepily.

"Don't go to sleep on me," I said, reaching for her loins. "I'm not finished with you yet, not at all, at all."

"How wonderful."

The sun was well up in the sky before I was finished.

I eased out of our bed carefully so as not to awaken my beloved and crept back to my own room. I must not miss my morning appointment with the MacDonaugh children.

20

I ATE A ROLL AND DRANK A CUP OF COFFEE IN THE COFFEE SHOP of the hotel. I glanced in the restaurant and saw Nora and the two young Ryan women. She seemed radiantly happy, happier than one could account for by the headlines about Parnell MacDonaugh's secret trip to Dublin at the time of his brother's death.

No shower after lovemaking? Or maybe a very quick one so she could keep a breakfast date.

"I'm off to Meath," I said.

"Hurry back," she said with an enigmatic smile.

Would she tell her young friends what had happened? Not likely. Would they guess? They might suspect, but they wouldn't know for sure. Good enough for them.

Then, as I was waiting for the doorman to bring my car, she caught up with me under the marquee.

"It was wonderful last night, Tim Pat." She took my arm. "But we must not do it again. We'll only end up hurting one another."

"I don't think so."

"I know so. Please don't ask again. I know I'll not be able to say no and then we'll truly make each other unhappy."

"If that's what you want . . ."

"It is, Tim Pat." All the sadness was back in her eyes. "It is. Promise you won't ask?"

"Whatever you want, Nora. Of course, I promise."

What had happened between her smile at breakfast and that moment, a space of only two or three minutes?

She probably remembered all the tragedy.

Well, we'll have to take care of that somehow or other.

County Meath is the heart of Ireland's dairy industry. The countryside and the farms look like Wisconsin. I paid little attention to the scenery because I was preoccupied with Nora, the woman who would *not* get away from me, whatever I might have promised her in front of the Shelbourne.

What would the children of Jim Lark MacDonaugh think if they knew that the highly recommended cop with whom they were about to meet had engaged in such behavior the night before with their stepmother?

They probably would be confirmed in their opinion of her and distrust the cop.

But they could not know how lonely their stepmother was, could they?

If they did, I reflected sadly, they could not have cared less.

Ms. Moire MacSweeney decided that I was irresistibly attractive. A bright-eyed and lively redhead of perhaps sixteen—months, that is—she squealed with joy as soon as I entered the room and held out arms to be picked up as soon as I cooed at her.

"The child is a terrible flirt altogether," her father, Cormac MacSweeney, said proudly, "just like her mother."

"Cormac!" His wife, who shared color and liveliness with her daughter, protested. "Won't Captain MacCarthy will be thinking I'm a terrible woman?"

"Not very likely." Her husband, a tall thin man with unruly brown hair and a wondrous Irish freckled face, laughed easily.

We were in the drawing room of the MacSweeney house in County Meath, a big and elegant, if rambling, country house. The trim lawns, carefully painted white paddock fences, busy trainers, and beautiful horses left little doubt that the MacSweeneys were affluent and successful horse breeders and trainers.

Agnes was perhaps twenty-seven or twenty-eight, her brother Dermot, the psychiatrist, maybe four or five years older, and Sean, the oldest, about the same number of years older than Dermot. Agnes was a short but generously constructed and vivacious redhead, a diminutive womanly clone of Jim Lark. Dermot, medium in height and stocky, was dark, wore rimless glasses, and stroked his thick beard periodically.

Sean was a couple inches shorter than me, slender, with a quick winning smile and determined blue eyes. He would, I figured, be a good man to work for until you betrayed his trust. The wives of the two men were more than presentable suburban matrons who listened attentively to our conversation with intelligent eyes that would miss nothing.

The three children were more American than Irish, except perhaps Aggie, who was readjusting to the speech patterns and the manners of the country of her birth.

M'lady Moire was the only child present.

Reluctantly I returned her to her mother, with whom she seemed perfectly content.

"Jim Lark would have been proud of her," Sean said easily. "Too bad he could not have lived to see her."

I calculated quickly in my head the numbers. Perhaps he would have seen her briefly in the hospital before he died.

"He knows about her, dear," said his wife.

"Indeed he does," Dermot agreed, "but we still must see that those responsible for taking away his life are punished, must we not, Captain MacCarthy?"

It was the signal to begin our serious conversation.

"You are making progress, are you not, Captain Mac-Carthy?" Sean considered me carefully.

"It was a crime which was committed eighteen months ago," I cautioned him, "and the trails are cold. I think certain patterns are emerging and that we may know shortly. But as I told Mr. Regan at the beginning of my investigation, I am not in a position to make any promises."

"We're angry, Captain." Sean's lean face was grim, resolute. "We are determined that woman will not profit from our father's death, no matter how long it takes, come what may."

"I can only agree," Dermot added. "Our father was a remarkable man. Like all children, particularly like all sons, we had an ambivalent relationship with him. But we respected and admired him. We enjoyed being with him. We do not intend to let someone snatch him away from us out of due season."

Even the buoyant Agnes was somber. "At first, we didn't

like her, then we trusted her, and even loved her. Now we all hate her. We want to see her punished for what she did."

"Our kids," Dermot's wife intervened, "were calling her Nana Nora. They're devastated that she killed Da."

The Irish are good haters, and this tight little band of survivors was determined to hate.

I had expected from previous testimony that the MacDonaugh children would be relaxed and likable young people. Perhaps they were sometimes, but certainly not this morning. There were depths of intensity and anger inside them that I would not have wanted to face.

Might that rage turn on a father who they thought was betraying them?

Why would that happen? Apparently they were all in reasonably good financial condition. But as I had said to Nora a couple of days before, you never have enough money. They were Dora's children as well as Jim Lark's. The two men resembled Dora more than they did their father. Might they have been on her side in family spats? Might they have thought he desecrated her memory by remarrying, especially the sort of woman he had chosen for his second wife?

Might they have felt that their mother was in great part responsible for Jim Lark's success? Might they have tried to save what they thought was properly her money from another woman's greed? Might they have tried to prevent a change in the will, if they knew one was coming?

They were in America, all except Aggie, when Jim Lark died. But Aggie's husband would know the criminal element in Irish society; horse breeders always did. Could they have arranged things from a safe distance and with perfect alibis?

Unlikely, but if they had, we would never find out unless we could discover someone in the criminal community who would talk. Presumably Tomás Clarke had already searched.

The only justification for these thoughts that raced quickly through my head was the intensity of their hatred for Nora, as if they wanted to convince me by the depths of their feelings toward her that she had to be guilty.

It was, I thought, just a little too much.

I upgraded their position on my list of suspects.

"I'm trying to reconstruct what went on a year and a half ago. I hope you don't mind if I ask you a few questions."

"Not at all," Sean agreed. "Anything which will help convict that woman we will be happy to do."

The way he said "woman" made it sound a worse appellation than did "bitch" or "bimbo" or "slut"—three words I had heard others use of Nora. To say nothing of "Miss Yo-Yo Pants."

"Did you have any suspicion that your father might change his will?"

"Not at all." Sean was to be the spokesman for the others. "We all had a long talk with him after the marriage—at his invitation, I might add. He could see that we had our . . . reservations. He assured us that he had taken the initiative, that she wasn't interested in his money, and that he would never change his will."

"Did you believe him?"

Dermot intervened. "The myth of the rich elderly man and the attractive young woman can be found in most cultures, Captain MacCarthy, precisely because it represents a phenomenon that is part of the human condition. One thinks of David admiring a naked Bathsheba from his rooftop. One realizes, of course, that it was no accident that Bathsheba was bathing on a roof where the king could see her."

"To be less mythical"—Sean picked up the conversation—"we didn't believe him. Or rather we believed that he was speaking the truth as he saw it, but we believed that he had been deceived. Now"—he grimaced bitterly—"we realize that we permitted ourselves to be deceived, too."

"He explicitly promised that he would not change his will?" I asked.

"If you had known my father," Sean replied, "you would know that he was a master of the Irish style of indirection—"

"Even fooled me sometimes," Cormac MacSweeney interrupted. "A cute man he was."

I sensed that the good-natured horse breeder had no taste for all the hatred.

"No small feat that, Cormac." Sean smiled briefly. "So he never said anything that you could later quote against him. As I recall, he said, 'Nothing will change in the financial area.' I'll admit that could mean anything."

"We were all taken in," Aggie protested, her green eyes flashing, "completely. She seemed so nice and Da was so happy with her that we began to figure that we were being old-fashioned and that we shouldn't begrudge him his pleasure."

"We feel guilty," Dermot continued, "because if we had been more alert, he might still be with us today."

Not a chance of that, I thought, but now is hardly the time to tell you.

"Do you have any idea of the reason for the meeting here in Dublin that day in January a year and a half ago?"

"None," Sean responded. "None at all. We didn't even know that he had flown across. We learned that he was out of the country only ... only when Arthur T. Regan called to tell us he was dead."

"Was that unusual?"

"Not to know he was traveling? He boarded a jet as casually as we would board the commuter train. He would tell us about such a trip only when it involved something we should know."

"It has been suggested that he wanted to make you the CEO of Jim Lark Enterprises."

"I know it has." Sean spat out the words. "But only by that woman. She would try to persuade us—through her lawyer because we will not speak to her—that he wanted the money to go to the foundation and me to become the head of the company on a long-term basis. But that is not in the will, Captain MacCarthy. We are mentioned only to be praised and to be given Polonius-like advice."

"One theory is that the purpose of the meeting was to tell the older members of the family that you were to succeed him as CEO."

"I know of no reason to think that."

"He never discussed that with you?"

"Captain MacCarthy, he talked about it every time we met, normally in the allusive fashion I have described. 'Why don't I slow down a bit, Seano, and let you run the damn show for me? Isn't it time for me to enjoy life a bit more?' "

"And you'd say?"

"I'd say that the day he would slow down would be a day we'd never see. Perhaps he'd get sentimental and say that after he was gone and I'd say that he'd outlive the lot of us."

"You didn't take his offers seriously?"

Sean MacDonaugh paused and drew a deep breath. "You could never be sure when he was serious and when he wasn't. I said to him a couple of times that I'd gladly take over Jim Lark Enterprises when he would give me a ten-year contract with complete control over the operation of the company. He'd laugh and say that was the kind of answer that he'd expect from a son of his. And that was that."

"You sound like you were a little exasperated by it all."

"You have to understand, Captain MacCarthy," Dermot endeavored to explain, "that his word games were both endearing and frustrating. We learned not to take him seriously until it was clear that he meant to be taken seriously. We became accustomed to the games, but I think I speak for my brother and sister when I say that we all found it tiring on occasion."

"And hilarious on other occasions." Sean took up his narrative. "That was the nature of the man. . . . I loved him too much, as I told him often, to work for him."

"Did he like that?"

"He loved it, poor man."

"So you had no expectation of someday standing in his shoes."

"I couldn't if I wanted to. And I wasn't sure I wanted to. I like my own job. It has a bright future. I wasn't sure that I would give it up even if there were an opportunity."

Yes, you would, I thought, you're his son after all.

"We all feel terrible, Captain MacCarthy," Aggie said. "We think we might have been able to stop it. We had the evidence that she killed her first husband. We gave it to him and he just laughed it off. Said he knew all about it. Maybe we should have pushed harder."

"That's our problem," Dermot agreed. "A problem I know all too well from my own profession. Guilt over death of a father and fear that we might have carelessly betrayed him."

" 'Im," said Ms. Moire, weary of not being the center of attention. She pointed at me. " 'Im."

She slipped out of her mother's arms and toddled in my direction.

"That's right, me dear," I said, lifting her up in the air. "I'm Tim."

" 'Im," she insisted.

I sang her one of the Irish-language lullabies my mother sang to us and my sisters sing to their kids. I had no idea what the words meant.

" 'Im." Moire laughed happily.

Her parents and uncles and aunts applauded enthusiastically.

And so the circle of hatred was broken temporarily.

On the way back to Dublin, I thought that the younger MacDonaughs were fierce people, worthy of their heritage and with not a little bit of Julia and the brothers in their souls. Oh, indeed, they were modern young people, well educated, and moderately sophisticated. But their fury was only a generation from the rocky soil of the West of Ireland. Were they capable of murder?

As capable as the brothers might be?

I couldn't say no.

And I didn't believe that in two years they had begun to warm to Nora. They had come to like her a little perhaps and to enjoy her grace, but the suspicions must have remained, deep and perhaps permanent.

Nora was too smart and too sensitive a person not to realize that. She must have been afraid every time she was with them.

In other circumstances they might be the pleasant young people of their reputation. When it came to the tight bonds of mother, father, and self, they were deep and potentially dangerous.

Their dislike of the woman who had replaced their late mother in her marriage bed was—or at least could be—explosive.

I drove back to Dublin with the deepest sense of foreboding that I had yet experienced during my investigation.

If I was forced to choose, I'd be more afraid of Sean MacDonaugh's anger than that of Brendan and the lads.

There were no faxes or messages in my box. I left the tape I had dictated while I drove back with one hand in the good bishop's box.

I also filched the extra key to Nora's room while the hall porter was busy ticketing some bags. Never tell when I might need to have it.

Right?

I paused at the door of her room on the way to my own. I heard the shower. I wouldn't bother her now.

I walked away a few steps, thought about it, and concluded that it would indeed be appropriate to bother her.

I opened the door and stole quietly into the room. Through the window the Dublin Mountains lurked in the distance, seemingly not displeased by what I was about.

The shower was still running. Her lingerie was stacked neatly on a chair. The woman was a good housekeeper.

Was I really going to do this?

I thought about beating a silent retreat.

Then I realized that opportunities like this don't come too often in life.

She won't mind.

Are you sure?

Pretty sure.

She'll be delighted.

You might be wrong.

I might at that.

Well.

Now or never.

So?

Now.

Put out a Do Not Disturb sign, eejit.

Oh, yeah.

And lock the door.

Yeah, I thought of *that*.

Taking a very deep breath, I pushed open the bathroom door and shoved aside the shower curtain.

She was holding a bar of soap and was most becomingly clad in suds. Her silver hair was piled tightly on the top of her head.

"You!"

" 'Tis."

"What are you doing here?"

She backed up against the wall in a defensive posture, but she did not try to cover herself. That would be graceless, and even offended, Nora would not be graceless.

"Catching you in your shower."

"That's obvious. Where did you get the key?" She edged along the wall, soap bar still in her hand, uneasy about the situation, but not ready yet to denounce it.

I knew I'd won.

"I stole it from the hall porter."

"Why?" She was leaning in the direction of fury, but not sure that she wanted to go that way just yet.

"In case"—I captured her and lifted her out of the tub —"I wanted a ride on the odd occasion."

She squirmed in my arms. "Won't you get your suit all wet?"

She was so very light and so very frail. I imagined the terrible hatred she must have experienced in her husband's family. I loved her very much.

"A ride, is it?" she protested. "Put me down this minute."

I then explained in the graphic terms of Dublin slang what I meant.

She giggled. "You learn the words quickly enough." She continued to squirm. "But this violates me privacy."

"Does it, now?" I slung her over my shoulder and carried her into the bedroom.

"Put me down!" she exclaimed, not loudly enough to be heard in the corridor, and pounded my back, not hard enough to impede my progress.

" 'Tis a ride I'm wanting and won't it be a ride I'm getting?"

"Don't be vulgar. . . . Oh, now you'll be soaking the whole bed. What will the maid be thinking?"

"Won't she be thinking that someone dragged herself out of the shower and had a good ride on the spread with her?"

I unloaded her from my shoulder and laid her gently on the bed. She was laughing now and her body was already twisting slightly in preparation for love.

"Do you do this to all your women?" She watched as I undressed, her eyes round and soft with desire. I felt the last shreds of inhibition slough away from me.

"Nope. First one . . . Anyone ever do it to you?"

"Never before." She sighed. "It's . . . kind of an interesting experience."

"You'd better get used to it."

"Turn off the shower, please." She giggled. "I don't want to flood the hotel and bring the management up here."

"Good idea."

I did just that.

When I returned, I paused and stared down at her.

"What are you looking at, eejit?" she demanded, her face crimson with a mix of pleasure and embarrassment, her limbs spread out in invitation and demand.

"Wasn't I thinking of John Updike's line about the naked body of a woman being the most beautiful thing a man is likely to see in the course of his life?"

"What a nice thing to say." She smiled contentedly and then she held out her arms to me and drew me onto her body.

Once again she was my concern. Once again I told her often how much I loved her. She did not question my assertions. But she did not respond to them.

Her body, however, did respond to mine, and then, with practiced and yet uninhibited ecstasy, she took command of our joint enterprise. She was much better than I at the art and craft of love, an accomplished performer who knew all the appropriate and carefully timed movements to enhance her pleasure and that of her lover. I had no choice but to react to her subtle and ardent invitations. I realized with a mix of inferiority and delight that she would always be better at the "ride" than I was. Her slender, sinuous body led mine in a skilled ballet of pleasure, a stylish dance of passion I would not have thought possible between a man and a woman save in my feverish fantasies. At the time I counted her superiority in the wanton waltz of our bodies joining and joined and unjoined and then joining again as pure grace. Only later did I wonder how she could have attained such proficiency.

"Would you be enjoying your little ride, Timothy Patrick MacCarthy?" she taunted me.

I tried to say that it would do till a better one came along, but my words were unintelligible. We laughed together, even our amazement now synchronized.

Everything will be all right now, I told myself when we had finished and I lay cuddled in her arms, my cheek against her breast—an affectionately indulged boy child. Everything will be all right.

I could not have been more wrong.

21

BLOOMSDAY WAS WEDNESDAY.

"It is necessary," Bishop Blackie told me when I en-countered him after my early-morning run, "to observe at least some of the rituals. I think that tomorrow we can con-clude this whole unfortunate matter with some ease."

"Parny?"

"Perhaps. I note with interest that the Dublin police report, however belatedly, that they are in contact with the police in Australia. I think we can count on them to be more careful this time."

"You listened to my tape about the conversations up in Louth."

"Indeed yes. Fascinating."

"Anything else to be covered?"

"I rather think not."

"What should I do today?"

He blinked at me and lifted a shoulder. "Amuse yourself in some innocent fashion. Doubtless we will see you and per-haps the enjoyable Nora at supper."

"She has some sort of meeting with someone today."

"So I am told."

What did he mean by that? Did he know about my something-less-than-innocent amusements the day before?

Who knows?

Who cares? I'm going to marry her and that's settled, even if she hasn't admitted it yet.

After our "ride" on Nora's spread, we both had dressed (in our own rooms), Nora in a belted and buttoned pastel dress and I in my best sport coat, and gone off to White's on the Green for supper.

" 'Tis said that the salmon here is grand," she had mused at the table, putting her rarely seen reading glasses back into her purse. "And haven't I the terrible hunger and thirst on me?"

"I wonder why."

She had looked around at the other diners anxiously. "Do I look like a woman who . . . who's just been doing what I've just been doing? Or"—she giggled—"had done to me what's just been done to me?"

"Woman, you do."

"Glory be to God." She had glanced around again over her tumbler of Bushmills. "What will they be thinking?"

"That I'm a lucky man."

She had touched my fingers. "No, darlin' boy, that I'm a lucky woman to have such a strong, handsome man."

I had eaten too much, including the sherry trifle, and drunk too much.

"Is the lust all gone from you now?" she had demanded as we walked back across the Green, arm in arm. "Has the drink destroyed it altogether?"

"Not if you don't want it to be destroyed altogether."

She had squeezed my arm. "Not at all, at all."

Then we had gone to my room, for variety's sake, she said, and frolicked most of the night.

At five o'clock, I had helped her dress and opened the door for her to sneak back to her room. "Sure, I've to meet a poor fella at half ten." She bussed my lips affectionately. "I'll see you before the day is over, darlin' boy."

I should run, I had decided, before I encountered Bishop Blackie on his way to observe some of the rituals.

I went back to my room, sad and worried. Too much sex, I told myself.

Yet I was afraid that I might somehow lose her.

I slept till early afternoon. Then I woke up feeling lethargic and dull.

I might just as well observe some of the rituals myself.

I ate a quick sandwich sent up from room service and left the hotel. I walked down Dawson Street and around Trinity, with a wink in the general direction of Molly Malone, whose mostly uncovered breasts were not unlike my love's.

I passed the Bank of Ireland, the building where the Ascendancy Parliament of Grattan met, and continued down Westmoreland Street toward the river and crossed the Liffey on the O'Connell Street Bridge, from which, in an earlier time, prisoners from the 1798 Rising were hung.

Too much history, as the good bishop had said.

In Joyce's day, I remembered, it was already called O'Connell Street by act of the Dublin Corporation—and he so called it—but it was only twenty years later when the Brits were gone that it officially stopped being Sackville Street and the signs were changed.

I walked up O'Connell Street, by the Gresham Hotel, and searched the north side of it from Cathal Brugha Street for the room of the last scene in "The Dead." Gabriel Conroy not unreasonably might have expected a little romance with his wife in a hotel room on a cold Dublin night. Instead he discovered that Gretta remembered an earlier and more rapturous love from which her lover had died of a broken heart (as had one of Nora Barnacle's young lovers). I imagined Gabriel looking out of one of those windows at the snow falling on the living and the dead.

I shivered.

I thought I had picked out the right window in the hotel, not that it mattered much because the Gresham had been destroyed in the first battle of the Irish Civil War (in which Cathal Brugha had died) and the present building was a reconstruction.

Besides, there was nothing to shiver about. Joyce believed that the dead were close to us and we to them, an ancient Irish notion encoded in the Catholic idea of the "Communion of Saints."

I continued east on Cathal Brugha Street and into Sean MacDermott Street. This part of Dublin—east of the Pro-Cathedral—is the area about which Sean O'Casey wrote in *The Plough and the Stars* and *Shadow of a Gunman* and his own memoirs—the poorest part of the city in those days, old Georgian homes subdivided into tiny slum apartments. Most of the buildings are torn down now, replaced by the Department of Education and car parks (parking lots to us Yanks), but it is still a gloomy and threatening area. Beggars, homeless people, and drunks appear frequently to torment the Yank's conscience and pocketbook.

Just south of this district was "Nighttown." ("Monto," the locals called it at the time, after Montgomery Street), the redlight district in which Mr. Bloom had taken charge of Stephen Dedalus and led him to safety on his trip home to Ithaca and Penelope (Eccles Street and Molly). The houses of prostitution had been torn down by the Free State government in the 1920s after the British garrison—the reason for a red-light district—had departed. The ugly public-housing projects that had replaced it didn't look like the kind of neighborhood a smart cop would want to walk through at night.

I walked up Gardiner Street, following the path of Bloom and Dedalus, across Mountjoy Square and by George's Church (whose bell Molly would hear later that night) to Eccles Street. Some of the old Georgian houses in the area had been abandoned, others were being rebuilt, and still others served as bicycle shops, Sinn Fein (IRA) bookstores, Catholic mission societies, and offices for oral surgeons. And pubs, pubs without numbers, pubs that made even the most gloomy street look lively, pubs that were less for drink than for play.

If Bloom's house at number seven had not been torn down to make room for a hospital, it might have been gentrified before the century was over, maybe even be a home to an advertising executive.

Three Japanese men, cameras around their necks, were studying maps, obviously puzzled.

"Where is number seven?" One bowed politely to me.

Not to disappoint them, I put on my phony Irish brogue. "Didn't they tear it down, now, to make room for Mater Hospital across the way?"

"So sad."

"Great Tragedy."

"Terrible waste."

" 'Tis." I sighed loudly. "But sure didn't they need a hospital?"

"As long as English is read"—one of them nodded gravely—"men and women will come to see number seven."

"Well, you go over to Duke Street and they have the door over in the Bailey Restaurant on Duke Street, and if enough tourists come, they might just rebuild the house, especially if you folks will give them the money. Number seventy-seven right here is supposed to be pretty much like old number seven."

The Japanese nodded politely, utterly baffled at the defilement of Eccles Street.

"Actually number seven was the home of J. F. Byrne—Cranley in *Portrait*—Joyce's most loyal friend. He stood by him through bad times and good and refuted the calumny that Nora had been unfaithful to him."

The three Asians nodded again, too polite perhaps to tell me that everyone knew *that*.

For a moment I knew who the killer was. I saw a face and the face made sense.

Then I lost it.

Knowing I'd remember it before the end of the day, I wandered aimlessly around some of the other markers on Leopold Bloom's trail through Dublin, encountering eager Yanks, intense Japanese, and courteous micks at every spot, the latter not too openly laughing up their sleeves at the first two groups. I passed the Wollen Mills store at the foot of the ha-'penny bridge and pondered the "hags with the bags" sculpture. Actually the Dubliners were inaccurate on this title. The women were not hags; and neither were the two young women, made of flesh and not of stone, sitting on the bench with them.

Nice touch.

Most of the buildings between the Mills and O'Connell Street were abandoned, prime property I would have thought. All Dublin needed to be an utterly charming city was a lot of prosperity. And, arguably, a hell of a big roof.

I recrossed the river on the Butt Bridge, just as Mr. Bloom

had done and walked along Sir John Rogerson Quay in his footsteps though much later in the day. The Liffey seemed dark and unhappy on its "riverrun" toward the sea and a new beginning. Was the Liffey as black as Guinness stout, I wondered, or was the appropriate comparison the reverse?

I cut back to Westland Row and walked under the railroad overpass again, this time in the same direction Bloom had walked.

I stopped at Sweny's Pharmacy, 4 Lincoln Place, at the bottom of Westmoreland Row, to buy a bar of lemon soap for my Molly Bloom.

A sign over the door informed the world that M. F. Quinn, MPSI, was the proprietor. Chemist's shops seldom move, as Bloom had said.

The shop, now forever immortal, was tiny, all brown-wood-and-glass cases. A carton of Brownley's Lemon Soap, wrapped in a tissue with green lines outlining lemons, was prominently displayed on the counter, under a protective glass cover.

"Big business in it today," the woman said to me.

"I can well imagine."

"Smells as nice as it did then," she said, as she popped the bar into a bag with a drawing of Sweny Chemist Shop.

I wondered how she knew how well it smelled then.

I put my change in a box for the Capuchin missions.

"God bless," she said.

"I need it," I agreed.

Out of regard for Mr. Bloom, I put the package in my hip pocket.

I walked along the edge of Merrion Square, with the National Gallery and the back of the Irish Parliament building on my right. Here was the spot that Bold Jimmy Joyce met Nora Barnacle on their first date, June 16, 1904. According to the story, she brought him to orgasm that first night. Not a shy or prudish young woman, to say the least. Three months later they fled Ireland—they were kids, he twenty-two and she twenty. It was a measure of his love for her that he chose that date for his story of Leopold and Molly Bloom and

Stephen Dedalus. They walked out to Ringsend Park on the banks of the Liffey, where he wondered whether he would ever find anyone to understand him, the words that Anna Livia Plurabelle, who was also Nora, utters as she flows into the ocean at the end of *Finnegan's Wake* to be reborn again at the beginning.

How he must have loved her. She was in all his books and at the end of all of them except *Portrait*—and there the reference to the "seabird" girl whose appearance on the strand at Clontarf changes Stephen's life is a reference to Nora, whose last name meant "seabird."

Quite a woman.

Could my own Nora have a similar impact on my life?

Well, I was not a Bold Jimmy Joyce, was I, now? And I was a good focking yabo to think of the comparison, wasn't I?

I walked by the restored government buildings on the bottom of Merrion Street, already illuminated by bright lights (and called by Dubliners the Chas Mahal after Charles Haughey, the prime minister (*taoiseach*) responsible for the display). Then, eager to see Nora again and to give her the lemon-scented soap, I turned toward the Shelbourne on Merrion Row and hastened by the old and slightly spooky Huguenot Cemetery. It was between six and seven, a mist was blowing in from the sea, and a fine "soft" rain was falling.

I came to a sudden, anxious halt. A large crowd of people gathered in front of the Shelbourne. As I hurried, heart pounding anxiously, to see what had happened, I realized that the crowd was largely staff and guests.

"What happened?" I asked a young woman in a maid's uniform.

"Isn't there a bomb inside?"

"A bomb! Where?"

"Aren't they saying it's in Room 309?"

My room!

22

"**W**ELL, WE FINALLY GOT MISS YO-YO PANTS THIS TIME." Tomás Clarke chuckled. "Dead to rights; the transmitter in her purse and the bomb in your room, under your bed, right where she put it. Just like the one that tore Jim Lark apart. It would have blown you all the way to hell and back and most of the people in the hotel, too. And no trace of who did it."

So she was the killer after all. Bishop Blackie had been wrong.

"How did you know about it?" I asked dully.

We were standing inside the Green, behind the "Wolfhenge" and shielded from the hotel across the street. The chief superintendent was having "a brief word" with me.

"Information received, boyo," he chortled. "Information received."

"A passing signal from a car phone could have detonated it," I murmured.

"Too true. We risked the lives of two of the best in the army bomb disposal squad to defuse it. Carry that thing out into the street and it could have killed as many people as an IRA car bomb."

"Yeah ... easy to defuse?"

"A piece of cake, my lads say. It wasn't intended to fool anyone. Just to send you to kingdom come. You must have really had the goods on her."

"No."

"We'll be wanting a statement from you about what you have, me lad."

"Nothing."

"Come on now, lad. You've no choice but to cooperate or we'll hold you, too."

"Where is she?"

"We've got her over on Harcourt Street. We'll move her to the Bridewell in an hour or two and she'll start to talk over there, unless I miss my guess. She turned hysterical when we arrested her, but we'll get it out of her before the night is over, no doubt about that."

A plant, I told myself, it was a plant. Why didn't I think of that instantly?

"Can I see her?"

"Can't do that, me boy. She's all ours till we get it out of her. Come along now."

No cop in his right mind would not suspect a plant.

He put his arm on mine. I shook it off.

"If we have to arrest you, we will, you know. What's the matter, you been riding Miss Yo-Yo Pants? I warned you that was a risky business. Come along now, we mean to have your statement."

I brushed his arm away again.

"Don't touch me again, you filthy jerk," I snapped at him.

That's when he hit me.

I can't imagine why he would do something like that, except that I've had the feeling that I wanted to do the same thing to a recalcitrant witness many times, especially when I'm tired and in a bitter mood.

I've never done it, especially to someone who was patently stronger than I am. But I know my own temptation of the minute.

Anyway, I succumbed to the temptation.

I hit him back, big macho deal.

He sailed backward about four feet and landed in the mud.

"Resisting arrest, boyo." He rubbed his jaw and shook his head. "It's the jail for you now. It's my word against yours."

He reached for his transceiver.

"I wouldn't blow that if I were you, Chief Superintendent Clarke," said the voice of doom out of the mists. "I witnessed the whole scene. I can testify that you laid hands on and then assaulted Captain MacCarthy without ever placing him under arrest and that he was defending himself. So it isn't exactly your word against his."

I did not recognize the voice until the speaker walked out of the gloom.

"Who the fock are you?"

"Bishop John Blackwood Ryan. I warn you, Chief Superintendent, that you are in the process of making a fool out of yourself."

Clarke struggled to his feet, still rubbing his jaw.

"You're no focking bishop."

"I warn you to be careful of your language in my presence."

The silver pectoral cross glittered dangerously in the twilight.

"I'll get you for this, MacCarthy." Clarke backed off, unsteady on his feet. "I warn you, you'll regret it."

"If there are any regrets, Mr. Clarke"—the good bishop advanced on him implacably—"they'll be yours. I serve notice on you that I hold you personally responsible for any harm, physical or emotional, done to Ms. MacDonaugh."

"We'll have a confession before morning," Clarke said sullenly.

"If you do, you'll regret it till your dying day. And, sir, if I may say so, in the colorful vernacular of this city, you are a nine-fingered shite hawk!"

So this was the real Blackie Ryan, a truly scary man. No wonder he hid behind the mask of a bumbling latter-day Father Brown.

"Come, Timothy Patrick, I think you need a small jar at the moment."

He led me across the street into the lounge of the Shelbourne.

Dazed, I followed after him.

"Ouch," I exclaimed as I sat on the bar stool at the Shelbourne.

"Ah!" The good bishop took the lemon-scented soap from my hand. "You are honoring the rituals of the day after all. Lamentably this is not the same brand."

"Lemon-scented soap," I proclaimed, "is lemon-scented soap."

"Arguably." He conceded my point.

"She didn't do it," I muttered as I sipped my drink of Bushmills. "It was a plant."

"Patently," he agreed, the old mask back in place. "Did I not tell you that she was innocent?"

"Yeah, but—"

"As My Lord Cronin, the good Cardinal Archbishop of Chicago says of me, I am rarely in error but never in doubt."

Was he making fun of me?

"For a moment I thought—"

"Naturally." He waved his hand to dismiss my guilt. "Unfortunately the device could have exploded anytime during the day, with you in the bed or not. The hotel could have been gutted with my sister and my niece at risk. This has gone too far. Quite unacceptable."

"They wanted to destroy the hotel?"

"Not at all, they wanted to destroy the numinous Nora. Put the bomb in your room. Slip the transmitting device in her purse, perhaps lifted briefly from the chair in a restaurant where she had laid it, and then make an anonymous call to the guard. Crude but effective. Is there a risk of killing a couple hundred people? No problem because Nora will be blamed. Mind you, they moved quickly after the plant because they have no desire to massacre, but they're willing to take the risk. Not that they would be all that unhappy to remove you from the scene, too."

"You know who did it?"

"Yes, of course. I admit that I erred intolerably not to have realized how desperate they are. Their behavior in this whole unfortunate matter has been that of those on the edge of despair. Hence they have engaged in unnecessary folly repeatedly."

"Why?"

"Guilt, Timothy, guilt; despair and panic-creating guilt."

Then I saw the face of the killer again. I also knew why the crime had been committed. I whispered the name and the reason.

"Capital, Timothy Patrick." The Bishop beamed. "Mike Casey the cop did not unjustly praise you."

"I was guessing," I admitted.

"We always guess at the beginning."

"You have proof?"

"Oh, yes. Surely. The killer made one serious mistake. . . . Now, if you will excuse me for a few moments, I will make certain representations in favor of the noble Nora. In her present understandably distraught state we must not leave her at the tender mercies of Mr. Clarke's team of interrogators."

He was gone for a half hour, during which I tried to persuade myself that I was a cop and not a potential victim of a terrorist.

Then the good bishop returned and with a sigh resumed the careful consumption of his drink.

"There was some resistance to my suggestion, some hint that I was interfering with the proper operation of the local authorities in a manner inappropriate for a bishop, let alone a bishop from beyond the seas. However, certain responsible people were persuaded, when I told them one or two facts, that discretion was advisable."

"So?"

"A woman officer of the embassy of the United States of America will remain with Nora all night and indeed until tomorrow. She will not be moved from Garda Headquarters on Harcourt Street, a much safer place because Mr. Clarke's superiors will not be able to pretend they don't know what is happening. A woman attorney will be present in due course. There will be no interrogation at which these persons will not be present. Mr. Clarke's mind rape will not work under such circumstances."

"You must have had to go pretty high to swing that." I felt great relief. She'd be all right till tomorrow when I would be able to see her.

"High enough." He glanced at his empty glass and looked around, apparently suspicious that someone else had been sipping from it. "Odd."

He signaled a waiter for a refill for both of us.

"Will she be all right?"

"Doubtless, especially since we shall rescue her by this time on the morrow at the very latest. She has survived worse traumas. Yet these incidents have a cumulative effect. We must prevent them from happening again."

"Can we?"

"Arguably. There comes a point where bravery becomes counterproductive."

"Tell me about it."

He blinked at me through his thick glasses.

"Indeed."

"What next?"

"Next you must go to your room, which I have asked the management to restore for you after the necessary depredations by the Army, and obtain a good night's sleep. We may need your alertness on the morrow."

"What will we do then?"

"We will breakfast at my table at half eight. Then we shall complete certain incidental inquiries. Finally we'll make our ultimate representations—very vigorously, I would add—and this matter will be brought to a successful if not particularly happy ending."

"I don't think I can sleep tonight."

The good bishop looked at the two empty glasses in front of me.

"I rather think you can."

I did.

23

THE BISHOP AND HIS YOUNG ASSISTANTS WERE ALREADY AT breakfast when, five minutes late, I joined them. The latter were wearing business suits and Trish her glasses, looking very professional.

"Matters are arranging themselves nicely, Timothy. I think I can promise you that the numinous Nora will be free before six this evening."

"When Uncle Punk says 'promise,' " Biddy informed me, "he means you'd better believe it."

"Arguably."

"What do we do?"

"My young assistants, suitably attired for the task, will make certain discreet inquiries of certain Dublin institutions. I, for my part, will visit Ms. Julia MacDonaugh and also make a certain representation to someone who is losing their taste for what is happening and wants a guarantee to survive the telling of truth. Then I will collect you at four for an appointment with a certain minister of the government who will be reluctant to accede to my suggestions but will, unless I am mistaken, agree to do so."

"What am I to do?" I demanded impatiently.

"Nothing. You've already done enough."

"What does that mean?" I asked angrily.

"Like you've already solved the mystery." Trish touched my arm sympathetically.

"Except for a few minor details." Biddy touched my other arm.

"Which we propose to clean up," her uncle concluded.

"How can I have solved the crime?" I demanded. "I know who did it, but not how it was done or how to prove it."

"You know both those matters," Blackie Ryan assured me. "Only you don't yet realize you know. Given another day or two, you would realize it, but we must not leave the enviable Nora at risk that long."

Why enviable, after all she had gone through?

"But—"

"The other side," he went on implacably, "is unaware of our involvement. Even if they were, they would not take it seriously. If you were up and searching again, they might risk some even more absurd demarche. Your presence in the hotel, perhaps seeming not to have recovered from yesterday's shock, will lull them for the hours required to dispose finally of this absurd matter."

"The Punk," Trish told me, "says they also serve who only watch and pray."

"He and John Milton," I said, a remark that seemed to trouble no one.

At four o'clock, the good bishop and I were shown in the office of the reluctant governmental minister. Bishop Blackie was wearing a carefully fitted suit, handmade shoes, and an episcopal ring fit for a very important cardinal.

The minister was a suave, faintly sleazy fellow who thought he could patronize the American ecclesiastic.

"We appreciate your interest, m'lord"—his voice oozed oil—"but, as I'm sure you understand, Irish justice takes its own course."

"I will endeavor to persuade you, Mr. Minister, that it is embarked tragically on the wrong course."

"I very much doubt that."

Such a little and seemingly unimportant bishop, not the kind of man one must take too seriously.

The minister laughed aloud when Blackie described the crucial evidence.

The good bishop went on implacably.

At the end the minister was thoroughly shaken.

"If all of what you say is true, m'lord," he said uneasily, "we will certainly have to take corrective measures."

"Consider these documents." Blackie pushed a pile of accounting sheets toward the cabinet official.

"Yes, quite. I'll have our men get after it the first thing in the morning. I must say, however, that we cannot honor the undertaking you have made with the person you just now quoted."

"Mr. Minister, that will not suffice. Ms. Nora Marie MacDonaugh will be released before six this evening or I will have to take certain drastic measures. Moreover, you will honor my undertaking, as you are pleased to call it, and be grateful that I was able to trade it for the information we all needed."

"This is untoward interference in the affairs of a sovereign state," the minister exploded. "Ireland is not a satellite of either the United States or the Catholic Church."

"Very well, Mr. Minister." Blackie Ryan rose to his full height of maybe five feet six inches. "You have here a copy of my evidence. I shall at this time bring another copy to the Merrion Road offices of the embassy of the United States of America."

"I don't care." The minister's face turned livid with rage. "Ireland will not be dictated to by anyone. We are not Israel. You don't own us."

Blackie waited a moment for the minister to realize what he had said.

"Arguably . . . then I shall have supper with a friend of mine from the *Times*. Not the *Times* of London nor the *Irish Times*, but *The New York Times*. The readers of that august journal will doubtless find this account of the mistreatment of a woman who is both innocent and an American citizen most interesting. It will no doubt lead to an increase in American tourism to this country."

We walked out in solemn procession.

"Got him." The good bishop chuckled. "Got the tosser."

At five minutes of six, a disoriented and haggard Nora was released into the custody of Trish, Biddy, and myself at the new red-brick *garda* headquarters in Harcourt Street. She was accompanied by, of all people, my friend Nessa.

While a very important Irish person embraced Nora and wept with her—a required ritual for which the two young women were also preparing—Nessa whispered to me, "Glad to see tough Tommy finally get it."

"Me too."

"She's a grand lady." A nod to Nora.

"All of that."

"Will you be taking good care of her?"

"Would I not?"

"Is it true that you knocked your man into a mud puddle?"

The exhibitionist in me could not resist. "Four feet into the focking mud puddle."

At seven o'clock an arrest was made.

The late news announced a tearful confession.

The mystery was resolved. I was given the full credit, along with a quote from me saying that attempts to involve terrorists in the north were totally unfounded and indeed part of the dodge that the accused had used.

Brendan would be pleased.

24

MY GOOD FRIEND MS. MOIRE MACSWEENEY BROKE THE ICE. " 'Im." She pointed an accusing finger at me.

"We have to stop meeting like this, young woman." I swung her into the air and she gurgled appreciatively.

Philomena, who had entered the death room unhesitatingly in the wake of the good bishop, barked her approval.

Everyone laughed nervously. Thinking the general amusement was for her, Moire gurgled again.

In fact the laughter was to ease the tension in the library at Aras MacDonaugh on Shrewsbury Road. The MacDonaugh children and their spouses had gathered to meet with Nora for an explanation of the solution to the mystery of their father's death. If they had felt guilt before, there was now guilt compounded because of Nora's putative innocence. Too many harsh things had been said over the last eighteen months for the tensions to dissolve easily.

Tea was being served by Julia MacDonaugh, ably assisted by Trish Ryan and Biddy Murphy, the latter two in matching sweaters and skirts, one light brown, the other light blue, and exuding the poise of young women who knew what they were about.

It was even better than Julia's tea when I had been in the house a few days—or was it a lifetime—ago. The sherry was much improved over the previous excellent bottle. Today we were pulling out all the plugs.

It was Bloomsday plus two and rain was pouring out of the low, racing clouds, the first truly awful day since I had come to Ireland. "Back to normal weather, sir," said the doorman at the Shelbourne as I had gone out for my morning run. It was the next week that Dubliners had in mind when they said, apropos of good weather, "Och, we'll pay for it next week, won't we?"

After my run I had eaten breakfast with Nora in the dining room of the Shelbourne. She was pale but self-possessed, in control of herself again. Skillfully applied makeup hid most of the strain in her face. But she was eating very little; she'd be thinner than ever before all of this was over.

"Did you sleep well, Nora?" I had asked.

"Pretty well. That nice physician that Bishop Blackie found gave me some Librium pills, but I preferred an Irish tranquilizer."

"Ah?"

"Bushmills . . . Three jars. Now, don't tell me I can't do that every night. I know that."

Her wit was struggling to surface. It would surely win before the day was over. Nevertheless the woman was in a state of exhaustion and emotional shock. It would take her a long time to work her way out of it. She was not likely to grant herself more than twenty-four hours.

"Tim Pat . . . we ought to explain to the children?"

"What children?"

"Jim Lark's children—Agnes, Sean, Dermot. They'll have read the papers and they won't be able to figure it out. I owe them an explanation."

"You don't owe them anything."

She considered. "I suppose you're right. Still I want to explain it all to them."

"That's different."

"Would you and Bishop Blackie be willing to meet with them and with me?"

"Of course."

I figured I had the good bishop's power of attorney. Besides, although I was officially the hero of the hour, I wanted a full explanation, too.

"Good. I'll set it all up. Tea on Shrewsbury Road this afternoon."

"Are you sure you're ready for it?"

"Certainly I am. I can't let myself fall apart now."

"You weren't in such good shape yesterday."

"That was yesterday," she had said impatiently. "The trouble then was I was so confused when they arrested me and found that terrible thing in my purse and said I was trying to blow you up. I was afraid that I had blown you up. I didn't believe you were still alive till I saw you last night."

Nothing wrong with our Nora, not at all.

Today was not the day to argue the point.

"I'm alive and well."

"I didn't want to kill another one. . . ."

"Nora!"

She hung her head contritely. "I know. Give me another night of sleep and I won't say such silly things. Really."

"You'd better not even think them," I said gruffly.

"Is it true that you slugged Chief Superintendent Clarke?" She smiled ever so slightly.

" 'Tis true. Bishop Blackie is my witness that he hit me first."

"You hit him hard."

"Not at all, at all. Only so that he fell back four feet into a mud puddle. If I had hit him hard, sure wouldn't he have sailed all the way across the Green?"

"Good enough for him!"

She actually laughed. But good humor faded away, and sadness, deep and abiding, returned to her eyes.

I had realized even before we met for breakfast (at her suggestion in a phone call to my room) that I would have to explain to her about Jim Lark's cancer before the news appeared in the evening papers. Now I had another reason to tell her: we would have to tell her children at tea that afternoon.

"Nora, there's something more you must know. I'll be blunt: Jim Lark was dying of cancer. He had a year to live. The first eleven months of it would have been a normal life, maybe a little tired. Then there would have been a rapid decline. Death, I am assured, would have been relatively painless."

She had gripped the edge of the table. "Why didn't you tell me?" she snapped.

"I found out only on Monday evening before the dinner party. There hasn't been time to tell you."

She had nodded. "Of course not. I'm sorry I blamed you. What I meant was why didn't he tell me?"

"He only knew, Nora, for two weeks at the most before he died. I don't know whether he would have told you or not. I'd guess, from the way he's been described to me, he'd have protected you from what he would have thought to be unnecessary worry until almost the end."

She had sighed. "I suppose you're right."

"I'm not sure that would have been wrong."

She had considered that as she signaled the waiter for another pot of tea. The finger she held in the air was quivering.

My poor Nora. You can't take much more of this. I would help you if you'd let me. But you figure that like all the other times you have to do it yourself.

"No," she had said thoughtfully when the new teapot had arrived. "In the final analysis it would not have been wrong. But it does change everything."

"And explains a lot," I had added.

"Yes," she had agreed, "a whole lot. I wonder how the children will react."

She loves them, too, doesn't she? They'll never ask for her forgiveness, never in a million years.

So that afternoon a large Mercedes limo had ferried us to Shrewsbury Road. The tension in the death room was almost unbearable.

At least everyone had greeted each other civilly.

Nora was wearing a simple charcoal-gray shift with white collar and cuffs, almost like a mourner at a funeral.

So we had eaten our sandwiches and sipped our sherry and tea while His Gracious Lordship, John Blackwood Ryan, sitting in what had been Jim Lark's chair behind the desk and oblivious to everyone else, had shuffled papers in a large manila folder Biddy had brought into the room for him. He was properly clad in his good suit and shoes and wearing his enormous ring and the freshly polished Brigid cross.

Philomena, apparently with a keen eye for ecclesiastical

dignity, had planted herself firmly at the good bishop's feet and did not budge from that position for the rest of the afternoon, save for an occasional sniff at Moire.

Heavy-duty.

Solemn high.

Then Mistress Moire had broken the ice. Nora looked at me. I was, it would seem, the deputed master of ceremonies.

"As you know, gentle persons," I began, "Mr. Arthur T. Regan sent me here to endeavor to solve the mystery of your father's death. As you also know, a solution was reached last night, one that I think I can say astonished everyone. I should state at the very beginning that the guard ought not to be faulted for not clearing up the matter long ago. There were aspects of the problem which would have baffled the best police forces in the world, of which the one in this country is certainly to be numbered. Moreover, as I have said repeatedly to the media, the tragic event of a year ago January was not the result of terrorist action."

When I had gone to my room after breakfast with Nora, the phone rang. I knew who it was before I answered.

"Good morning, Brendan."

"Ah, now, aren't you the clever one!" Brendan had whooped. "You ruin my opening line, which was that I was sure you'd recognize my voice."

"To which I would have said that I never forget a voice."

"I'm on the run, in a manner of speaking. I just wanted to tell you that we're proud of the way you handled the whole thing."

"Thank you, Brendan."

"Maybe we'll meet again."

"I hope you live long enough so we can meet again."

"Wouldn't I be hoping the same thing myself?"

And the line was dead.

On Shrewsbury Road I continued my canned introduction. "I was fortunate to secure, quite by chance, the services of Bishop John Blackwood Ryan of Chicago, who was here doing research for a book he proposes to write about James

Joyce. Bishop Ryan has a very distinguished reputation in Chicago for solving puzzles."

The line was that he had helped me. Which was to laugh, but that was the line.

"He was ably assisted by his half sister, Patricia Anne Ryan, and his niece, Brigid Marie Murphy."

Both those worthies nodded gravely.

The six people seated opposite us were growing more interested. The *équipe Ryan* seemed intriguing.

Guys, you don't know the half of it yet.

"I have asked the bishop to summarize our investigation, because he has had, as you may imagine, a good deal more experience than I have had at public speaking."

A low giggle from Biddy, silenced instantly by a quick glare from her aunt.

"Bishop Ryan." I sat down.

Blackie looked up like he was utterly mystified, quite unaware of where he was or what he was supposed to say.

But there was no trace of doubt in his voice when he began.

"I have two pieces of information which I must share with you before I continue. The first is that Ms. Nora Mac-Donaugh has also been cleared of suspicion of the murder of her first husband. Or rather, to be more precise, she has made available to us information on that case which she has had all along but did not share with others out of exemplary respect for her husband's memory and for the feelings of his mother and father while they were alive. Trish, if you will, please pass out copies of this affidavit and then collect them after our guests have read them."

Our guests indeed. The bishop would no longer be staying at the Shelbourne when he was in Dublin.

Dermot MacDonaugh glanced at the paper and nodded gravely. "It rings absolutely true, m'lord. I've had cases like this. The person is bent on self-destruction. There is nothing that can be done to prevent it. Only hesitation for another day can change his mind. When there's no hesitation . . ." He shrugged.

"Why did you keep this secret so long, Nora?" Sean MacDonaugh asked hesitantly as he gave his copy back to a waiting Trish.

"After my in-laws had died, I felt it was no one's business but my own and Rony's."

"Did Dad know about this testimony?"

"If he did, I didn't tell him. I'm sure he must have checked me out pretty thoroughly before he asked me to marry him. He believed only in carefully calculated risks, as you remember. So I assume he knew."

"The second piece of information," Blackie continued implacably, "is also of a medical nature. Biddy, if you would . . . you may keep this document if you wish. I'm sure Dr. MacDonaugh will want to speak with the relevant medical personnel at Beth Israel Hospital. In brief summary, your father had incurable cancer and would have died within the year. That does not excuse those who needlessly shortened his life."

The three children and their spouses gasped.

"About a year is right." Dermot MacDonaugh stroked his beard. "Rare enough and not painful, even at the end. But"—he hefted the paper—"a death sentence . . . Did you know, Nora?"

"Not till Captain MacCarthy told me at breakfast this morning. Jim Lark's physician assumed that the autopsy had revealed the existence of the . . . the disease."

"He would never have told us," Dermot said firmly. "Not till the very end."

"I agree," Nora replied.

I looked at the faces across the room—taut, drained, grim. And guilty.

Biddy and Trish distributed biscuits, tarts, and sweets—and more scones and heavy cream. They gave me one of everything without being asked. Then they refilled the teacups and the sherry glasses. They didn't ask me about the sherry either.

Nora waved them off.

As they were finishing, the faithless Moire squirmed off her mother's lap and toddled across the room to the bishop.

He picked her up, rested her on his knee, and rearranged his papers. Philomena sniffed at the child again and returned to her prone position at the bishop's feet.

"We did that once," Biddy whispered in my ear. "Trish and I. He's magic with kids and I can't quite remember why."

"Because he's a kid himself," I whispered back.

She nodded solemnly. "That's what my mom says."

"I think it possible," Blackie continued while his little friend played with the silver Brigid cross, "to reconstruct a scenario of what he had intended to do in the months still allotted him.

"It is safe to assume that if the scheduled family meeting had occurred that afternoon, he would have informed the older generation that he was retiring from active direction of the affairs of Jim Lark Enterprises in favor of his son Sean. The older generation had the right to hear from him first. He would have offered them a very generous settlement in the form perhaps of trust funds, if they signed a quitclaim against all further money from him and his heirs. I assume he had no illusions about how they would behave."

"Scapegraces," said their sister ominously from the corner of the room.

"Arguably. I presume that if they had demanded more, he would have given them that, too. But he wanted clearly to establish that while he felt an obligation to them, the next generation should feel no obligation. Does that sound reasonable, gentle souls?"

Six heads nodded solemnly. Mistress Moire went peacefully to sleep on Blackie's knee.

"He would have assumed on the basis of previous conversations with you, Mr. MacDonaugh, that you would become his successor under proper circumstances. I suspect that after the meeting he would have phoned you almost at once and made you an offer you could not refuse. He would also have doubtless made a settlement in benefit of your children—in addition to the stock you own in his various companies. Does that not sound probable?"

"It would have been a generous offer," Sean said sadly.

"He was almost more generous than one expected him to be. . . . Then he would have called Derm. He always believed in the proper order."

"Dr. MacDonaugh, how would you have reacted?"

"I presume he would have told me that he was retiring to take life a little easier and devote more of his time to the foundation. I would not have believed that he would be able to take life easier, but I would have been delighted that the, if you will, succession crisis had transpired so gracefully."

"I'm quite sure he would have given you an explanation something like that."

"Then," said Cormac MacSweeney, "your man would have come up to Meath to see herself and me, ride some of our horses, and tell us the same things."

"I will go on record," Blackie went on, "as saying that as marvelous as this young person is, I do not at the present time have any intent to take her home to Holy Name Cathedral rectory."

General laughter.

"He would have taken advantage of his time in Dublin," Blackie continued, "to have a heart-to-heart talk with Councillor Quaid and perhaps with efficient Ms. McNulty. I rather imagine he would swear everyone to secrecy so that he could return to New York to face Mr. Arthur Regan, a confrontation he probably feared more than any of the others, including that with the brothers."

He paused. No one argued.

"Now, I'm sure you perceive what has transpired. The will was written before the event. If he had lived to make all the settlements he proposed to make, including, I presume, a generous one to Ms. Nora MacDonaugh, the monies remaining in the estate for distribution would be much less than they are now. What was left would have gone to her for contribution to the foundation at a time and place of her and her tax lawyer's choosing. The result would have been a will that would have surprised no one and bothered only a few, none of whom are presently in this room. Do I make myself clear?"

There was stirring around the room as Blackie's analysis began to sink in.

"Now everything begins to make sense," Sean Mac-Donaugh said, his voice excited. "Complete sense."

"He made the will"—Blackie carefully removed another paper—"both as a guarantee against immediate unforeseen disaster and as a final resolution of his finances when his year of grace came to an end. He did not anticipate the immediate disasters and hence did not realize how the will would be understood in that eventuality."

"Dear God," Aggie exclaimed.

At the sound of her mother's voice, Moire stirred uneasily.

"I think, Ms. MacSweeney, I had better remove completely the temptation to make off with this admirable child by returning her to the proper arms."

"Thank you, m'lord." Agnes smiled up at him, another victim of the good bishop's winsome charm.

"To continue. We have now re-created with tolerable confidence what was supposed to happen during and after the meeting. The meeting, as you know, all too tragically did not occur. I deem it safe to say that our knowledge of what the meeting was to be about does not enhance our understanding of what prevented its occurrence. That has been the barrier to understanding why your father died before his time. The meeting and the will, as such, had nothing to do with his death. As we shall see, a misinterpretation of the reasons for his sudden trip to Dublin is what led to his death."

Blackie had established his wisdom. Everyone was listening attentively now, hanging on his every word.

"We must start with the matter of the locked room. If the reason for the sudden meeting was an accidental obfuscation in our search of what happened that afternoon, the locked-room explosion was a madcap attempt to throw dust in our eyes. It succeeded all too well, giving those who had conceived its reason to try again with nearly tragic results for Ms. Nora MacDonaugh and possibly Captain MacCarthy and scores of people in the Shelbourne Hotel, myself, be it noted, included.

"I had the advantage of hearing an accurate description of this house before I had seen it. It seemed from that rather unique perspective that the solution to the puzzle was rather obvious. However, like the solution to the bafflement of the sudden family meeting, it at first appeared not to advance our understanding of the central mystery: Who killed James Larkin MacDonaugh."

"You knew how my father was murdered but not why?" Sean MacDonaugh asked in dismay.

"Let us say that knowledge of how at least gave us some hints as to why. Consider a possible scenario for the how. A potential killer comes into this office. For one reason or another its occupant chooses to have a few words with this person. The person is anxious for reasons we will specify subsequently. He—and we will not imply that the pronoun tells us the gender of the potential killer—is extremely nervous. He is afraid of the bomb he carries in his attaché case, although he has been carefully instructed in its use. He also fears murder, never having done it before. He must make up his mind in the course of the conversation to detonate the bomb. For reasons we can only surmise, he decides that he must proceed with his devilish—I use the term literally—scheme.

"Before he arms the bomb, he has shown the man behind the desk the mechanism." Bishop Blackie picked up the TV remote control again. "Perhaps with the suggestion that Jim Lark Enterprises might develop such a device in its electronics factory in County Waterford. He is careful to handle it with tissue paper himself so as to leave no fingerprints at this point. He may argue that it is a delicate instrument that must be handled with care.

"He then arms the bomb, a simple and quickly executed task that could be done behind the top of an attaché case as he pretends to search for papers, and places it, perhaps under a stack of file folders, on this desk. All that remains is to press the button on the transmitter, much like this TV remote control, which will send a signal to the bomb."

The men and the women in the library were somber as they heard this quiet description of evil.

"He has been warned that explosive devices like this one are unpredictable in their force. He must seek protection for himself before he transmits the signal. However, he knows where he will go. He has ascertained that the explosive material is unlikely to shatter the massive oak doors of the library. He assumes that this includes"—Blackie rose from the desk and stumbled over to the bathroom door—"the solid door to the bathroom, a relic of the days when this door led to the concealed third stairway. Doubtless this door persevered because it was part of the decor of the library.

"He asks permission to go to the room for a moment. Inside, surely with fingers trembling, he puts on a glove, one would do, and presses the button. He experiences a moment of terror, both because he realizes what he has done and because the force of the blast shakes the door so powerfully. Perhaps he is knocked off his feet."

"He detonated the bomb from the WC?" Cormac MacSweeney asked in disbelief. "Wasn't that a terrible risk?"

"He was driven by his situation to take terrible risks," Blackie replied. "Or rather his perception of the situation. Now, however, what is done is done. He opens the door and sees the devastation that he has caused. He is momentarily sickened perhaps, but he must go ahead with his plan. Not looking at the remains of his victim, he steals across the devastated library and puts the transmitter on a shelf where it will be seen immediately by those who will eventually force their way in. He then locks the door with a key he happens to have, wipes traces of his fingerprints from the key and anything else he has touched, including the doorknob to this room, and then makes his escape."

"How does he get away?" Dermot MacDonaugh asked.

"From the beginning"—Blackie sighed—"it seemed obvious that his escape had something to do with the abandoned stairway. You will remember that when the house was remodeled, a decision was made that the mores of our time no longer permitted the master of the house a protected if not altogether secret passage from his dressing room or his library, by use of which he could exit with less risk of detection when on the way to an amorous adventure, or to be fair, perhaps to some local church to say his night prayers."

"Protestant church." Cormac MacSweeney, whom I was beginning to like a lot, broke the ice.

"Presumably. However, we must note for the record that the behavior we postulate is ecumenical in its incidence. . . . In any event the stairs were removed and the stairwell was converted into bathrooms on this and the next floor, increasing notably the number of such facilities in the house in response to modern customs. A glance inside this room will reveal to you that the ceiling is much lower than the ceiling of the library. One does not have to be a brilliant detective to suspect an empty space above and perhaps a passageway."

"Didn't the *garda* think of that?" Sean MacDonaugh asked.

"Surely they did. But a cursory examination of the ceiling revealed it was solid. Moreover, since the old doorway on the ground floor had been sealed up, how could someone have escaped once access to the stairwell had been accomplished?"

"Yes, m'lord." Agnes shook her head in amazement. "How did he get out, if he it was?"

"I had been informed"—Blackie continued to stand in the doorway to the bathroom—"that there had been installed in the bathroom above, serving the master's dressing room, a sunken whirlpool and a sunken bathtub. . . . Was that at your late husband's suggestion, Ms. MacDonaugh?"

"No, but he was pleased by it. A grand idea, he said."

"I have little personal experience with such devices, but some of my siblings seem to be devoted to them, for what purposes need not concern us at the moment. However, I am aware of two facts about them. The first is that they do not sink into another plane of being. If they are at floor level, then there is, axiomatically, empty space beneath them. Secondly these mechanisms tend to malfunction. Hence it is necessary for plumbers and electricians to have access to them."

"A trapdoor upstairs," I exclaimed, playing straight man despite myself.

"Indeed. Ms. Julia MacDonaugh was good enough to permit me access to the house yesterday and serve me one of her splendid teas."

That worthy snorted, but nonetheless seemed pleased with herself.

"My first step was to pull back the plush carpet from the floor of that luxuriant room. Naturally I discovered the trapdoor I had anticipated. Of necessity it was wide enough to permit entry to a workman to repair the whirlpool. The stairwell, like everything in this house, was built to endure the ages, as were the beams on which the staircase had rested and on which now the two heavy, ah, luxury items rested. There was, you see, a compartment." He pointed at the wall above the doorway to the bathroom, between the two floors. "As you might imagine, I did not trust my ability to climb into that compartment and then extricate myself from it, but I did ascertain that there was more than enough room for a person to pass through it, and attain the third, or if you will, second level of the house."

"The carpet . . . ?" Nora asked. "It was tacked down."

"Normally it was. However, the tacks had been removed, presumably on some other occasion when the house was empty, in case this plan became necessary."

"How did he get through the ceiling?" I asked. "Didn't the guard check it?"

Hadn't I checked it?

"If everyone would come to the bathroom . . . Biddy, would you for the moment take charge of the sleeping princess? There is not room inside for all of us. Some of you may watch from the door. Captain MacCarthy, you are of sufficient stature to test the ceiling if you stand on the toilet bowl. Does it seem solid?"

I was the dog man in the dog-and-pony show, so I did what I was told.

"Absolutely. Solid plaster over laths, I should think."

"Precisely . . . You may step down, Captain. Here was the weakness of my solution to the locked-room puzzle. I could account for how someone could ascend to the third floor, but not how he could escape this floor. However, I had been told that a new shower head and new faucets had been installed in the bathroom. I presumed that this installation had taken place at the same time as the room upstairs had been renovated. Is that correct, Ms. MacDonaugh?"

"Yes, Jim Lark was delighted with the change. He never used the shower in this room because of the old plumbing."

Blackie pushed back the thick blue shower curtain around the tub.

"Note the new shower head and faucets and especially the ceiling above them."

"Plasterboard," I said, "neatly fitted and suspended from above ... All right, I'll climb up on the tub and push.... You're right, Bishop, the panels slide away easily and there's enough room for a man to push his body through." I hoisted myself on the cross beam above the ceiling, a remnant of the old stairwell, and pulled myself through the opening I had created in the ceiling.

Then I dragged myself into the chamber, if one could call it that, between the two stories of the house. The space was cramped and smelled of bromine from the filter to the hot tub, but there was enough room to move around. On either side were the walls of the two tubs. Above me was a trapdoor to the next floor. Hanging on to one cross beam with one of my feet on another, I carefully slid the two plasterboard panels back into place.

I should have thought of that, I told myself. Well, too late now.

I pushed the trapdoor. It yielded slowly because the carpet above it impeded its movement. Nevertheless, when I shoved hard enough, the door opened wide enough for me to hoist myself through it as I forced the carpet back with my head.

I pulled myself into the "luxuriant" room, as Blackie had called it, closed the trapdoor, rearranged the carpet, and went into the master bedroom—trailed by the image I had on my first visit of the naked woman in the shower.

Slick.

Blackie was talking again when I returned to the library.

"One can therefore see that passage from this story to the next was possible to a resourceful and athletic person, which would include a number of the suspects, who knew the structure of the house, and who was brave enough or frightened enough to run the risks of a misstep."

He was seated behind the desk again with his stack of papers.

"How would this person get out of the house?" Nora asked. "The guards would come looking for an explosion in a few minutes. Wouldn't it be too great a risk to appear in the street? Even if the guards hadn't arrived, someone might have seen him, linked him to the explosion, and remembered him."

"Let us imagine this person slipping rapidly through the bedroom level of the house and down the back steps through the servants' quarters. Someone else may be in the house. He might have encountered you in the master bedroom, a risk he was forced to take. Your prospects for survival under such circumstances would have been poor. Perhaps he had seen you slip out to purchase the materials for tea. But there might have been a servant. Perhaps he knows that there are no servants there. However, by now our person is on a maniac high. He is convinced of his own invulnerability and the fated success of his intricate scheme. In any case he exits through the kitchen door of the house and scurries into the garden."

"Even if he has a key to the gate," Nora said, "and I presume that he does. The gate leads to Shrewsbury Road and he has the same problem as if he strolled out the front door of the house."

"Indeed. At first I thought he had followed the very risky strategy of hiding somewhere in the house till dark and then slipping out into the night. But he would then depend on a moment of negligence among the guard who he knows patrols the house. Then I reasoned that there would be little point in the master of the house having his private entrance and exit if he then had to walk out on Shrewsbury Road where everyone in the house might see him if they happened to be looking through the front windows. There must be, I argued, another entrance to the garden.

"As fortune would have it, the gardener was at work when I visited Ms. Julia MacDonaugh. I took counsel with him as to the availability of another gate. There indeed was one, he told me, a stone gate set in the back wall of the garden, but it had not been used in years, maybe decades. The lock was probably rusted, so it couldn't be opened. We investigated the gate, a narrow opening in the wall obscured by vines. There was no lock and the gate swung open easily. Our person had slipped out the gate and into the walled and wooded lane—an alley we would call it in Chicago, separating the property from the athletic fields behind the house and the back gardens of homes on Aylesbury Road. He would have walked rapidly down the alley and entered the car he had parked on Aylesbury Road to make his escape. In January in Ireland, the sun has already set at that time and dusk is far advanced. He is confident that he can escape unnoticed. Indeed, that is just what he did."

"Dear God," Sean MacDonaugh murmured. "He must be crazy."

"Or driven by enormous energies," his brother the psychiatrist added. "It's all possible and it certainly happened. But the chances he was taking—"

"Were commensurate with his fear. There might have been other ways to commit murder and seem to get away with it. But our person is clever, very clever, perhaps too clever by half, as the local idiom puts it. He enjoys the game."

Everyone was silent for a moment, trying to digest the facts with which they were being assaulted.

"Note that our friend did not intend to incriminate Ms. Nora MacDonaugh. Rather, the intent was to make it look like a terrorist crime. Before he came into the room, he probably assumed that she would be here in the library with her husband, a fact which would make the crime seem more despicable and of the same sort as the one in which Lord Mountbatten and his family were destroyed. That she was not present interfered with that aspect of his scheme, but had the benefit, perhaps unanticipated, that suspicion would fall on her."

"Oh, Nora," Aggie exclaimed, "how terrible!"

"I'm still alive, thanks be to God."

"Why the key and the transmitter at the door of the room?" Cormac MacSweeney asked.

"Obfuscation. Terrorists were to be blamed, but he also wanted to create the illusion of a possibility of suicide, hence Jim Lark MacDonaugh's fingerprints on the transmitter. Perhaps he intended to leave the transmitter near the body to strengthen that illusion. Unfortunately for that part of his plan, Mr. MacDonaugh was too close to the bomb when it went off."

The good bishop paused, awaiting other questions. Since there weren't any, he continued.

"What about Uncle Parn's trip from Australia?" Aggie asked. "Was he involved in the crime?"

"There is no telling," I replied, "what he had in mind when he flew here from Perth. Perhaps only to plead with your father for help. Perhaps to do something much more violent. As it turned out, someone beat him to it."

"Doubtless you perceive," Bishop Blackie continued, "that the resolution of the locked-room puzzle does not by itself tell us who the person was. Or that is the superficial reaction. Michael Davitt MacDonaugh is in the vicinity. So is Nora MacDonaugh. So is Julia MacDonaugh. So, at some remove, are Clare McNulty and Paddy Quaid, though the offices in their building are at too long a distance to transmit the signal. Moreover they testify to each other's presence in the offices at the time of the killing. Anyone, however, could have come to the house on that fateful afternoon and entered the library while Nora MacDonaugh was shopping. Some member of the family or of the board could have flown over secretly. Or, alternatively, a highly paid and resourceful professional killer, well informed about the layout of the house and on retainer until a window of opportunity appeared, might have executed the strategy. Hence we knew the how but neither the why nor the who.

"I overstate the matter somewhat. There were strong hints of the who, but we still need to know the why. Captain

MacCarthy provided that when he discovered the strange affair of the Irish cream."

"The Irish cream?" several of our guests exclaimed.

"Indeed. As some of you may remember, Mr. MacDonaugh had the notion of offering to the public a liqueur to rival Baileys Irish Cream. He elected to call it Jim Lark Irish Cream. A considerable amount of money was put into the research and development of the product, but it had not yet been put on the market. Ms. Nora MacDonaugh, prejudiced in favor of the project naturally because it was a pet idea of her late husband whom she very much loved, was prepared to admit to Captain MacCarthy that the cream, even now better than Baileys, as she thought, still needed something extra to lure the public.

"The captain, using the picturesque local idiom, suggested in my presence that in fact the mixture could be compared roughly to, ah, liquid excrement. Neither I nor my efficient sister and niece could refute that suggestion."

"So . . ." Sean MacDonaugh had seen it all and now understood yesterday's arrest.

"So I concluded that Jim Lark Irish Cream was a fraud. The samples given Nora MacDonaugh and perhaps her husband before her could have been cooked up in a kitchen. Someone had taken the money expended on research and development and used it for other purposes. The account books registered the money paid for the projects and the canceled checks had been returned. But the recipients were either persons and firms which did not exist or those who were part of the scheme. Someone has stolen several million dollars by diverting money from a nonexisting project. We made a number of inquiries yesterday and were able to confirm this fact. We now knew the why and the who and were able to make suggestions along these lines to the proper authorities."

Blackie raised his hands as though it had all been a simple matter.

"Paddy Quaid!" several of our guests shouted.

"But he had an alibi, didn't he?" Nora was parchment pale despite her makeup.

"As is patent from the fact he has been arrested, his alibi is false. I visited Ms. McNulty yesterday and suggested to her that it was time for her to tell the truth, and that if she told it now, she could save herself certain inconveniences in the months ahead. She admitted to me that she had lied to protect the former lord mayor, with whom she was, ah, on intimate terms, as certain parties had suggested to us that she might be. How much of the rest of the plot she knew is conjecture. It is difficult to see how she might have been oblivious to the diversion of funds. Moreover, her hatred of James Larkin MacDonaugh, based on an illusion that he had sought her favors and then spurned her, is so great that I have no doubt that she was aware of the general outlines of the murder, too. These matters are relatively unimportant. She will be left to heaven's judgment, since she has already testified that she lied when she provided the alibi for the sometime lord mayor. I would add that he may deserve her betrayal because I suspect that he became, ah, intimate with her to guarantee himself an alibi should he eventually need one."

"Moreover," I interjected, "it had also been suggested to us that there was a link between the crime and the story Mr. Joyce tells in *Ulysses*—a house being dishonored by a false lover. The house, as is well known, was in fact owned by Mr. Joyce's closest friend, a rather convoluted allusion, I admit."

"The house was owned by J. F. Byrne." Bishop Blackie had grasped the allusion, too, probably before I had. "The hint said that we should watch for the best friend."

"The dirty bastard," Cormac MacSweeney commented through clenched teeth.

"The affair of the Irish cream merely confirmed strong suspicions I already had," Blackie went on. "Who would know the internal details of this house better than the man who had supervised its various remodelings for James Larkin MacDonaugh?"

"Why did he need the money?" Sean MacDonaugh asked. "Didn't he have enough already?"

"No one has enough money." It was my turn at last. "There is reason to suspect now that he had been taking money from Jim Lark Enterprises from the beginning, small sums at first, then larger ones. We will never know for sure, but he may well have instigated the kidnap plot ten years ago with a dissident branch of the IRA. He justified his theft to his collaborators on the grounds that the money was going to the IRA and that Jim Lark owed this money to the cause. He also must have paid his collaborators handsomely. That will all come out in the full-scale investigation now being conducted by the Irish government. We have reason to believe that small amounts of the money did go north, but most of it remained in his hands—till he lost it in his own ventures."

"What ventures?" Dermot MacDonaugh asked.

"Patrick Quaid had a strange and ambivalent relationship with his friend from the days on the hurling team. He worshiped him and was forever grateful to him. On the other hand he felt that he himself was the better speculator of the two and that he was largely responsible for Jim Lark's success. So, while Jim Lark generously rewarded Paddy Quaid's efforts, the latter always wanted success of his own. He also needed money for his political campaigns. Of course Jim Lark would have given him the money, but Paddy Quaid's pride would not permit him to ask.

"We may never know how many unsuccessful risks he took on his own. These last years it has been almost too easy for him to lose money—the presence of the Financial Services Center down the road from his offices in Liberty Hall gave him computerized access to a worldwide gambling casino. A few questions yesterday revealed that he was a major trader and a major loser. The Irish government will fill in the details."

"So he thought we were onto him?" Nora said sadly. "But we weren't, Tim Pat. Neither of us had any idea."

"That is the irony of the murder"—Blackie sighed heavily—"as the sums he diverted grew larger, Mr. Quaid's guilt and fear of discovery became almost paranoid. Your late husband probably discussed his sense that something was wrong with him on a number of occasions. The sometime lord mayor took these comments to be indirect accusations; your late husband called Mr. Quaid from the airport and asked him to stop by the house for a conversation. An unexpected call, an allusive invitation—Mr. Quaid thought that the moment of truth had come. So he executed a scheme he had been planning for a long time. Ironically all that James Larkin MacDonaugh wanted to discuss was the change in command in Jim Lark Enterprises. He may have said something about the Irish-cream project and thus sealed his fate."

"Dear God!" Nora buried her face in her hands and began to sob.

"That's what happened on Bloomsday." I brought the explanation to a close. "Nora visited him and asked him some pointed but hardly suspicious questions about the progress of the Irish-cream project. He was already nervous because of my investigation, so he or Ms. McNulty slipped the transmitter into her purse. One of his people dashed over to the Shelbourne and put the envelope with the explosives under my bed. When Paddy was sure of that, he promptly called the guard. In the meantime, as Bishop Blackie has noted, if Nora out of curiosity pushed a button, or if the guard pushed it by accident when they arrested her, or if a random radio signal had activated the explosives, any number of people inside and outside the hotel may have been sent to their eternal rewards, and perhaps in tiny pieces. He was so terrified of public exposure as a thief and then as a killer and his fall from grace as a political leader, that he no longer cared how many people he killed."

"On the other hand"—Blackie ended our discourse—"his guilt over the murder of a man who had been his closest friend for more than four decades caused him to break down and confess everything only two hours after he was arrested, especially when, for reasons of her own, his sometime lover chose to tell the guard that she had lied in providing him with an alibi. He received more coverage on the late news last night than in all his political career."

Nora continued to weep. I was glued to my chair. What could I say or do to ease the pain of renewed grief?

Aggie MacSweeney knew what to do.

"Nora," she wailed, and embraced her stepmother, "I love you. I want you to be my mother again and Moire's Nana Nora."

Nora rose and hugged Aggie in return. "I'm not your mother, Aggie."

"Yes, you are, isn't she, Cormac?"

"She is," that stalwart countryman agreed.

"Forgive me, please," Aggie begged.

"Of course, of course. Don't cry, Aggie. Everything is all right now."

Nora was now consoling the other woman.

Naturally.

Then there was general weeping and sobbing as the whole clan embraced Nora and begged forgiveness. Again she it was who consoled them.

Finally, Ms. Moire, awakened by the noise and in an unpleasant mood, was carried to her new Nana Nora. An easily appeased young woman, she snuggled comfortably into Nora's arms.

Biddy and Trish were crying, too. As was I.

"Amazing," I said.

"Come here, you wonderful old woman." Nora reached for Julia, who was standing shyly in the background of this happy family reunion.

Slowly, tears pouring down her face, Julia came to her. Nora embraced her in one arm and continued to hold Moire in the other. Three generations of matriarchs.

"Happy are the peace makers," Blackie Ryan agreed.

"She's really good at it," I agreed.

"Who?"

"Nora."

"But," said the bishop, "this gathering was your idea, was it not?"

I continued to receive credit for work that was not my own.

Now I must not fail at work that *was* my own.

25

I BLEW IT WITH NORA.

I told myself I was being discreet, giving her time to recover from the multiple shocks and the reopened wounds.

The truth was I didn't quite know how to help her. Looking back, I can see that the only help she might have wanted was my being with her. I didn't have to say anything.

So while the MacDonaugh family sorted out its tearful reunion and its plans for the future—and the rains continued to pour on Dublin's fair city—I returned to the Shelbourne and studied papers, notes, transcripts, and audits. I didn't bother to find out whether she was staying below, as the locals would have put it, on Shrewsbury Road or coming back to her room at the Shelbourne.

I spent most of Friday with the Irish government people in a modern office block at the castle. Somehow the bishop and his staff were dispensed from all such responsibility and were preparing to return on Sunday on the Aer Lingus flight directly to Chicago.

"Consider at the castle," the good bishop informed me, "that from its beginning until the Brits surrendered the castle to Michael Collins a few months before his death, this city was ruled by a foreign power of one sort or another."

"Like Chicago having a Republican mayor for all its history."

The Irish investigators were very polite—perhaps because they had heard rumors of how I behave when I'm riled—and very skeptical. Moreover communication was impeded by the fact that they spoke a different variant of English than I did, one filled with allusions, winks, nods, indirections, and convoluted questions.

Deep down I suspect that they resented the "focking Yank"

who had solved their mystery for them, with the help of an ineffectual-seeming cleric and two young women.

We eventually straightened things out.

The deputy commandant of the *garda*, a man with a thick Kerry accent, finally leaned back in his chair and sealed it all. "Wasn't your man a bleedin' tosser from day one?"

"You have enough leads now to keep you going for a while."

"Ay"—he sighed—"and we'll have to follow it all up. . . . Well, we owe a deep debt of gratitude to you and yours, Tim Pat, don't we now?"

We shook hands. "Send me a fax when you next come to Chicago, and I'll buy you dinner, Eamon."

"I'll do just that."

Whether he will or not remains to be seen.

They implied that "poor Tommy" Clarke had needed a rest for a long time and would doubtless have plenty of time to relax out in West Clare, where he had been posted.

I had a couple of pints at O'Neill's, the Trinity College pub, and admitted to myself as I listened to the young people that I was an aging and probably incorrigible bachelor.

The rain continued to pour down in torrents. Now it was accompanied by a bitter wind, which swept across the Green and blew raindrops against my face like grains of sand on a windy day at the beach.

Biddy, whom I met when I entered the Shelbourne, informed me that, "You know, like Nora is back here and not on Shrewsbury Road."

"Good," I said. "I'll give her a buzz."

"Will I see you at Grand Beach this summer?"

"Fersure."

The second answer was true. The first was true when I said it, but it became untrue when I returned to my room.

What do you say to a woman who has been through so much and is coming apart at the seams?

Like I say, I blew it.

I bumped into her on Saturday morning—literally. Despite

the rain, we were both running around the Green in opposite directions and we collided.

"Nora! I'm sorry." .

"I think it was my fault." She sighed. "I guess I can't think and run at the same time. I'm all right, really."

Just the same she let me lead her to a bench. We were both wearing shorts and T-shirts and were soaking wet.

For a few moments we gasped for breath. Then I took her hand.

She pulled it away.

"It's over, Tim Pat, all over."

Serves you right. Eejit.

"It doesn't have to be, Nora."

"Yes, it does. . . . I don't have any regrets for what we did. You are the sweetest and most wonderful man I've ever met or ever likely to meet—"

"I'd make a good husband."

"Not for me."

"Could I ask why?"

"I've tried marriage twice. I don't propose to try it again. . . . Besides, I don't want to jilt you like the others did."

"We're both losers?"

"*No!* Don't say that!"

"I love you, Nora." I reached for her hand and she pulled it away again.

She turned away from me.

"I'll always love you."

"You'll get over it, Tim Pat. Eventually you will find a good woman and be happy with her."

"Shite, Nora, stop playing the focking fiddles!"

That got her attention.

"What?"

"I don't like the heroic martyr role. You're good at it and you've played it a long time, but it's worn-out now!"

"What do you mean?" Leaning toward me with her eyes blazing, she was furious.

Well, that was progress of a sort.

"You've got on the average forty years of life ahead of you. Don't retreat behind a widow's mask. You have too much to give to life and too much to get from it."

We were both soaked to the skin. We needed a hot shower and a small drop even if it were morning. Both the shower and the drink together.

"I'm not retreating from anything." She turned away.

"Bollix," I said, slipping into the dialect of the land. "You've told me more about yourself than you've ever told any man. I've held you in my arms. I've been inside your body. I know you can't live without love."

"I've done fine so far."

"This adventure should end in a wedding."

She was horrified by the suggestion. "There will *not* be a wedding. That's final!"

"I'm not a stray, Nora. I can bring as much to marriage as you."

"That's irrelevant," she shouted. "How dare you say I collect strays!"

I thought she'd stalk away. But she didn't. Instead she sat next to me, rainwater running down her face, her head resting on her chest.

"I don't want it to end this way, Tim Pat. I want us to part friends."

"Do you think after all that has happened we can be merely friends?"

"I suppose"—she sighed her loudest County Mayo sigh— "that it isn't realistic."

I hadn't made much of an argument out of it. My South Side Irish wit has never performed very well in closing dialogues with women.

Besides, what kind of a nine-fingered shite hawk would press a woman who had been through so much so recently for a decision about marriage?

Hell, I told myself, she wouldn't have made a very good wife, anyway.

We sat there on the bench, buffeted by the wind and the rain. I knew it was all over, but I didn't want to leave her.

Probably she felt the same way. We conspired to prevent the final curtain from falling.

I broke the silence. "I bought you a bar of lemon-scented soap at Sweny's. Father Blackie says that it's not the same brand Bloom bought for Molly."

She took the soap. "You were just carrying it around in your running shorts, were you, now?"

"I was."

She held the soap in her hand. The rain fell on it, curling back the wrapper. A bit of suds appeared. The faint scent of lemon wafted by my nostrils.

"It smells like lemon," she said, hefting the bar judiciously.

"The bishop says it's not authentic."

"Lemon scent is lemon scent," she said firmly.

" 'Tis." I sighed like a native. "Focking lemon scent is focking lemon scent."

Her stately breasts, sharply outlined under her wet T-shirt, moved up and down as she responded to my sigh with one of her own. Desire and disappointment, the sick emptiness of an opportunity lost, tormented me.

"When is Bishop Blackie going back?" she asked with yet another very loud sigh.

"Tomorrow."

"We should probably ask him if he can stay a few more days. The young women, too."

"Why?"

"Until we can fly your mother and father over."

"Why are we going to fly them over?"

"For the wedding, you bleeding amadon!"

"What wedding?"

She was grinning at me now. "Sure, the wedding we're not going to have, what other wedding would I be talking about?"

"Are you trying to tell me, woman, that you've changed your mind about a wedding?"

"Well"—she took a deep breath—"wasn't I saying to my-self you don't mean all that nonsense you're telling your poor darlin' man and you're only saying it because you're scared and if you keep it up you might lose him and himself such a marvelous lover with all them wonderful things he does with you in bed and the thought of them makes you shiver and you'll have to apologize and tell him you were talking shite and will he please give you another chance and love you for the rest of your life, won't you, now?"

She leaned her head on my chest and sighed again.

"Are you trying to tell me in a characteristic Irish way"—I put my arm around her—"that you *will* marry me?"

Which, as both Bold Jimmy Joyce and mild (sometimes) Blackie Ryan would have pointed out, was the same response Mary gave to Gabriel.